JONNY THOMPSON

Murder at Winkleberry Farm

A Limestone Manor Mystery

To everyone still reading.

1

"It's hot," Kitty said as she fanned herself with her hand and stepped out of the Hearse and onto the gravel driveway of the Winkleberry Farm's visitor parking lot.

Cliff had to admit the air-conditioned bus was much more enjoyable than the sweltering June heat.

"I suppose we should be grateful that Hans was able to secure us a spot so close to the entrance then." Bunty gave the big man a pat on the back. He was sitting in the driver's seat, his infectious smile still brimming with energy at the prospect of the day.

"Don't thank me. It was lucky that Pieter was able to hold the spot for us." Hans chuckled, and Cliff wondered if "lucky" was the right word. Miraculous might have been a better descriptor, considering the state of the parking lot.

The lot had been so jammed with vehicles that many people had given up all together and resorted to parking up and down the sides of the dirt road that led to the hundred-acre farm.

"Well, at least it's a nice day," Cliff said, feeling the sun against his face as he held the railing and stepped off the last step. He preferred the heat over the cold, and the way he figured, a person wasn't allowed to dislike both. Sure, you could prefer a more temperate climate, but he'd decided some time ago that if he was only allowed to dislike one of them, it was going to be cold, since the cold brought the aches and pains of getting older with it.

"What it is, is a nice day for *gardening*." Mrs. Chen squinted to look around at the throngs of people walking past them through a set of wooden archways with a large celebratory banner that read: *Celebrating Winkleberry Farm's 75th Strawberry Festival.*

Cliff didn't go as far as to roll his eyes, as Kitty had, but he, like the rest of the house, wasn't about to be fooled into engaging in this conversation again this morning.

It was no surprise to any of them, considering Mrs. Chen told everyone daily, that the annual county garden adjudications were happening the next week and for the first time in three years Mrs. Chen's garden was in the running for the top prize. Along with a full-page spread in the local newspaper, the winner would be pictured in the town and country newsletter and brochure. And that was to say nothing of the $1500 gift certificate to Hennigan's Garden Centre, that, as Mrs. Chen kept explaining, would cover her annual upkeep cost, and then some.

"I know you hate to miss a day, Mrs. Chen, but I appreciate you coming. Who knows, maybe you will find something in their garden centre." Hans closed the door to the Hearse and joined the rest of the house as they took cover under the shade of one of the large maple trees which lined the driveway.

"I can't imagine what would make my design better." Mrs. Chen gave Hans a confident smile. "And don't thank me. Thank Cliff." She tucked her cane behind her back and pulled herself up to her full height, which wasn't altogether that striking. Certainly not as striking as the smile she had on her face.

Hans looked at her with confusion and then over at Cliff, who wore a mildly guilty expression as Hans's eyes narrowed on him.

"He said if I came, he would help with the weeding this week." She walked over and gave Cliff a pat on the arm. "An offer I will certainly take him up on."

Hans looked as though he wanted to say something, but Cliff waved it off. "Happy to help."

"You said there would be food," Gerald said, his fingers fidgeting as they slowly rested on his belly. The short rotund man had already begun shuffling over towards the entrance. He glanced around, looking at everything, and Cliff suspected nothing, at the same time. Despite showing some signs of awareness, Cliff had suspected Gerald preferred to live in his own mind. Although Cliff often wondered what that mind might look like.

"We only just ate lunch, Gerald," Kitty said, shaking her head in an unapproving way.

"Correct," Gerald said, taking another tentative step towards the entrance, "but I don't see what that has to do with a light afternoon snack?"

"Well, don't you worry about food, Gerald. Pieter mentioned all kinds of food here this afternoon. The farm went all out for their anniversary."

"I still can't believe it's been seventy-five years," Cliff said, shaking his head. His eyes drifted over to the large, brown, timber-clad barn that appeared to have been converted into some sort of shop, complete with a red tin roof. It was much bigger than Cliff remembered, which was fair, considering the last he was here, he was maybe nine years old and all that had been here was a small wooden hut and fields of fresh strawberries.

They still had the fields of fresh strawberries, but they also had a wildflower meadow, a small garden centre, a pasture with various animals, honeybees, hayrides, and, at least for the day, rows and rows of the local vendors their farm had worked with over the years.

"Are we really that old?" Cliff asked.

"Yes." Sol chuckled, patting his forehead with a pocket hanky. "You said something about pie?"

"Sol Keen, you will not be eating pie this afternoon," Kitty said as she smacked her husband across the arm.

"It's strawberry festival, Kitty. You can hardly expect…" Sol began, but Kitty tilted her head and glared at him.

"You're supposed to be watching your sugar intake. Remember? Or was the doctor not clear on that?"

"He said cut back. Not stop. One piece of pie will hardly—"

"I plan on holding on to you for as long as possible, Mr. Keen, and if that means playing bad cop, I will," Kitty said, giving his arm a little squeeze, which deflated Sol, if only a little.

"Fair enough, my love. Perhaps a frozen one for dessert this week?" Sol asked in a small voice that made him sound more like a child asking for an allowance than a grown man requesting a treat.

"I suppose that would be a fair compromise. Besides it would be a shame not to support the farm," she said with a wink.

"Speaking of pies." Gerald turned and walked straight for the entrance, no longer caring to wait around for someone else to make the first move.

But his efforts were short-lived, as he was stopped abruptly by a large man, who Cliff supposed was in his sixties, with graying hair but a surprisingly athletic frame. He was followed closely by a smaller, thin man wearing rounded glasses and a suit.

"Uncle Pieter, it's a good offer."

"I said not now, Hendrik." The man put up a hand to stop the younger man from saying anything else. "Look, it's a celebration. Go…celebrate." Pieter waved a hand in the festival's general direction, and although Hendrik looked frustrated, he managed a slight nod of his head before turning on his heels and storming off towards the festival.

"Hans! I'm sorry about that," Pieter said, gesturing towards Hendrik before opening up his arms to give the big man a hug.

"Pieter!" Hans embraced the younger man. "Was that Hendrik? He's gotten so big."

"He has. He's also developed a lot of opinions, which he believes are always right. One of the spoils of law school, I suppose." Pieter looked back over his shoulder towards Hendrik, who was still walking away. "Though, obviously, they don't teach manners at his fancy school," Pieter joked. "Speaking of which, Hans, who are you friends?"

"Pieter, this is Gerald, Cliff, Mrs. Chen, Sol, Kitty, and Bunty. They are my housemates."

"Of course, the infamous Limestone Manor. It's a pleasure to meet you all!" Pieter said with a broadening smile.

They each took a turn saying their hellos, even Gerald, although by this point, he was nearly completely distracted by the calling food stands.

"Everyone, this is Pieter VanWinkle. His opa was the man who started Winkleberry Farm."

"Correct, although I have to admit it was my oma who made sure it continued."

"A long-standing family farm," Hans offered.

The expression on Pieter's face was less than enthusiastic, though it only lasted a moment before his smile returned. "So happy you were all able to make it," he said.

"Thank you for the parking. I'm not sure my old knees would have been able to handle the walk up," Hans said as he patted his thighs.

"Well, we couldn't have asked for a better turnout," Pieter said, looking at the hundreds of people who were funnelling into to the farm's entrance.

"Your oma, and opa would be proud." Hans placed a hand on the man's shoulder.

"Thank you, Hans. That means a lot—"

"Dad!" a young woman shouted as she ran over, waving her arms in the air and looking a bit surprised. She wore a red plaid shirt with her sleeves rolled up and a name tag pinned to her chest that Cliff had no hope in reading from that distance.

"Is that Mari?" Hans asked as he squinted and gestured towards her.

"Yes, it is," Pieter said, staring at her with both pride and concern.

"I remember her when she was just this big." Hans bent over to put his hands down well past his hips.

"She's bigger, that's for sure, and as it turns out, she's quite the help around here," Pieter said with a half-smile.

Cliff didn't know why, but when he watched the younger man, he got the distinct impression he seemed a little distracted. Though Cliff had never organized a festival before, so he figured that might have something to do with it.

"Dad!" Mari shouted again. "It's Lucas."

Cliff noticed that the disappointment in her voice was mirrored in Pieter's reaction.

"No rest for the wicked," Pieter said, resting his hands on his hips. He looked tired as he stared at the ground for a minute.

"Everything okay?" Hans asked.

"Yes. Of course. You know Lucas. Probably just some confusion over who's manning the hayrides." Pieter chuckled to himself, though Cliff wasn't convinced he was telling the whole truth, and from the look on Hans's face he imagined the big man felt the same way. "Honestly, everything is fine," he reaffirmed as he placed a hand on Hans's shoulder. "Just a lot of moving parts today." Pieter started to walk away. "Please, enjoy yourselves, have fun, and thank you all for coming today. Should be one for the history books," Pieter said as he crossed his fingers and ran off inside.

"Does this mean we can go in?" Gerald asked, though he'd already started to head in before anyone answered.

"Shouldn't we make a plan?" Kitty asked.

"I thought the plan was to come here?" Sol asked.

"Obviously, Sol, that is the plan. But what do we say we meet back at the Hearse around three thirty? That gives us two hours to walk around. That work for everyone?" Kitty looked at her watch as she tried to shield it from the sunlight.

"Yep," Gerald said, as he spotted a couple round the corner with a plate of food. He sniffed the air and disappeared before anyone had a chance to say anything to him.

"I swear there is something wrong with that man," Kitty muttered.

"He's passionate, I'll give him that," Bunty said. She looked like she was about to say more, but she was suddenly distracted by a wooden sign hanging in the distance that read "High Quality Local Wool," with an arrow pointing towards the barn. "That was two hours, correct?" Once she received a nod, she, too, disappeared into the crowd of people.

One by one, the members of the house began to spot various attractions to distract them. Mrs. Chen spotted a large green house, which she assumed to be the garden centre, and Sol and Kitty decided to pick strawberries before heading over to the tractor pull. Cliff assumed this was a compromise for both parties.

Then it was only Cliff and Hans who were left standing by the main entrance. Cliff, who had not known what to expect from the day, was blow away by the laundry list of events that he could take part in to occupy his time, and he was not going to admit to anyone that he found it very overwhelming.

"What did you think about that?" Hans asked, catching Cliff a little off guard by the near randomness of the question.

"Ummm…I'm not sure…" Cliff looked around. "I suppose when you've been together with someone for so long, you have to find a way to share your time?" Cliff shrugged.

Hans looked at him, his brows furrowed.

"Well, I imagine Kitty is the one who wants to pick berries, and Sol might be more interested in the tractors, but I wouldn't want to presume anything."

"Oh right." Hans chuckled. "No, I wasn't talking about that, though I suspect you might be on to something there." He was still looking around, as if he was trying to find something. "I was talking about Pieter. You don't think he appeared a little…off?"

Cliff thought back to the interaction with a slightly more critical eye now that he was being asked. Although Cliff had only just met the man, he was confident enough to know he held a keen eye for matters such as these. After all, he'd been a detective in the Toronto Police Department for over thirty years before becoming a private investigator and consultant. Making assumptions about people and how they carried themselves, even if he'd only just met them, was somewhat of a specialty for him at this point.

"Hard to say," Cliff said, thinking back on the conversation. "Who's Lucas?"

"Pieter's younger brother. He's a bit of… Well, he's always been a wild card. Had his fair share of ups and downs, I suppose. He has a sister, too, Cynthia, but she moved away a long time ago. I think she lives somewhere out west. They had a bit of a falling out when Pieter was left the farm and, well, everyone else got nothing. Let's just say not everyone was happy about it."

"I suppose inheritances are always hard on families."

"It's a shame, really." Hans shook his head.

Cliff gave some more thought to Hans's previous question. Obviously, there was much more to this family dynamic than Cliff could possibly know.

"I suppose Pieter did seem a little strange, but then again, a festival like this is a massive undertaking and bound to come with more than a few surprises." Cliff gestured to the events that surrounded them. "I have to imagine that organizing something like this would be very stressful for anyone."

"I'm sure you're right," Hans said, forcing a smile.

"I'm sure everything is fine, Hans. He's probably just stressed. But if you're really worried about him, you could always ask," Cliff said with a shrug.

"No, no, I'm sure I'm just being a little paranoid. I guess I'm more nervous for him than I thought."

"Why would you be nervous for him?" Cliff asked, feeling a little confused now. "What do you mean?"

"Well, remember how I told you that I sold my farm to a young family?" Hans tilted his head knowingly towards the farm.

"You mean you sold Pieter *your* farm?" Cliff vaguely recalled the brief conversation he and Hans had had about having to sell it many years ago.

Hans had pretty much been running the farm alone, and since his only daughter, Isa, had chosen the route of educator rather than farmer, and her son, Jan, the local reporter for the town newspaper, might have been the furthest thing from a farmer, Hans had decided to sell the farm.

"Yes. Though at the time, I wasn't sure they could handle it. Pieter and his nephew Flynn were looking to expand *their* family farm, and I always liked Pieter, but Flynn I knew less about, only that he is young and very ambitious."

"But you sold it to them anyways."

"It was either him or the Badger," Hans said, putting more than a little disgust behind the name.

"Who's the Badger?" Cliff asked.

"I guess you could call him a corporate farmer. Buys up everything he can. He owns pretty much all the land we saw on our way up here.

All but the handful of farms Pieter and his family own."

"Why don't you like this…Badger?"

"His real name is Mike Wilderman, and let's just say I've heard stories that he doesn't always play fair when it comes to getting his hands on what he wants."

"What do you mean?" Cliff asked.

"Nothing. I just mean rumours, nasty ones. Like forcing contractors to limit supplies to smaller farms, sabotaging sprinklers, calling in compliance issues to hold up deliveries. That sort of thing."

"That's awful."

"Well, no one's ever been able to prove anything. All we know for sure is, once the Badger sets his eyes on your farm, things seem to fall in his favour and not yours," Hans said with a shrug.

"Why do you think he could be the reason for Pieter acting strange?" Cliff watched Hans's eyes drift over to the parking lot where they landed on an all-black, jacked-up Dodge Ram truck with, what Cliff assumed, were illegally tinted windows.

Hans pointed over towards the giant monstrosity. "Because that's the Badger's truck."

2

Hans was still half distracted when Cliff finally left him, surrounded by a group of young famers getting ready to compete at a livestock show. Cliff, who hadn't spent much time around farm animals, save for a few years in his youth when he'd helped out on his uncle's farm, wasn't particularly interested in learning the nuances of what differentiates a good-looking dairy cow from a bad one.

But he was happy to see that it had come as a much-needed distraction for Hans, who still hadn't managed to wash the look of concern from his face, no matter how much Cliff had insisted that it was most likely all in his mind. But considering Cliff wasn't fully convinced himself, he could hardly blame Hans for his apprehension.

Cliff had his own reasons for wanting something interesting to happen. He'd been living back in St. Marys for a little over a month now, and it was just a little over three weeks since he and his housemates had managed to unravel a murder and save the town from a biker gang who wished to destroy it.

He hadn't realized it at the time, but it had all been rather exciting, and had possibly distracted him from the reality of what living back in a small town would be like. When he had initially moved home, he'd thought he was taking up a room in Hans's house. He hadn't realized the house also contained five others, along with Hans. Such knowledge likely would have dipped him into the "never returning" category around coming back to St. Marys.

On top of all that, he was only given a week from his arrival to decide if he wanted to sign a document that committed him to the house for at least a year. Between the murder, being arrested, and finally moving back to town, it may have been safe to assume that Cliff's judgement had been off at the time. All of the excitement may have gotten in the way of the realities of being home.

He only believed this because, since he'd signed the papers, things in town were back to normal. It was slow and easy going for a man who'd spent most of his life chasing criminals in Toronto. He'd become just another old timer walking around a small town, with nothing more to do than twiddle his thumbs, play cards, and occasionally sneak off to lose a lawn bowling match. It was a sport he still hadn't managed to get much better at and, thanks to Gerald's constant reminders, he knew just how terrible he was. Things were…dull.

He supposed he may have been content. It was a very simple life and without much stress. But he was starting to get the impression that he might have done himself a major disservice. He wasn't all too sure he was ready for quiet and content. Stress had been such a constant companion in his life, he was beginning to wonder if the lack of it was driving him towards the mundane.

This all twisted around in Cliff's brain as he walked through a row of makeshift booths trying to sell him all manner of homemade goods, while simultaneously he contemplated what Pieter might be worried about.

He'd been so lost in thought he didn't even notice when he bumped into a tall, blond man taking a photo.

"Sorry," Cliff said absently as he moved to step around him.

"No prob— Cliff?" the voice said through a chuckle, causing Cliff to pause his lamenting and look up at the tall reporter he recognized well.

"Jan?" Cliff gave the young man a gentle pat on the arm, since his shoulder was too high for Cliff to bother with.

Jan was Hans's grandson and the local reporter for *The Town Gazette*, which, from the look of it, he'd been taking photos of some of the booths for.

"What are you doing here?" Cliff asked, despite having surmised the answer himself. It felt like the right question to ask in the moment.

"Well, I'm sure you read the article I put in the paper last week about Winkleberry Farm's 75th Anniversary and their festivities." Jan gave Cliff a proud smile.

Cliff had *not* read the article, though he vaguely remembered skimming over it on the way towards the crossword.

"Of course," Cliff said with a smile. "Well-written."

"Thanks. Well, I wanted to come and do a follow-up piece on the farm. I thought it would be good to let the community know there is more happening in town than just minor ball." Jan chuckled. "What about you? Opa never told me he was going to come to this. Though I should have guessed. Is he here?"

"He is. Somewhere," Cliff said, looking around absently. "Though I'm surprised he didn't tell you, since it's been pretty much all he's talked about this week. But it would appear that, from the looks of the event, your article was a success."

"I think there is more to it than just my silly article. Though it did get shared more than a hundred and thirty-seven times on Facebook, so that's something."

"Impressive," Cliff replied, though it was a reactionary response to the joy on Jan's face rather than actually knowing if that was good at all. Cliff had never been good at the internet, nor did he have any desire to look at things on the Facebook.

"Yeah, I think it will be good for them. You know after…" Jan started, then looked as though he had said something wrong and stopped.

"What?" Cliff asked, trying not to sound too curious.

"I shouldn't. Wouldn't want to gossip."

"Posting about gossip in the newspaper isn't ideal, Jan," Cliff said raising a finger. "Running an idea by someone you trust, while you discover the truth, is an entirely different thing altogether."

"Really?"

"Of course. Consider me a sounding board." Cliff felt a wave of excitement creep across him as the idea of more information on this little farm peeked its head out at him.

"Well, it's just that, from what I heard, Winkleberry Farm might be in a little trouble. Financially. I remember Opa telling me his concerns about the farm being able to expand, and rumour has it, if they can't pull off a miracle this summer, they may be forced to sell," Jan said, trying to keep his voice low as his brows raised at Cliff, whose own face must have looked ponderous with the new information. Jan studied him carefully. "What do you know?"

"Nothing, Jan. You know me."

"I know you don't like to share all of your information with people."

"I don't like sharing *partial* information with people," Cliff corrected.

"What's the difference?"

"I like to let the dust settle on my thoughts before I present them." Cliff shrugged.

"Come on, I told you what *I* know," Jan said, his voice sounding more like a child than an adult reporter.

"I don't know anything. I swear." Cliff crossed his heart. "But out of curiosity," Cliff began, and Jan's ears perked up at this. Cliff needed to be careful about how much he gave away. Despite Jan's childlike demeanour, Cliff knew from firsthand experience that he was surprisingly sharp. "What do you know about Mike Wilderman?"

"You mean the Badger?" Jan gave his head a shake. "Pretty much what everyone else knows. Started off as a small-town farmer before he began buying up all the land in the area. I guess you would say he was the first industrial farmer in the region. Though by all accounts, he can be rather ruthless. When he gets his eyes on something he wants," Jan added casually. Though it wasn't long before something switched in Jan's brain, and Cliff could see the wheels turning. "Wait, you think the Badger is after Winkleberry Farm?" Jan's eyes went wide.

"That's *not* what I was saying," Cliff insisted, though it was hardly convincing, even to himself, let alone Jan. But his comment was quickly overshadowed by some shouting in a nearby tent.

"I told you to stay the hell away!"

Cliff turned to see a bulky, middle-aged man stumble out of a nearby tent. He was the picture of what Cliff would have guessed a farmer to look like, in his blue jeans and brown cowboy boots, and a button-down plaid shirt, complete with a large black Stetson. He had a dark, stubbled beard that showed off his white teeth. In front of him, and still shouting, was Pieter, whose face, even from a distance, appeared bright red as he pressed his palm hard into the other man's chest.

"Don't you ever come back here. Do you understand?" Pieter's teeth were clenched.

A young woman appeared from the tent dressed in a similar uniform to everyone else Cliff had seen working at the farm. She grabbed for Pieter's hand and attempted to pull him away.

"I don't suppose that's…?" Cliff started, but Jan was already nodding before he finished.

"Yep. That would be the Mike Wilderman a.k.a., The Badger," Jan said, as he absently took a photo of the ongoing situation. Leave it to the reporter to never truly let a story fall.

"Who's that?" Cliff asked, gesturing to the women tugging at Pieter's hand.

"Looks like Aria. I don't know her very well, just know that she's been working for Pieter the last few years. I think she came over from Holland. Not sure."

Pieter rested one hand on top of Aria's and squeezed it briefly before pushing it aside. He looked as though he wanted to do more than shout at the other man. He clenched his fists together, and his face still flushed red. He opened his mouth to speak again but stopped when another woman stepped in between the two men.

Cliff couldn't get a good look. Her long brown hair was blocking her face, but she appeared to show the two men something. The Badger raised his hands up and took a step away. Then she focused her attention on Pieter. After a couple seconds and some quiet words, Pieter still didn't look happy, but he was now more aware of all the eyes staring at him.

Slowly, he unclenched his hands and leaned in to say something quietly to the Badger before Aria grabbed Pieter by the hand again and dragged him off in the opposite direction, though not before sharing a few words of her own.

"So, they really don't get along then," Cliff said, still watching Pieter as he disappeared behind a line of tents.

"No. Though in fairness, not many farmers do," Jan chuckled.

Cliff shifted his attention back to the woman who had broken up the argument, as she, too, shared a couple of words with the Badger, who didn't appear all that discouraged by the confrontation. In fact, he appeared to enjoy the attention he was receiving from all the people still looking over at him, smiling, and even waving, as he pushed his brimmed hat up a little higher to show off his face before dismissively dusting his hands off and walking away.

"I wonder what she said to him?" Jan said quietly to Cliff.

"Not sure, but she handled it well." Cliff took a few steps closer, and the woman finally turned to face them.

"Oh god, no!" Jan said, turning away and pretending to look at the nearest booth, which just so happened to be a collection of women's leather purses.

This left Cliff alone once again as Lou finally spotted him, waved, and ran over.

"Cliff! It's so good to see you," Lou said as she started to come in for a hug, which was a little awkward, considering Cliff wasn't much of a hugger. If Lou noticed his discomfort, she didn't let him know it.

"Lou, it's great to see you too," Cliff said, surprised that he found himself believing it. Perhaps that was because Lou had been such a big help solving the mysterious death in town, considering she was the only person in the Ontario Provisional Police who was willing to listen to his suggestion, and had been integral to discovering who was behind the murder.

It was sheer happenstance that they had even met in the first place. She'd been tasked to escort him home when he'd first arrived in town, which was supposed to be a punishment. But now he would even go as far as to consider her a friend in town. A friend who might be able to help an old man bring some excitement to the current mundane existence he found himself wrapped up in.

"What was that about?" Cliff asked. But if he thought he was going to get any information he was wrong.

Lou was clearly not on duty today, having abandoned her blue-and-black uniform for more casual cowboy boots and a sundress. Between her hair being down and the sunglasses she had on, Cliff hardly recognized her.

"Just silly men." Lou waved a hand dismissively. "You know I can see you, Jan. Right?" She looked over Cliff's shoulder.

"Oh? What? I didn't… Lou? Wow!"

This was painful for Cliff to watch. He couldn't even begin to understand how Jan must be feeling, though that did little to stop him.

"So good to see you. You look really great…and in boots. And those…"

"Sunglasses?"

"Yes. Nice."

"Smooth," Cliff said. "Looks like you handled that well?" Cliff attempted again, gesturing towards the Badger, now standing in front of a vendor and laughing as if nothing had just happened. Perhaps, for him, nothing had?

"Best to shut that stuff down early," Lou said, shaking her head.

"Yeah. And you really did shut it down," Jan said with a smile.

"Thanks?"

"You're welcome." Jan bowed his head, before thinking better of it and stopping. This only managed to make him look more awkward. He must have felt it, too, as his eyes closed heavily.

"Right, well. I wouldn't have expected to see you here today?" Cliff jumped in, saving Jan from himself, but, to his surprise, it was Lou who appeared uneasy. She shifted nervously on her feet and looked around.

"Me? I read about it in the paper and thought it would be a fun day."

"You read my article?" Jan asked, surprised.

"I read *an* article. I'm not sure who wrote it. Don't even know what paper it was in, if I'm being honest," Lou said, giving Jan a shrug.

"Oh."

"You come alone?" Cliff asked.

"Yeah. Well, sort of. I—"

"I got you lemonade, since you said you didn't want a soda," said a rather large gentleman, who handed Lou a biodegradable cup.

"Oh, thank you," Lou said with a half-smile. "Dan, this is Cliff and Jan. Cliff, Jan this is Dan. He's…"

"Massive?" Cliff offered, which caused Lou's face to turn bright red.

"Thank you. It's part genetic and part hard work," Dan said. He stretched out his arms and scanned them, not that this was entirely necessary, considering every inch of Dan's body looked to be covered in either muscles, tattoos, or both.

"You look very familiar." Cliff gave the big man a once-over. "Would I have met you before?"

"Not likely," Lou said quickly before Dan could answer.

"So. Dan. Are…ummm…you police?" Jan said, though from the sounds of it, he was having trouble getting the words to come out of his mouth properly.

"No," Dan said with a smile, and Jan looked a little relieved, though it didn't last long. "I'm with the London Fire Department."

"Really?" Jan said, and Cliff could have sworn Jan was trying to stand up a little straighter than normal. Jan opened and closed his mouth, clearly trying to figure out something to reply with, though he didn't appear pleased with the line that eventually erupted from his mouth. "Ever run into burning buildings?"

"All the time," Dan said without hesitation. "Kinda goes with the territory, you know." He sipped his drink. "Like you and photos?" Dan tilted his head as he glanced at Jan's camera.

"Yes. Well, no. I take photos for the paper, but I also write the words…articles with the corresponding image."

"Corresponding image?" Cliff mumbled to Jan, shaking his head.

"Yes, so I pretty much handle most of the St. Marys paper," Jan said, trying to shrug it off like it was no big deal.

"Jan's a great writer," Cliff offered, feeling a little bit bad for Jan's apparent awkwardness.

"Thanks, Cliff," Jan said, and for a moment he almost went back to normal.

"Did *you* write the article about this festival?" Dan asked, pointing towards Jan and getting excited.

"Yes! Yes, I did." Jan beamed.

"Yeah, you're good. Remember, Lou, you made me read it the other day."

"Did I?" Lou said, shrugging it off. "I don't remember if that was the article."

"I knew it!" Jan pointed towards Lou, wearing a smug look of amusement on his face.

"Yeah. I'm almost certain that was it," Dan said, and he appeared to really be thinking about it, for a moment. "Yeah, Jan, right?"

"It's *Jan*," Jan said, emphasising the soft J sound. "It's Dutch."

"Right, yeah, of course," Dan said, turning to Lou. "I read it the other morning at your place."

This appeared to strike what little wind he had right out from Jan's sails.

It also appeared to be the last little straw for Lou, too, as she grabbed Dan by the arm and started to pull him away. "Well, it was great to run into you both. Been too long, Cliff. We should grab a coffee soon."

Dan, who seemed oblivious to everything around him, smiled as he sipped his drink. "Nice to meet you both." He waved, leaving Jan and Cliff alone once again.

"That went well," Cliff said, turning to keep walking through the vendors.

"You think?" Jan shook his head. "Felt strange to me."

"Yeah, I was kidding. It was awkward," Cliff chuckled.

"I agree. I mean, lying about reading my article…come on," Jan pointed out, looking over for some sort of confirmation from Cliff, which he did not get. "Okay, fine, I might have handled that a little better."

"You think?" Cliff said. "Have you talked to her at all since you wrote that piece about her for the paper?"

Jan had written a great article in the paper, praising Lou and all the hard work she did in helping to solve the last murder in town. In fact, it had gone over so well with her superiors that they had offered her a promotion, which she took, as long as it meant she wouldn't need to leave the area. Cliff wasn't entirely sure why she had wanted to stay, since her family was up closer to Kenora, but she had.

Cliff imagined the article should have evened the scales with the previous article Jan had written about Lou, which had contained some private banter that Lou had told him about while they'd been out on a date. Needless to say, they did not have a second date, and Jan had been trying to crawl himself back into her good books ever since.

"I don't understand what she sees in him," Jan said, which would have made Cliff laugh, had it not been so ridiculous.

"You mean besides the fact that he is very, very good-looking?"

"You think *he's* attractive?" Jan shook his head.

Cliff smirked. "I think society thinks he's attractive, Jan, and I would wager a guess Lou does as well."

"Different taste, I guess. Some people like the lean look." Jan ran a hand down the front of his body. Then he caught a glimpse of the time. "Shoot! I have to go, they're about to start the finals of the nail competition, and I'm supposed to take photos."

"Nail competition?" Cliff asked.

"Yes, competitors see who can drive a six-inch nail into a railway timber with the fewest strikes, in the fastest time."

"You're kidding," Cliff said.

"Not at all. It's actually incredibly challenging. You'd be surprised."

"I bet I would. Well, good luck," Cliff called as Jan ran off into the crowd.

Cliff looked around, wondering just what else was happening at the festival, when he caught sight of the Badger, who was being pulled by the arm between two tents by a man in a brown plaid shirt.

I wonder where he's off to in such a hurry?

The thought alone was enough to cause Cliff to shake his head. "I really need to find a hobby," he said to himself as he continued off down the row of tents.

3

Cliff hadn't managed much more than adding to his waistline as he wandered around the fairgrounds without any real plan. He'd been sucked into the various food vendors, particularly the old-fashioned donut stand that he told himself he didn't really need but got anyway.

He didn't have a plan and, worse still, he was incredibly aware that, despite there being so many activities, he hadn't found a single one that interested him. He found himself jealous of his housemates, each of whom had found something to help occupy their time while they were here.

Mrs. Chen had squirreled up in the greenhouse, and when Cliff had passed, he found her engaged in a discussion with one of the gardeners about the benefits of annuals versus perennials with regards to the overall aesthetics of a garden. Cliff hadn't stuck around long enough to see which one was right.

Bunty was talking to a local wool distributor about getting a discount for their upcoming church fundraiser. Kitty and Sol argued over the value of quantity or quality of strawberries picked while they watched some sort of tractor show. Hans, who had more hobbies than Cliff could shake a stick at, had seemed to distract himself in the animal show pen. Even Gerald, despite the heat and the man's obvious affinity for sweating, had cozied up next to what appeared to be a massive smoker and was discussing the merits of various types of wood smoke.

Each one of them found themselves engaged in conversation about a topic they were interested in. Whereas Cliff, who lacked a hobby or anything to keep him distracted from the day-to-day, wandered around, picking away at treats while he watched people move through the festival.

It wasn't like he hadn't tried to be interested in stuff. He liked gardening, but not enough to do it every day. The same went for reading or cooking or cards. He was a man who liked a lot but didn't like anything enough to feel he could do it all the time. He supposed that would have been one of the reasons why he never got a tattoo. Every time he'd ever thought about one, he could never imagine looking at it forever.

"You look lost," said a voice that startled Cliff from his internal contemplation.

He looked around and spotted a woman he supposed was in her sixties, wrapped in light, flowing material that Cliff thought would be very warm in the heat, although she didn't appear to be sweating at all…unlike himself.

"Who, me?" he asked.

She nodded giving him a thin smile. She wore dark eyeliner that made it appear as though she was looking through him and not at him.

"No, I'm pretty sure I know where I am."

"Somehow I doubt that very much," she said, flashing him a toothy grin.

Cliff looked around at the surrounding vendors, feeling like he was going mad or something. He had been wandering around for some time, and he might not know where the entrance was from here, but he didn't think he would go as far as to say he was lost.

"You have a lot on your mind." She said it more as a fact than as a question.

Cliff was puzzled by the accusation. He opened his mouth to speak, but stopped, taking a moment to look around until he spotted the folded sign by the entrance of the small red and gold tent she had set up. He read: "Physic Readings, Tarot Cards $20. Unlock Your Path to Happiness."

"I'm okay," Cliff said, waving a hand in her direction as he went to carry on his way. *Where am I going?*

"You recently made a big decision in your life, and you're wondering if it was the right one," she said, once again catching him off guard.

He would have refuted the idea if it wasn't altogether true.

"I don't believe in fortunes," Cliff said, stopping to face the woman, whose eyes studied him as if picking him apart.

"I know," she said sincerely.

He didn't think she was offended, although she didn't take her eyes off him either.

"That doesn't mean I'm not correct."

"Maybe, but isn't everyone always making some kind of big decision?" Cliff suggested.

"I don't know. Are they?" The woman shrugged.

"I think so." Cliff shook his head, wondering why he was still engaging with this woman. For some reason, he couldn't convince his feet to keep moving.

"Does that mean your decision is any less important?" she asked him.

"No. I just mean you're trying to hook me into spending money in your tent. I'm just saying it's not going to work," Cliff said, trying to sound confident.

"Is that what I'm doing?" She tilted her head off to one side.

"Well, isn't it?" Cliff asked.

"I saw a man who looked like he was asking himself a lot of questions.

Questions he didn't have answers for." She shrugged. "Is it wrong to want to ask?"

"No. It's just… Like I said, I don't believe in fortunes," Cliff repeated, though, at this point, he got the feeling he was trying to convince himself and not her.

"Okay," she said, waving a hand.

Cliff turned slowly on his heel to walk away. Then he paused, turned back around, and opened his mouth to say something, but stopped, shook his head, and frowned.

"I hope you find the answers you're looking for."

"I'm not looking for answers," Cliff shot back.

"Interesting," she said, turning to head back inside her tent.

Cliff watched her, as the urge to walk away combatted with his curiosity. Why was this interesting, and why did she think he had unanswered questions? He did, of course. But that was hardly the point. He'd spent his life as a detective, and the one thing he knew about most people was they all had questions they needed answered about something.

Reluctantly, Cliff took a step inside the tent, and when he did, he was hit with a nice, cool blast of chilled air. It was a refreshing difference to the heat outside.

"Why is it interesting?" he asked.

"Isn't everything in life interesting? If it wasn't, wouldn't things be boring?" she asked.

"Sure. Yeah. I guess so," Cliff said, trying to find his words again. "But why is mine interesting?"

"I don't know, is it?" She took a seat in a comfy chair that faced Cliff and the entrance.

"You just told me you thought it was interesting."

"Is that what I said?" she said with a disarming smile.

"I might be too old for this." He shook his head. "You got me all confused."

"I'm not trying to confuse you. I said you looked like a man who was contemplating a recent decision. Unraveling questions is kind of what I do."

"It seems to me that you like to trick old people into your tent," Cliff said, folding his arms across his chest.

To his surprise, she laughed. It was healthy, vibrant even, and it caught him so off guard he didn't know how to respond.

"Is that what I did to you? Tricked you? You followed me in here. I didn't ask you to come in or invite you to join me. You made it clear you didn't want to hear what I had to say. And unlike yourself, I respect boundaries." She set her hands on a small wooden table in front of her as she leaned in towards him.

Cliff looked around the small space and thought back on the conversation and realized she might be right, although it hadn't been his intention at all. But now that he was thinking about it, he was having trouble understanding what his intentions even were.

"I'm sorry. You're right. I shouldn't have just come in."

"But you're here now. And it's cool, and I'm quiet today. So why not have a seat?" She gestured to the chair across from her." Cliff opened his mouth to protest, but she raised a hand to stop him. "Yes, I know you don't believe in fortunes. That's fine."

Cliff took a look around the tent. It was sparse, save for the two chairs and the round table in the centre. At the back of the tent, Cliff noticed the small air conditioner that was running, which let out a soft humming sound and kept the room at a chilled temperature.

He stepped over to the chair and sat down before he had a chance to overthink what it was he was doing, staying in the tent with this person.

"You think you can see the future?" Cliff asked, which released another laugh from the woman.

"Do you think if I could see the future I would be in this tent? That I wouldn't use my gifts to win the lottery and live out my days in a tropical paradise, drinking fruity drinks and basking in the sun?" she asked, brows raised.

"I suppose not," Cliff chuckled.

"I interpret things. Cards, visions, glimpses of people, past, present, and futures. Although nothing is clear. I just have a way of…"

"Telling people what they want to hear?" Cliff offered up.

"No. Not always. I just offer them what I see. What they choose to do with that information is entirely up to them," she said, not at all insulted by Cliff's line of questioning.

"Well…" Cliff started, realizing he didn't know her name, "what do I call you?" He felt awkward about the phrasing of that sentence, as if she had a name, like Tabitha the Incredible.

"Rosalind."

"Were your parents Shakespeare fans?" Cliff asked, recalling a Rosalind in at least one of the bard's plays.

"They were English majors, yes," she said. "And yourself?"

"Cliff," he said, holding out his hand to introduce himself.

Rosalind took it. "Nice you meet you."

"You as well," Cliff said. "So, you told me I recently made a decision and I'm second-guessing it."

"I did," Rosalind said.

"Why?"

"Because you have. Haven't you." Once again, Rosalind posed it more as a statement than a question.

"I suppose so," Cliff said. He went to continue, but Rosalind held up a finger.

"Why don't we see what the cards have to say?" She pulled out a deck of cards from a drawer under the table.

Cliff had never seen tarot cards before, but he had to admit the design on the well-worn cards was very detailed.

"Sure. Why not?" Cliff relaxed back in the chair. After all, what else had he been doing, other than wandering around the festival waiting for the time to meet everyone back at the Hearse? At least here he was cool.

Rosalind grinned as she shuffled the deck of cards and placed them on the table, gesturing for Cliff to cut the deck. Cliff leaned in and split them, doing his best to cut the deck right in half. He wasn't sure why, but it had been a habit of his from his days of playing bridge. He'd never actually known how accurate he was, but he liked to imagine he was close.

Picking up the cards, Rosalind took care in placing the lower cut cards on top and knocking the top of the deck with her knuckles before picking it up. She still hadn't said anything, and Cliff, who was still rather skeptical of the whole thing, wasn't about to start talking about his life, only to give her more fodder for her mind games.

Smiling, she flipped a card over, tilting her head at the card before placing four more around it, starting at the top and working around clockwise, before finally ending with three cards face down at the bottom. Rosalind looked to be examining the cards individually, making curious sounds at each one and, to his surprise, never looking up at him to see his reaction. Though he supposed that was because he had no idea what any of the cards meant.

"Very fascinating, Cliff," she said at last. "You have lived an exciting life, although I see that it has been lonely."

Cliff opened his mouth but stopped.

Rosalind continued. "Don't feel the need to say anything. The cards tell me a lot about you, Cliff."

"Such as?" Cliff wondered.

"You enjoy puzzles. Solving things. It consumes you, perhaps some sort of research...no, that's not it. Police or detective. Yes, a detective.

Your life was your work, though from your past, I would say it was because you were running away from something or…someone?"

Cliff had to struggle not to say anything. Although he wasn't willing to say she was right, it was hard to say she was wrong. He wasn't quite sure he'd been running away from anything. He'd left his life in town to have a better future, a future away from all the problems he had with growing up in a small town like St. Marys.

"This card means death," she said, pointing to the one in the centre.

"Hopefully not too soon," he joked, though he could feel his pulse quickening.

"Not you. Not yet." She smiled at him, and he couldn't tell if he was relieved or not. "But this death seems to follow you around. It can have all kinds of meanings, but this one aligns with your past, present, and future. Perhaps it's the death of an old idea, or a love maybe. But whatever it is, the cards also show rebirth in its wake. But, in order for you to achieve this, you have to let old ideas die." She looked up at Cliff, who must have looked confused, because she added, "It might not make sense now. But it will. You just have to be open to change. Which I can see is against your nature."

She smiled, gesturing to another of the cards. "Also, I see many close people in your life. Perhaps too close. You may feel suffocated. There will be a time when you must choose if you are willing to embrace this new life or return to the comfortable," she said, still smiling.

Cliff wasn't sure if this was helping him to understand or hurting.

"It appears you will be tested as well. You lack purpose, and I can see walls that have been built up for your protection. But those same walls prevent you from truly becoming who you were meant to be. The person you want to be," she said with a shrug. "Not sure if you can relate or not, but hey, I just read the cards."

Cliff sat, unmoving, but listening intently, trying hard not to say anything as Rosalind spoke, though he could only imagine what his face must look like, since he was still processing all the death talk. Cliff was used to death. He'd been around it his entire life. But it didn't mean he enjoyed the idea of it happening to him.

"So, I need to let things around me die?" Cliff asked.

"Not exactly. Like I said, the cards give me a glimpse, and what I see right now is two paths, one is longer than the other. But in order to reach this path, you have to be willing to let some part of you die. Possibly some part of your past. This is the only way to open yourself up to the future."

"You know, this is all very cryptic."

"Oh yeah, I'm very aware." Rosalind chuckled. "However, what would the fun be in life if someone told you all of the answers? Sometimes we need guidance, and then it is up to us to decide how we want to interpret that guidance."

"You think I need guidance to let go of my past?" Cliff asked.

"I've only just met you. To say I know anything about your life other than what is in front of me is absurd. I'm just here to tell you what I see. Do *you* think you need to let go of your past?"

"The past defines us," Cliff said with a shrug. "Wouldn't letting that go change who I am?"

"Perhaps. Perhaps not." Rosalind shrugged. "We can never forget our past, and our experiences, and you're right, everything you've done has made you who you are today. And from what the cards tell me, you are a very capable man, Cliff."

"Thank you." Cliff leaned back in his chair while he thought about it. "Can you tell me what this event is? The one that will bring me to my crossroads?" He felt a little strange now that he was sitting in this tent, talking to a woman he, only moments before, had written off as a con artist. Though if she was, even he had to admit she was an impressive one.

"You of all people should know it's not one event that changes the course of our life, but rather a series of micro-challenges that build towards a final decision."

"Why me, of all people?"

"You spent your life solving puzzles. When is a problem ever just one problem?"

"Sounds more like a riddle to me."

"Perhaps it is. Perhaps I'm just a crazy woman spouting nonsense." Rosalind shrugged, causing Cliff to laugh.

"I wasn't going to say anything," he said, holding up his hands in defence. He noticed the final four cards on the side. "What are those?"

"Those are your near future, but if you want those, it will cost you twenty dollars." Rosalind held out a hand and raised her brows.

"In for a penny, I suppose," Cliff said, as he leaned to his side and pulled out his wallet and took a green twenty from inside.

"Good man. And for what it's worth, I'm rooting for you, Cliff." Rosalind waved a hand over the star formation of cards on the table.

"I suppose I am too." Cliff put his wallet back in his pocket and rested his hands on his lap. "So, what do you see?"

Rosalind flipped the cards. "I see someone seeking your help. They are in trouble, trouble you are good at sorting out." Rosalind leaned in to scan the cards. "But you need to be careful. I see danger for you, and someone you care about. I see countryside, perhaps fields, maybe? And a family tied in knots and your presence unwanted." Rosalind looked up at Cliff. Unlike him, she looked concerned by what she was reading.

"So, you're saying I'm going to try and help people who won't like me?" Cliff laughed. "I'm used to that, especially when it comes to solving puzzles."

"You are certainly well-equipped. But for you to succeed, you will need to rely on the help of others." Rosalind looked up at Cliff. "And from what the cards are telling me, this is not in your nature."

"Not sure you need to be a fortune teller to get that one," Cliff said with a grin. He was treating this as he did any other parlor game, trying to get amusement from it. Although normally parlor games didn't have another human on the other end, looking as though he was a fly hovering near a trap.

"Does the phrase 'the earth laughs in flowers' mean anything to you?" she asked him.

Cliff thought it sounded familiar, but he couldn't pin why. If it was something he was supposed to know, he certainly couldn't think of it now.

"No, not really."

Rosalind shrugged. "Might be something, might be nothing. I'm not sure."

"You just read the cards," Cliff said.

"Exactly."

"So, this news, how soon can I expect to get it?" Cliff asked.

Just as he said this, there was a scream of terror from somewhere outside. It was faint, and between the air conditioner and the heavy fabric of the tent, Cliff wasn't confident he'd even heard anything.

But Rosalind's face paled.

"What is it?" Cliff asked.

"I think, sooner than you might imagine."

4

Cliff stepped out from the tent, unsure of what he should be feeling now that he was outside. Based on the expressions of everyone around him, confusion appeared to be the common state. He doubted, though, that it was for the same reasons.

"What's going on?" Cliff asked a passerby.

It was a young woman who appeared to be on a date. She and the person she was with shrugged, and then, like everyone else, turned to face the origin of the commotion. It was as if everyone wanted to know the reason for the hysterical cries for help. But everyone also was afraid of getting any closer.

"Cliff!" It was Hans's voice.

Cliff turned to see the big man moving through the crowd of people, coming up beside him.

"What's going on?"

"I was just asking myself the same question," Cliff said, looking around.

"You heard the yelling though, right? I wasn't imagining that?"

"No. Someone was most certainly yelling." Cliff took an initial step towards the heart of the commotion. In the distance, a small gathering of people had started to form around one of the outbuildings farther up from them. "Only one way to find out, I suppose." Cliff waved a hand and starting walking towards the crowd.

"I hope it's not anything serious," Hans said, taking a few long strides to catch up to Cliff.

"That would be nice," Cliff said, though he doubted very much that was the case, considering the gut-wrenching cry he'd heard, even from inside a thick canvas tent with the air-conditioning running. Cliff wagered it was likely everyone heard it.

Cliff and Hans walked up to the crowd and were blocked from moving any closer. Unfortunately, as was a natural response from crowds, nearly everyone there wanted to get closer to get a glimpse of what was happening.

"See anything?" Cliff asked, hoping his huge friend might have a better perspective from where he was, which was nearly a head taller than himself.

"Looks like all the commotion is coming from that building up there, but no, I can't see what's happening." Hans shrugged.

Luckily for Cliff, he had years of practice getting through crowds, so it didn't take long for old habits to kick in. Pulling out his wallet, he held it open and started shimmying through the crowds of people.

"Police? Move, please. Please, move," Cliff said, holding out his wallet. People began to part slightly to let him pass.

Hans, who must not have wanted to get left behind, began moving along with Cliff, periodically exclaiming, "I'm with him," as he passed.

A few moments later, the pair had broken through the crowd and were standing at the front, a respectful distance from the entrance of the building. At this point, Cliff didn't know what he should be doing. From the looks of it, a couple of people had taken care to stand by the door. Cliff didn't know them, but they looked to be employees of the farm.

"I can't believe people moved for you," Hans whispered in Cliff's ear.

"The most important thing is to sound like you should be here. Most people will just accept it," Cliff said with a shrug.

"But isn't it wrong to tell people you're the police? Isn't that a crime?"

"I didn't tell people I *was* the police." Cliff turned to give his friend a smile. "I just held up my wallet and *asked* if there were police. If people presumed I was the police and not *looking* for the police, then that was simply a miscommunication."

"Sounds misleading," Hans said rolling his eyes.

Cliff shrugged. "You're welcome to go back there."

"Well, I'm here now."

Cliff shook his head, amused, then scanned the crowd until he saw the person he was looking for poking their head out from the crowd and walking over to the tent.

"Opa!" Jan yelled as he skirted across the crowd.

"Jan? I didn't know you were here," Hans said, embracing his nephew in a big hug.

"I did." Cliff smiled wryly, as Hans tossed away the remark.

"Are you doing a piece on the 75th anniversary?" Hans asked.

"I was. But I think this might be the bigger story, now," Jan said, adding, "unfortunately," after seeing the sad look on his Opa's face.

"Well, we don't know what's going on yet," Hans said optimistically. "You haven't heard anything, have you?"

"Only just got here, and they won't let me inside," Jan said.

"Who won't?"

"The staff. And well…"

"Lou," Cliff offered, realizing she would have been here immediately. "Yes."

"Lou's here too? Busy morning, Cliff," Hans mused.

"I ran into them while I was walking around," Cliff said casually as he leaned over, looking to catch a glimpse inside, secretly hoping Lou might spot him.

"How did it go? With Lou?" Hans asked Jan.

"It was okay," Jan said, at the same time Cliff said, "Bad." The pair looked at each other and then over at Hans.

"I just mean…" Cliff started to correct himself but didn't have a strategy of where to go next, so he looked to Jan to fill in the missing pieces.

"Better. It could have gone better," Jan offered. "She was here with a date."

"A date? With who?"

"A rather large firefighter," Cliff said.

"Would you call him large?" Jan said, looking as though he was having trouble chewing a sour grape. "He was big, for sure, but I don't know if I would go as far as to say *large*."

"Fine, he's big," Cliff said shaking his head. He felt for Jan, but sooner or later he was going to have to take a risk and talk to Lou again if he ever wanted to try and make things right.

"How big?" Hans asked. "That guy big?" He gestured to a figure looking confused near the tent.

Cliff nearly laughed out loud when he spotted him. "Yes. Exactly him," Cliff said. "That's Dan."

"He is big," Hans said, shaking his head and then, catching sight of Jan's slack mouth, he quickly added, "Sorry, Jan."

"Sorry? Why? I think it's great she's dating. I just hope that means we can put our past behind us and move on. Be amicable. And all of that," Jan said, not sounding all that convincing as he rambled to himself.

Cliff watched until he spotted Lou. She finally poked her head out from inside the tent, and he saw his chance to call out to her.

"Lou!" Cliff waved a hand.

She looked concerned as she walked over with Dan a half step behind. "Cliff. I should have guessed you'd be nearby."

"I think everyone is nearby, Lou," Cliff said, giving her a shrug.

"We all heard the scream. Is everyone okay?" Hans asked.

Lou opened her mouth to speak but then spotted Jan standing there. "May be best if I don't talk too much about it."

"Is that because of me?" Jan asked.

"You mean the reporter with a pen and paper, ready to take photos?" Lou said, the sarcasm dipping off her tongue. "Yes."

"We all just want to know what's going on, Lou," Jan said, gesturing to the crowd.

"And you'll have to wait along with everyone else for a statement."

"When will that be?" Jan asked.

"When we have a statement."

"So, you're waiting for the police to arrive then?" Jan asked in a very unwanted reporter kind of way, which caused Lou to raise a brow. "Fair enough. I'll wait."

"Are you going back in?" Cliff asked.

Lou nodded and then narrowed her eyes at Cliff. "No," she said, waving a finger, "I can't. You're a civilian."

"I'm not saying give me a badge. Just let me see what's happened. A second pair of eyes never hurts."

"Couldn't hurt," Dan said, shrugging. "You mentioned him being helpful before."

This brought a smile to Cliff's face and a look of disappointment to Lou's.

"What?"

"It's Dan, right?" Hans said, getting a curious look from Lou in the process, but if she was going to asked how Hans knew his name, she shook the idea out of her mind.

"Yes," he said, stretching a hand out towards Hans. "I'm Lou's…"

"Friend. He's…my friend," she said, putting a stop to wherever that conversation was heading. "Why do you even think I'll need help?"

"A hunch," Cliff said casually.

"And what gave you this…hunch?" Lou smiled.

"A fortune teller," Cliff said. He ignored the collection of confused faces appearing in front of him. "It doesn't matter. I just think you're going to need me."

Lou looked hard at him for a long moment and appeared to be weighing her options before finally landing on a decision. She held up a finger. "Fine, but you keep quiet, and you don't speak unless I ask you something."

Cliff mimed locking his lips with a key and tucking it in his pocket.

She turned to head towards the tent with Dan beside her. Cliff went to follow but felt a big hand on his shoulder. He turned to look at Hans.

"What about me?" Hans asked.

"It's probably best if you stay here." Cliff gave a thin smile and placed a hand on Han's shoulder.

"What about me?" Jan asked optimistically.

"Only if you want Lou to beat you up," Cliff joked.

Jan stopped in his tracks and honestly considered the idea for a moment. "I'll wait here with Opa," he said finally.

"Safe call," Cliff said, moving to catch up with Lou. He glanced back and caught the worried expression on Hans's face.

"You'll tell me what happened though, right?" Hans whispered.

"Of course," Cliff said quickly before turning to approach the building.

When Cliff entered, he spotted a pair of employees who both appeared to be holding back tears, standing guard by the entrance. At first glance, Cliff noticed the door, which was currently open, had a surprisingly complex lock on it. Cliff found this curious considering the tiny barn-like building didn't appear to be all that important, so far away from the main building.

The red-faced employees moved aside after Lou explained who she was. Cliff and Dan followed, staying close enough that no one seemed to guess at their reason for being there.

The building was larger than Cliff would have guessed from the outside and looked to be some sort of storage unit for all the extra supplies for the festival and the farm. There was a long corridor down the centre of the room. On either side were rows of shelves packed full with numerous boxes labeled for everything from napkins and cups, to stacks of various canned drinks. Nothing that Cliff thought warranted the massive lock on the front door. Then he spotted the source of the cries.

At the end of the corridor were two people Cliff had never met and, had it not been for Hans, he might never have recognized. The first was Mari, who was clearly the cause of the cries that Cliff, and presumably the rest of the attendees, had heard around the farm. Her face was flushed red as she pressed her head into the chest of, who Cliff assumed must be her cousin, Flynn. His own face looked angry and resolute as he stared down at the body sprawled out on the floor only a few feet from where they stood.

Cliff, who was no stranger to crime scenes, felt a pang of guilt, as he watched the pained expressions on their faces. Perhaps it was because he had a small, yet somewhat personal, connection with the pair standing there, although it was more likely the feelings of guilt at knowing how much this was going to hurt Hans. He was immediately grateful he'd had his friend wait outside.

Because even as Cliff moved closer to the body, he knew exactly who it was. It was Hans's good friend, Pieter VanWinkle, who lay dead on the ground.

5

Cliff's personal feelings about the body lying prone on the floor were cut short as he instinctively reverted to his previously familiar role as investigator and began to examine the area around him. He still didn't know what had happened to the man, and he wasn't prepared to start making assumptions until he had a better sense of the room around him.

"That's..." Lou stopped short of the body on the ground, her own expression going dark as she spotted the unmoving figure.

Pieter VanWinkle, from everything Cliff had gathered, was well-known in the surrounding area as being a good man, but also for the fact that his family farm had been an institution in the community for as long as most people could remember. Clearly even Lou, who was a transplant to the area, understood what this would mean.

"Yes," Cliff said, trying to keep his own emotions in check.

"Is he...?" Dan asked, and Cliff wagered, being a firefighter, Dan was no stranger when it came to seeing death on the job. Firefighters often saw the most horrific things while working, but still, no one ever "got used to it," Cliff knew.

"Yes," Cliff said, shaking his head as he took a few steps away, giving the body on the floor a wide berth.

"What are you doing?" Lou whispered, reaching out to grab Cliff's arm. "You really shouldn't be here."

But Cliff's eyes never left the body as he started to pay a little more attention to the things around it.

"I'm already here, Lou," Cliff said, giving her hand a pat. "What do you see?"

"I see two people who just lost a family member," Lou whispered into Cliff's ear.

"That's a side effect. What do you see?" Cliff asked again, shaking his head.

Lou looked confused.

"They shouldn't be here."

"No, *you* shouldn't—" Lou started.

But Cliff turned and took her by the hand and looked into her eyes, hoping his own eyes conveyed the confidence he certainly wasn't feeling himself. Although years of keeping his composure had taught him one thing. Someone has to stay calm.

"Lou," Cliff said his voice low and even, "there is a body on the ground. We need to clear the area. Have Dan move them, take them to an office maybe, somewhere they can sit down and not talk to anyone until more police arrive. Who knows how many people have already been in here. We need to know who they were as well."

"You think this was…?" Lou said.

Cliff shook his head before she could say the words out loud. It would do no one any good to overhear even the slightest thought of this being anything more than an unfortunate accident.

"We don't know what it was," Cliff said carefully. "All we know is that there is a man dead. We need to isolate this area, sooner rather than later."

Lou took a deep breath and straightened up, giving Cliff a nod.

"Hello," Lou said, coughing to get the strain out from her voice as she approached Mari and Flynn.

Cliff couldn't hear what she was saying to them, but her tone was low, and from the looks of things, they appeared to be nodding, which was a good sign.

A few seconds later, she called Dan over. His face was unreadable as he approached Lou. After a few brief words, he led the cousins away, with one of the employees who'd been standing uncomfortably in the corner of the room. They all appeared relieved that Dan was leading them out.

"I told Dan to stay with them until the police arrive," Lou said when they were alone. "I also told him to tell the two employees out front not to let anyone who isn't the police in here." She shook her head, clearly unsure if she was doing it right.

"You're doing great, Lou."

"I don't know what the hell I'm doing, Cliff," she said, shaking her head. "Pardon my language."

"I'm not Kitty, Lou. And I've heard worse," he chuckled. "You're doing a great job. The important thing is just to keep track of everyone who was in and out of here. Whoever comes is going to want to know that."

"We just saw him earlier," she said, her hand covering her mouth slightly as she glanced down at the body.

"Try not to think about that. Not yet."

Cliff took a step and spotted for the first time the only thing that justified the large locks on the door. A small safe, about one metre high, pressed up against the back wall. He hadn't seen it before, since it was blocked by Mari and Flynn.

"What is it?" Lou asked.

Something on Cliff's face must have given his thoughts away as he turned to look at her before gesturing to the safe, which, at least from where he was standing, was clearly cracked open.

"You see that?" Cliff stepped around Pieter's body. He was ignoring the reality that he would have to be the one to tell Hans what had happened to his friend and the pain it was most certainly going to cause him.

"It's a safe," Lou said. Moving to follow him, she tilted her head to look at it.

"Notice anything strange about it?"

"It's open."

"Why is it open? What was in it?" Cliff asked, though it was more out of habit than anything.

One of the things Cliff had always enjoyed about his work was answering questions. In his mind, he never saw himself *investigating* anything so much as just asking and then answering a series of questions. If he was able to ask the right questions and find the right answers, eventually he would find his way to the ultimate conclusion. Although every investigation always started with the simple, more innocuous, questions, like "What was in the safe?"

"You think it was a robbery?" Lou asked.

"Too many variables to think like that," Cliff said. "Think smaller. What do you see? What doesn't make sense?"

Lou shook her head. "I don't understand."

"Of course you do, Lou. You're smart. Use that brain of yours and those eyes. Look around."

"I see a body," Lou said hesitantly. "A dead body."

"Be specific, what about it?"

"How are you so calm right now?" Lou asked.

"I'm not," Cliff said chuckling, "but my emotions won't help me right now. I'll process those later. For now, we need to pay attention to the situation at hand." Cliff placed a hand on Lou's shoulder. "Take a breath. Calm yourself."

He waited for Lou to take in a deep breath. She held it for a moment before letting it go. She by no means looked to be a hundred percent, but at least she no longer appeared to want to jump out of her skin, which was a step in the right direction.

He gave her another moment, then gave her shoulder a light squeeze. "Good. Now what do you see?"

Lou blinked a couple of times and took another deep breath before she started surveying the room around them. "There isn't any blood. So, he wasn't shot or hit with anything. So how did he die?" She squinted in thought, looking around the room. She knelt down on the ground and looked closely at Pieter's face.

Cliff knelt beside her, though he wasn't able to get that low. Still, he was able to see the face, made all the more visible as Lou pulled out her phone and flashed a light on it. Pieter's face was red and puffy and, if Cliff hadn't just met the man that day and seen what he'd been wearing, there was a chance he might not have recognized him at all.

"Maybe he was strangled?" Lou asked.

"Nothing around his neck to suggest that," Cliff said, gesturing to the neck.

"But he could have choked, a reaction to something maybe?" She looked up at Cliff, who shrugged. "Why is the body this way?" Lou asked, standing up and gesturing to Pieter's body, which was lying sideways and pointing towards the side wall.

Cliff pointed to a fallen stack of boxes beside his body. "He fell trying to support himself?"

"But it looks like he was crawling. See?" she said, looking at his arms. "He's moved past the boxes. "Why would he be crawling over here?" Lou got down closer, pausing briefly to point at a pool of pink liquid, which had leaked under one of the stands.

"What is that?" Cliff asked.

"Looks like…a milkshake maybe?" she said, trying to get a better look at the pink puddle. "Weird." She slowly dropped herself down to the floor and shined her flashlight along the ground, being careful not to touch or move anything.

"See anything else?"

"I don't… Wait…" She adjusted herself on the floor. "I see…ummm."

"What is it?" Cliff asked, feeling a rush of excitement at the idea of finding another clue.

For a moment, he nearly forgot where he was and what he was doing; it was just another case. But he wasn't a police officer anymore, and this wasn't his case. Nor was it just another body that he could leave in a file. This was someone his friend cared about, and he was dead on the ground.

"It's an EpiPen!" Lou said standing up with excitement. "He was reaching for an EpiPen. Perhaps this is all just some sort of unfortunate accident," she said, sounding hopeful.

Cliff had to admit that would be much simpler. It wouldn't comfort his friend much, but it would be easier to handle than the alternative. But there was something about it all that didn't quite add up for Cliff, like why was the safe open and why would there be a spilt milkshake but no cup?

"For the love of god," said a voice Cliff recognized coming from the entrance.

Cliff turned to see Captain Marks standing there, his lips closed tightly, as he glared over at Cliff. His brow was wet, though that wasn't much of a surprise for a man standing in his full, navy blue, OPP uniform in the middle of summer. "Why is this man anywhere near my crime scene?"

"Good to see you, too, Captain," Cliff said, glancing over at the large man, who, for good reason, wasn't a huge fan of Cliff. After all, Cliff and the other residents of the Limestone Manor had worked behind his back to solve a crime he didn't even know was happening. Because of this, his promotion had been, "postponed" while they sorted out what happened.

"I thought you were gone!" he said wiping the sleeve of his uniform over his forehead.

"Not yet. Actually, I'm sure you'll be happy to hear that I've committed to a room at the Limestone Manor for the year, Captain." Cliff grinned when he caught the annoyed look on Captain Marks's face.

"Lucky us," he said, letting out a heavy sigh.

"Sir, Cliff was helpful in locking down the crime scene," Lou said, though she didn't appear all too comfortable with the statement.

"I see. So you thought you would utilize some volunteers, and a retiree?" He gestured towards the front door and the Winkleberry staff members, then over at Cliff.

"I did the best with what I had." She sounded more confident now, or perhaps it was just more annoyed. Either way, Cliff appreciated it.

"Lou… *Officer Polaski* did an excellent job," Cliff offered, though he knew his input would do little to help her here.

"Oh well, I'm grateful she held up to your standards," Captain Marks said, letting the sarcasm linger in the air.

Cliff had hoped he wouldn't have to cross this man's path again, but here he was. *What does he expect from me? To do nothing?*

"Who is he?" the captain asked, nodding to the body on the ground, as another two uniforms came in from the outside, no doubt relieving the two sad employees from the front door.

"Pieter VanWinkle, sir," Lou said, her professionalism slipping in, as her entire demeanour shifted with the captain's presence. "He was found by his nephew, Flynn Stroud."

"Where is he?" Captain Marks asked.

"He's, umm, with his cousin. We moved them to one of the other buildings. They have an office there, and we thought it would be better place for them to wait until you arrived," Lou said.

"Oh, did we now?" The captain looked between Lou and Cliff, shaking his head. "So, who do we have looking after them? No doubt one of your friends there at the rock manor? Hell, you may as well bring the rest of them in."

"No, sir. It's, umm…Dan. He's a firefighter from London. He's, umm…well…my date, sir."

"Christ, Polaski, your date? What is this?"

"With all due respect, Captain. We're at a family festival in the middle of the day, and a body has turned up. Considering your response time was what? Twenty-five…thirty minutes?" Cliff said, making a show of looking down at his watch, though in truth, he had no idea how long it had taken them, but he was hedging his bets. "I'd say Lou used the resources she had on hand to lock down the area and contain the situation as best she could. And if you think there was some way she could have improved on her actions taken, I suggest you lay those out in your report. Though I can't imagine how you could have fared much better, sir." He added this last bit with a thin smile, catching the two officers behind Captain Marks pursing their lips, attempting to stifle their amusement. Cliff was impressed they managed to keep it together, even as Captain Marks began to fumble around with his words.

"Well, we're here now. Perhaps you can walk us through what you found," Captain Marks finally said to Lou through gritted teeth.

Cliff was sure that embarrassing the man likely wasn't the best way to handle the situation, but he didn't like the way he talked to Lou, and Cliff had spent his entire career surrounded by men like him, who felt like they could use their position to tower over people under them. Cliff hated it and wasn't afraid to let people know they were wrong.

"I think it's best if I go, now that the cavalry has arrived," Cliff said, gesturing towards the captain and the men behind him.

"I think that's best," Captain Marks agreed dryly. "Time to let the police do their job."

"Agreed," Cliff said as he walked towards the entrance.

"Cliff, wait!" Lou said, running after him, which received an eyeroll from the captain, which Cliff ignored.

"What is it, Lou?"

"Would you do me a favour?"

"Sure"

"Dan…ummm, his truck is at my house. And, ummm, I think I'd like to stay, but…" Lou looked so uneasy, Cliff was beginning to feel bad for her.

"What do you need, Lou?"

"Can you give him a ride home?" she asked nervously, which gave Cliff a good chuckle.

"Of course," Cliff said, turning to walk out of the building.

"Mr. Shaw," Captain Marks said before Cliff reached the door.

Cliff stopped and turned to face him. "Yes, Captain?"

"Please. Stay away from this investigation."

"Of course," Cliff said, giving the man a nod.

Just so long as you figure out what happened to Pieter VanWinkle, Cliff thought as he walked away.

6

"What happened?" Kitty asked from her seat in the Hearse.

Like everyone else who was at the farm, she had heard one of the morbid versions of what had happened that had swept around the celebration. Between the police arriving and the unexplainable reason as to why the festival was shut down in the first place, all manner of rumours had begun to spread around. Though only Cliff and Dan, who was squeezed into one of the seats at the back of the bus, really knew what was going on.

Cliff had remained quiet about the whole thing, since Pieter had been Hans's friend and, despite not wanting to be the one to tell him, Cliff had thought it was better that his friend heard it from him instead of anyone else.

Since Cliff had told him, Hans had gone very quiet and not said a single word to anyone. As such, the entire group was beginning to get restless about what had occurred.

"Perhaps now's not the best time to pry, Kitty," Sol suggested from the seat beside her. No doubt he too was wondering about Hans's silence and had concluded it was not good news.

"It's a shame they had to shut the whole festival down," Bunty said. "After all the hard work the VanWinkles put into setting it all up."

Cliff couldn't be sure, but he thought he heard sniffling from Hans as he drove the Hearse down the bumpy country road. Bunty must have heard it, too, as she quickly changed the topic.

Turning in her seat, she glanced back at Mrs. Chen who was seated behind her. "I see you got something special." Bunty forced a smile.

"I suppose it wasn't a waste of time, after all," Mrs. Chen said, her finger grazing the petals of a large orchid.

"Very lovely plant. Will it go in the garden?" Bunty asked.

"No, this one will just be for me in my room. It's a sign of good luck and, frankly, I'm going to need it if I don't get back in my garden soon," Mrs. Chen said, shaking her head.

"I'm sure it's already better than you think." Bunty smiled. "I know I love it, and the judges will too."

Behind Mrs. Chen sat Gerald, who chewed away on a large bag of kettle corn. He sat across from, looking confusedly at an equally confused-looking Dan.

"Gerald, you know it is possible to chew with your mouth closed, don't you?" Kitty said, turning to look back at him, her face scrunched up with an annoyed expression.

Gerald, on the other hand, appeared unfazed as he looked down and shoved his hand into the bag, scooping up another big handful.

"Yes. I do," he said, shovelling the corn into his open mouth.

Kitty scoffed and turned away, as Gerald continued to chew loudly.

"Who are you?" Cliff heard Kitty ask, when she finally turned in her seat to take a look at Dan in the back.

"Kitty, that's Dan. We told you that," Sol said, placing a concerned hand on Kitty's, which she promptly swatted away.

"I know his name, Sol. Do you think I'm losing my mind?" she asked.

Cliff smiled as he watched Sol open his mouth to speak, but think better of it and shake his head instead.

"Good. I'm simply asking *who* he is. He looks very familiar."

"You know a lot of young men, Kitty?" Mrs. Chen smiled.

"Don't you start that, Mrs. Chen. Or you will need more than that plant for good luck."

"Someone is snippy today," Mrs. Chen said, as she caressed her new plant.

"I think Kitty's just jealous, Mrs. Chen." Bunty looked towards Cliff and gave him a little wink.

"I do not like whatever this is. I was simply trying to understand who he is. Since this is a longer car ride, and we can't talk about the elephant in the room, I figured I'd focus on the handsome young man instead." Kitty turned towards Dan, whose face had flushed red as he tried to catch up with whatever was going on.

"Umm…" Dan cleared his throat awkwardly, undecided whether he should be answering the question or not. "I'm Lou's boyfriend."

"Lou has a boyfriend?" Kitty asked, suddenly very interested.

"I believe she said *friend*," Cliff said.

"Who's a *boy*," Hans added, and Cliff was thankful he was still present.

"I guess we haven't really had that conversation yet." Dan's face flushed an even brighter red.

"Conversation?" Mrs. Chen asked. "Shouldn't you either know or not?"

"I'm not sure. Should I?" Dan asked.

"Things might be different now, Mrs. Chen," Kitty said. "Kids these days tend to overcomplicate things."

"Overcomplicate things?" Dan asked.

"Well, considering I asked you a simple question, it should be a simple answer, no?" Kitty asked, her brows shooting up.

"I'm not sure Lou is all that simple," Dan offered.

"Fair point," Kitty said. "She seems like the kind of person to get in her own way."

"Come on, this is Lou we're talking about here," Cliff covered, feeling an overwhelming desire to stick up for her. "She's a brilliant policewoman, and she'd make a damn good detective if she ever wanted to."

"Wonderful," Kitty mused. "Of course you would understand those things." She looked at Cliff, who was concerned about the direction this conversation might be heading.

"Run away, Cliff," Sol said chuckling.

"Hush you." Kitty smacked Sol's arm. "I'm simply saying that, of course, Cliff would admire those qualities in Lou. They are all the wonderful qualities he processes and made him great at what he did."

Somehow, Cliff felt as though he was being praised and insulted at the same time.

"Lou's a great cop," Dan interjected.

"That point is not in question," Kitty said.

"I'm not sure I'm following." Dan pressed a hand to his forehead before running it through his hair.

"I'm just saying that, isn't it interesting how Lou, who is a very confident woman, might find it difficult to discuss where she is in her personal life?"

"Perhaps she didn't want us talking about it," Sol offered.

"I wasn't." Kitty put a hand to her chest. "Dan brought it up."

"I did?" Dan asked.

"Yes. All I wanted to know was where I recognized you from. Your questionable relationship status with Lou was entirely your own design."

"It was?" Dan looked as though this conversation was making him dizzy, and he seemed to be trying to think of something but couldn't quiet find it.

"Don't overthink it, son," Sol offered.

"Perhaps we should leave the poor man alone," Cliff offered.

"Happily," Kitty said, folding her hands together and resting them in her lap.

For a brief moment, the Hearse was incredibly silent, save for Kitty's foot tapping on the ground. Finally, she turned and blurted out. "Are you from town?"

A collective gasp was heard from nearly every occupant of the Hearse.

"Less than a minute," Sol said.

"A new record," Gerald laughed.

"Shush! Both of you." She peered narrow-eyed towards Dan.

"No, London," Dan said.

Kitty shook her head while she examined him. "And you're police, like Lou?"

"Fireman," he said, and before the words came out of his mouth Kitty's eyes lit up with realization.

"Mr. October!" she said, clapping her hands. "I knew I recognized you."

Dan still looked confused for a moment, but then his face softened as he smiled broadly. "Yes," he exclaimed as he slapped his knee and laughed. "I'm surprised you recognized me."

"Well, it was difficult with all the clothes on, but you have a remarkable jawline, my boy."

Cliff wasn't sure, but from the redness in Dan's cheeks, he wondered if she had winked at the man.

Everyone on the bus had now turned to look at Dan and Kitty, who appeared to be sharing a private moment that everyone wanted to now be a part of.

"Who is Mr. October?" Mrs. Chen finally asked.

"Yes, Kitty. And why would him wearing clothes make him more difficult to recognize?" Sol added.

"Jealousy is not a good colour on you, Sol Keen." Kitty grinned, flustering Sol.

He began stammering. "I'm not... I'm just... Never mind." He finally gave up and turned back to look out the window. Cliff could tell from the way his head kept flinching to the side that he was still listening.

"It's nothing like that. Just one of the fundraisers for the church every year."

"Not just the church," Dan interjected. "We print them for all kinds of charities."

"Print what?" Bunty asked.

"The Firemen's Calendar, of course," Kitty said with a smile. "Dan was Mr. October last year. He's practically a celebrity."

"I don't know if I would call us that," Dan said, blushing. "We just like to give back to the community."

"He's in the shirtless calendar you waste money on every year?" Sol asked.

"If you mean he's one of the male models in the calendar I purchase to show support for our church every year, then yes. He is."

Sol shook his head.

"I wouldn't mind seeing this support for God," Mrs. Chen said, tilting her head as she looked back at Dan.

"Mrs. Chen!" Bunty said, giggling herself. It reminded Cliff of the young schoolgirl he'd once known.

"Don't pretend like you don't want to see it yourself, Bunty."

"Why, I never!" Bunty laughed as she began to reexamine the contents of her yarn bag.

Gerald who, as per usual, had disappeared into the background, crumpled up the empty bag of kettle corn and licked his lips. "You know, I used to be a model," he said, so nonchalantly that everyone, save for Hans, who was driving, turned to look at him. Not a single part of him looked to be kidding, and yet Cliff assumed this *had* to be a joke. Although there was so much Cliff didn't know about Gerald it was hard to say for sure.

"You, Gerald? Were a model?" Bunty finally asked, saying what everyone else was obviously thinking.

"Did a movie too. Wasn't any good though," he admitted with a shrug.

"I can't tell if he's kidding or not," Kitty said.

The skepticism didn't seem to bother Gerald at all. He simply shrugged before resting his head down on the bag of groceries he had. That quieted the car down as everyone took to looking out the window.

After what felt like a long time, Cliff heard Hans cough from the driver's seat before he glanced up into the rearview mirror, catching Cliff's eye. In that moment, Cliff could see his eyes were red and puffy.

Cliff had offered to drive the Hearse back for Hans after he told the big man the news, but he had refused, and Cliff wondered if this allowed him the privacy he was likely looking for. Cliff saw something else in his eyes as well. *Resolve?*

"It was Pieter," Hans said quietly from the driver's seat, glancing up in the mirror towards everyone in the back. The gravel road was bumpy and loud and it made it nearly impossible for anyone other than Cliff—and from the way Bunty had covered her mouth, her too— to hear. "Pieter's body was found at the festival. He died," Hans said finding his voice a little.

This time the news was heard by the rest of the housemates, who shared in a moment of shock.

"Oh my. That's terrible, Hans. I'm so sorry." Kitty shook her head, her hand pressed against her heart.

"That poor man," Mrs. Chen said. "He was so young."

"Are you okay, Hans?" Bunty asked.

Hans let out a sigh and shook his head. "I'm not sure," he admitted, his cheek tugging tightly at his lips. "You'd think I'd be used to death by now, but..."

"It's different when you think people have time," Sol said, receiving nods of agreement from everyone. Even Dan was nodding.

"What happened?" Kitty asked. Though her voice was much more timid than it had been before, like she wasn't expecting there to be an answer.

"I'm not sure. Cliff told me."

"You were there, Cliff?" Bunty asked.

"Not *there*, there," Cliff said, trying to shut down the idea that he knew more than he did.

"But you went inside?" Kitty asked.

Cliff felt suddenly uncomfortable with all the questions, not the least of all because Hans was still listening. However, when Cliff looked over at his friend, he was surprised to see him nod. No doubt he was equally as interested in what happened as the rest of the house.

"I saw Lou going in and thought she might need some help. I saw his body on the ground and a few of the things that Lou spotted in the area. Hardly enough to come to any conclusions."

"You must have seen something though," Kitty said. She was leaning in towards him, as was pretty much everyone on the bus. Even Dan was leaning in so that he could hear better.

"Sure, I managed to make some observations…but…" Cliff regretted his words, as curiosity began to build on the faces around him. He knew all about it. It was like a dog with a bone; it would torment you until you figured it out.

"We know you saw more," Mrs. Chen said, shaking her head, "so stop pretending like you didn't and tell us already."

"Honestly. I didn't see much." Cliff shrugged, though he knew that wasn't entirely true. He'd seen quite a bit in the short time he was there. Enough to create all of the suspicion he needed to want to stay longer, to really see where all the pieces fell. But that was no longer his job. He wasn't a detective anymore.

"You're no fun." Mrs. Chen leaned back in her seat, as did everyone else.

The only one who didn't turn away was Bunty, who watched him curiously for a long moment before pulling out a little journal and scribbling something on one of the pages.

Cliff tried to keep his mind off the whole affair, and he was doing a subpar job of it, when he felt something hit his arm. He glanced down and saw a neatly folded-up piece of paper on the seat beside him. He glanced over at Bunty, but she was clearly half pretending to look out the window and half glancing at him to make sure he picked up the paper.

Cliff picked up the note that was folded near perfectly into a tiny square. He unravelled it and started to read the note jotted on the page. *You're lying*, it read.

Cliff once again glanced over at Bunty. He could see her watching him from the corner of her eye, a brow raised.

Meet me in the library tomorrow morning, 6 a.m.

Cliff refolded the paper and slipped it in his pocket, slightly amused by the cloak and dagger of it all. Though he knew in his heart that this wasn't a game, and that Bunty was right, he *was* lying.

Because he was beginning to suspect that Pieter VanWinkle had been murdered.

7

"Good morning," Bunty said. She sipped her tea in the library with Skittles, the house's grey tabby, curled up on her lap, his head popping up briefly to inspect Cliff as he walked in, before nuzzling back into Bunty's lap.

Cliff had never been much of a cat person, and the last month had done little to change that. Although, as it appeared to stand, Skittles had not gotten the memo and was perfectly content to occasionally circle Cliff's leg. A comfortable place, Cliff thought, for their relationship to begin.

Despite the early hour, most of the house was up and about. Cliff spotted Kitty and Sol reading the newspaper in the living room while they drank their coffee, and Cliff couldn't be sure, but, given the soft humming noise, he guessed Hans was already in the basement working in his woodshop. That, and considering the man had spent most of his life waking up at four in the morning for chores on the farm, and with the recent news of Pieter's death, he doubted Hans had slept much, if at all, the night before.

Cliff spotted Mrs. Chen filling a small watering can at the kitchen sink, which he supposed would be for watering her plants in the sunroom while she formulated a plan of attack for her outside garden that day. It was a habit he had found she'd been doing more often these past couple of weeks.

Gerald, the last member of the house was…well, Cliff didn't know what Gerald did in the mornings. For all he knew, he was still fast asleep. But then again, Cliff didn't think that even sleep could part that man from his meals.

The night before had been very quiet. They dropped Dan at Lou's house, where Kitty had refused to let him leave without making him promise to get her a signed copy of that year's firemen's calendar, which luckily hadn't taken long, since he appeared honoured to do it. Hans then silently drove them all home, where they changed and waited for Gerald to finish dinner, which was a delicious wild mushroom risotto, using some of the ingredients he'd picked up at the festival.

Despite Cliff's many attempts, Bunty remained steadfast in her decision to talk about nothing until the next morning. Cliff couldn't understand the reason for the secrecy, though he suspected it had something to do with respecting Hans, who was clearly still unnerved by it all.

"Good morning, Bunty," Cliff said as he sat down across from her in one of the room's large, wingback chairs. He gripped his morning coffee in both hands, blowing the top of it while he waited. When she didn't say anything, he chuckled to himself and continued. "This is all rather cloak and dagger, isn't it?"

"I wanted to give myself time to think," Bunty said, taking a sip of her tea.

"And what do you think now that you've had some time?"

"The same as I did last night," Bunty said, her brows lifting.

"You don't think it was an accident," Cliff asked.

"Correction. I don't think *you* think it was an accident." Bunty smiled thinly.

"And why would you think that?"

"Call it a hunch," Bunty said.

"So now you're having hunches about crimes. Should I be concerned?"

"Only if you've committed a crime, Mr. Shaw." Bunty's lips curled into a smile.

"You weren't even there. You didn't see the body. How could you…?"

"You did," she said. "I believe you saw more than you were letting on last night." She tilted her head as she leaned in to get closer, causing Skittles to leap off her lap, having decided it was a little too much movement for him. He vanished around the corner and into the hallway.

Cliff opened his mouth, prepared with all conviction to say he *hadn't* seen more than he was letting on last night, but then he'd be lying. There were many things he didn't necessarily like about the crime scene, including the missing milkshake container. It might not have been altogether weird, but it did imply that Pieter wasn't alone at the time of his death. If that was the case, who was with him, and why wouldn't they have called for help? That, combined with the open safe, which Cliff hadn't had a chance to examine, made it all feel strange.

"You did see something!" Bunty said, whispering as she pointed at Cliff. "I can tell you're…contemplating."

"Okay, fine. There may have been some things off. But it could also be nothing." Cliff held up a hand when he saw Bunty's eyes light up.

"But it could be something," she stated eagerly.

"You might be worse than me. You know that?" Cliff leaned back in his chair and let out a sigh while he tapped the side of his coffee mug thoughtfully. He ran through what he knew about where the body had been, and he had to admit it wasn't a lot. He paused and looked at Bunty. "What?"

"Well? Are you going to tell me what you saw?"

He could see the eagerness in her eyes. It was the same look he saw in young detectives. But Bunty wasn't a young detective, nor was he, and that made navigating this difficult. But still, there was a tug inside of him to share what he'd seen with *someone*, if only just to make him not feel like he was crazy.

"Fine," he said.

He slowly laid out the room where they found Pieter's body, making certain to only state the facts, rather than shrouding it with his own personal assumptions about what it all could mean. He had to admit, he was very curious to know what Bunty might unearth, given the same information. He was also pleasantly surprised when he had finished how well he'd done, considering he hadn't taken any notes. *I suppose I haven't lost all my skills yet.*

"Interesting," Bunty said when Cliff finished.

They both leaned back in their chairs. Bunty's face was a mixed expression of careful consideration and obvious uneasiness at imagining a dead man at a crime scene. Then again, Cliff wasn't a mind reader, and perhaps he was just putting that on her.

"Why?" Cliff asked, cocking his head.

"Well, if I'm right, it means someone watched as that poor man died. But who could do that?"

"You'd be unnerved by what people are capable of." Cliff shook his head. "What else?"

"Ummm…" Bunty thought a moment. "I would wonder what was in the safe that was so important."

"Maybe it was nothing. Maybe he had an allergic reaction and that's it. A tragic, unfortunate accident that took a man's life." Cliff shrugged. "I certainly wasn't allowed to stay long enough to find out. Not after Captain Marks arrived," Cliff chuckled.

"Is that man still upset that you solved his case? You would think he would be thanking you."

"First of all, *we* solved the case," Cliff said, knowing that he would never have managed to do it without the help of Bunty and the rest of the house, especially after he'd been arrested for interfering in a police investigation. Without Bunty's ingenuity, they might never have managed to save the town at all. "Second, in my experience, most people don't thank you when you help them lose a promotion."

"He should have been better at his job." Bunty smiled. "As for the body, of course I would prefer that Pieter's death be an unfortunate accident, and maybe we will need to just wait and see what the police find?" Bunty didn't look all that convinced of this line of thinking, though she was right, there was nothing they could do until they learned more.

"I'm sure, by the end of the day, they will have it all sorted out," Cliff said leaning back in his chair and sipping his coffee.

"I'm sure they will," Bunty replied.

However, by early afternoon, nothing more had been discovered about Pieter's death. No rumours or hints of speculation came up at all surrounding it. Not even Jan had heard anything, and Cliff had checked in twice. Any more and it would be certain that Jan would start to believe Cliff was hiding something more than just general curiosity.

He did wish Lou would get back to him to help ease his mind a little, but so far, she had maintained radio silence. He wasn't sure if that was for the best or not, although the longer he was forced to wait, the longer his brain had to imagine the worst-case scenarios.

Cliff suspected Bunty was in the same boat, having also followed up with him a couple times. Each time, he reiterated how she would be the first to know if he ever heard anything.

To take his mind off thinking about it, he accepted Mrs. Chen's not-so-subtle invitation to work in the garden.

"You can spread one of those bags over here," she said, gesturing to a small patch of freshly worked garden.

"Just the one bag? You should have given me a challenge." Cliff slung one of the bags of compost over his shoulder. It was heavy, and he was not the young man he once was, which he noticed immediately, as he nearly toppled over when his trick knee suddenly decided to act up. He might have fallen completely over had he not been able to brace himself on one of the arbour's posts.

"Careful, Mr. Shaw. I wouldn't want you getting injured when we have so much work to do." Mrs. Chen gave him a smile as she patted the ground around where she wanted him to lay the compost.

"Save nothing for my wellbeing." Cliff took a moment to adjust himself and the bag on his shoulder. Once he was convinced of his stability—at least as convinced as he was likely to get—he hauled the bag over to Mrs. Chen. Hauling felt like the optimal word.

"Naturally, I care about that as well. But you can rest after the judging," she said with a thin smile.

Cliff dropped the bag beside her with a thud. "So did you enjoy the festival? Before the…well, you know." Cliff gave his shoulder a rub. He hated feeling old. Worse, he hated doing anything that reminded him just how old he really was. It wasn't like the old days when he could just do whatever he wanted without remorse. Although he supposed that logic was also why his knees, along with many other parts of his body, ached continuously.

"I was pleasantly surprised. Which I suppose was unexpected and nice. I guess it is possible that, sometimes, we can all be wrong… occasionally," she said, pointing at Cliff with her spade.

"How is your lovely new plant anyways?" Cliff asked.

"That plant is currently housed in my room. Perhaps, one day, I will attempt to plant some in my garden, but for now, this garden is perfect. And if it isn't, well then, it's too late to change anything now."

"Why's that?"

"I listed all the plants I would have in bloom prior to the contest. I curated this whole project last year, and now it is all about seeing my vision through to fruition." She stabbed her spade into the bag of compost before ripping it open with her hands, a technique Cliff thought was impressively creative.

She began pulling out handfuls of the stuff to place around a brown speckled, yellow and pink flower Cliff had never seen before.

"That's impressive," Cliff said, taking a moment to rub his knee.

"I'm always impressive," Mrs. Chen said. "Except when I'm not, of course," she amended. "But, fortunately, that is rare."

Cliff allowed himself a laugh but stopped when Mrs. Chen turn to look at him and he realized he wasn't sure if she was joking or not. Although he'd only known Mrs. Chen for a short while, he had come to realize that she might, in fact, be one of the wittiest people he'd ever met. Although it was hard to gauge, considering it was so dry he had trouble understanding when, if ever, she was being serious. Perhaps that was part of her charm.

"How do you think your garden will hold up this year?" Cliff asked, looking around at what he perceived to be a very exquisite-looking garden. He had, in the past, kept a handful of houseplants, which he cared for in his apartment in Toronto, and now and again, he would help out by watering the much larger collection of plants Mrs. Chen had propagated in the sunroom of the Limestone Manor. But he never imagined in his life that he would be living in a place where real gardening would be happening. He only wished he had better knees for it.

When he first arrived, he hadn't truly appreciated just how much time and effort Mrs. Chen put into her hobby. But seeing her work, particularly in the past few weeks leading up to the Perth County Home Garden Competition, he was beginning to recognize not just the skill and patience of Mrs. Chen, but also the fact that her so-called hobby looked more like a full-time job. A job she appeared to thoroughly enjoy.

"I would be disappointed with anything outside the top three. Though, I admit that, like all great works of art, the final decision comes down to individual taste and, since the judging is anonymous, it is hard to build around the taste of a ghost," Mrs. Chen said as she packed the fresh earth down around the base of the flower.

"Must be difficult to design something without knowing who you're trying to impress, I suppose," Cliff said.

"Not entirely." Mrs. Chen pushed herself up from her knees to examine her work. "Grab that bucket and spade, will you?" She gestured to the items by the other bags of compost. "May as well slip on a pair of gloves too. Things are about to get dirty," she added with a grin.

Cliff moved over and picked up the items, spotting an extra pair of gardening gloves in Mrs. Chen's woven basket, and he picked those out as well.

"What do you mean *not entirely?*" Cliff asked as he slipped on the gloves and picked up the bucket and spade before turning to look back at Mrs. Chen, who was scouting the garden for something specific.

"Well, you said I don't know who I'm designing it for," she said, dusting off her hands. "But that isn't entirely true. Sure, I don't know who will be judging my efforts—there is no way of knowing that. So, all I have the power to do it create a final product I would be proud to show myself." She turned to look at Cliff. "That, Mr. Shaw, is what I am doing here."

"You're creating something you like?"

"Indeed. Since I like myself and my tastes, why shouldn't I design something I like to look at?" She chuckled.

"And what exactly goes into a good garden design?" Cliff asked.

"Excellent question. Some people think it is about beauty, using the space to highlight the pieces you admire or enjoy the most."

"I'm assuming you don't do that?" Cliff asked.

"Sometimes," Mrs. Chen answered thoughtfully. "But my true desire is to tell a story. I want the garden to lead you. Allow your eye to catch hints of what is coming. Punctuations of colour, morning vs. afternoon light. Each step should be a surprise to your eyes. The ultimate achievement is to present something that stops you in your tracks. Gives you the moment you need to really take in the mystery of it all."

Cliff looked around the garden. He didn't have the heart to say that all he saw were plants. Maybe that was because he didn't know what to look for, or maybe it was because he didn't possess the scope to understand the majesty of what Mrs. Chen was doing, no matter how much he would have liked to.

"The earth laughs in flowers," Mrs. Chen said, as she knelt, running a finger through a flower.

"What was that?" Cliff asked, the words flicking a light on in his brain, though he didn't understand why. *Something about that phrase.*

"It's from a poem I used to read when I was learning English. I'm afraid I don't remember much of it now, but I always loved that line," she said thoughtfully. "Such a beautiful way to think about our world and our role in it."

"It's Emerson, isn't it?" Cliff recalled the poem now from his youth, and how they would repeat it in English class. "Flowers are the earth's way of expressing joy." It was coming back to him now, his time in school, and his odd encounter at the festival with the strange woman in the tent. The fortune teller had quoted that to him. He hadn't remembered it was a poem. But he did now, along with its meaning of how humans only have a short existence on earth. Not something he though much of as a boy, though he supposed it took on an entirely different meaning as an old man. *But why would that be important to me now?*

"You're trying to see it, aren't you," she asked, standing to look up at him.

"Trying and failing, I'm afraid," Cliff admitted, though he was unsure which question he was answering.

"There is no failing. You can't fail when you look at a painting. It just there. The trouble is when you try to *see* something."

"Isn't that the point?"

"Is it?" she asked. "You solved mysteries, right?"

Cliff nodded.

"When you solve them, do the answers only come to you when you try to find them?"

Cliff had to genuinely think about that for a moment, wondering if this was a classic chicken or the egg question. But given his recent run-in with a crime scene, he had to suppose not. Or else he might have jumped to conclusions. If this was something he did subconsciously he didn't know.

"I suppose not."

"We are so often tricked into trying to see what is right in front of us, that we miss everything else altogether. But," she said, gesturing to the garden, "when we allow our brain to wander, it often leads us in the right direction." She shrugged.

Something on Cliff's face must have shown his confusion, because she walked back over and gave him a pat on the shoulder and gestured behind him.

"Take this plant here. Without me to point it out, without turning around, there is nothing to tell you it's there." She waved back the way they had come as she pulled his arm and began to guide him back down the grassy pathway. "As we walk, our eyes are met by the shadow of this tall lilac tree. We may get distracted by its flowers, before following the trunk down towards the small bushes of wild daisies, which pull us further along the pathway towards the pond and the bridge." Mrs. Chen gestured towards the tiny wooden bridge he knew Hans had built for her a few years before.

They used it to traverse the small koi pond Mrs. Chen had built in the centre of the garden. When they reached the other side, he was still following her, but still wondered if he saw what she saw, if he saw the story of her garden as she gestured to more plants along the path.

"It would only be natural for one to get carried away, distracted by the vibrant salvias, the bearded irises, or the cupid's dart. But if one was curious enough to turn around," she said, spinning Cliff again, to peer down at some orange flowers he hadn't even noticed, as they were tucked into a small alcove surrounded on three sides by manicured hedges. "They will be rewarded by this hidden gem. It's a Peruvian lily." Mrs. Chen gave Cliff a pat on the back. "All of the best stories reward curiosity. It is fine to follow the path, but it is sometimes worth it to stop and have a look around."

Cliff still wasn't entirely sure if he understood exactly what Mrs. Chen was trying to say. He somehow managed to find her both direct and indirect at the same time. That didn't mean he wasn't confident about one thing. She certainly knew how to tell a story, and if that was her goal for the judges, he had no doubt in his mind she would succeed in this garden challenge.

"Anyone ever tell you you have a unique way of speaking?" Cliff said.

"No," she answered, turning abruptly to walk back across the garden. "But I hope your knees are feeling better after that rest, because you are going to need them." She turned to give him a wide grin.

Cliff chuckled to himself as he felt a buzz in his pocket just as his phone beeped.

He reached in and pulled it out, looking at the screen, which had a new message on the front. He opened the phone, surprised to see it was from Lou:

I have news. Meet for coffee tomorrow, 9 a.m.? Usual spot?

Cliff read the message twice, trying to figure out how and why he kept getting messages from women to meet him mysteriously at set times. But considering he wanted answers, he wasn't about to say no. As for the issue of the usual spot, Cliff had only one idea where that might be, considering he and Lou had only met for coffee one other time.

He closed his eyes as two things crossed through his mind. The first was trying to imagine what could be so important that she wanted to meet him rather than just sending him a text. The second was whether or not he was going to tell Bunty about the meeting.

He knew the answer to the first would be solved by showing up and finding out, which is why he replied, *See you there.*

The second was slightly trickier, since sooner or later, he would be forced to tell Bunty that he had met with Lou, regardless of what she said, and because it was Bunty, there was little chance of lying to her, since she had a habit of seeing right through him. But also, it was Bunty, and she wasn't the kind of person you lied to easily.

"These weeds aren't going to remove themselves, Mr. Shaw," Mrs. Chen called after him, pulling him from his internal debate.

I have till tomorrow, Cliff told himself as he put the phone back in his pocket, hoping that Mrs. Chen's advice might kick in, and the answer would come to him if he distracted himself with work. At least he thought that's what she'd meant. He still wasn't sure.

8

"This is so exciting," Bunty said, clapping her hands as they walked down the hill on Jones Street towards the river.

Cliff had caved first thing that morning when he'd gone down to get his coffee. To his credit, he'd managed to keep it to himself the entirety of the night before, but Bunty had seen some sort of mask on his face, because he'd continuously caught her staring at him before turning away sharply any time he tried to meet her eye.

That morning, she'd surprised him when she called him out in the library. She'd been patiently knitting in her chair, a hot cup of tea at her side, when without glancing up from her stitch, she had shouted as he walked by, "You're hiding something!"

That was all it had taken for Cliff to spill his guts to her about Lou, and the message, and his pitiful reasons for not telling her about it immediately.

To Bunty's credit, she was neither annoyed nor angry. She simply carried on, as if the delay in her discovery had never occurred. In no time, Cliff had gone from lone wolf, wandering into an odd, clandestine conversation with the local police, to a ragtag team of two.

"I think it's best if we try not to speculate on anything," Cliff said, raising a hand to try and calm Bunty down, although he had to admit her enthusiasm was palpable.

"Of course, I just never imagined how exciting these things would be. Is this what it was like for you all those years as a detective?" she asked.

"It was different," Cliff said, feeling a smile coming to his face. "You're very excited for someone looking into someone's death."

"I know," Bunty said, sounding almost ashamed of her reaction. "Am I a bad person?"

Cliff was taken aback by the seriousness of her question. There were many words that Cliff would use to describe Bunty, but never could he ever think of describing her as a bad person.

"No. You're curious," Cliff said, shaking his head. "It is a good skill to have in what I did." He stepped up to the corner, watching as the early morning crowd of people hurried in and out of the post office. Well, "crowd," might be a little too generous, he thought to himself.

Having spent most of his adult life living in Toronto, crowds tended to take on a different meaning than they did in St. Marys. What might have been hundreds in Toronto translated to under a dozen in this rural community.

"But someone's died," Bunty said, as if the realization of this was only now dawning on her.

"Sometimes people die," Cliff said with a shrug. "Some have simple solutions; others are more complex. Our job is to figure out which one it is."

"*Our* job?" Bunty said, giving Cliff a mischievous smile.

"I meant *my* job. The one I used to do."

"Of course you did," Bunty chuckled, as the pair waited for an opening before crossing the street. "Do you miss it? Being a detective?"

Cliff thought about it for a moment. "Yes and no," he finally said. "I was good at it. I think I miss that."

"To lack purpose, is to lack hope," Bunty said.

"Who said that?"

"I did." Bunty smiled. "Right now."

A beat later, Cliff began to laugh. "I liked that."

"Everyone gets one, I suppose." Bunty smiled.

"I just worked for so long. It was all I did. And now…"

"You don't know what to do with yourself?" Bunty asked.

"Yes. And being back here, in St. Marys."

"It must be a shock, I'm sure."

"Yes," Cliff sighed.

"You come by it honestly." Bunty shrugged, "It's man's greatest weakness."

"So, it is a man thing. Perfect."

"Not only men. That would be naive. But I believe it plagues men more than women," Bunty said so casually that it caught Cliff off guard.

"Care to explain your insights?" Cliff felt the question came out more defensively than he would have liked, especially since he knew Bunty wasn't being malicious. He doubted she had a malicious bone in her body.

"Sure," she said, and if she caught his defensive walls being built, it didn't appear to bother her much. "Men, in the general sense, lose the ability to adapt to life. Take you, for example. You spent most of your life working as a detective. When it came time to retire, rather than quit, you became a private investigator. I'd hardly say that's a big leap from what you were doing before. It was comforting, and it provided you with purpose," Bunty suggested. "But this is the first time in your life where you have not been doing anything that gives you purpose. You must feel lost."

"I suppose a little. But I would hardly say it's just because I'm a man," Cliff chuckled. "You're saying women are better at finding purpose?"

"No. We are better at adapting to change and creating purpose for ourselves, rather than only finding it in our work." She said it as if this was simply a matter of fact.

"Why would you say that?" Cliff asked.

"Well, I have my theories."

"Go on," Cliff insisted as they reached the next intersection at Water Street. It took a few moments for some cars to pass, creating an opening for them to cross.

"Well, and keep in mind this is a general observation..."

"I'll keep that under consideration." Cliff chuckled, amused that, even now, Bunty was more concerned about insulting him than being right.

"Well, I would hardly say the opportunity for women, at least for our generation, was great," she said, raising a hand to stop Cliff's interjection. "There were exceptions to the rule, but I would be curious to know how many female detectives there were in the Toronto Police Department during your time there. Now, I'm sure it's changing, but for a long time, the purpose for most men was to go to work and provide for their families. It was a service, but it was singularly focused. You did one thing for your entire life. You worked towards being great at what you did. There is honour in doing that. But there is a price to be paid as well. Once that purpose is taken away, what are you left with? Do you feel whole, living in this town, or is this possibility of a mystery the first time you've felt normal since you arrived?" she asked.

Cliff shrugged and let out a sigh. "I suppose I could be a little bored."

"Boredom is what kills us." Bunty shook her head. "Without something to challenge ourselves, we lose sight of what matters. You just have to be open to change."

What's that? Cliff thought, feeling a small sense of déjà vu.

"Cliff!" Lou shouted from the bench as she waved towards to the pair.

"Perhaps we put a pin in this for now," Bunty said with a wink, as she waved over at Lou.

The last thing Cliff wanted to do right now was to put a pin in this conversation. After all, Bunty was somehow managing to express everything he had been feeling this past little while since moving to town. It was as if he was trying to shuffle his way through a dark void but had no idea which direction he should be going. He was simply wandering around aimlessly.

He had chalked this up to being back in St. Marys, and a general feeling that living in town just wasn't for him. But deep down, he knew that wasn't the case. He'd been very apprehensive about moving into the house with so many people at first, especially considering it had been a very long time since he lived with anyone, and he may not be ready to admit it quite yet, but he was happy to have people around. At least, he wasn't alone.

"How are you, Bunty?" Lou said, both women reaching in for a hug. "I'm a little surprised to see you here."

"Every good detective has a slightly smarter partner." Bunty winked.

"Easy, I did invite *you*, remember."

"Only because Lou didn't have my number, I'm sure," Bunty said, taking a seat on the bench beside two coffees.

"Sorry, if I'd known you were coming, I would have picked you up a coffee," Lou said, reaching down to pick up the two coffees and handing one of them to Cliff.

"It's tea for me, dear, and, not to worry, I had mine at the house," Bunty said, as Lou sat down beside her.

Cliff squeezed onto the edge. He'd thought about standing and facing the two women, but his knee was tight from the walk, and he was too old to want to stand for an indefinite amount of time. Though he imagined the three of them squeezed onto the bench must be a funny sight for anyone walking by. Thankfully, there weren't many, just a young man, who had paused briefly to let his curly black-haired dog pee against one of the nearby trees.

"What's up, Lou?" Cliff said, looking over at Lou wiggling around, now squeezed between the pair of seniors.

Lou looked at Cliff, then over at Bunty hesitantly.

"Don't worry about me. Mum's the word, dear." Bunty mimed zipping her lips closed. "Consider me an interested bystander."

"I'm not sure how many interested bystanders I'm allowed to talk with," Lou said, pausing to blow on her coffee.

"The answer's none," Cliff said, sipping his own coffee. "But we've walked all the way down here and, well, if you're going to bend a rule, I suppose it doesn't matter how far." He shrugged.

"Not really the reassurance I was looking for," Lou said.

"If it makes you feel any better, I've assumed that this isn't a cut and dried death. That there is a possibility that—"

"Your instincts are right," Lou said, not waiting for Cliff to finish his thought.

Cliff began to shift uncomfortably. It was one thing to think something was happening; it was another thing entirely to hear that he was right. If it was murder, that inevitably meant that someone was the killer. An obvious conclusion, and yet it was something that always turned Cliff's insides upside down.

"Poor Hans," Bunty said, mostly to herself, and Cliff couldn't help but feel a little guilty that his first reaction hadn't also been towards his friend and what this news was sure to do to him.

"Who do you think did it?" Cliff asked, unsure if this was territory Lou was prepared to talk about or not.

"There are three camps at the station. The first is an accident. Which looks good in theory, but there are some…inconsistencies with that narrative that not everyone, including myself, are all that sold on."

"Let me guess, the captain's not all that thrilled about there being a murder in town," Cliff asked.

"No one is thrilled, Cliff. It's a murder," Lou said, her head shaking at him.

"Fair point. I just mean—"

"I know what you mean. I just think perspective and all that," Lou said.

Cliff raised his hands in defense. "I get it. What are the other theories?" he asked, desperately wanting to change the topic from him to anything else.

"Second theory is Mike Wilderman," Lou said.

"The Badger?" Cliff recalled the name of the man Hans hadn't been all too thrilled about seeing at the festival, and also the minor scuffle he'd had in public with Pieter beside one of the stalls. It had only been a short argument, though it was enough for Cliff to get a sense of the mutual relationship between the two men.

"And the last one?" Bunty asked, a tight expression painted on her face as she studied the uneasy look Lou shot between the pair.

"It's Mari VanWinkle. His daughter."

9

"Absolutely not. She's his daughter," Bunty said, objecting to the idea that the police found this worthy of investigating.

"Well, that is unexpected." Cliff tapped the top of his coffee cup. His brain was racing around, trying to fill in the blanks, only it was much easier than he would have liked to admit.

"You can't honestly believe that, can you?" Bunty asked incredulously.

Cliff, on the other hand, knew the statistics well enough to know that most murders were committed by someone who knew the victim. He'd long ago stopped trying to trust what he did or did not believe.

"Only six employees had keys to access the shed where Pieter's body was found," Lou said, shaking her head.

"Was Pieter one of them?" Cliff asked.

Lou nodded.

"Well then. He could have brought anyone in there with him, couldn't he?" Bunty asked, still adamantly opposed to this idea.

"I suppose, he could have," Lou said, giving the idea some careful consideration. "The only catch is that we found Pieter's key for the shed hanging on a hook in his home. He'd forgotten it that morning."

Bunty didn't look too thrilled by that.

"I'm assuming you spoke with the Bad— Mr. Wilderman. You saw their argument as well as I did. That couldn't have been about nothing?" Cliff asked.

"Yes. Apparently, Winkleberry Farm has had a rough couple of years. They attempted to expand their holdings, and well, they haven't been able to cover the payments on money they borrowed."

"So Mr. Wilderman offered to buy them out," Cliff asked.

"Yes. But Mr. VanWinkle had been claiming that Wilderman was purposefully using *his* farms to stifle their ability to grow."

"How?" Cliff asked.

Lou pulled a little notepad from her pocket and flipped through the pages until she landed on the one she was looking for. "Apparently, it had to do with their quota? And delayed deliveries."

"What does that mean?" Cliff asked.

Lou shrugged. "I was only able to copy some of the notes taken. Farming isn't really my forte."

"Dairy farms are highly regulated in Canada," Bunty said. "Basically, a farm's quota is the amount of butterfat they are allowed to produce and sell to the market each day. Say your farm's quota is ten kilograms. You can only sell ten kilos worth of butterfat to the market a day. Then it becomes a little more nuanced in there, because the farm board then dictates how that milk is used, and there are different prices for different products like milk, cheese, yogurt. All that money is pooled up and distributed to the farms based on their contribution. There are speciality markets like certified organic that would be paid more but also have more regulation. So, depending on what your designation for the dairy is, it could cost... well a lot. Last I heard it's about $25,000 per kilogram, maybe more."

"Wow." Cliff let out a little whistle. "So what? They set limits on what people can produce? What if they make more?"

"Then they toss it. And they are fined if they produce less. Quota is basically gold in Canada. It can make or break a farm, and because it's so regulated, getting your hands on more is always difficult. Big farms tend to snatch it up whenever they can."

"So you think Wilderman was buying up quota so Winkleberry Farm couldn't?" Cliff asked.

Bunty rocked her head from side to side. "It's a possibility. They could also be leveraging their size to prioritize feed deliveries to his farms before Pieter's. His hundred-plus farms are a bigger client then Pieter's what? Three family-owned plots?"

"I can see where you're going with this, but I told you Mr. Wilderman wouldn't have had a key for the shed," Lou reminded them. "Besides, all of this feels like more reasons why Pieter would want Mr. *Wilderman* gone, not the other way around. What good does it do Wilderman to have Pieter gone?"

"I don't know why people kill." Bunty shrugged. "But if Pieter somehow had proof that the Badger was doing any of this, then perhaps he threatened to go to the police," she said, matter-of-factly.

"Well, unfortunately, not everyone in my department thinks the same way as you Bunty," Lou said.

"What about you?" Cliff asked.

"Clearly there was something going on between them the other day when he was at the fair. You saw me break up their confrontation. Hard not to think there is a connection. But an argument doesn't mean he was willing to kill him."

"Fair enough. So why Mari?" Cliff asked.

Lou began to shift uncomfortably in her seat. "I can't tell you that," she said, after a few agonizing seconds.

"What do you mean, you can't tell us?" Bunty asked, though from the expression on Lou's face, Cliff was beginning to understand what this was about.

"You're warning us," Cliff said, when Lou couldn't look over at Bunty to answer the question.

Lou nodded. "I know Hans was friends with the family, and well,

I thought… I don't know what I thought." Lou shook her head and buried her face in one hand, as her fingers tightened around her coffee cup.

Bunty's frustration vanished, and her eyes took on a sympathetic expression as she rubbed circles along Lou's back. "I'm sorry, Lou."

"Look, Lou, you know there is no good way to break news like this to anyone. But we will make sure we keep an eye on Hans," Cliff said. "I also understand that you can't tell us anything about what you've found."

"No, I can't." Lou looked up, giving him a head shake. "I'm already breaking the rules being here, and considering what happened last time…"

"You mean when we used the information to save the town from making the worst mistake in its history?" Bunty said in a very matter-of-fact way.

"Yes. A happy conclusion that nearly lost me my job," Lou said.

"But you didn't lose your job," Bunty said. "In fact, didn't you get a promotion?"

"I know how this sounds," Lou said, clearly struggling with some internal conflict about what to do.

"You don't have to tell us anything you don't want to," Cliff said, taking a sip of his coffee. "This is hardly an ideal situation. But you did message me for a reason, and I don't think it was just so we could take care of Hans." Cliff sipped his coffee again and leaned back in the bench. He closed his eyes, feeling the cool air on his face and the morning sun on the back of his neck, and for a moment, it was very peaceful, despite everything going on.

"How do you even know he was killed?" Bunty asked.

Cliff opened his eyes to glance over at Lou. *Good question, Bunty.*

"That is one of the assessments," Lou said. She looked like she was preparing to say something but having second thoughts about it. Her eyes flickered between Cliff and Bunty.

Cliff thought for a moment about what he'd observed during his brief time at the crime scene and tried to understand what would make him draw the similar conclusion. There were more than a few oddities in the room.

"How did he die?" Cliff finally asked.

Lou didn't look like she was going to reply, but then thought otherwise. "Asphyxiation. His throat sealed up. We think it was from some sort of allergic reaction."

"Allergies? So why would you think someone tried to kill him?" Bunty asked.

"Because we found traces of peanut oil in a melted pool of a milkshake that was spilt on the ground. We think someone put it there on purpose."

"Perhaps it was an accident," Bunty offered.

"Maybe." Lou shrugged. "And if it was, then I'm sure we'll figure it all out."

Cliff wasn't all that reassured by her reaction.

"Thanks, Lou. We appreciate the heads-up," Cliff said, standing up and turning to offer a hand to Bunty. She took it.

"I still don't see why you think it was Mari?" Bunty said, shaking her head, as Cliff helped her to her feet.

Cliff glanced down at Lou, who looked like the frustration was starting to build. She tapped the top of her coffee cup, clearly struggling with something.

"Fine. But you can't tell anyone, okay?" Lou said, standing up to whisper conspiratorially. "We think she was after his will. Apparently, Pieter had planned to leave the farms to Flynn, his nephew. But, from all accounts, he's the reason the farm was failing in the first place. Some of the employees overheard Mari and Pieter fighting about breaking up the farms, leaving her with the family farm and Flynn with the rest. But Pieter didn't want to break it up."

"What about Hendrik?" Cliff asked.

"We spoke with him. Apparently, he's wanted nothing to do with the farm for some time. He has his own thing going on."

"But…" Bunty began to say.

"Sounds like you have your work cut out for you, Lou," Cliff said, placing a comforting hand on Bunty's arm as he moved to walk away. "We appreciate the heads-up, and we will keep an eye on Hans." He gave Lou a thin smile as she stared back at him with mild confusion.

"But, Cliff…" Bunty said as they started to walk.

Cliff shot her a look at that he hoped said *not now*, and once they were far enough away from Lou, who was still looking at them curiously, he whispered to Bunty. "I know what you're thinking."

"Do you now?" Bunty said, her eyes rolling slightly.

For a moment, Cliff wondered who this person was and where the usually quiet woman knitting in the library had gone.

"Yes. If Hendrik wanted nothing to do with the farm, then what was this supposed offer he was presenting to Pieter? Am I right?"

Cliff watched as Bunty's lips curled at the edges. "It had crossed my mind," she mused. "But why not tell Lou?"

"Sometimes it's better to have all the facts before you start telling people what you think you know."

"What are you suggesting?" Bunty said, her elbow nudging his side playfully.

"I'm suggesting we start trying to get our own answers," Cliff said, as they moved cautiously through a small parking lot that was nearly completely empty, despite the early morning.

"You don't really think Mari is capable of killing her father, do you?

"From my experience, most people don't know they're capable of killing anyone until they do." Cliff felt a sigh fall out as he thought back to his years of murders in the city.

"Even me?" Bunty asked, her brows jumping up at him.

"Especially you," Cliff chuckled. "I'm sure that, beneath that calm demeanor and gentle disposition, is a complicated and mysterious woman capable of so much more than I can envision."

"And in those visons, you see me killing people?" Bunty laughed as Cliff's face went red hot. "It is always the quiet and unassuming ones, isn't it?" She winked.

"Not everything is like your books," Cliff said.

Bunty shrugged. "Some things are."

"Fair enough. By the way, how do you know so much about farming?"

"Bill worked in sales. Farming equipment, seeds, pretty much anything and everything you would need to farm," Bunty said with a shrug. "But, also, you tend to pick up a few details in this town if you keep your ears open." She smiled.

"I can only imagine what those ears must have heard over the years," Cliff mused.

"You would be shocked, and I bet more than a little surprised. I'm no Kitty, but…" she shook her head as if recalling a few details from her past before giggling to herself.

"Quiet and unassuming," Cliff said again as they crossed back on Water Street and headed for home. He was still unsure if, or how, he planned to tell Hans about Mari, but perhaps he would think of a plan before he got home.

10

By that afternoon, neither Cliff nor Bunty had found the best way to tell Hans about Mari and the police's suspicion about her involvement in her father's death. Although neither had they heard anything about Mari in the news, Cliff suspected Jan would find out about it first, since that was the kind of interesting news that would find its way into the paper or Jan's online blog.

This didn't make it any easier when Cliff heard Hans slumping up from the basement, where he had no doubt been trying to occupy his time by working on one of his projects.

"Hans? How are you doing?" Cliff called out, getting up from his place on the couch and walking into the kitchen. He ignored Kitty's raised eyebrows, as though she were imploring him to give Hans some space. In the kitchen, Cliff found Hans twisting the top off the jar of peanut butter.

"Ummm…" Hans murmured as he considered how he wanted to answer Cliff's inquiry, though Cliff suspected he already knew the answer. Between the untucked shirt and trail of woodchips left in his wake from the woodshop, it was clear the typically neat and tidy man was not okay.

"Do you, umm…?" Cliff moved to his friend and twisted off the top of the jam jar, getting a nod of appreciation as Hans pulled out two slices of bread and set them on the counter. "Want to talk about it?"

Cliff asked, giving the big man a pat on the back.

"I know I should be used to these things," Hans said, letting out a heavy sigh as his shoulders drooped down from the hug they'd just been giving his ears.

"This is different," Cliff said firmly, shaking his head, although he could tell this did little to appease his friend's feelings.

"I know," he said, with less conviction than Cliff would have preferred.

Cliff wasn't used to being a consoling person. In the past, his job had required him to deliver bad news to good people, occasionally about a loved one. It was part of his position. It had been what he'd signed up for.

However, in those instances, Cliff had been able to maintain a level of distance. Granted, it was never easy to tell someone that a person they cared about was dead; therefore, Cliff had always found it more beneficial to get to the point and show a little patience as they came to grips with their new reality. But Hans wasn't a stranger. He was Cliff's oldest friend, and he suspected that patience alone wasn't going to be enough.

Cliff watched as Hans slathered one slice of bread with peanut butter and then the other with jam before smooshing them together and taking a lackluster bite.

"There is something I need to tell you," Cliff said, drumming his fingers on the kitchen counter. Hans tilted his head to look at him, still chewing on his bite of sandwich. "I want you to know I don't want to. But I think I should because....well...I do."

Hans took another bite of his sandwich, sighing when a dollop of peanut butter and jam fell from it onto the counter. "Perfect," he said running a finger over the mixture to clean off the counter as he glanced around to see if anyone other than Cliff was watching. When he was sure no one else was, he licked his finger. "Don't tell Kitty," he whispered.

"Don't tell Kitty what?" Kitty said, her eyes narrowing on Hans and then at the crumbs on the counter and finishing with a disapproving sound for the woodchips leading up from the basement. "Hans, you're making a mess."

"I know and I'm sorry, Kitty, I just needed a distraction," Hans said, his eyes searching for sympathy, which Kitty eventually wielded in his direction.

"I'll let it slide today," Kitty said.

"You'll let it slide for as long as the man needs, Kitty," Sol said as he entered the kitchen.

Kitty shot him a look that would have stopped any other man in their tracks, but for a seasoned veteran of such looks, it barely appeared to affect Sol as he went over to fill up the kettle.

"Anyone need coffee?" he asked, still ignoring Kitty's murderous eyes.

Both Cliff and Hans raised their hands as the water filled up the electric kettle in Sol's hand.

"I don't think sulking around is an entirely useful way to spend one's time," Kitty said.

"Have you heard anything yet?" Sol asked, ignoring Kitty's comment altogether, which caused another huff of hot air from her.

"Not yet," Hans said. "I'm not sure if that makes it worse or not." He took another bite of his sandwich, and Kitty watched, unamused, as the crumbs fell to the ground.

Cliff, on the other hand, felt a tightness in his body as he thought about the fact that he did have information for him, information he didn't really want to share, though he knew he should.

"Such a shame," Kitty said. "Makes you wonder what they're doing over there." She gave Cliff a calculated look that made him wonder if Bunty had shared with Kitty what they'd learned that morning from

Lou.

"About that," Cliff said taking a deep breath, "I may have some information on what's umm…happening." He grimaced, feeling as though he was keeping this massive secret when he'd only just learned about this information that morning. But still, somehow, it felt like some minor betrayal.

"You do?" Hans asked.

"Yes. I spoke with Lou this morning," Cliff said, surprised when Bunty stepped in from the hallway.

"*We* spoke to Lou," she corrected.

"Why did you both talk to Lou?" Hans asked, looking between Cliff and Bunty.

"Together," Kitty added.

Cliff caught the corners of her lips curl a little and could feel his face start to flush. He tried to ignore the feeling and carry on.

"Lou thought it would be nice to share some details with us," Cliff said, trying to play it off casually.

"What is happening in here?" Mrs. Chen said, stepping into the kitchen from the sunroom, where, from the looks of it, she'd been reading a book, which she carried in one hand, with an empty tea mug in the other.

"Bunty and Cliff went to talk to Lou about Pieter's death, and they didn't tell Hans," Sol said. "Hot water?" he added, glancing down at Mrs. Chen's empty mug.

"Yes, please. Why weren't you going to tell Hans? It was his friend, after all." Mrs. Chen tilted her head, her eyes narrowing in on Cliff, then Bunty.

"We were going to tell him," Cliff said, looking over at Bunty for assistance, but when it didn't come, he added, "We just didn't know how."

"Why not?" Hans asked.

"Well, it's just…" Cliff began.

Gerald stepped into the kitchen, his eyes wide as he wore a very puzzled expression on his face. "No," he said, shaking his head feverishly.

"Sorry, Gerald? We don't speak confused," Kitty said, slightly amused by her own joke.

But Gerald distinctly was not. "This is the kitchen," he said, as if that cleared up his confusion.

"We are aware of where we are," Mrs. Chen said.

"I need to get started on dinner," he said, tapping his fingers nervously against his thumbs.

"I'm sure it can wait a few minutes while we chat, can't it?" Kitty asked.

Sol put a hand on her arm, as if reading Gerald's mood mildly better than his wife was.

"Is that what you think? I suppose you wouldn't mind eating a little bit later tonight then? I suppose you would be more than happy to be late for your bridge game tonight? Or your book club, Bunty? Or badminton, Sol and Mrs. Chen? It is a busy night, and I have a pork tenderloin that I've been marinating since yesterday. But in order for me to prepare the vegetables and the pork, and the sauces that will tie it all together, I'm going to need"—he made a show of glancing at his watch and tapping it as if counting—"two hours and forty-five minutes, which, by my clock, starts now." He raised his hands slowly as he turned to walk out of the kitchen, shaking his head. "But, by all means, feel free to occupy the kitchen for this conversation. If you need me, I'll be shredding potatoes in the library. Like a normal person."

It was the first time Cliff had ever heard the man speak more than a handful of words at one time, let alone display any form of passion that wasn't general frustration at Cliff's lawn bowling skills. Cliff knew Gerald appreciated food, but he never truly understood how much until now, and just how good he was at planning around the busy schedules of the rest of the house.

"We get your point, Gerald," Kitty said, as the kettle finished boiling and clicked off.

"I still can't believe he knows our schedules," Mrs. Chen mused.

Sol filled her mug, before he filled up a large French press and carried it off to the living room.

"You wouldn't really peel potatoes in the library, would you?" Bunty asked, genuine concern on her face.

"Only if you gossip in the kitchen," Gerald said, a thin smile crossing his face.

"It's not gossip," Cliff said a little too defensively, though he felt silly doing it, as Gerald shooed him out of the kitchen.

"You never cease to surprise me, Gerald," Hans mused as he slipped out of the kitchen and into the living room.

As was usually the case, Kitty and Sol sat in their tall chairs that faced one another at an angle towards a cribbage board with a small notepad on the table. Cliff wondered just how many games the pair had played and if they managed to tally all of them. Almost more importantly, who was winning.

Bunty and Cliff sat beside them on the leather couch, while Mrs. Chen sat across in another leather chair. Hans was the only one who didn't move towards a seat. He just leaned up against the window to look out it.

"So," Hans said, taking a deep breath and turning to face Cliff and Bunty. "What did you learn?"

Cliff looked at Bunty, who gave him a nod. He slowly started to go over everything they had discussed, with Lou focusing mostly on the fact that Mari was considered to be a suspect, which immediately caught Hans by surprise. A reaction that never dissipated, even as

Cliff, with the help of Bunty, tried to explain the rationale behind it.

"Absolutely not," Hans said firmly.

"I know it seems impossible," Cliff said, raising a hand as if to remind his friend that this wasn't his idea.

"Because it is," Hans said matter-of-factly.

"That doesn't mean they're going to stop looking at her," Cliff said, taking a deep breath.

"Why haven't they arrested her, then?" Kitty said, her hands in her lap, listening carefully.

"They would only be able to hold her for twenty-four hours before they would need proof she was connected." Cliff rocked his head from side to side. "Best guess is they only have circumstantial evidence against her, which makes it harder to hold her for longer."

"So what? We just sit here and wait for them to take her?" Hans asked.

"That is, *if* they take her. For all we know, Lou is wrong, and they were just looking into her because she found the body and they want to rule her out. If she really didn't do it, then it shouldn't be a problem," Bunty offered, though even she didn't appear confident in the statement either. If Lou went out of her way to let them know this, it was very unlikely that they weren't interested.

"Shouldn't be?" Hans asked latching onto the big question mark in Bunty's comment.

"I think we should focus on the fact they haven't taken her in. That's good news," Mrs. Chen said, her eyes flickering between Cliff and Bunty.

"Potentially," Cliff said, not wanting anyone, particularly Hans, to get their hopes up.

"What if she *did* do it?" Sol asked. He raised his hands in defence as both Kitty and Hans turned on him. "What? I'm just saying, if the police are looking into it and find enough proof to arrest her, isn't there a chance that she *is* the one who did it? I just think it worth mentioning."

This sentiment was clearly not shared by many of the residents in the house, but Cliff had to admit it was a reasonable assumption to make. Cliff knew from experience that many people believed something wasn't true just because they couldn't understand how it was possible. How someone they knew could do something so terrible. But Cliff knew better. He'd seen it time and time again. It wasn't as if he was immune to the idea that the police could be wrong or get fixated on a piece of the puzzle that fit the narrative they wanted. But that didn't mean it was happening now.

"Sol's right," Cliff said, not wanting to leave the man stranded on his own, as he shared in some of the glares himself. "Look, it might not be the popular opinion, but that doesn't mean that it isn't true. We have to assume there is more information at play here than we possess."

"So what do you suggest we do then? Sit back and watch them tear this young woman down?" Hans asked, though it sounded more like a plea than anything else.

Cliff felt awful. He could see the pain behind Hans's eyes. Cliff had known that Pieter's father was a close friend of Hans, and he obviously had a soft spot for Pieter and his family. After all, he'd trusted them enough to sell them his farm. But Cliff couldn't fully understand the pain in his friend's eyes.

"Hans, you have to be open to the reality that, in order to get to the bottom of who killed Pieter, you might not be happy with the results. We don't know what happened, but…" Cliff stopped and shook his head.

"I understand," Hans said, looking torn about whether he actually believed that statement. But he found a way to meet Cliff's eyes. "But I owe it to Pieter to figure out what happened to him. Even if I don't like the outcome." Hans sighed weakly.

"So, we find out what happened for ourselves," Kitty said, clapping her hands together excitedly.

"Are you talking about interfering in a police investigation?" Sol asked, looking around the room, eventually landing on Cliff. "Because the last time we did this, you ended up in jail."

"I'm aware." Cliff shuddered, remembering his time spent in the tiny cell in the St. Marys jail. It wasn't the worst accommodations he'd ever had, but it wasn't the best either.

"And you're willing to risk that again?" Sol continued.

Cliff glanced once again at Hans, and he knew he didn't have the heart to tell his friend he wouldn't help. Which meant only one answer.

"Yes." Cliff did his best to sound confident in his decision.

The room went quiet for a moment, and Cliff saw a smile form on Hans's lips, the first one he'd had seen since Hans had learned that it was Pieter whose body had been found at the festival. This was enough for him to know he was doing the right thing, no matter how much he would have preferred to keep himself away from the trouble. Cliff had the skills to help his friend, and that meant he had an obligation to do what he could. Even if it meant skirting the law once again.

"Now that that's settled," Kitty said, "what do we do?"

"We need to create confusion, stall them," Bunty said, her head tilted up to the ceiling as she appeared to think through some ideas.

Cliff hadn't noticed her before—his focus had been squarely on Hans—but now he could see that the idea wheel in Bunty's mind was turning, and he wondered what must go through that woman's head to keep her always one step ahead of the rest of them. Her quiet demeanor was simply a front for her calculating mind.

"What do you mean?" Hans asked, though Cliff didn't need an

explanation for him to start leaning into her train of thought.

"Great Idea," Cliff said, tapping the centre of his head while he pondered the problem.

"And for the rest of us who may *not* understand?" Kitty asked.

"They want to point the finger at someone else, hoping the confusion will offer up enough time to find out who actually did it," Mrs. Chen said, her hand tapping the top of her cane. "Am I right?"

"Yes," Cliff said, not surprised that Mrs. Chen was also following along. It was usually the quiet ones, who spent more time listening and thinking, that surprised Cliff the most.

"How do we do that?" Sol asked.

"Talk to Mari," Gerald called out from the kitchen. How he heard any of the conversation from the kitchen, when he so often complained about not being able to hear anything at all, was beyond Cliff. But still, the man had a point.

"Gerald, should we discuss your ability to hear when it's convenient for you?" Kitty asked, turning to shout into the kitchen.

"Sorry, what?" Gerald shouted back, not bothering to poke his head into the living room.

A roar of laughter came from everyone but Kitty, who shook her head, annoyed.

"I swear that man is going to be the end of me," Kitty said.

"Inshallah," Gerald called back from the kitchen.

The word was clearly unknown to everyone but Bunty, who giggled.

"What was that gibberish?" Kitty asked.

"It's Arabic," Bunty said pressing a finger to her lips to fight back a laugh. "It means, 'God willing.'" She smiled as Kitty's frown deepened.

"How does that man know Arabic?" was all Kitty could think to say, her head continuing to shake.

"How that man knows anything is a mystery to me," Sol mused.

Nods of agreement about Gerald's mysterious person rippled

around the room. But the respite from the conversation hadn't stopped Cliff's mind from working through Gerald's suggestion, and he knew he was right. If they wanted to get to the bottom of this, they would need to go to the source. They had to find a way to talk to Mari VanWinkle.

11

"Hold these," Mrs. Chen said to Hans, whose left arm was already wrapped around two large flowering plants.

"Sure thing." He blew a flower away from his mouth, as he reached out to take the other flower from Mrs. Chen.

"So much for not buying anything," Cliff whispered to Bunty as they walked a few steps behind, keeping their eye out for Mari.

Hans had already confirmed that she was working today, despite everything that was going on. Cliff supposed, during times of crisis, some people like to shut themselves up while others needed to go on with it. Mari appeared to be the latter. Given that she was even at work this morning meant the police still hadn't decided to bring her in, which was lucky for them.

"It was a tall order to ask her to come and expect her not to buy anything. I've never met anyone more passionate about plants than Mrs. Chen," Bunty chuckled.

"Seems like a lot when none of them will make it into her garden." Cliff shrugged. "Did you know she has to plan it out the year before?"

"Some of her plants are several years in the planning. Every year, she redesigns the entire garden. She truly is an artist," Bunty said.

Cliff could hear the admiration in her voice. This was the first time he'd talked to her one-on-one since their chat with Lou and, since then, he'd had something on his mind but didn't know how to bring it up.

"Yesterday…" Cliff started, but Bunty jumped in.

"Yes. I'm sorry about that. I didn't mean to—"

"No. I think you may be right. I *am* bored, although I'm not sure what to do about it. It appears everyone has something they enjoy doing, and frankly, all I've ever been is a detective. I'm not sure I have anything else," Cliff said shaking his head.

"Don't be ridiculous, of course you do," Bunty said.

Cliff laughed. "If you have any suggestions, I'm all ears."

"I can't tell you what to be interested in, Cliff. That's something for you to discover," Bunty retorted.

"I like crosswords." Cliff shrugged.

Bunty laughed, but immediately covered her mouth as her face flushed red with embarrassment at doing so. "Sorry."

"It's stupid, I know." Cliff shook his head, letting his hands fall to his sides.

"It's not stupid. But I think you should think bigger. What's something you've always wished you could do more of but never had the time?" Bunty asked.

Cliff opened his mouth but realized he didn't have anything to say. In fact, his mind was running a complete blank. Perhaps it was being placed on the spot, or maybe he truly didn't have anything, and the thought of this hurt more than anything.

"Cliff!"

"Sorry, I'm thinking," he said.

But when he looked over, he realized Bunty wasn't looking at him at all. He followed her eye line, spotting the reason for her outburst just as she said, "I see Mari."

"Mrs. Chen, we need to borrow Hans for a moment," Cliff said, pulling the big man away from the table lined with small houseplants.

Mrs. Chen didn't appear bothered by the interruption. She waved a hand in their direction and picked up one of the tiny plants and ran her fingers along its green leaves.

"Think maybe you can…?" Hans started to say as they walked through the rows, glancing down at his arms full of plants.

"Yes, of course," Cliff said, taking one of the medium-sized plants, while Bunty took the smallest one, leaving Hans with only two plants to manage.

"Thank you," he said, letting out a sigh of relief. "I think we'll need a cart if we let Mrs. Chen stay here any longer." Hans glanced over his shoulder at the other woman, who was discussing something with a red-shirted employee. "As much as I appreciate the respite from holding these," Hans said, "what are we…?"

"Mari is here," Cliff said. "Bunty spotted her walk in, and we figured it would be easier for us to all speak with you there as well. Might be odd to be asking about her family when we've never met."

"What am I supposed to say?" Hans asked, and despite having the plants removed from his arms, Cliff thought the man had already begun to sweat a little.

"Just ask her how she's doing, what's happening. We'll jump in if we think of anything."

"Doesn't it feel wrong to pry?" Hans asked. "Her father just died."

"And you just lost a friend. And if we don't get to the bottom of this, she might be the one who's blamed for it all," Cliff said, which seemed to ease Hans's mind.

A look of resolution swept across his face. It wasn't the first time Cliff knew in his heart that Hans might be the kind of person who truly couldn't see the worst in people. A gift that Cliff had lost many, many years ago. He envied it.

"Don't worry. Just be yourself and ask how she's doing. Remember, we're just trying to understand what could have happened." Cliff gave the big man a reassuring pat on the back.

"Hans?" Mari said, glancing up from behind a table filled with tiny, ornamental garden gnomes performing a variety of tasks, like bowling or setting up a ladder. Her eyes were puffy and red, as if she'd recently been crying. When she spotted Hans, it looked as though the floodgates would open up again at any moment, but she managed to contain herself, to Cliff's surprise.

Mari ran around the table to meet them and gave Hans a big hug, which appeared to catch him off guard a little.

"Hi, Mari," Hans said, wrapping one big arm around the young woman, while he protected the two plants in his other arm.

"It's so good to see you," she said.

Both Cliff and Bunty could tell she was fighting now to hold back tears.

"It's good to see you too," Hans said, looking a little flushed. "How are you holding up?" he asked once she appeared to settle in and push her emotions away.

"Not so good," she said, shaking her head. "I just can't believe it." She wiped her eyes with the sleeve of her shirt until Hans pulled a white handkerchief out of his breast pocket.

"Here," he said, handing it over.

"Thank you." She took the white handkerchief and dabbed at her eyes.

Hans switched the plants back around in his arms, and Cliff was jealous of how much strength his friend still managed to have.

"I thought coming into work would make it easier, but I'm not sure," she said, sucking in a deep breath through her nose and holding it a moment before letting it out. She shook her head, caught somewhere between mild amusement and sheer exhaustion. "They said he might have been murdered." She looked up at Hans, her brow furrowed. "I just can't believe that."

Hans stole a glance back at Cliff, and the gesture did not go unnoticed.

"Did the police talk to you too?" Mari asked.

Cliff made a mental note. *So, they've already spoken with her.*

That shouldn't have been a surprise to Cliff. If Lou and Captain Marks felt Mari was of interest, it would make sense they had already interviewed her. But from the way she was talking about it, she clearly didn't think that, somehow, she would be the one blamed for his death.

"No," Hans said, forcing a thin smile as he looked down at Mari. "I just wanted to come and check in on you."

"That's really kind of you," Mari said.

Cliff could see the pained expression forming on Hans's face, likely from the idea of withholding his true motives from Mari.

"I'm sorry, I'm being rude, who are your friends, Hans?" She gestured towards Cliff and Bunty.

"These are my housemates, Cliff and Bunty," Hans said, opening himself up and using the arm with the smaller of his two plants to gesture towards the pair behind him.

"Dad said you lived in a house with some other people. Kind of a funny arrangement, isn't it?" Mari asked.

"No," Bunty said, at the same time Cliff replied, "Yes."

"Cliff's new to the house. He's still trying to find his bearings," Bunty said with a thin smile. "But for the rest of us, it works well. It's important to be around people you like, especially at our age."

"Sounds a little bit like my days at Guelph," Mari said, "only I would assume less parties?" Despite clearly being upset, she chuckled.

"Maybe just a reimagined idea of partying," Hans joked. "When you get to be our age, partying tends to be a little more…subdued."

"So how *did* you hear about Dad? Jan tell you?" she asked.

"No, it wasn't Jan," Hans said.

Mari took a step back from Hans to eye him up suspiciously.

"Cliff used to be a detective, and, well…"

"You're a detective? Could you find out what happened to my dad?" Mari asked, sounding a little too hopeful for Cliff's liking.

"Umm…I'm not…well, I can't promise anything, but Hans has asked me to look around. But…" Cliff said, shaking his head.

"But what?"

"Are you sure you want us to get involved? I mean, this is a very personal matter." Cliff felt a little surprised at how easy it was to chat with Mari. She was either very good at covering up what she did, or she was genuinely interested in what happened to her dad.

"If you think you can help him, of course I want you to investigate it. I just don't know what you're going to do. I mean…" She shook her head as if trying to wrap her brain around it all.

"Like I said, I can't promise anything and, well, things like these are personal. Having people look into it can be awkward," Cliff insisted.

"From what I've seen so far, no one is looking at anyone. It's been two days since they talked to me, and from what I've heard, they haven't been speaking to anyone else, really. Just seems strange to me," she whispered.

"We heard this as well," Cliff said. "Which is why we wanted to come and talk to you actually."

"Me? Why me?" she asked.

"Well, I'm curious to know what you said to the police." Cliff looked around at the small garden centre, which was by no means crowded. But there were more people inside than Cliff would have liked, especially with the conversation he was hoping to have with her.

"They wanted to know about my relationship with my dad."

"What did you tell them?" Cliff asked.

"The truth. That we had a good relationship. Obviously working together was challenging, and we didn't always see eye to eye on things, but that's the nature of the work. In hindsight, it all seems so unimportant now, after, well…" She stopped, blinking back tears. "I just wish I could have seen him again, talked to him, told him I was sorry." She shook her head.

"What were you sorry about?" Cliff asked.

"It's just…" She pinched the bridge of her nose. "It's just, that morning, we got into a big argument. We each said some things we didn't mean, but still. Knowing that would be the last time I was going to talk to him, I wouldn't have been so…difficult." She sighed.

"You told the police about your fight, I'm guessing?" Cliff asked, glancing over at Bunty and Hans.

"I'm not sure I would have called it a fight, but yes, of course. They're the police. Besides, if the movies have taught me anything, it's that the truth always has a way of coming out. Figured honesty was my strongest bet," Mari said.

Cliff plastered on a thin smile as he nodded. "It is definitely good of you to tell the truth."

But something in his face must have given him away, because Mari narrowed her eyes on him. "What is it?" she asked, looking first at Cliff, then over at Hans, and then Bunty.

"It's nothing, Mari," Hans said, unconvincingly.

"You didn't just come here to check on me, did you?" Mari asked, her eyes fixed on Hans. He was one person she knew well enough to know he kept his heart on his sleeve.

"Of course, I wanted to check on you," Hans said. He opened his mouth, as if to say more, but stopped as his head dropped, defeated, to his chest.

I need to teach Hans how to keep a better poker face, Cliff thought.

"Hans did want to check on you," Cliff offered, waiting until Mari's attention was with him, "but I wanted a chance to speak with you myself."

"Why?"

"Because Hans has asked me to help find out who killed your father," Cliff said.

"So what? You thought you would come here and ask me what I know?" Mari asked, an edge in her tone.

"Yes. I thought you would be a good person to start with." Cliff wished he'd had a better plan with how to go about saying what he was doing. Because, as it stood, the entire thing felt a bit flimsy and awkward. Everything he wished it wasn't.

"Why me?" Mari asked skeptically.

"You know things, like who else has access to the shed. You also might have some insights into what happened that day with your father. Who he talked to, things like that."

Mari's eyes narrowed slightly on Cliff as she studied him. She did not look overly convinced by the time she spoke, but she wasn't walking away either.

Off to a good start.

"It was a busy day. We had everyone running around. Hell, even Flynn and Hendrik were there, and Hendrik is useless at these things. Though I suppose he had other reasons for wanting to be here." Mari flinched at the statement and glanced up at Cliff, as if she'd said something wrong.

"What reason was that?" Cliff asked.

Mari looked worried for a moment as she wrung her fingers together. "It's nothing," Mari said. "Forget I even said anything."

"Mari, please—"

"With respect, I don't even know you," she said, turning to walk away.

But Hans reached for her shoulder, placing a calming hand on it. "Mari, wait," Hans said, his voice soft and gentle.

She turned back to face him. "I'm not here to put the blame on anyone, Hans, especially not my family. No matter how much they piss me off sometimes." Mari shook her head feverishly.

"I know you don't want to, but I really think you should talk to Cliff," Hans said calmly.

"Why? Why on earth would I trust him?"

"Because he's here to help you."

"Help me? Why would I need help?" she asked, her tone rising, and Cliff caught a couple people looking at them now.

"Perhaps there's a place we can speak to you in private? I swear I just want to help if I can," Cliff said, trying to sound reassuring. He looked over at Bunty, who also noticed various eyes turning to look at them now.

"Not until you tell me what's going on here." Mari's eyes worked their way from Cliff to Bunty before finally resting on Hans. "Hans, please." Her voice was soft.

"Mari, we think…well, we heard…" Hans's voice was getting trapped in his throat, and Cliff was about to jump in for his friend when he felt Bunty brush past him.

She took Mari's hand gently in her own. "We believe the OPP have reason to suspect you of trying to kill your father."

"What?" Mari asked, her face pure shock. "Why would they think… me?" Mari was shaking off the idea like wet hair.

"That's what we're trying to find out, my dear. We need your help to learn who may have killed your father."

"Sorry it's a little cramped," Mari said as the four of them squeezed into the small office. It was just large enough to hold a small desk, a chair, a few filing cabinets, and an old seventies-looking couch that appeared to have been very well used over the years and was reminiscent of Cliff's early years in Toronto.

Cliff, Bunty, and Hans all went into the office, and while Bunty and Hans took a seat on the couch, Cliff remained standing. He paced, as best he could, around the room, looking at various poster boards filled with notes and schedules for the farm. He wasn't sure what he was looking for, but it had been ingrained in him over the years to remain standing while he worked. For one, pacing helped keep his brain active, and the moving around gave him a nice change in visual stimulus. He never knew what might jump out at him during an investigation, but he always found being physically engaged to be helpful.

They had invited Mrs. Chen to join them, and despite her reluctance to come in the first place, she appeared to be very happy wandering around the greenhouse and gardens, examining the plants. When she had asked them how long they thought they might be, none of them were able to give her an answer. It was obvious to all of them that she was eager to get back to the house and, more importantly, to her own garden, the one she had routinely reminded each of them that they'd agreed to help in that afternoon.

Clearly, she would not forget those promises, although from how well the conversation appeared to be going with Mari, Cliff was beginning to wonder if those promises had even been necessary. Not that he wouldn't honour his commitment. He was a man of his word. No matter how much the thought of it hurt his old bones.

"I was a little surprised when I heard you were coming in at all," Hans said as Mari shut the door to the office and squeezed past Cliff on her way to her swivel chair at the head of her desk, which was pressed up tight against the wall.

"You sound like my staff," Mari said as she sat down. "But when I was at home, the only thing I could think about was how much it hurt."

Cliff felt as if he was watching a little girl swinging around in her chair, lost. *Perhaps she is?*

"At least here I can keep busy, and, well, everything here reminds of him. It's like he's still here in some ways," Mari said, shaking her head. "I know it sounds silly."

"It doesn't," Bunty said, giving the young woman a warm smile.

"We're sorry to bring it up with you," Hans said.

"If you think you can help find out what happened, I'm more than happy to help. I thought that's what I was doing with the police, but…"

"I know it's difficult, but they're only doing their job," Cliff said, hoping it sounded reassuring. "Maybe if you tell us what you told them, we can get to the bottom of it." Cliff smiled weakly, knowing that, from the sounds of it, if Pieter had been killed and it wasn't Mari, then it was likely someone she knew.

"I can try." Mari stared up at the ceiling, trying to remember the details from the day. "Everything was so chaotic that morning. You would think with so much time to prep it all, that things would move smoothly, but these things have a way of surprising you." She chuckled, but it was hollow and held a lot more than just a small memory. "I thought Dad seemed stressed. I mean, I knew this was important to him, but still."

"Stressed how?" Cliff asked.

"I'm not sure. Just a feeling maybe." Mari shrugged. "He just kept saying how great the day was going to be, but not in an excited way more like…I'm not sure…" Mari thought for a moment. "Like he was trying to convince himself it was going to be fine."

"How much do you know about the farm?" Hans asked.

Cliff turned with a puzzled look towards his friend. From the expression on his face, Hans appeared to know more than he had originally told Cliff. He made a mental note to ask him about it later.

"Just what Dad told me. That things were tough. I assumed it had something to with the other farms. I mean I know Winkleberry Farm has never made a huge profit, but I've always assumed it was doing fine. Why? What did you hear?"

Looks like I won't have to wait after all, Cliff thought.

"Your dad told me he was approached by the Badger to buy his farms—"

"I wouldn't let that bastard near our farms."

"You know him?" Cliff asked.

"Yes," Mari scoffed. "He's a creep."

"What do you mean?"

"Let's just say he has a tendency to hit on any girl with two legs." Mari shuddered. "Just ask any woman unfortunate enough to cross paths with him at the pub." Her disgust was palpable.

"I know the type," Bunty said, sharing an understanding nod with Mari before asking, "Do you think your dad would have sold him the farm?"

"My dad hated him. I couldn't see why he would ever sell that man anything," Mari said with solid conviction. Although from the sounds of it, Cliff got the impression that she might not have all the information about just how desperate Pieter might have been, especially given the look on Hans's face.

"What about the shed?" Cliff asked. "Who all had access to it?"

"Not many people have keys. Myself, Dad, Uncle Lucas, Flynn, Aria…" Mari tapped her head thoughtfully. "I think maybe Hendrik has one too. Although Dad forgot his at the house that morning."

"You told this to the police?" Cliff asked.

"Of course," Mari said.

Cliff vaguely recalled Lou mention finding Pieter's key on the hook at the house. He also made a larger mental note to get himself a paper and pen, considering his brain wasn't what it used to be. He was surprised when he turned to see Bunty jotting something down in a tiny notebook. He looked at her, tilting his head. Her face flushed red as she glanced up at him.

"You don't mind that I'm taking notes, do you?" she asked, half to Cliff and half to Mari, who shrugged, indifferent to it all. "I think better with notes," she said.

"I was just thinking the same thing," Cliff said, smiling at her as she finished jotting down her memo.

"So, the only people with keys to the shed are you, your dad, your cousins, your uncle and…who exactly is Aria?" Cliff asked.

"A manager," Mari said. "She's been with us for a year now. She came over from Holland looking for a job and Dad gave her one."

"Is that normal?" Cliff asked.

"Yes," Hans and Mari said at the same time.

"Dad knew her mom. She umm…passed away. I think he just felt bad. Wanted to give her a fresh start over here," Mari said.

"Other than her, it's just your family then who has access?" Cliff asked.

Mari nodded, her face darkening with understanding. "I know what you're thinking," she said, "but…" She stopped, appearing unsure of what to think about all of this.

"We're just gathering information." Cliff tried to reassure her. "I don't like jumping to conclusions until I have all the information."

Mari nodded, though Cliff didn't think she looked all that convinced.

"There is something I don't understand," Hans said, shaking his head and slowly looking up at Mari. "None of this makes me think you did anything wrong. So why do the police seem to think that you had anything to do with your father's death?"

Mari looked down at the ground as she wrung her hands together on her lap, sucking in a deep breath through her nose before looking back up at Hans, her eyes reddening as she struggled to fight back tears. "I um…we…Dad and I argued that morning. It was the, umm…last time I spoke to him."

Everyone remained quiet, their eyes fixed on Mari as she swivelled side to side uncomfortably, struggling to get the words out.

"I lied…sort of. I did know the farm was in trouble, but I only found out that morning when Dad told me he was considering selling," she said, her hands clenching together. "At first, I thought he was talking about the other farms, but then he told me Hendrik had made an offer for Winkleberry Farm, as well and…well, I kind of lost it. I couldn't even listen to him anymore. I mean my cousin doesn't even like the farm. It's small and not overly profitable, but it's been in our family for generations, and the thought that my dad would just sell it like that, made me so angry. It sounds stupid, but I always thought that I would get the farm. Flynn could keep the other ones, sell those to Hendrik if he wanted a farm, but this one was special. I just thought my dad understood that. But I was wrong." Mari let out a heavy sigh.

"I'm sorry," Bunty said, glancing up from her notepad to look at Mari.

"Now, I have to live with the reality that our last conversation was so…awful." Mari shook her head.

"Your relationship with him is not defined by one conversation," Bunty said reassuringly.

"Thank you, but you didn't hear the conversation," Mari said quietly.

"I don't have to. I can see what your father meant to you. Which means he did too." She offered Mari a warm smile.

Cliff understood that Bunty was trying to be kind, but this didn't change the fact that she'd had an argument with him prior to his death, which did little to push the needle in her favour.

"Who else knew he was planning on selling the farm?" Hans asked, pulling Cliff out from his thoughts. It was a good question, since it was highly unlikely that Mari would be the only one in the family upset by the prospect of selling.

"All of us. It wasn't something Dad was able to hide for long. As per usual, I think I was the last one to find out. Except for maybe Hendrik, but I don't know."

"He must have cared a little," Bunty said, jotting down a note as she looked up, all eyes on her now as her cheeks pinked slightly at the attention.

"I agree," Cliff said, but he seemed to be the only one who knew what she was talking about.

"What do you two know that we don't?" Hans asked.

Cliff looked to Bunty, giving her the space to continue on with her thought.

"When we saw Hendrik at the farm, talking to Pieter, he told him it was a good deal and that he should take it," Bunty said.

"I remember that now," Hans agreed.

"I assume that was the offer for the farm." Mari shrugged.

"What exactly does Hendrik do?" Cliff asked curiously.

"Investments or something. I know he's told me, but it's not really my thing," Mari said.

It was strange to Cliff that she wouldn't know, but maybe she just wasn't close enough to him to care to know. Still, he put that little kernel of knowledge in his memory for the time being.

"I know he travels a lot. Hendrik's never been one to stick around."

"He's your cousin, correct?" Cliff asked.

"Yeah. His Mum is Dad's sister, though they don't speak much, or at all really," Mari admitted.

"Why's that?" Cliff asked, his mind wandering now with curiosity. He was looking for a reason to not have Mari as a suspect, and siblings who didn't talk was usually a good start.

"When Grandad left the farm to Dad, she wasn't overly thrilled. Never really got over it, I suppose." Mari shrugged.

"And where is she?"

"Why?"

"Just trying to get as much information as I can, really." Cliff wasn't in the habit of telling people why he was asking questions. The reality at this point was that he was just trying to fill the pool with information. Eventually, he would have to decide what information was important and what wasn't. But from the questionable look on Mari's face, he supposed she believed it was something else.

"She couldn't have been involved. She lives out west. She calls to talk to Flynn. But doesn't really come around. *Ever,*" Mari emphasised.

"Fair enough," Cliff said, thinking about it for a moment before something else dawned on him. "How did your cousins end up working for your dad if he doesn't speak with his sister? Can't imagine she loves that."

"She doesn't. The boys came to visit when they were younger. My dad offered them each a job, which pissed Aunt Cynthia off more than anything. But the boys liked it. Well, Flynn did. Hendrik just needed a little money for school. So, he would work in the summers and then live in Toronto. Went to U of T."

"Why did your dad offer them jobs?" Cliff asked. He began to feel a lot like his old self again as he paced the room, letting the information sink in, at least what he hoped was relevant, while disregarding the rest.

"He felt guilty, I guess. Never really liked that his dad left it all to him. But then it was just a small farm. He helped make it what it is today. Still, he told me once it was the least he could do. I suppose I kind of understand."

"What about your aunt, did she love the farm?" Cliff asked.

"Not sure. But considering she stopped talking to my dad because of it, I imagine she didn't hate it."

"You have an uncle too?" Bunty asked, reading over her notes, glancing over at Cliff. "Sorry," she grimaced.

"No, you're alright," Cliff said, kicking himself for not thinking of that as well. Mari's aunt wasn't the only one who got nothing from the granddad. And Cliff knew that Lucas was on site.

"Yeah, Uncle Lucas has been here since the beginning," Mari said.

"And he wasn't angry about not getting the farm?"

"No. Well, I don't think he was." Mari shrugged. "He just stayed on, working with Dad for over twenty years. I think he was happy to not have to worry about any of it. Just take his pay and..." Mari dusted her hands together. "You know?"

"I think so." Bunty jotted something down in her notebook, while the room fell silent for a moment.

Mari looked at them all again. "If you don't have—"

"Sorry," Cliff said, raising a hand as a thought occurred to him.

"Yeah?" Mari asked.

"Well, it's just something I was curious about. If your cousin Hendrik didn't like to work for the farm, why was he here for the festival? Just being nice? And why does he have keys to the shed?"

12

"Maybe being nice. Maybe showing my dad he cares about the farm." Mari laughed uncomfortably. "I stopped trying to understand why Hendrik does what Hendrik does a long time ago. As for the keys, just left over from working here, I guess." She shrugged, but then frowned as a thought must have entered her mind. She nervously chewed on her bottom lip.

"What is it?" Cliff asked, watching the expression on her face shift awkwardly.

"Nothing. Probably," Mari said.

"Mari, I understand that it's hard to tell us everything, but we do want to help. And the more we know the better," Cliff said, walking to stand by her desk.

"I just can't understand why anyone would kill…" Mari shook her head.

Tears welled in her eyes. Cliff knew from experience that, whatever strength she was accessing to give them this information was weakening, and soon her walls would be boarded up and it would be unlikely Cliff, or any of them, would get anything useful from her.

"It's not fair, what happened to your dad." Cliff stepped closer to lay a reassuring hand on her shoulder. "And I understand why you don't want to talk about this. I do," he said softly. "But you need to tell someone what you know, the good *and* the bad, if the truth is ever going to come out and let us find out what happened."

Mari looked up at Cliff and then over at Bunty and Hans, each of whom appeared to wear a similar pained expression on their faces. Cliff understood that neither of them had much experience talking about the dead in such a casual manner, and for Hans, it would be particularly difficult, considering this man was his friend.

Mari took a deep breath and looked up towards Cliff. "My dad was a calm man," she started softly. "He rarely let his emotions get the better of him. But there was something about that day that seemed to set him on edge. It started with the Badger, Mr. Wilderman. He shoved him and was shouting. I'm not sure. I wasn't there, but Aria said she had to pull him away."

Unlike Mari, Cliff had seen this little confrontation. He hadn't been aware of what it was about and, from the sounds of it, neither was Mari, but she wasn't finished.

"Then he got into it with Uncle Lucas." Mari shook her head. "He's had his issues."

"You just said he didn't care about the farm," Bunty said.

"I said I didn't *think* he did. But apparently, they'd got into it about it at some point. Flynn said he heard them shouting about the farm."

"Flynn heard them arguing?" Cliff asked.

"Apparently," Mari said. "And Uncle Lucas, well…" Mari looked at Cliff, then over at Hans, who looked as though he already knew what she was going to say. But she didn't continue.

"Well, what?" Cliff asked.

Mari's eyes flicked over to Hans again, whose head fell to his chest. Whatever this information was, Hans knew about it.

"We don't really talk about it. I mean no one ever talked about it," Mari said weakly, "but he, umm, well, he apparently…"

"He killed someone," Hans said weakly, and all eyes turned to stare at him.

"Sorry," Cliff said, shaking his head. "You're saying that Lucas VanWinkle killed someone?"

Hans looked up slowly, his eyes meeting Cliff's. Cliff could see the pain on his face. "Yes. I am."

13

The Hearse was silent as Hans, Cliff, Bunty, and Mrs. Chen all drove home. The empty seats in the back were filled with tools, plants, and fertilizers that Mrs. Chen picked up on her light visit to the garden centre.

"Why do you all look like you've seen a ghost?" Mrs. Chen finally asked. Her cane was resting on her lap as she looked out the side window.

"We found out some information," Cliff said softly, his own eyes still lingering on Hans, who looked oddly guilty as he gripped the steering wheel.

After that little bombshell, they'd left Mari alone in her office, and it was painfully obvious from the sounds of weeping as they shut the door that whatever strength Mari had been holding onto that morning had washed away with their conversation.

Cliff knew it was never going to be easy, but what he hadn't counted on was Hans keeping secrets from them as well.

"Wasn't that the purpose of the trip?" Mrs. Chen asked.

Cliff gave her a nod.

"And yet you don't look pleased."

"Hans had some information about the family that he forgot to mention," Cliff said.

"It wasn't my information to tell," Hans said weakly.

"Hans, your friend was killed and his brother killed someone."

"It's not what you think," Hans said softly.

"What is it then? Because from the sound of it, Lucas and Pieter didn't get along, and he has…a history," Cliff suggested.

"Perhaps it's best if you don't jump to conclusions until Hans tells us what he knows. Maybe it's nothing," Bunty said, although she didn't look convinced by her words at all.

"I'd nearly forgotten all about it," Hans said, shaking his head. "It all happened so long ago."

"But what happened?" Mrs. Chen asked, sounding a little more intrigued by what was happening now that she was no longer roaming the grounds for garden supplies.

Hans's eyes flicked up in his mirror to glance back at Cliff. He opened his mouth to speak but stopped before eventually letting out a huff of air. "It's complicated and I likely don't know the whole story."

"Hans, this could be important." Cliff didn't want to sound too pushy, but also, his curiosity was getting the better of him, and he desperately needed to know what was going on.

"Remember, this is just a piece of the puzzle. And we won't know which piece it is until you tell us," Bunty said, her notepad out on her lap. Her eyes widened at Cliff, and she tilted her head towards Hans.

Cliff relaxed, his shoulders dropping away from his ears, where he'd been holding them. "Bunty's right. We're trying to gather all the information, that's all," Cliff said, feeling a little bad that it fell on Bunty to remind him what was important before getting there himself.

He kept forgetting that he wasn't a detective anymore, nor was he working with other police. These were his friends, none of whom had a history of solving crimes. Hans was a farmer, Bunty was a librarian, and Mrs. Chen was…actually, Cliff didn't know much about her past, considering she mostly kept herself to herself. This was something Cliff admired about the older woman. Still, as far as his understanding went, he wasn't sure she'd spent a lot of time solving crimes either. No, if Cliff was going to get anywhere with them, he would need to remember that this was all new to them. Which would mean exercising a degree of patience. Something he was never known for in the workplace.

"I can only tell you what I know. And I'm telling you now, it's not a lot," Hans said, his eyes firmly on the road. He turned the wheel to avoid a hole in the dirt road, causing everyone to rock to the side. "Pieter's dad told me about it once. It was a good forty years ago maybe now. Lucas and some friends were coming home from a field party." Han's voice sank.

Cliff had a feeling he knew where this story was leading. It wasn't a new story by any stretch, and an unfortunate side effect of small-town life. From the dark expression on Bunty's face, he could tell she was thinking the same thing.

"Lucas was driving, with Pieter and a few others in the truck as well. They had people standing in the bed, they'd all be drinking and, well...his tire hit a lose patch of gravel and he lost control of the truck and swerved into a tree. Everyone in the truck got banged up pretty bad, but it was worse for the people in the back. They were tossed out into the woods. One of them died and another two were badly injured," Hans said weakly.

"Jesus," Cliff said. "That's awful."

"It was tragic. The entire community was shaken by it. But Lucas was a minor at the time, so he was sent to a detention facility. He was there for a couple years, and then, when he got out, he was different. Johan, their father, said he didn't think Lucas ever fully recovered from it. He just stayed and worked on the farm." Hans shook his head.

"Sounds like it was an accident," Bunty said.

"A horrible accident," Hans agreed, his hands regripping the wheel, and Cliff thought Hans appeared a little more pale than he had a moment before.

He's not telling us everything.

"There's more, isn't there?" Cliff asked as the Hearse pulled up to a stop sign, sliding to a halt on the gravel.

For a moment, the van stayed put, despite there being no other cars on the road in either direction.

"Yes. But this was just…well it was never, actually…you know…" Hans's voice was breaking.

"Hans what happened?" Cliff asked, his voice gentle. He could see his friend struggling to understand what, if anything, he should say.

Finally, whatever inner war he was waging appeared to end as he let out a reluctant sigh. "There was a rumour that went around saying it wasn't Lucas who was driving that night." Hans turned in his chair so he was facing the rest of them in the Hearse. "It was Pieter."

…

The midafternoon sun beamed down as Cliff and Hans carried bags of fertilizer towards the back garden, where Mrs. Chen and Bunty were sitting on tiny collapsible benches with a tool Cliff had, up until today, called a "three-pronged hand thing." Hans had been quiet since they got back to the Limestone Manor, and Cliff knew the big man felt guilty, despite not having anything to be guilty about. However, from the smile forming on his face, the manual labour of working in the garden seemed to be having a positive effect on him.

Cliff had tried reassuring him that all he did was tell them what he knew. It was up to Cliff, and now the rest of them, to figure out how useful that information would be. At the very least, it meant that it was worth taking a trip to speak with Lucas, though they'd decided it had been enough investigating for one day. Besides, part of the agreement with Mrs. Chen to use her as an excuse to visit the garden centre was that they would help her weed the garden that afternoon. It was turning to out to be more difficult than Cliff had imagined, and he wasn't even sure they'd needed the excuse.

"How does she do this every day?" Cliff asked Hans as he wiped the sweat from his brow. "I feel like I'm putting one foot in the grave right now."

Hans wiped his own brow, though from the look of the big man he was handling the effort a little better than Cliff, but not by much. "It's the sun that will get you," he said smacking his lips together, and Cliff could feel his own lips feeling a little parched as well.

"It's a marathon, not a sprint," Bunty said.

Cliff was impressed when he looked over at her. Her legs were crossed, while her bum rested on the stool under her, as she methodically combed the garden with her hand and cultivator. Mrs. Chen, on the other hand, was nowhere to be seen. Her stool was empty, and Cliff wondered where she could have run off to.

Bunty had a handkerchief wrapped around her head and, unlike the two men, she looked relaxed and not drenched in sweat.

"I would happily never run a marathon," Cliff said, rubbing his knees, which felt tight just looking at Bunty on the ground.

Bunty laughed. "I just mean, you're working like you want it to be done, doing as much as you can, as fast as you can, as if that will make it finish faster."

"Won't it?" Cliff asked.

"No." She smiled. "You should know better than to just use brute force, Hans."

"Tell that to the ninety-odd acres I used to sow, Bunty," he chuckled.

"You mean the one you used a *combine* to tear through? And the *airplanes* to spray your fields?" she said, tilting her head. "You wouldn't call that brute force."

"I'd call it effective."

"I'm with Hans on this."

"That may be true. But this garden is about pleasure, not efficiency," Bunty said.

"I don't see why it can't be both?" Hans moved over to take a seat on the cast-iron bench nestled between two sculpted hedges.

Cliff joined him, and they must have looked like a funny pair, squeezed onto the tiny bench.

"No matter how hard you work, weeds will always work harder." Bunty gestured to a dandelion in the ground. "The only thing you can do is be consistent. And consistency means longevity. Burning yourself out on day one doesn't do you any favours."

"I hadn't realized this was a multi-day event."

"You both promised Mrs. Chen you'd help prep the garden for the competition. It's next week," she said, lifting a brow.

Cliff and Hans turned to look at each other. From his friend's expression, Hans felt the same way Cliff did, that they might have missed something in that previous discussion.

"Wait, do you mean we're going to be out here every day?" Cliff asked.

"You said you'd help." Bunty shrugged. "What were you expecting?"

"To help *today*," Hans laughed.

"I'm not sure my knees could hold up another day," Cliff mused.

"Well, have fun explaining that to Mrs. Chen." Bunty picked up another tiny tool beside her and used it to pry out the dandelion.

"She can't expect—"

"Can't expect what?" Mrs. Chen asked as she came out of the house holding a tray with a pitcher of fresh lemonade and four cups. She placed it down on the matching cast-iron table with two chairs, across from Cliff and Hans, who, seeing the fresh juice, stood immediately to help themselves.

"Thank the heavens," Hans said, approaching the table.

Mrs. Chen poured him a glass and handed it to him, before doing the same for Cliff.

"I'm not sure how you do this every day, Mrs. Chen," Cliff said, taking a long drink from the lemonade and letting the cool, satisfying liquid refresh him.

"I find it relaxing," she said. "But I have to admit, having you all help should make this all go a lot faster." She handed a cup to Bunty, who'd moved to sit in one of the chairs, then poured herself one.

"About that," Cliff said. "I'm not sure how much of this I can do before I'm no longer helpful. Or alive for that matter," he chuckled.

"I wouldn't expect you all day, Cliff. Don't be ridiculous," she said, waving a dismissive hand in his direction.

"Oh good." He smiled warmly. "'Cause with everything that's going on with Pieter, I just feel like it could be busy."

"Of course," Mrs. Chen said, taking a sip from her glass before continuing. "A couple of hours a day should do the trick."

Cliff wondered if his face looked as stunned as Hans's.

"That isn't going to be a problem, is it? I mean, you did say you would help with the competition after all." Her smile faded slightly.

Cliff glanced over at Bunty, who was clearing trying to suppress a giggle as she took a sip from her glass. When she met his eyes, all she could do was give him a little shrug and a wink.

"Of course, we're going to help," Hans said. "It's just we're, ummm… well, it's just…" He glanced over at Cliff for help.

"We're not used to this kind of work. We might have to do it in small chunks, is all."

"I see," she said looking between the two men. "If you don't want to help…"

"No, that's not it," Cliff said, suddenly feeling guilty, though he was sure now that he hadn't fully understood what he was agreeing to at the time. Truly, he had no one to blame but himself, but still, it didn't make this any easier. "We agreed to help. And we will. I just might need to ease into it a little." He rubbed his knee, and Hans slouched forward and rubbed his back, though Cliff didn't know if this was because it actually hurt, or whether the big man was also trying to get out of a full day's work.

"Same," Hans said. "A couple…hours a day should be good, once we, umm…"

"Figure out how to pace ourselves," Cliff finished for him. He thought Bunty was going to spit up her drink, though the quiet, reserved woman was too polite for something like that. Instead, she just choked a little.

"Bunty? Are you okay?" Mrs. Chen asked, giving the other woman a pat on the back.

"Yes, excuse me, I'm sorry. I'm not sure what came over me." She smiled and patted her chest.

"Well, you've all been very helpful. Perhaps we call it a day?" Mrs. Chen suggested, looking at Cliff and Hans. "I can see you might need a break."

"If you think that's for the best." Cliff finished off the rest of his drink, hoping he might find more inside.

A few minutes later, Cliff, Hans, and Bunty were back in the house. Cliff hadn't realized just how wonderful the air-conditioned rooms would feel after working outside. He was looking forward to taking the rest of the day off. He felt exhausted as he slumped down on the living room sofa.

He was surprised not to see Sol and Kitty in their usual spot until he remembered they would be playing bridge for the next few hours. That was opportune for him, since he had little desire to speak with anyone about much, and he knew from experience that Kitty would want a full report on what happened with Mari.

Cliff watched Hans collapse in the chair across from him, while

Bunty sat next to him on the couch. Mrs. Chen, despite claiming that they'd done enough work for the day, remained outside, tackling a section of the garden she had deemed "stubborn."

"I'm pooped," Hans said, chuckling. "I feel like I haven't worked that hard since I was a boy doing chores on the farm."

"It's the heat that gets you," Bunty said, shaking her head. "You boys should have really covered up from the sun," she admonished.

Cliff barely had the energy to agree with her as the cool sofa threatened to pull him into a midafternoon snooze.

"Who do you suppose we should talk to next?" Bunty asked, shifting Cliff out of his near slumber and back into the room.

For a moment, he was puzzled as to what she could be talking about, until understanding kicked in. "How are you able to think about that right now?"

"How are you not?" Bunty countered.

"I can think of a few reasons," Hans mused as he patted his legs.

"It's tricky," Cliff said.

"Why's that?" Bunty asked.

"This isn't *our* investigation. We can hardly just go around question-ing people. We're not the police," Cliff said, then felt guilty at being so abrupt when he saw the disappointed look on Bunty's face. Even Hans, who Cliff knew was finding this entire ordeal to be less than desirable, looked disappointed at this prospect. "I said it was tricky, not impossible," Cliff corrected, which appeared to lighten their faces.

"How did you do it when you were a private investigator?"

"I had a licence to do that."

"What about being a concerned citizen?" Hans asked.

"I'm afraid that's not really how it works," Cliff said.

"So we can't talk to people?"

"I didn't say that," Cliff said. "It's more like they don't have to answer any of our questions."

"What do we do, then?" Hans asked.

Cliff rubbed his temples while he tried to activate his tired brain. The reality was that investigating was never going to be easy, but he didn't have the heart to tell Hans or Bunty this. Even with all the resources the police department had, over twenty percent of all murders—if that's even what this was—were unsolved in Canada, and those that were, were more often than not, committed by someone who knew the victim.

Yet another reason why the police might feel Mari could be involved. She knew the victim and had motive, which he knew would be a win in their books.

But I can't say this to Hans, or it will destroy him.

"We take what we know, and we work back from that. Then, perhaps we talk to Lou. Maybe she can tell us more about what the police have. Maybe all they wanted to do was talk to Mari."

"It must be a good sign that they haven't brought her in, though, right?" Hans asked.

"They will wait until they have something concrete to charge her with. The last thing they want is to not be absolutely sure," Cliff said, realizing during this exchange how unused he was in having to manage the expectations of others. Typically, he was on the other side of it all, working with people who understood the nuances of the system. Bunty and Hans had little knowledge of how the police department worked, outside of what Bunty read in her books.

"So we just wait?" Bunty asked, and Cliff caught the look of disappointment in her eyes, though unfortunately, that was most likely all they could do right now.

"Well, we know that only five people besides Pieter, had access to the shed: Mari, Lucas, Flynn, Hendrik, and Aria. We know that all of them were there that day. Perhaps if we can find a reason to speak with each of them…?"

"Without making it feel like we're questioning them," Bunty offered.

"That would be ideal," Cliff agreed, feeling the wheels in his brain trying to turn but getting stuck with each rotation, as he continued to repeat things over in his mind. "Perhaps it's best if we sleep on it." Cliff tried to stifle a yawn, covering his mouth with a fist. "See what happens…"

The front door opened, and Cliff turned to see Jan barge in. He was sporting a blue button-down shirt and brown khaki shorts. His short blond hair was tucked under a navy-blue Tilley hat, as he rapidly licked a small, dipped ice cream cone, attempting to avoid it melting all over the front of his shirt.

"Opa?" he said, licking around the edge of the cone.

"Jan?" Hans waved from his chair, as he was obviously not ready to stand up quite yet. "What are you doing here?"

"I was in the neighbourhood." He gestured with the small cone Cliff figured he got from Rob's Dairy. "I thought I would come in and see how you were doing. You know with…umm…yeah." He shrugged awkwardly.

"You're a good kid, Jan," Hans said, giving the young man a nod of appreciation. Despite not being able to say it out loud, the entire room understood the intention behind his visit.

Jan was a familiar face around the house, since he was often used to help move things around, or drive people to appointments when there were conflicts with those who could actually drive the Hearse, so he was always welcome. Cliff was continuously impressed with the young man's desire to help out, not only with Hans, but with everyone else in the house as well. All he ever asked for in return was access to the contents of their fridge and what seemed to be an endless supply of peanut butter and jam sandwiches.

"Any news?" Bunty asked.

"Well, I heard the police are looking into Mari VanWinkle." Jan grimaced.

"We know," Hans said, giving Jans a reassuring smile.

"How do you…?" Jan asked, looking from Hans to Cliff and Bunty before stopping. "Have you been…? You know…?" Jans brows rose slightly.

"We're not doing anything," Bunty said, unable to hide the slight smile on her face.

"What else do you know?" Jan asked.

"Not much," Cliff answered before anyone else felt the need to jump in. Cliff liked Jan, but at the end of the day, he was a journalist, and it was his job to write about what he discovered. Which was why it was better for the time being to keep their information to themselves, something Cliff was very used to doing. Though, from the puzzled looks on Bunty's and Hans's faces, they were not.

"You're not telling me something," Jan said, his eyes narrowing.

"It's best if we keep what we find to ourselves until we know what's going on," Cliff said.

"But—"

"We promise to tell you more when we have actually information to tell," Cliff said, raising a hand to let Jan know that he wasn't going to get anything out of any of them.

Jan appeared a little like a wounded bird, but he nodded his understanding.

"Well, I have news," Jan said, his mood shifting slightly, "and obviously this stays between us," he continued earnestly, licking his ice cream, which threatened to drip on the floor. He held up a finger as he quickly devoured the remains of the cone.

The idea of chewing on ice cream made Cliff's head hurt just thinking about it, and from the pained expression on Jan's face, he wasn't too prepared for it either.

"Brain freeze," he said, as if his half-closed eyes and the grimace on his face weren't clues enough of his struggles. He shoved his thumb into his mouth, pressing it hard against the roof.

"What are you doing?" Bunty asked.

"I-t he-l-ps," Jan said, struggling to speak around the thumb in his mouth. He looked odd, but it must have worked, as a moment later, his shoulders dropped, and he returned to normal. He removed the thumb and looked around, as if preparing to wipe it on his shirt, then thought better of it. "One second," he said, raising a finger before running out of the living room towards the kitchen.

"I'm not sure I've ever eaten anything that fast," Bunty chuckled.

"My teeth aren't even real, and they still hurt," Hans said, which sent a round of laughter through the room, as the sound of running water came from the kitchen.

A moment later, Jan returned.

"What were you saying?" Cliff said, sending a quick reminder his way.

"Right. Well, there has been some talk around town that Winkle-berry Farm was in trouble," Jan said, sounding conspiratorial.

"We heard that too," Hans said. A defeated look passed over his face.

Jan noticed and stopped, like he wasn't going to continue, but Hans waved him on.

"But have you heard why?" Jan asked, brows lifted.

"Because Mr. Wilderman was trying to sabotage the farms," Bunty offered up.

Jan seemed taken aback, clearly not expecting them to know. "How are you all so well informed?" Jan asked, chuckling softly.

"Hard work," Bunty said mischievously.

"So, I suppose you heard the rumour that Flynn Stroud has been stealing money from the farm too," Jan said, as if it were a passing thought.

"What?" Cliff, Hans, and Bunty all said at the same time, causing

Jan to jump a little in surprise.

"Apparently not." Jan grinned, happy to know something they didn't.

"What exactly do you mean?" Cliff asked.

"Well, apparently the safe at the farm was also broken into, and a few things were missing. Pieter's will was one of them, the deed to the farm, and—"

"The company's financial records," Cliff guessed, receiving a nod from Jan. Cliff leaned back into the couch and let this information sink in for a moment.

"Why steal those things?" Bunty asked.

"More importantly, why do they have a handwritten ledger?" Jan said, shaking his head.

"That's what I did," Hans said, folding his arms across his chest. "Worked well enough then."

"But it's… I'm not…" Jan stumbled over how he wanted to approach this particular line of thinking, which is why he looked appreciatively at Cliff when he jumped in.

"Is there any proof to these accusations that Flynn was stealing from the farm?" Cliff asked.

Jan opened his mouth, but then stopped and shook his head, "No. Not exactly. Apparently, rumour has it, someone overheard Flynn in a bar, talking to the Badger, trying to level with him about buying the farm. When the Badger questioned him about some discrepancies in his books, Flynn got all angry, blaming the Badger for road-blocking any chance of success." Jan shook his head. "Needless to say, the conversation took a turn at that point and ended with Flynn grabbing the Badger by the collar and saying some particularly rude words."

"So this part of a story someone heard in the bar?" Cliff asked.

"Well, yeah," Jan said, less confident now. "But I did investigate it. Apparently, Flynn recently purchased a brand-new truck and was looking at purchasing another farm. Which seems like an odd thing to do when the farms you have are failing…doesn't it?" Jan asked, glancing nervously over at Cliff, who sat thinking for a moment.

"It is," he finally said, giving Jan a little relief.

"But that doesn't mean he was stealing, does it?" Hans asked.

"No," Cliff said.

"But it does make you question why the financial records were stolen from the safe," Bunty said.

Cliff tried to think for a moment, but his brain was foggy. It had already been a long day, and soon he knew Gerald would be getting prepped for dinner, a meal he, for one, was very much looking forward to. His body was sore and, somehow, in one day, he'd gone from knowing nothing about Pieter's death to having both Lucas and Flynn as new suspects for them to look into. But for right now all he wanted to do was rest.

"Perhaps," Cliff said slowly, "now is not the time to jump to conclusions." The room deflated around him. "Let's sleep on this and reconvene tomorrow with fresh eyes and bodies," he said, habitually rubbing his aching knee.

"But what about—"

"Cliff's right," Hans said, and Cliff thought he saw some relief in him as well. "A good sleep might be just what we need."

Jan didn't look thrilled at the prospect of leaving, but he also didn't object. Perhaps he saw the weariness in all of them, as even Bunty stifled a yawn.

"A sleep then," she said, "and tomorrow we figure out what's actually going on here."

Her smile was firm, and Cliff returned one of his own, though he didn't have the heart to tell her that it was unlikely they would be solving this mystery by tomorrow. After all, they'd only being looking into it for one day, and already it was a mess of confusion, with not just one, but *three* people who apparently had motives for Pieter's death, and that was before they'd even talked to everyone. *Who knows what else we will find once we start lifting stones?*

14

"Good morning," Bunty said, as Cliff slumped into the library, his hands gripped tightly around his coffee mug.

He slowly manoeuvred himself in front of one of the open, high-back chairs.

"Or have I spoke too soon?" she asked, as Cliff placed a steadying hand on the corner of the chair to ease himself down into it.

It had not been a good morning, and it was only seven a.m. He'd allowed himself to sleep in a little, although he still felt as though he could have spent the entire day in bed. His body was so stiff from the running around and working in the garden the day before. He was particularly sore in his shoulders and legs.

"I don't think I've been this stiff in nearly twenty years," Cliff said, shaking his head. He eased the coffee cup up to his mouth.

"I did tell you to take it easy." Bunty's brows rose in amusement.

"Never try to plan for tomorrow's challenges," Cliff said.

"That's ridiculous." Bunty laughed out loud, catching Cliff off guard.

"What?" Cliff asked, surprised.

"That is a terrible saying. You should always plan for tomorrow's challenges." She had so much conviction in her words, Cliff almost felt embarrassed.

"Doesn't the Bible say something about this? Tomorrow will take care of itself, and all that?" Cliff said.

Bunty's eyes narrowed on him. "I believe that means we can't plan for everything. So don't try to," she said, shaking her head. "But the work we do today can and will affect us tomorrow."

"So, what do you suggest?"

"Pil—"

"Don't say pills," Cliff said, raising a hand as he shook his head. *Pain and stubbornness.*

"Fine. Though I'm unsure I have ever met a man as…bullheaded on a subject as you," Bunty said, picking up her tea from the side table and blowing on it before taking a sip. "Perhaps you could try stretching then. It helps the muscles."

"Who has time for that?" Cliff chuckled.

"I do," Bunty said, her lips curling at the edges.

"Please, when do you stretch?"

"Every morning and every night for about ten to fifteen minutes," Bunty said proudly.

"Are you serious?" Cliff asked, his eyes wide as he tried to remember the last time he would have possibly stretched for any reason other than a physical examine with the doctor. He leaned forward, feeling the muscles tighten in his back, and he wondered, if he attempted to touch his toes, would he ever be able to stand up straight again?

"Of course. I've adjusted myself over the years, but sooner or later, we all have to accept we're getting older. Denial only gets you so far." She winked.

"I'm not in denial about getting old. I just don't like it." Cliff smiled weakly. "In here"—he tapped the side of his head—"I'm twenty-eight."

"But out here"—Bunty waved her hand at the rest of his body—"you're eighty-two."

"Don't remind me," Cliff said, trying to ignore the steady pain thrumming throughout his body.

"It would appear you are currently being reminded," Bunty chuckled.

"Every day? The stretching? Really?" Cliff asked weakly. "And it helps?"

Bunty studied him for a moment before she placed her tea back down on the table and stood up. Wordlessly, she raised her hands up in the air, before rolling down and letting her hands touch her toes. When she rolled back up, she was smiling at him. Cliff watched in awe as he tried to imagine himself bent over in any fashion and coming up with such ease. He would be lucky, at the moment, if he was able to rise up from the *chair* with as much grace as Bunty just presented to him. She leaned over and picked up her tea and sat back down.

"Impressive," Cliff said, shaking his head in disbelief.

"It's the small things over time that help us the most, Mr. Shaw."

"I'd hardly say what you just did was small." Cliff laughed, feeling weakened by his own minuscule movements.

"You could get there. You just have to put the work in," Bunty said and when Cliff looked at her, he could tell she meant every word of it, though he couldn't quite believe that himself.

"I just hate stretching," Cliff said, feeling the excuses wash over him, knowing instantly what it was. *Stubbornness.*

"More than you hate not stretching?" Bunty asked, her head tilting, as if examining Cliff and his body all at once.

Cliff had always told himself how much he hated to stretch, though when he was younger, he'd forced himself to do it, more because, when he did, things always seemed to not hurt as much the next day. But that had all been when he was younger, playing sports and running around, not from simply walking around a garden.

"Take it easy, Marcus Aurelius," Cliff joked, which got a smile from Bunty. Cliff figured the reference would go over well with the town's retired librarian. Although Cliff had never read it in its entirety, he was familiar with the Roman emperor's work, though Cliff couldn't help but feel like he was simply reading the personal journal of a man trying to contemplate his own existence. Something like that sent shivers down his spine, the idea that someone would ever get a hold of a personal journal. Not that Cliff was in the habit of jotting down all of his little idiosyncrasies. "You've made your point," Cliff conceded.

"I can show you a few stretches. If you ever feel like you want help," Bunty said sipping her tea.

Cliff was about to refuse, feeling more than a little embarrassed by the idea of getting help with something so trivial as stretching. But, somehow, he managed to even surprise himself.

"That would be nice. Thank you," he said warily, taking another long sip of coffee.

"So…" Bunty remarked as she leaned back in her chair casually.

She examined him as they drank silently. He'd wondered when she would bring it all up, and he'd been waiting for it since he sat down, but now that she was preparing to present him with the question, he wasn't sure how he wanted to respond.

Cliff's body had completely given out the moment he managed to find his bed the night before. It was a blessing, considering he'd done nothing for the rest of the day and had managed to avoid thinking or talking about the murder over dinner, despite knowing that both Hans and Bunty were very keen to come up with a strategy for what they needed to do next. Even with all that time to think, Cliff hadn't managed to come up with any actionable plan that was satisfactory.

"Sorry, I didn't mean to rush into it," Bunty said.

When Cliff looked up at her, he wondered just how much his face must have given away his concern.

"No, I'm sorry." Cliff sighed. "I've just been…well…" Cliff thought for a moment, while he tried to come up with the right words to explain how he felt, something that was never easy for him. "I was a detective, I always knew how to proceed. But now…"

"You're not sure what to do," Bunty offered.

Cliff nodded.

"Well, as someone who was never a detective," she said giving him a big smile, "I'd say there is no reason why anything should be any different."

"Are you suggesting we just go and speak with people? Ask them intimate details about their lives so we can try to figure out if they're the ones who killed Pieter VanWinkle?" The words sounded even more absurd when he spoke them out loud.

"Yes," Bunty said, and Cliff couldn't tell if she was just having a go at him or not.

"But why would anyone want to speak with us?" Cliff said, feeling a bit like he was the one new to all of this, and Bunty was the expert, though he knew, fundamentally, that was not the case. Yet he couldn't get over the confidence Bunty had with something so speculative.

"Well, we tried finding a reason to speak with Mari, and as it turned out, she was very happy to tell us what was going on. All we got from asking Mrs. Chen to be our cover was a week's worth of work in the garden." Bunty smiled.

Cliff's body did not need much reminding of what he'd given for that particular help. Though he was happy to work in the garden, he would need to make mental notes about following the lead of Bunty and Mrs. Chen, instead of Hans, who, despite complaining about being sore, hardly looked to be suffering much this morning when Cliff had run into him in the kitchen getting coffee. The big man was as lively as ever, happily tinkering away in the basement.

"Not everyone may be as forthcoming as Mari was," Cliff said.

Bunty shrugged. "Perhaps not." She took a sip of her tea, her eyes studying Cliff for a moment. "But perhaps it is exactly that easy. Have you ever stopped to think that they also want to know what happened to Pieter?"

"Of course. But that doesn't mean they're going to be all warm and fuzzy with us snooping around their family's business," Cliff laughed.

"That remains to be seen," Bunty said. "At the end of the day, the only person who doesn't want us to find out the truth is the person who did it."

"There are many reasons people hide the truth, Bunty, regardless of whether or not it makes them sound guilty," Cliff said, from some deeper understanding that people lied for all kinds of reasons, despite those reasons not always making sense in the moment. It was usually a means of self-preservation.

"Well then. We just have to do a better job at getting them to tell us the truth, won't we?" Bunty said, as if this was as simple as asking what aisle you find the salt in, but he did admire her conviction. Something about the woman's contrasting confidence made him laugh. "Is something funny?"

"I've just never had a partner with such undying convictions," Cliff said, taking a sip of his coffee.

"Is that what we are?" Bunty smiled ruefully, causing Cliff's cheeks to flare up.

"I just mean, that we are working together…as partners. To…you know…figure out what's going on here. And that…"

"I know what you meant, Cliff. I would be happy to be your partner on this case." She gave him a warm smile, tilting her head slightly, as if examining something interesting on the ceiling. "Seventy-three seems a good age to start something new, doesn't it?" she chuckled.

"Never too late, I suppose." Cliff smiled as he thought about it for a moment. Here Bunty was starting something knew for the first time at seventy-three, and he still couldn't do anything more than what he'd done his entire life. *Am I just a one trick pony?*

He pushed the sentiment to the back of his mind for now and thought instead, about the fact that he had no idea if this plan would be successful or not. Unlike Bunty, Cliff had spent his entire life trying to understand what made people tick and why, finding the right questions to ask and then, eventually, assuming he did his job right, getting to the root of those questions to find the answers he was after.

Mari VanWinkle had more or less told them everything they wanted to know, but he doubted that would be the case for everyone they spoke with about the incident. Cliff also wasn't able to tell how much of what Mari had told them they could trust, even with all of her "honesty." There were reasons the police had decided to look into Mari in the first place, and just because she had given them a small understanding of what was happening in her family, it didn't erase the fact that she, like the others, may have had her own reasons for being angry with her father.

"So, boss," Bunty said with a smile, pulling Cliff out from his thoughts, "where exactly do we go next?"

"Please don't call me boss," Cliff said, feeling incredibly awkward at the reference to a title he'd forgone a long time ago. "How about, partner?" Seeing the smile on Bunty's face made that title even better in his mind.

"I can live with partner," Bunty said. "So what's next?"

"Now we start pulling on some threads." Cliff took in a deep breath, not loving where this next direction was going to take them, but they needed to start somewhere. "Now, we speak to Lucas VanWinkle."

15

"How did you know he'd be here?" Bunty asked as she pushed open the main door to peer inside the Creamery. It was nearly empty, save for a couple of booths filled with some construction workers on lunch.

It was a little past one p.m., and normally this would have been too early for Cliff to ever step into a bar, unless, of course, he was having lunch. But he was still very full from the Belgian waffles with fresh strawberries that Gerald had cooked up for the house that morning. Cliff had to admit the man's cooking was absolutely a selling point in his continuing desire to live at the manor.

"Hans said Lucas has been here a lot since Pieter's death," Cliff whispered, glancing around and spotting a lone figure sitting slouched over the bar. "And Sol mentioned Pete saw him here as well."

Cliff had met Sol's friend Pete after he'd helped them out with the young boys who'd found themselves wrapped up in a dangerous game with the Scorpions, a local biker gang. Luckily for them, they had managed to get out relatively unscathed, just some minor detention and some community service. Considering that the other boy who had crossed the gang wound up dead, Cliff thought this didn't sound so bad.

"From what I've heard, he spent more than enough time here *before* his death too," Bunty said, as she reached into her pocket to pull out a notepad.

Cliff raised a hand to stop.

"What?"

"Best if we try to keep this casual. The less it feels like an interrogation the better." He nodded towards the notepad.

"Fair enough," Bunty said, though Cliff could tell she would have felt more comfortable taking notes. It was in her nature to be organized and thorough. But if she was going to get into the sleuthing game, she would have to learn how to roll without a plan. "So what *do* we do?"

Cliff shrugged, which caused Bunty's brows to furrow. *Case in point,* Cliff mused.

Without a word, Cliff walked up the stairs to the upper landing and past the group of guys finishing up their lunches, sensing Bunty close behind him as he pressed up towards the bar.

"Mind if I sit?" Cliff asked.

As he reached for the stool to the left of Lucas, the man glanced up and peered around at the line of empty bar stools before looking over at Cliff, clearly confused by his desire to be so close, despite the many options afforded to him.

"Free country," Lucas said, not sounding too thrilled at the idea. He rocked a bottle of beer between his hands.

To Cliff's surprise, Bunty took the seat on Lucas's right, pulling herself up to the bar. This move seemed to surprise Lucas a little, also.

The bartender, a short gray-haired man, walked up. "What can I get ya?"

"Orange juice for me," Bunty said with a smile.

"Soda water with lime," Cliff said.

Their orders gave the bartender a look that was somewhat less than thrilled.

"And we'll get his next beer," Bunty said with a firm nod.

Always with the surprises, Bunty.

The bartender looked towards Lucas, who appeared equally confused by the offer but not confused enough to turn it down.

"Coming right up." The bartender turned to grab some glasses from behind the bar.

"Thanks for the beer, but if you don't mind, I'd like to be alone," Lucas said.

Cliff could hear some slurring in the man's voice, despite the early afternoon. He placed a hand on the counter, as if he were about to move elsewhere, when Bunty placed her hand on top of Lucas's.

"We were sorry to hear about Pieter," she said softly, her tone taking away what little steam the man had, as he looked around and finally sat back on the stool.

"You knew Pieter?" he asked Bunty. His back was turned to Cliff as the bartender placed the drinks down on the bar.

Cliff pulled out a green, twenty-dollar bill and slid it over towards the man, thinking that should be enough to cover the drinks. He didn't seem to argue as he picked it up and left them alone.

"Not very well, no. But we live with Hans VanDosen. You know him, right?"

Lucas chuckled. "Of course, I know him. Hell, we bought his farm. Well, Pieter did, and that dear little pissant of a nephew of ours," Lucas said, his voice edging on disdain. "Sorry, I'm not really good company at the moment." He waved a hand before finishing his old beer and reaching for the new one.

"That's fair," Bunty said softly, politely adding, "Would you mind if we asked you a couple of questions?"

This caused Lucas to stiffen a bit. He sat up in his stool, as best he could at this point.

"You with the police?" he asked.

Cliff could sense the man's walls going up. Not for the first time did he wish they'd brought Hans with them to help build up their trust with this man a little. But Hans had had plans to go to Lucan to acquire a few slabs of hardwood that he'd purchased, and he would be gone for most of the afternoon. Meanwhile, he and Bunty had used this opportunity to talk to Lucas as an excuse to take a break from the garden, which they'd been working in since before breakfast. Cliff's back was still tight from the day before, and he had no idea how it was possible for Mrs. Chen to work so tirelessly in it. Not when he was feeling so exhausted after just a couple of days.

"We're a little old to be police," Cliff offered, though it didn't have the desired effect he'd hoped for. If anything, Lucas seemed more nervous.

"Then what kind of questions do you want to ask," Lucas said, his eyes drifting to his full beer before taking a swig and letting it fall back to the table, "if you're not police?"

"Hans asked me to look into Pieter's death," Cliff said, trying to sound casual about the whole affair. *Well, as causal as I can sound asking a man about the death of his brother, I suppose.*

"Isn't that what the police are for? Figuring out what happened to my brother?" Lucas said.

To Cliff's surprise, he thought he caught a crack in the armour the man was using to hold himself together. At the mention of everything going on, something shifted. Something Cliff couldn't quite put his finger on.

"You're right. We're not the police," Bunty said softly, "but that doesn't mean we don't want to understand what happened to Pieter. I'm sure you must too?"

"Knowing the truth doesn't bring him back, does it?" Lucas glared over at Bunty, who froze in the man's glare.

"No, it doesn't," Cliff said weakly, getting Lucas's frustration turned back on him.

"Well then, what the hell good does it do me to talk about it with two strangers I've never met?" Lucas said, putting a hand on the bar to push himself away from it. "All I wanted was to have a drink on my own. Try not to think about all this crap." He shook his head.

Whatever crack that had appeared had mended itself with raw, cold anger. Cliff couldn't blame him. After all, what good could it possibly do for him to talk to Cliff and Bunty? He was right, they weren't the police, and what good, if any, would come from it?

"Did you do it?" Cliff asked.

The bluntness of the question appeared to shake the man, as he faltered during his movement to get up. Lucas stared blankly at the bar top for a long moment, his hand gripping tightly around his bottle of beer.

"Did I what?" Lucas asked slowly, and when neither Cliff or Bunty said anything else, he shook his head. His voice began to rise a little, drawing the attention of the bartender, who was looking a little worried, though Cliff didn't know if it was for them or his bar. "Did I have something to do with Pieter's death? Is that what you mean?" His eyes burrowed into Cliff, then into Bunty, though she looked as taken aback by the question as Lucas.

"Yes," Cliff said evenly. "Because someone did. Someone who knew him well enough to know that slipping peanut oil into his smoothie might kill him. Someone who had access to the storeroom, someone who might have some reason to be angry with him. Why shouldn't I think it was you?"

"Because I loved my brother!" Lucas said, the words coming out so angrily the bartender took a step back and the group of men in the booth glanced their way.

"You had no reason to hate him, or resent him for anything then?"

"No, I didn't," Lucas said, standing now, so he could look down at Cliff, who was used to people's emotions rising, though from the concerned expression painted on Bunty's face she was not.

"So, there was no resentment for having to cover up for him when those kids were killed? The accident that put you in juvenile detention, while he took over the family farm?" Cliff asked, pulling at the only thread he had that might push Lucas to the edge.

The comment did send him reeling, hitting Lucas like a cold winter wind. He shuddered at the mention of it before finding his footing again.

"You don't know what the hell you're talking about," Lucas said, and Cliff got the impression he was biting back more than a few choice words. But he still wasn't attacking Cliff, so he took that as a good sign.

"Then tell me. No rumours, nothing. Just the truth about what happened."

"Everyone knows what happened," Lucas said.

"Do they? Or do they know what they were told?"

"I made my peace with this years ago," Lucas said, though Cliff couldn't tell if this was some sort of admission or just another way of getting them to leave.

"I—"

"I would appreciate it if you would leave me alone now," Lucas said, his hands flexing into fists, as he seemed to be only just keeping his temper under control. Lucas appeared to be in his late fifties, and there was little chance that, even in his prime, Cliff would have been able to stop this man. He was bulky, with fists the size of grapefruits and, despite the belly on the man, he was clearly a byproduct of hard manual farm work. Like Hans, he was just built differently.

Which is why antagonising the large man was a last-ditch effort. But Cliff knew that emotions often got the better of most people not used to processing them. He'd succeeded at getting him emotional. Now he just needed him to slip up. But he had to cap it off and not allow it to escalate further. Assuming he hadn't already pushed it too far.

"We will go," Bunty said calmly. "But you were right, we're not the police. Which means you have nothing to gain or lose from telling us anything. All we're interested in is getting to the bottom of what happened to Pieter. And if we heard this rumour, then you can bet, given the nature of small towns, that the police will too. Then what?"

Cliff was impressed. For a person who looked as though she wanted to vomit, Bunty was incredibly good at keeping up. Even if she did appear a little pale.

"She's right. I know it doesn't feel like it now, but I swear, we're just trying to help. Just trying to get your side of the story," Cliff said, switching tactics now that Bunty had calmed the flames a little.

"What does any of it matter? He's gone," Lucas said, his earlier pain welling up again.

"You don't want to know what happened?" Bunty asked.

"Of course I do… Pieter was my brother," he said, looking at Bunty as he wiped an eye and took a long sip from his bottle. "But the past is the past."

"We never forget our past. We can move on, bury it deep, but we can't forget it." Bunty placed a hand on Lucas's, but he pulled his away.

"I did," he said coldly. "And if you think I'm going to talk to you about it, you're out of your damned minds." He looked at Bunty before turning back to Cliff. "Now get the hell out of here."

He waited for Cliff and Bunty to get up to leave before he pulled his stool out and sat back down, waving for the bartender to get him another drink.

"For what it's worth, we are really sorry about what happened to Pieter," Cliff said.

Lucas never turned back to look at them, but he didn't shout anything rude either, so Cliff stole the silence.

"We just want to help find the truth, if we can. If you change your mind, and feel like talking about it, you can reach out to Hans." Cliff turned to leave, catching a glimpse of Lucas's head dropping to his chest before they disappeared out the door.

"That didn't go well," Bunty said, shaking her head, a confused expression on her face. "Good cop, bad cop?"

"Something like that. I appreciated you helping to calm him down." Cliff took a deep breath.

"Wait. So you didn't plan that?" Bunty asked.

"Not exactly, no."

"Then why would you push him like that?"

"Sorry, I shouldn't have brought you in for that. I should have known he would be—"

"I didn't say I didn't want to be there. I asked why you did it. There is a difference, you know." Bunty smiled.

"He has no reason to talk to us. Whether he did it or not, the best way to get a sense of where he is in all of this is to see him emotional."

"Well, you certainly got him there." Bunty smiled. "I thought he might knock your block off."

"For a moment there, so did I," Cliff said, feeling rather lucky that it had played out the way it had. It wouldn't have been the first time someone has punched him, but given the size of the man and Cliff's age, it might have been the last. Luckily, most people, no matter how angry, aren't prone to hitting octogenarians.

"Though I'm not surprised he wouldn't want to talk about any of that. Must be awful."

"Exactly. Why would he want to talk to us?"

"Because we're unbiased?" Bunty suggested.

"Are we? Is anyone?" Cliff asked.

"I'd like to think I am," Bunty countered.

"Even if you are, he doesn't know that," Cliff said as they walked down the ramp towards the driveway before crossing Parkview towards the sidewalk.

"Well, why would he trust us now?" Bunty asked.

"We don't need him to trust us," Cliff said. "We just need him to want to talk to us more than the police."

"You think he would lie to the police?" Bunty asked.

"Not lie, necessarily. But avoiding things is human nature. His past with his brother, for example. It was so long ago, so why bring it up?" Cliff asked. "Like you said, people don't just forget the past."

"It would make him look bad."

"It does. And the last thing anyone wants is to look bad in front of the police. So, you avoid the topic. All we did was put the idea in his mind that people talk. And if you talk to enough people, someone is bound to talk about the incident and what may or may not have happened. Then what? He didn't lie, but he also wasn't forthcoming with the information either. How does that make him look?"

"Guilty," Bunty said.

"He was never going to be open with us. The truth is, we got lucky with Mari being so forthcoming with us about what she was feeling. Though something tells me she has the reverse problem of the Lucases of this world."

"She says too much?" Bunty chuckled.

"Yes, exactly. So why should Lucas talk to us? We're no one to him. But now he knows we're another option."

"You think he would trust us after that ambush?" Bunty asked.

"Again, it's not about trust. We just need him to want to talk to us. And when the pressure is on him to make a decision, who do you think he is going to want to speak to? Us or the police?"

Bunty shook her head. This was beginning to feel a lot like a logic puzzle, though they didn't usually revolve around a man's death.

"Most of the job is gathering up as much information and pressing as many buttons as you can until either someone slips up or the answer is so obvious it practically slaps you in the face," Cliff said.

"That happen a lot? The slapping in the face?"

"Yes," Cliff said, the corner of his face twitching slightly, "but it doesn't always come with the obvious conclusion."

"Bunty!" a voice called out from behind them, back towards the Creamery.

Both Cliff and Bunty turned, and Cliff's stomach sank when he caught sight of a tall woman, with a light shawl wrapped around her shoulders, walking towards them. She didn't need to approach any closer for Cliff to know immediately that this was Annie, Bunty's sister, and the woman who broke Cliff's heart when she refused to leave town with him over fifty years ago, which effectively broke off their engagement. She had been the love of Cliff's life, and she broke his heart. And now here she was, running up to him.

Not me, us.

"Annie?" Bunty asked, and Cliff could sense her glance his way and the sudden, uncomfortable feeling that washed over everyone as Annie stopped a couple of feet from them.

"Cliff?" Annie asked, perhaps surprised to see her sister with him, or him in general, Cliff didn't know either way.

"Annie. Hi," he said, happy he found his words this time, considering the last time he'd run into her, he'd barely managed to speak at all.

"Hi," she said, a smile forming on her lips, and with it a slew of long-forgotten memories he wished could have stayed locked away for the rest of his life. "What are you two doing?"

"We were just at the bar," Cliff said hastily.

"A little early to be drinking, isn't it?" Annie joked.

"No…we weren't…we were…"

"We were talking to someone there, for a little project we're working on," Bunty said, and Cliff was grateful for her being there.

"You two are working on a project…together?" Annie asked, her head falling to one side.

Cliff tried to understand the puzzled look on her face and what it meant. *Is she jealous?*

"It's nothing, really," Cliff said, attempting to downplay their meeting, though he felt guilty when he spotted the frown on Bunty's face.

"Well, I'm not sure what you're doing now," Annie said, looking towards Bunty, "but I'm off to get a coffee, if you're interested. Cliff, you're obviously welcome to join if you'd like."

"No," Cliff said a little too quickly, feeling a touch overwhelmed as he slowly attempted to backtrack. "Sorry, I mean, no. It's just, I told Mrs. Chen I would help in the garden this afternoon, and I would hate to leave her stranded," he lied, and if Bunty knew he was lying, she said nothing, thankfully.

"Such a shame. Elizabeth?" Annie said, using her sister's full name, and Cliff wondered if this was a family thing, though based on the subtly annoyed look on Bunty's face, she didn't like it.

"Sure, it's just, Cliff and I had some things we were going to discuss…"

"We can talk about them when you get home?" Cliff offered.

"This have to do with your little project?" Annie asked.

"Yes," Cliff said, turning to look at Bunty. "A little time to think about it doesn't hurt. We can talk about it tonight at the house. If you'd like, that is," Cliff amended.

"Tonight then," Bunty said, giving Cliff a thin smile as she stepped forward and clasped arms with Annie.

The pair walked back towards the green bridge.

"Goodbye, Cliff," Annie said, giving him a wave over her shoulder.

"Goodbye," he said, feeling a slight pain in his chest, though he felt it was more from the balled-up, unresolved issues he felt at seeing the previous love of his life than it was from the potential of a heart attack. Though, given the awkwardness still lingering around him, he might have settled for a heart attack instead.

A beat later, he turned, trying to ignore what just happened, and instead focused on two other thoughts. *What do we do next? And does this mean I have to help Mrs. Chen in the garden?*

Cliff was thankful after arriving back at the Limestone Manor that no one was around to see him enter the house. He felt exhausted from the morning in the garden and the walk downtown, and the last thing he wanted was to get roped into more work.

So when he was able to get into the house and up to his room unseen, he wasn't surprised by how quickly he was able to fall asleep, especially as the cross breeze formed by the two sets of windows on either side of the house created a pleasant current that washed across his face while he lay on the bed.

He figured it must have been a little over an hour later when he woke to a red-winged blackbird that had decided to perch itself on a branch directly outside of his rear window. As far as alarm clocks went, it was as good as any.

He removed the small, quilted blanket from his legs and refolded it back at the foot of his bed before making his way downstairs. It was a little after three p.m. now, and he could sense already that Gerald was in the process of getting dinner prepared for the house, something with lots of garlic, from the smell of it.

Cliff made it to the bottom of the first flight, catching sight of Mrs. Chen as she closed the door to her room and peered back at him, giving him subdued smile.

"I remember there was a time in my life when I could make it through a whole day without a nap," Cliff said, watching as Mrs. Chen pulled her cane off a small handle Hans had made for her to hang it on.

"I don't," she said, grinning. "There are few things in this world I enjoy more than a nap." She made her way towards the main stairs. "You, Mr. Shaw, have missed out."

Cliff followed closely behind her as they slowly made their way down the last set of stairs, each of them taking care to grip the handrail as they did.

"You've always napped?" Cliff asked curiously. He'd always felt like it was a waste of time during the day, eating up the time for more important things he could be doing. But now, eating up time was not an issue he suffered from, and therefore, not something he had a problem eating away at. What else was he supposed to do?

"Of course. I love it. Our brain," she said, pausing briefly to tap the side of her head, "needs a chance to process what it is taking in, and it never hurts to give our bodies a break either. Sleep is a necessity, not a thing to be dismissed as a simple choice. It's as vital as walking up and down stairs." She gestured to the final few steps below her. "Something that I *do* miss is being able to take more than one step at a time." She continued down, pausing to let her second foot follow suit.

In that moment, Cliff realized that, despite living in the house for over a month, he still knew very little about many of his housemates, save for a few superficial facts.

For instance, he had no idea how old Mrs. Chen was. He'd assumed, because she had chosen to live in this house, that she must be around the same age as Cliff and Hans, who were both eighty-two. But he knew Bunty was a few years younger and so was Gerald. Cliff figured the rotund man was mid-seventies, but even that was a wild guess.

Looking at Mrs. Chen now, he figured she could be anywhere from seventy-five to ninety-five and neither answer would have surprised him.

"Will you be off to the garden this afternoon?" Cliff asked as they reached the bottom of the stairs.

"Not this afternoon. I will walk around and begin to make notes on what else needs to be worked on before the judging next week," she said. "A garden is, after all, supposed to be walked through."

"Sounds like a wonderful plan," Cliff said, happy that his lead-in to the garden wasn't met by more recruitment into its weeding. "When is the judging? Do you know?"

"They will announce times this weekend. But I suspect maybe Wednesday or Thursday," Mrs. Chen said, sounding both excited and nervous at the same time.

Cliff had never entered a garden competition. He'd never *lived* anywhere with a garden. Not since he was a boy. But he imagined that there must be a lot of pressure in wanting it to be perfect for the judging, especially since, from what Cliff had gathered, Mrs. Chen had been developing her garden for a couple of years now. Something that Cliff could barely comprehend.

"Well, I, for one, think you've created a masterpiece back there," Cliff said, giving her a nod.

"If only you were the one judging then." Mrs. Chen smiled, her bluntness causing Cliff to chuckle.

"If only," Cliff said.

He watched Mrs. Chen move to the door and replace her house slippers with her garden shoes before opening the door and stepping out into the midday sun.

"Cliff?"

Cliff turned to see Bunty sitting in her chair, knitting something that he knew would be extraordinary, despite the modesty of the woman about her skills. She'd made him a hunter-green cable-knit sweater when he'd finally agreed to live with them. He'd only worn it the one time, given the heat of summer, but even from that single use, he knew the exceptional quality with which she did her work.

"Bunty," he said, stepping in and shooing Skittles off the chair before taking the seat across from her. "Did you have a good tea with Annie?" He forced himself to remain casual about the whole thing, despite the turning in his stomach.

"It was good, thank you," she said, giving him a thin smile. "I recognize that it must be…strange to see her." Bunty set her knitting needles down in her lap and looked over at him, a gesture he took for sympathy, since he knew she had no problem knitting without looking at it at all. So, feeling the need to give him her full attention was not something he took for granted.

"It's fine," Cliff lied.

It was awful to see Annie again, and it was even more difficult to live in a house with her sister, of all people. And although Annie and Bunty could not be more different, at least from what Cliff could remember of Annie, he still, on occasion, was reminded of their connection. Today was a perfect example.

"Still, I'm sure it's hard," Bunty said, pausing to examine Cliff a moment, "coming back to town after all this time and having to run into her. I…well, I couldn't imagine." A tight smile creased her face.

"It certainly has its challenges," Cliff said, wishing he hadn't come into the room and had avoided this entire awkward encounter. But it was too late to do anything about it now, other than accept the situation he was in, since leaving at this juncture would only serve to add to the feeling of uneasiness he had discussing it.

Thankfully, however, the moment didn't last long, as there was a knock at the door, which Cliff was more than happy to volunteer to answer.

"I wonder who it is?" Bunty asked.

Cliff was also curious, since the only people who knocked at the door were the occasional people seeking donation for charity or delivering a package. Perhaps the occasional promotion, for better internet or TV, which was always rejected, since no one in the house had a desire to change a system all of them already knew how to work.

"I'm not sure," Cliff said, as he approached the door, turning the handle and opening it up a crack to peek outside. "Lou?" Cliff opened the door a little wider to let their officer friend inside the house. "What are you doing here?"

"It's nothing official, I hope," Kitty called out from the living room.

Cliff hadn't even known she was sitting there, but now that curiosity has curled its way into the home, of course, Kitty wouldn't be too far behind.

"Nothing official," Lou said, though from the look she was giving Cliff he suspect that wasn't entirely true.

"It's good to see you, Lou," Cliff offered, as she wiped off her boots off on the mat.

"You too," she said, pulling out a manila envelope that was tucked under her arm as she looked at it curiously, saying, "I have this for Kitty?" She looked as confused as Cliff by the package.

"For me?" Kitty poked her head around the corner at the mention of her name. She glanced down at the folder, her eyes narrowing in on it. "What is it?"

"To be honest, I have no idea." Lou shrugged. "I was hoping you might be able to tell me." She handed the folder over to Kitty, who eyed it warily. "All I know is that Dan left it for me at the apartment this morning with a little note that said it was for Kitty. *The one at the old people's home.*" Lou reread the note in her hand, trying not to laugh at the somehow appalled and gleeful expression on Kitty's face.

"Let me see that." Kitty grabbed the envelope and the small note and read it. "I think we need to have a word with him about his penmanship," she said, glancing up at Lou, as if it were her responsibility to fix it, "and I'm not sure I like the tone of *old people's home*," Kitty said, affronted.

"We are old, Kitty," Sol pointed out, "and this is our home. Give the man a break."

"You know what I mean, Sol. How would you like it if someone called you old?"

"People call me old all the time," he countered.

"That's because you *are* old," Kitty said.

"What does that make you?" Sol asked.

"Married to an old man, I suppose." Kitty smiled, clearly feeling quite good about herself and the joke.

"Are you going to tell me what it is?" Lou asked. Clearly this was something she'd been holding on to all day and respectfully appeared not to have opened it, despite her obvious desire to know what it was.

"Only a promise kept, I hope." Kitty pulled at the edge of the envelope and tore it open. She peeked inside and smiled. "Oh, yes. The ladies at bridge are going to be very, very jealous."

"Why?" Cliff asked, now feeling swept up in the mystery of it all.

"Don't play her game, Cliff," Sol shouted, "you'll only be disappointed."

"Oh, shut up you," Kitty chastised as she reached in and pulled out a calendar.

"Sorry, is that a calendar?" Cliff asked.

"I told you!" Sol shouted. Cliff imagined the man sitting in his chair, reading the paper while he waited for Kitty to finish up whatever this was so that they could carry on with one of their endless games of cribbage.

"This isn't just a calendar." Kitty smiled.

"Oh my god, is that...?" Lou said, covering her mouth as she suppressed a laugh.

"Yes. It. Is," Kitty said slowly. She dropped the calendar down, showing a large man wrapped up in a firehose, with nothing but his overalls and helmet on, his hairless body showing his rippling abs and a large chest, and complete with a signature at the bottom. "And he got them to sign it like he promised."

"Like who promised?" Lou asked, now looking very much confused.

"Mr. October," Kitty said, giving Lou a wink. "I always knew you had it in you." But the remark appeared to go right over Lou's head.

"I don't know what…" Lou said, but her thought was cut short when Kitty flipped to the picture of Mr. October, or to Lou's amusement, her would-be boyfriend straddling a fire pole, riding it like a cowboy as he waved his helmet in the air.

"What the…?" Lou said, tilting her head, as if somehow that would better explain the angle of what the man was doing.

"Don't tell me you didn't know," Kitty said, waving a hand in Lou's direction.

"I had no idea," Lou said, honestly, though she pursed her lips and nodded approvingly. "Not bad, Dan."

"It's gets better, dear." Kitty winked, giggling to herself.

"I'm not sure where you plan on hanging that thing," Sol said. "Because I certainly don't need the reminder in our room."

"Don't be a fool, Sol," Kitty said, peering at another page and turning it sideways to appreciate the entire imagine. "Art like this would be wasted on you." She gave Lou a knowing smile. "This is for the ladies at the church. We have our own dressing room." She winked again.

"What is this you're looking at?" Bunty asked curiously, as she approached Kitty from the side and peeked over her shoulder. "Oh my!" Bunty's cheeks flushed red as she covered her mouth and giggled. "Such…ummm…a lovely young man," she finally said after a minute.

"You couldn't be more right about that, Bunty." Kitty nudged her with her elbow, sending another flash of red into her cheeks. "Thank you, Lou." Kitty closed the calendar and hugged it against her chest like she was Bunty with one of her rare books.

"Not a problem," Lou said, smiling as Kitty returned to Sol.

Cliff peeked in just in time to see Kitty place the calendar on the table and smack Sol's hand when he tried to look at it. "Not for you, Sol."

"Only curious," he said, raising his hands in defence. "Wasn't sure what all the fuss was about."

"Wouldn't you like to know?" Kitty picked up her cards and laid down a four of hearts. "Four," she said, as if the little disruption from their game of cards had never actually occurred.

This suited Cliff just fine, because it gave him the opportunity to turn and talk to Lou, with Bunty now beside him.

"You're not just here for the calendar, are you?" Cliff asked.

Lou shook her head and tilted it towards the door. "Have a minute?"

"Depends. Are we in trouble?" Bunty asked, picking up on Lou's demeanour at the door.

"That depends on what you tell me next," Lou said, stepping out the door.

Cliff turned to look at Bunty, whose bright cheeks had faded, and now she just looked worried.

"I'm sure it will be fine," Cliff said, not fully believing his own words as he slipped on a pair of shoes.

Bunty did the same, then the pair stepped outside to follow Lou, who had just made it off the front deck when Bunty closed the door, whispering to Cliff as she did. "Your confidence is underwhelming."

17

"You two have something you want to say to me?" Lou said.

Cliff couldn't help but hear the condescending tone in her voice, something he did not care for.

"Not if you insist on talking to us like we're children," Cliff said as they rounded the corner and headed into the back garden, where Lou stopped and turned to look at Cliff and Bunty.

"You're right," she sighed. "It's been a long week."

"Everything okay?" Bunty asked.

"Not overly, no." Lou ran a hand over her hair, which had been pulled back into a tight bun.

"I'm sorry to hear that," Bunty said.

Cliff was impressed with her ability to let things slide. He, on the other hand, could feel his shoulders wrapping tightly up around his ears like a dog's hackles, as he prepared to take the defence with Lou.

"Thank you. But I'm not here for that."

"What are you here for, Lou?" Cliff asked.

"I want to know why on earth you were talking to Lucas VanWinkle at the Creamery this morning," she said.

Cliff had suspected this, but still, he had to admit he was rather impressed by how quickly the news travelled back to Lou and the OPP.

"We just wanted to ask him a few questions," Cliff said.

"Why?" Lou asked.

"Is it a crime to ask questions?" Bunty asked.

"Yes," Lou said, just as Cliff replied, "No."

Cliff's eyes narrowed on Lou for a moment before she folded her arms tightly against her chest.

"Okay fine, it's not a crime, but it is a little strange to be asking someone questions while there is an active investigation going on," Lou said. "You understand why people might be a little bit…?"

"Whiny?" Cliff offered.

"I was going to say sensitive," Lou offered, though Cliff noticed she was trying hard to hide the smile at the side of her mouth. "You know Captain Marks has it out for you, Cliff. Why push this?"

"I'm not worried about Captain Marks," Cliff huffed, though from the look on Bunty's face she could not say the same. After all, he'd previously gone so far as to lock Cliff up for a weekend the last time Cliff stepped on his toes.

"You should be. He's not entirely relieved to have to delay his promotion after everything that happened with the Scorpions."

"Whose fault is that?" Cliff shot back, feeling rather cranky, since he'd only just woken up from a nap and wasn't at all prepared for this level of conversation right now.

"Look, I'm not here to talk about that. I just heard that voices were raised at the bar and that you two"—she gestured to Cliff and Bunty—"were seen with Lucas VanWinkle. I want to know why."

"Hans asked me to look into Pieter's death, and after you told us about Mari… Well, we thought it would be good to ask around to the others who held keys to the shed."

"You're investigating his death?" Lou asked, eyes flaring up.

"I didn't say that." Cliff raised his hands. "I said we were asking around to get a better idea of what might be going on."

"That sounds a lot like an investigation!" Lou spat out.

She turned to walk further into the garden. Thankfully, Mrs. Chen must have been elsewhere in the garden, since Cliff couldn't see her, but still he doubted Lou would want this getting around, and as she could just be tucked away in any number of little alcoves, he raised his hands.

"Perhaps it's best if we bring it down a notch."

"Fine," Lou said, though her face looked far from agreeable.

"Technically," Bunty said raising a finger, "an investigation involves a formal or systematic examination, or research. I would hardly say there is anything formal about what we were doing." She smiled weakly.

"You know what I mean, Bunty."

"I do. I'm just wondering if you do?" she said, tilting her head.

"You can't go around asking people about someone's death, you two."

"Who says that?" Bunty asked, and Cliff was beginning to be amused by, not just Bunty's word prowess, but her direct nature. Up 'til now, he'd only ever been on the wrong end of it.

"Me. Us. The police!" Lou said, though she didn't sound nearly as confident as she presumably would have hoped.

"I told you. Our friend asked us for our opinion on the matter. And we are all looking for the same result, correct?" Cliff said, waiting for Lou to give a reluctant nod. "Great. So perhaps we should stop bickering and agree that the only thing that is important right now is finding out what happened to Pieter."

"I agree," Lou said.

"Good." Cliff nodded.

Lou opened her mouth, as if she was preparing to say more on the matter, but then she closed it, narrowing her eyes in on the pair of them. "I don't like this," she said, her finger gesturing between them.

"Too bad," Cliff said with a smile.

"Shouldn't you at least want to know why we were talking to Lucas?" Bunty asked.

Cliff turned to give her a glance, but she either missed it or didn't care.

"I have to admit, I was a little surprised. We ruled him out a while ago," Lou said.

"Why?" Cliff asked before Bunty could jump in with the information they had.

"Well, he had nothing to gain from the Pieter's death. As far as we can tell, he was the only one, well, besides Aria. It seems a little radical to want to poison your boss after they pretty much paid for your relocation into the country," Lou said, shaking her head.

"What did the others have to gain?"

"Well, Mari stood to inherit the farm. At least she was…" Lou looked at Cliff and shook her head. "I really shouldn't be telling you any of this."

"Mum's the word," Bunty said, zipping her lips shut.

"This is sensitive information."

"Why don't we make you a deal, we tell you what we know, and you tell us what you know?" Bunty offered, which, in theory perhaps, sounded like a better deal than it actually was, considering neither Bunty nor Cliff had much information at all. All they had was a twenty-year-old rumour. But something in the way Bunty was looking at Lou made Cliff believe she knew this as well. To his surprise, Lou appeared to be thinking about it.

"Okay, fine. But you have to promise me you won't do anything stupid with it."

"Wouldn't dream of it, dear." Bunty smiled.

Lou looked around the garden before she moved over to sit on the double glider swing. The memory of sitting Lou and Jan down flashed in Cliff's mind. Only, this time, it was Lou doing the talking while he and Bunty listened.

"Well apparently," Lou said as the swing rocked back and forth, "Pieter had always felt bad that his sister was never put in the will for their farm. At least Lucas was provided a job for as long as he wanted it. But the sister, Cynthia, was cut out completely. Pieter had wanted to give Mari the farm with a similar deal, only this time, it would be Flynn, Lucas, and Hendrik, who would have jobs for as long as they wanted or needed. Plus, they would all get a small piece of equity in the farm in case it was ever sold. But Mari would still have majority control in the farm. Well, obviously this didn't go over well with the cousins, specifically Flynn, who'd put all his efforts into the new farm expansion."

"You mean the expansion that wasn't going all too well?"

"Yes. But rumour had it that Pieter had multiple offers for the farm. Mr. Wilderman being one.He was exploring options to pull them out of debt. But given his history with Mr. Wilderman, and the rumours he'd been actively trying to roadblock the farms from success, we think it was unlikely Pieter was ever going to sell it to him."

"I think I'm a little confused," Bunty said, tapping her leg, and Cliff was sure she wished more than ever that she had her notepad with her to jot things down.

"I'm not surprised. We have so many rumours and counter rumours that it's hard to know what to believe. We had conversations with Pieter's lawyer, who confirmed he had two offers, and he hadn't ruled either one of them out with him. But we have Mari and some of the family saying he would never sell."

"Wait, so what was this other offer?" Cliff asked.

"This is where things get interesting," Lou said, sounding almost giddy at the thought of all this information.

Cliff remembered how that felt; there was no better feeling than having as much information as possible to start chipping away at.

"This is where things get interesting?" Bunty chuckled.

Cliff also knew that feeling of being overwhelmed by what he learned. Later in his career, he found that the only difference between being overwhelmed and underwhelmed was how you were able to piece it all together at the end.

"Yes, you see, Hendrik mentioned that he'd had a discussion with Pieter that would settle all their financial issues. He wanted to make a small investment in exchange for equity in the farm. This would have changed everything about who owned the farm."

"Sounds like a generous offer," Bunty said.

"It does. Unless you're Mari, who just went from primary ownership in the farms to potentially losing control of everything. According to Flynn, all she'd ever wanted was the family farm, she didn't even care about the other ones. But a new ownership agreement would have meant she would have almost no say if the boys wanted to sell the farms. She'd go from owning three farms to a small fraction. Bit of a blow to go from nearly everything to potentially nothing. Wouldn't you say?" Lou said, asking for some reassurance.

"Maybe," Bunty said after a while. Like Cliff, she must have been thinking about the fact that Mari seemed to only care about the family farm. At least that was the impression they'd got.

"Maybe? You wouldn't be pissed?" Lou asked.

"Easy on the language, young lady."

"Sorry, Bunty. I just meant you don't think she would be mad?"

"Mad enough to kill her father?" Cliff asked, unable to hide the skepticism in his voice. "But"—Cliff held up a hand to fight the crossfire Lou was clearly settling in for—"even if we did believe you, all of this is just speculation. Does anyone have any actual proof of what was going on with the land? After all, who cares what he *might* have done? If Pieter did change the will, then there must be a record of it somewhere. And if he did, then what does it say? What actual evidence do you have?"

"That's the kicker," Lou said, dropping her voice conspiratorially. "The safe," she paused to give the word time to sink in. It did not. "Oh fine, well, according to Pieter's lawyer, he had mentioned wanting to draw up a new will recently. No, we don't know what those changes were, just that he did want to change it."

"You think this unseen draft was stolen from the safe?" Bunty asked.

Lou confirmed with a nod.

"That's why you believe Mari was involved, because if Pieter wound up dead, the old will would be finalized, and she would get ownership of all three farms and could do whatever she wanted with them?"

"Exactly," Lou said. "Now you understand why she's been our primary suspect."

"But without the other will, there's no proof that any of what Flynn or Hendrik are saying is even true. For all we know, they made it up to blame Mari, because they were upset about not getting anything," Cliff countered, which appeared to suck the wind from Lou's sails.

"Which is why we're trying to find the will," Lou conceded.

"But you haven't found it on Mari yet? Which is why you haven't officially brought her in, because you still don't have any real evidence that she was the one to do it?" Bunty said, talking more to herself than anyone else.

"You have to admit, it paints a pretty picture," Lou said.

"The devil is in the details," Bunty said with a thin smile.

"I don't understand. Why do neither of you appear to be on board with this train? I'm telling you, we know that Mari and Pieter had a big argument at the farm just a couple days ago. Some of the employees heard them shouting about 'what was fair' and 'promises'. Those were just a couple of the phrases heard. We also know that, the only way Mari was ever going to be able to afford the farm, was if it was given to her."

"Wouldn't she still have to pay land transfer tax?" Cliff asked, feeling like he was missing something. He'd spent all his time working in the city, where most people were given a cottage or a house. None of that stuff was straightforward. There was always a catch, usually something financial. But he had no idea what in the world people needed to do if they were gifted a farm.

"No. The government waives transfer tax fees on farms which have been transferred in a will to a family member, as long as they continue to operate the farm as a farm."

"Sounds like a good deal," Cliff chuckled.

"Sometimes," Bunty said.

"What do you mean?" Cliff asked, feeling very far out of his element, but judging from the expression on Lou's face he wasn't the only one.

"Well, take this farm for example. You can transfer the farm for free. Three farms, four people, how do you divide it? What if you don't want to run a farm? Do you give it away for free? Because farms aren't profitable in the way other companies are. The value is in working them or selling them. What happens when four people can't decide what to do?"

"Wouldn't you make money from renting it out?" Lou asked.

"Sure, but at most, you might be talking about twenty thousand a year. Which is a far cry from the million or so you would make from selling it," Bunty countered. "Also split between them all? So, if Mari inherited the farms, she could continue to work them, maybe even sell off the new farms to keep the family farm going. Which brings us back around to why? Why would Mari kill her father over a little bit of money and a couple of farms that aren't profitable? I mean when we talked to her—"

"I'm sorry, you what?" Lou said, sounding shocked before shaking her head. "Of course you did." She let out a hollow laugh. "What did you find?"

"She just doesn't seem like the kind of person who cared about money," Bunty offered.

"I'm with Lou on this. People do terrible things for money all the time," Cliff said, knowing from his own experiences working as a detective in Toronto just how true this was. "Even still, things don't really look to be adding up on this."

"Why? What do you know that we don't?" Lou asked.

"Nothing," Cliff said, sending Bunty a glance from the corner of his eye, one that was clearly not missed by Lou.

She placed her hands on her knees and leaned in closer, her eyes narrowing on him. "What happened to I tell you what I know and you tell me what you know?" Lou asked, not even trying to hide the frustration in her voice as she glanced down and took note of the time.

"Have somewhere to be?" Cliff asked.

"Technically, I'm on lunch," she said, shaking her head, "which means I don't have time for any of these games, Cliff. Tell me why you don't think Mari VanWinkle had anything to do with this, and why you felt the need to talk to Lucas VanWinkle about why he might."

"Firstly, it's not that we don't think Mari had anything to do with it," Cliff said, which received a curious look from Bunty, who turned to face him.

"We don't?" she asked.

"No. We don't. No matter how nice we think she is, that doesn't mean anything. The list of reasons Lou just laid out should be enough to question her. She potentially had a lot to gain from her father's death, especially if the old will stands and there is no dividing of the farm." Cliff pinched the bridge of his nose. "But without this will that was supposedly stolen from the safe, we can't know for sure how much of this is a story and how much of it is just angry family members. At least I assume that's where you got your information?"

Cliff glanced over at Lou, who thought for a moment before giving him a nod. "Right, so without knowing what was on this thing, we can't rule out anyone."

"If the will did have him breaking up the land, why would anyone else want to get rid of it?" Lou asked. "That doesn't make any sense."

"Neither does a riddle, unless you know the answer," Bunty said, her face looking more resolved about the idea of Mari not being innocent than he had given her credit for.

"Exactly," Cliff said.

"Fine. But this doesn't explain why you wanted to talk to Lucas. As far as we can tell, he's a little rough around the edges, but he might be the only one besides"—Lou stopped and opened up her notebook and flipped through a couple pages until she found what she was looking for—"Aria, who appears to have nothing to gain from his death."

"There are more reasons than just money that people kill, Lou," Cliff pointed out.

"What are theirs?"

"I don't know much about Aria, other than she appeared pretty close to Pieter at the festival, while he was in that spat with Mike Wilderman," Cliff said.

Lou started to look confused. Though he caught the realization in her eyes when the memory must have come back to her and she nodded.

"Right, that was Aria," she said.

"You haven't talked to her?" Cliff asked, surprised.

"It's only been a few days, and honestly, everyone has been caught up on Mari and finding whatever was in the safe. That's what seemed important," Lou said, her tone defensive.

"Well, considering there were only six people with a key to get inside, I think it would be prudent to talk to all of them, no?" Cliff asked, ignoring her obvious frustration with where this conversation was heading.

"We know all of this," she said, shaking her head. "And, of course, we plan on talking to each of them. But we thought priority should be given to understanding what was inside the safe." Lou sounded annoyed. Cliff was certainly pushing a nerve here.

"How do you know that whatever was in the safe is even relevant. Or worse, what if it's already destroyed?" Bunty asked.

"We don't," Lou said, letting out a frustrated breath. "Look, I get it, you think we should be talking to more people. But you're evading my earlier question, why did you feel like you should talk to Lucas?"

"There was an accident when he was a kid. A couple kids were injured and one was killed, apparently. Lucas was a minor and spent some time in a juvenile detention centre. But they were lenient on him because he was a kid. He served his time and then he returned to worked on the farm."

"He was charged with manslaughter?" Lou asked her eyes wide. "How do we not know this?"

"Not quite manslaughter. It was a different time, Lou. Likely charged with something like reckless driving resulting in death. Something like that. And because he was a minor, he could have asked the courts to remove it from his record after twenty years, so you might not even see it in your system now," Cliff said.

"Okay so, we can't see it and this all happened, what…?" Lou thought for a moment.

"Forty years ago," Bunty chimed in.

"Right. Why would it matter now?"

"Because…" Cliff said, looking over at Bunty, feeling a bit guilty about sharing this information, but he knew he had too.

"Because," Bunty picked up for him, "there was a rumour that it wasn't actually Lucas driving the car; it was Pieter. And Lucas just took the blame for it because he was a minor."

"Jes—" Lou stopped short at the look Bunty gave her. "So, you think Lucas has been harbouring this fact for his entire life and finally decided to act on it?"

"I don't know what to think," Cliff said softly. "All I know is that, if there is any truth in the story, then Lucas has a lifetime of reasons he might have wanted to see Pieter dead."

A silence drifted between the three of them while the information sank in.

Lou leaned back against the swing, causing it to rock gently. Finally, she let out a small breath and shook her head. "You're sure about this?"

"As sure as anyone can be about rumours. It's not like Lucas was open about discussing any of this with us."

"Well, I can't do anything with this information, even if I wanted to. How would I ever explain how I got it?"

"Same way we did," Bunty asked. "Someone told you. All you need to do is confirm he does actually have a record, right?"

"I suppose. But still it's just…" Lou blinked hard and shook her head. "I don't know. It was such a long time ago, and well…"

"I agree. But our job is to take all the information available to find out what happened to Pieter."

"*My* job," Lou corrected. "It's *my* job to find out what happened. You're retired, and you were a librarian, Bunty. Neither of you should be talking to anyone about this," Lou reminded them, her tone taking a sharp edge.

"I agree," Cliff said, gently putting a hand on Bunty's arm to stop her interjection. "It isn't our job. But we are concerned about the outcome, and we live in a free country and can talk with whomever we want."

"You're playing a dangerous game here, you two. If Captain Marks finds out either of you are out there asking questions…" She shook her head. "Well, I don't think you'll like what he does."

"I'm sure we won't," Cliff said.

"Which is why it's best if he doesn't find out?" Bunty gave Lou a disarming smile.

"Cliff's a bad influence on you, Bunty," Lou said, shaking her head.

"I think you may have our roles reversed," Cliff said under his breath. Bunty jabbed an elbow in his side.

"Let me look into this Lucas thing and figure out what I can find out. Okay?" Lou offered. "But in the meantime, maybe don't do anything that might ruffle any feathers. Maybe we leave this one to the police?"

"Of course," Cliff and Bunty said in unison.

This did little to convince Lou, as she just stared at them. Glancing down at her watch, she stood up from the swing, re-tucking her uniform to get rid of the wrinkles.

"Fine." She smiled, tilting her head as if she wanted to say something, but then thought better of it. Instead, she nodded. "Okay," she said, and, turning, she began to walk away, leaving Cliff and Bunty alone on the swing.

"Wait," Cliff shouted, a thought clinging to his mind that never really added up.

"I really need to get back." Lou turned back, checking her watch.

"I know. It's just something Bunty mentioned."

"I did?" Bunty looked confused.

"What was is it, Cliff?" Lou asked.

"If the farms are divided up, it complicates everything for Mari, true. But doesn't it also mean that it's very likely the farms would be sold?"

"I don't know, Cliff, what's your point?"

"Mike Wilderman," Cliff said.

Lou, from the initial expression her face, looked as though she wanted to smack him, but slowly the information seemed to dawn on her.

"Fair point," she said turning to walk away again. "I'll look into it," she shouted back.

Once Lou was far enough away and had disappeared around the corner of the house, Bunty turned to look at Cliff.

"You think Mike Wilderman would snatch up the farms."

Cliff and Bunty jumped, and Cliff thought for a moment his heart might stop.

As he turned, he saw Mrs. Chen, her head popped up from behind a hedge.

"My lord, Mrs. Chen, you scared us," Bunty said, while Cliff tried to get his breath back.

"You two have apparently been up to more than just helping me in the garden." Mrs. Chen smiled.

"We're just trying to help Hans," Cliff said.

"Sure you are. Interesting case, this one. Seems very confusing."

"It is," Bunty said, before turning to look at Mrs. Chen. "Just how long have you been back there?"

"Long enough to know the two of you aren't going to stop looking into things." She chuckled to herself. "Am I right?"

"We're not. Are we?" Bunty asked, unable to hide her own disappointment at the thought.

"Of course we're not." Cliff smiled, his mind already running around with the new information they'd gathered from Lou, as he looked from Mrs. Chen to Bunty. "And I think I know who we need to talk to next."

18

"Are you sure this is such a good idea?" Bunty asked Cliff as she, Hans, and Gerald walked into the small parking lot in the centre of town, which was currently bustling, by small-town standards, with early morning risers, all searching for fresh produce.

It had been Cliff's idea to head down there after Hans had mentioned that Flynn Stroud would have a booth there. It had surprised Cliff that Flynn would choose to set up a stall at the town farmers' market that popped up every Saturday morning, considering Winkleberry Farm had a permanent location, and Flynn, by all accounts, was more interested in large-scale agriculture than small local produce. Although, given the frustrated expression on the man's face as he lugged in crates of produce with Mari and Aria, perhaps Cliff's assessment of the man had been right.

"If you can think of a better way to talk to Flynn without causing suspicion, then I'm all ears," Cliff said, looking over at Bunty, who appeared to think it over for a moment, though chose to say nothing.

It was by no means a large farmers' market. Cliff had been to a couple in Toronto when he lived there. Having farmers haul their goods to the centre of Toronto often came with a hefty price tag, along with rows and rows of packed stalls in the St. Lawrence Market. Cliff had found it difficult to enjoy, with thousands of people packed in, trying to make the most of all the fresh produce.

The St. Marys market was smaller, to say the least, with less than twenty stalls set up, and, given the early hour, there were only a few dozen people wandering around, scanning the selection, while the vendors finished setting up their stalls.

"Shoot!" Hans said, pulling his foot out of a small hole—or what appeared to be a small hole—which was filled with water. It was one of the many puddles that had formed in the parking lot and around town after the torrential rainfall the night before. "I can't get over how much it rained last night."

"You're telling me," Cliff said, shaking his head. "I left the bedroom windows open, thinking it would be nice to have the breeze. Bit of a shock in the middle of the night when I woke up to the rainforest café hammering in," he chuckled.

"Suppose you don't get those much in the city," Hans said, with a hint of jest in his voice.

"Oh, we get storms," Cliff said, looking up at the big man, "but thunderstorms like that don't happen outside of the Bible, I'm sure."

"Just you wait," Bunty laughed. "I think you'll be in for a big surprise this summer."

"You're kidding," Cliff said.

"Obviously you don't remember your childhood much. But don't worry, you will," Hans laughed.

"I thought the house was going down."

"The Limestone Manor is solid as a rock," Hans said.

"But not *actual* rock," Cliff said, poking fun at the ridiculous name his friend had decided to give the building they lived in, since there were countless homes in the area that were made of limestone, which the town was famous for. Yet not a single stone was used in the construction of their yellow brick house.

"It's catchy," Hans huffed.

"Has this been here the entire time?" Gerald asked, looking around at the various vendors all unloading their selection of goods and foods.

"Every Saturday morning, Gerald, since…" Hans thought for a moment. "Well, a while," he finally said, chuckling to himself.

"How is it no one has ever told me about this?" Gerald asked incredulously. "Did none of you think that, perhaps, there might be some advantages to having access to this kind of food in our house? The meals I could have been making." It was as close to anger as Cliff had ever seen the man get, which still only teetered on the edge of frustration.

"Damn this town and its lack of communication. Where are the news bulletins or shoutouts about what is happening? You would think they don't want people to come."

"It's advertised in the paper, I think. Also, maybe they just suspect people already know about it." Hans shrugged.

"Who are these people?" Gerald asked. "And why are they not screaming this information from the rooftops? How is it I knew there was a market in Stratford before I knew about the one here?"

"Maybe because it's bigger?" Bunty offered.

"This town should be celebrating its unique tininess. We the people need to know what is going on around these parts," Gerald said, surprisingly passionate and wordy.

"You could always join the committee and maybe be the one to promote it?" Bunty suggested with a smile. "I think you would have a rather…unique perspective."

"I couldn't possibly. I've got too much on my table as it is," Gerald said, though Cliff felt as though he saw the wheels starting to turn in the man's head. "Let's see what we're working with." He rubbed his hands together as his eyes narrowed in on the stalls around him, and he started walking over to the nearest one, that appeared to be a small selection of apple ciders.

"That man is certainly passionate about his food," Cliff chuckled.

"I would be nervous for the committee if he decided to turn his attention to it," Hans joked.

"Though it might be nice to have more people coming down, perhaps some food options?" Bunty said. "I trekked out to the St. Jacobs Market a few times, and it was the size of a small village. Clothes, food vendors, an entire outdoor section. The whole thing was rather impressive."

"We can't all do that, Bunty," Hans said.

Cliff was beginning to feel a little out of sorts, considering this was only the second market he'd ever been to, and the first could hardly be considered small. It was easily twenty or thirty times larger than the one here, and he'd never seen or heard of the one they were discussing now. But if he'd learned one thing over his many years of living, it was that, when you are in any doubt about what is going on, sometimes it was best to smile and nod. All the while, his mind flickered back to his primary objective, Flynn Stroud.

Flynn was resting on the tailgate of his truck, looking back at the rest of the crates he still had left to unload, while Mari and Aria where busy setting up the stall itself. It may have been nothing, but there was something about the way Flynn's eye kept turning to stare at Aria as she passed him. This time, she carried a Winkleberry Farm produce sign with a complete price list of everything they were selling.

It was hard to say exactly what kind of relationship the pair had, but given the uneasy way Flynn looked over at her, Cliff got the impression something was going on. His assumptions were strengthened when it appeared Aria was doing everything in her power to avoid any type of interaction with him.

At first, Cliff wondered if there was some sort of romantic connection between the pair. It wasn't altogether out of the question. Cliff understood that some things had changed from when he was young man, but Flynn was about thirty-three years old, and Aria couldn't have been much older than twenty. Perhaps that was odd these days, but not unheard of, especially since they likely spent a lot of time together, potentially finding a common interest in working on a farm. But if this were true, then from their demeanour around one another now, whatever connection might have been there was gone, and had been replaced by something entirely different. Something Cliff wasn't quite prepared to put a name on yet.

"Well, I think we both agree that more could be done to the market," Cliff heard Bunty say amicably to Hans, who nodded his agreement. Cliff had missed where that conversation had gone, not that it mattered much. He was there for one reason and one reason alone. To find an opportunity to talk with Flynn.

"I have to say, it's rather impressive," Bunty said.

Cliff turned, only to realize she was talking to him.

"Sorry, Bunty. What do you mean?" Cliff said to his would-be partner.

"Well, I mean, look at them." She gestured over towards Flynn, Mari, and Aria, all moving around, prepping their stall.

"I am," Cliff said, feeling a bit like an idiot and more than a little confused.

Bunty laughed and shook her head. "I only mean, it's impressive what they are doing. It can't be easy for them to be here. Not only did Pieter just die, but there is a good chance that one of them might have killed him. You don't think that, if the roles were reversed, you wouldn't want to shut yourself up in your home and not see anyone until it was all over?"

"Well, considering all I want to do *most* of the time is shut myself up in my room and not see anyone, I would hardly say I'm the right person to ask. But yes, I'm sure all of this must be very difficult to manage," Cliff replied.

"The farm doesn't stop because you want it to," Hans said.

Cliff spun round just in time to see the sadness that briefly crossed behind the big man's eyes.

"It's your life, it's their lives. Without them there to keep it going, everything shuts down."

Cliff tried to recall what Hans had been like after the death of his wife, Adria. Cliff hadn't been around much then, and he'd only actually met Adria twenty or so times over the years, and it was often just in passing. But from everything he could remember, she was an incredible woman, and Cliff knew how difficult it had been for Hans afterwards. But, like the VanWinkles, Hans had put his head down and carried on with his work, leaving his time for mourning her death for after the busy season. Though Cliff questioned whether or not he'd ever actually grieved.

"That's when the vultures move in," Hans said, grabbing Cliff's attention once again and giving a nod towards another stall that Cliff hadn't noticed yet.

Mike Wilderman stood leaning with his back against his truck and, like the three of them, he was focused on the Winkleberry Farm stall as well. But unlike Winkleberry Farm, The Badger had a team of people moving everything around for him. Cliff couldn't help but notice the minor discrepancy in prices between the two vendors, with Wilderman Farms having a good thirty percent markup on all his goods. It just added to the list of things Cliff didn't like about the man.

"I'm surprised he would even have a stall here," Bunty said quietly. "He doesn't seem the type for farmers' markets, or one to talk to people, for that matter."

"He'll do anything to make a buck," Hans said bitterly. "I hear he's already been over to Winkleberry Farm twice to offer to buy them out. Greedy little—"

"Hans!" Bunty blurted out before he could finish on, what Cliff assumed, would be a very colourful note, especially given the redness in his cheeks now that Bunty had called out to him.

"Sorry, Bunty. That man just boils my blood," Hans said, trying to shake off the feelings he was having. "It takes a certain kind of person to strike before the body's even been laid in the ground." He shook his head.

"Any word on when that will be?" Bunty asked, in a crude attempt to switch the topic away from Mike Wilderman.

Still, Cliff couldn't help keeping his focus on the smug-looking man standing there as though he didn't have a care in the world.

Although Cliff wanted to believe that maybe this horrible man played some part in Pieter's death, he couldn't figure a way that was possible. Not only did he not have access to the building where Pieter was found—and Cliff couldn't imagine that Pieter was in the habit of inviting him anywhere—he also appeared to be one of the few people who didn't openly have something to gain from his death. Especially considering now that Pieter was gone, there was no telling who owned the farms at this point, or what any of them would do with his offer. At least until they found his will, and Cliff highly suspected that they wouldn't.

"They won't be able to bury him until the investigation's closed," Cliff said absently, after he saw Hans shrug his shoulders towards Bunty.

"That's such a shame. Hard to have closure with something like this looming over you," Bunty said with a sad smile.

"I just hope all of this gets cleared up soon and these poor kids can move on."

"You forget that one of these poor kids might be the reason Pieter's dead," Cliff said, his comment getting a mild look of shock from Bunty and Hans.

For a moment, Cliff had forgotten that he was no longer in the police service but was talking, instead, to regular people who had spent a majority of their lives shielded from the grim world associated with murder investigations. It was one thing to get to the bottom of an investigation. It was another thing entirely to alter your perspective of the world and know, deep down, that good people were capable of doing terrible things. It was something Cliff no longer had the privilege of lying to himself about.

But that doesn't mean I need to rob them of it too.

"Potentially, that is," Cliff corrected himself, though from the looks on their faces, it wasn't enough to erase the thought from their minds. The idea had already nestled itself into their heads and, once the seed had been sown, it was difficult to prevent it from growing.

"One thing at a time, I suppose," Bunty said, giving a firm nod and looking up at Cliff and Hans. "The question I have at the moment is how do we talk to Flynn without making it obvious we're trying to ask him questions?"

Cliff and Hans looked between one another, then over at Bunty, none of them appearing to have a solid plan. In the past, Cliff could always just walk up and ask what he needed to ask, but given what had happened with Lucas, he doubted that tactic would be enough to get him through this little charade.

"More importantly, how do we get him alone to chat?" Bunty asked.

"I might have a way of doing that," Hans said, tapping his chin thoughtfully, "though it would be best if we had someone distract Mari." He looked at Cliff.

Both their eyes landed on Bunty, who folded her arms in protest.

"How did I get to become the distraction?" she asked, looking between them.

"You're not the distraction, you're just…" When Cliff couldn't find a better way of phrasing it, his shoulders slumped, and he shrugged lightly. "A distraction, yeah. Do you mind?"

Bunty didn't look entirely thrilled at the prospect, and Cliff had to admit that her attention to detail was something he would miss. But there was no doubt in his mind that, of the three of them, it was more likely that Hans would be the best at making Flynn feel comfortable. After all, Hans was a farmer, and one of their farms had been his. To Cliff's appreciation, Bunty appeared to come to a similar conclusion, and her features dropped as she resigned herself to the role she was about to play.

"On the upside, this will give you the opportunity to speak with Mari again, now that we have this new information. Perhaps you can find out more about what's going on in her mind, or what she believes was in that safe?" Cliff offered, which seemed to give Bunty something to think about.

"That's not a bad idea, I suppose," Bunty said. She turned to head off towards the stall. "Have fun, boys." She gave them both a wink over her shoulder, and Cliff couldn't help but recall the quiet woman she had been when he first moved into the house. Clearly, she was starting to enjoy herself, and Cliff had to admit he was starting to as well.

He turned to look up at Hans. "So, what have you got in mind, big man?"

19

"How you holding up, son?" Hans asked, placing a hand on Flynn's shoulder as the three of them found some space away from the stalls, and almost as importantly, away from Mari and Aria, who continued to move crates of produce around.

Once again, Cliff was reminded he was no longer living in the big city, but a rural town. Which is why he shouldn't have been surprised to learn that Hans's plan was quite literally to approach a young man he knew and start a conversation. After all, he'd known Flynn for years and even sold his farm to Pieter. Why would it be unusual to check up on him? And with Hans in tow, perhaps they wouldn't find themselves with another Lucas VanWinkle disaster on their hands.

"Good," Flynn said, though, from the uneasy shifting in his feet, his body was telling an entirely different story.

An exaggerated laugh startled the group as Cliff turned to see Gerald speaking animatedly with a young Amish couple who appeared rather uncomfortable. Though they were still managing to smile and nod to the pudgy old man, his wicker basket, that he'd borrowed from Mrs. Chen, was already filling up with various goods.

At least one of us has found some success today.

"It's a lot to be dealing with," Hans offered.

"You don't know the half of it," Flynn chuckled awkwardly. "The farm feels like a shit storm." He looked up and raised a hand apologetically. "Pardon my language."

"No worries, son. I can only imagine what's going on over there at the moment."

"Hans, it's a mess. I'm not even sure what's going to happen, the farm is…well, it's not great, I'll say that. Whoever…" Flynn stopped and looked away for a second. His eye caught Mari's briefly, and then he shook his head, not wanting whatever thought was burrowing in his mind to live there. Then, turning to face Hans and Cliff again, he continued. "Whatever happened to Uncle Pieter." His words near silent now. "Him dying has done a number on us, and I'm not sure what exactly we're going to do about it."

Hans gave the man a pat on the back. "I'm sure it will all work out. The police will figure out who is responsible soon enough."

"I'm not so sure that's going to help us," Flynn said, looking defeated. "They seem to think it was one of us who killed him. But why on earth would any of us want that? We're family, for Christ's sakes."

"I'm sure there is a perfectly good explanation for all of this," Hans offered, though it felt a bit hollow even as he said it.

"Nothing about this is good." Flynn shook his head. "The farm's in trouble, Hans, and if we can't do something about it soon, I'm not sure there will be anything left to sell when the dust finally settles."

"What do you mean?" Hans asked.

"I mean, every part of our business right now is down. Uncle Pieter could only do so much. He'd only just started to show me how to handle our books, since he refused to switch over to doing anything digitally. I thought it was a terrible idea, and I was right."

"He was always a sucker for the old ways," Hans laughed.

"Yeah, it wouldn't have been a problem, except that the old ways were stolen from the safe, along with some other documents."

"What do you mean, stolen?" Hans asked, and Cliff was surprised at how adept his friend was at feigning ignorance about the knowledge he had.

"Apparently, someone took his ledger, and possibly a rewritten will. At least that's what we think it was. No one knows for sure. We do know they stole the company records. Why? Who the hell knows," Flynn said, shaking his head. "Now, we have to try and figure out what we're going to tell the banks. On top of all that, we didn't earn nearly as much as we hoped from the festival before all the commotion, and since then, sales at the farm are down by nearly forty percent. Apparently, people don't want to take their kids out to an active crime scene."

"What about the dairy and the cash crop?"

"Don't even get me started. We're stalled out on that. Our most recent shipment of feed has been delayed, and the weather's been brutal. It's either sunny as all hell or we have torrential downpours like the one we had last night, flooding the fields. I mean, we're doing what we can, but you know what it's like," Flynn said.

"I thought rain was good?" Cliff asked, feeling a little out of his element with all the farm talk. He was thankful for Hans being there. *Perhaps I should have let Bunty come instead of me. At least she knows more about farming.*

"It is. But too much of it all at once floods the field, and then we have to wait until the water drains before we can get back in there," Flynn said. "Not to mention the rain redistributes the seeds we've already planted. It's a mess out there right now. Our only blessing is that everyone on this side of seven is in the same boat." His eyes flicked over towards Mike Wilderman, who shot him a cringeworthy smile. "But he's got so many farms to fall back on to help pick up the slack. We have the two we planted, and neither of them is giving us much hope."

"What about insurance?' Hans asked.

"Insurance?" Cliff asked.

"Even farms need insurance, Cliff," Hans chuckled.

Cliff tucked his head back in his shell, realizing he was very much out of his element on this one.

"Fair enough. But waiting on a settlement with that lot will take time. Time we don't have. Not to mention, everyone's going after a claim, and I'll give you one guess who's going to get priority, and it ain't two-farm Charlie over here."

"Pieter had mentioned you were interested in selling the farms to the Badger?" Hans asked.

Flynn's face went red in the cheeks. "It's not…" he started, but he slowly nodded. "I mean before, sure. It wasn't a great deal, but it would be enough to get a little money for us. He would get the farms, and we could stay on as managers, and we'd get to keep our team. The only catch is he would get rid of Winkleberry Farm and turn it into something more profitable. That might not be a bad thing, but good luck trying to convince Mari of that," Flynn said. "And Hendrik for that matter. I never figured him for the sentimental type, but he had some strong words to say about selling the family farm to the Badger."

"I thought Hendrik wanted to sell the farm?" Hans asked, glancing over at Cliff, who also started to remember Hendrik saying something to Pieter about it being a good deal.

"Umm…not sure. He was talking to Uncle Pieter a lot recently," Flynn said, looking utterly confused by the idea.

"I might just be mistaken," Hans said. "I just thought I overheard him talking with Pieter about a deal. But maybe it was about something else."

"Weird. If he did have some sort of deal going with Uncle Pieter, then I didn't know about it."

"What about Mari? What did she think?" Hans asked, and Cliff was impressed at the way Hans was managing the conversation. Even from his perspective, it didn't seem like he was being overly intrusive, more like an interested bystander.

I suppose he is.

"Like I said, she's too stubborn to sell that place." He laughed before pausing for a moment, appearing to sit on something else he would like to say but not knowing if he should. He must have made a decision, as he chose to lean in towards Cliff and Hans and whispered, "But maybe she would think differently about it, knowing the price tag. Now that she owns them, perhaps stubbornness can only take you so far."

"Farther than you think, kid," Cliff said, giving his knee a rub, catching an odd glance from Flynn. "Do you really think your cousin is only in it for the money?"

"I don't know what Mari does it for. But for a few million? Who knows what people will do. And frankly, she's been acting really strange since it all happened. Like she knows more than she's letting on."

"What do you mean?" Hans asked.

"I don't know, it's hard to explain, but she's…"

"Hope I'm not interrupting anything." Mike Wilderman stepped up to the makeshift circle the three of them had formed, pressing himself in alongside them like he was meant to be there.

"You are," Flynn said angrily.

"Easy there, hotshot. Just wanted to come send my condolences. Despite stopping by, I haven't had a chance to talk to you, or anyone in your family, for that matter, since Pieter's terrible death last week. Such a shame something like that could happen to such a good man." The Badger shoved his hands into his pockets, further intensifying the calm demeanour of a man used to taking up space no matter where he was.

Even Cliff, who had not known the man long, could tell a lot by the way he conducted himself, and knew that even he would like to punch this man in the face.

"And given all the rumours around town that he may have been murdered"—he shook his head in mock shock—"your family must be a wreck."

"Shut the hell up, Badger," Flynn said, taking a step in, causing the Badger to throw his arms up.

"Easy there, Flynn. I'm just saying what I heard. Don't shoot the messenger and all that."

"If I hear you've been spreading lies about our family, Badger…"

"I think you'll find this town does enough talking without me having to say much."

"What do you want, Badger?" Hans said, his massive fist clenched and held against his side.

"With you, Hans? Nothing," he said, tilting his head at the big man, before his eyes drifted down. He smiled at Hans's tightened fists, before dragging his eyes back over towards Flynn. "You, on the other hand, I just want to offer some assistance."

"How's that?"

"I heard through the grapevine your feed supply was delayed. I was only going to mention that I may have a little extra we could sell ya."

"Sell us the feed you bought up to screw us?" Flynn asked, appearing to bite back some other choice words.

"That is a very dangerous accusation. This is a fickle business, and my number one priority is and will always be the health of my farms. I'm sorry if your little hobby farm can't manage itself. That's why I continue to keep my offer on the table, for whenever you feel you may want to start playing in the big leagues."

"It's not a league if you're the only one playing," Hans snapped back.

"I can't help it if I'm really good at winning, Mr. VanDosen. And don't be angry at me because you chose to bet on the wrong horse," he said, flashing a sideway smirk.

"Perhaps it's best if we depart before anyone does something they might regret," Cliff said, stepping between the two men.

"I'm sorry, I don't believe we've had the chance to meet. Mike Wilderman." He shoved out a hand for Cliff to take, which he did. "But you can call me the Badger. Hell, everyone else does." He laughed.

"Clifford Shaw."

"Aww, yes. I've heard about you," he said, his eyes narrowing slightly. "Aren't you the one who had the argument with Lucas VanWinkle at the Creamery the other day?"

"We talked, yes," Cliff said, trying to keep his cool without letting anything slip.

"I heard you did more than talk." The Badger laughed. "Interesting friends you keep." He nodded over towards Flynn.

"You talked to Uncle Lucas?" Flynn asked, and Cliff turned to see Flynn's eyes shift between Cliff and Hans and the Badger. "Why?"

"Cliff here is a retired detective. Perhaps he fancies himself still in the game?" The Badger shrugged his shoulders as he turned away. "You have my number, Flynn. And the offer still stands." He moved away, looking more smug than ever.

"You're a detective?" Flynn asked, looking towards Cliff then over at Hans. "Is he?"

"I was, kid. And I've been asking some questions because I'm curious about what's going on here. That's all," Cliff explained, hoping he sounded casual. Though Flynn didn't appear to be enjoying the casual nature of Cliff's *conversation.*

"You think *I* did it? That I killed Uncle Pieter?" Flynn asked, taking a step back. "Is that why you wanted to know all that stuff?" He looked at Hans, whose anger had receded and who was now looking a little pale.

"No," Cliff answered for him. "We just want to understand what's going on. We know the police are handling it, but sometimes it's nice to have another perspective."

"And you think you deserve that perspective? What gives you that right?"

"Nothing," Cliff said calmly. "But I do think I have an outsider's perspective. It's something I think this town lacks. Wouldn't you say?"

"Stay away from me and my family," Flynn said, pointing a finger at Cliff.

"Don't you think what's important is finding out what happened to your uncle?" Cliff asked.

"You're not the police. You're an old man with nothing to do." Flynn's words slapped Cliff across the face like it had been his hand instead.

"Easy, Flynn." Hans said, holding his palms up in front of Flynn in a vain attempt to calm him down. "You're angry! But if you're angry, be angry at me. I'm the one who asked Cliff to look into this."

"You did? Why?"

"Because Pieter was my friend. And if someone killed him, I want to make sure that whoever is responsible for his death is found. If Cliff can help make that possible, then you can bet that I'm going to ask for his help. I would have thought you'd want the same thing," Hans said.

"You know I do, but…"

"But nothing. If you want to be mad at someone, be mad at me." Hans hooked a thumb back at his chest. "But you leave him out of this." He tilted his head towards Cliff, who had never felt so grateful for the big man as he did right now. "The Badger is trying to rile you up. Hell, the man just tried to sell you your own feed back to you at a higher price, and you sit here and get mad at a man who's only trying to help solve your uncle's death? Cool your head, Flynn, and when you're ready to talk about this, we'll be here. Come on." Hans turned and placed a hand on Cliff's back, leading him away, leaving Flynn to stand in his own silence.

"That didn't go so well," Hans said shaking his head. "Sorry."

"What? I should be thanking you," Cliff said as he released a breath and felt his chest drop as he once again relaxed. "And I think that went rather well actually." He smiled, until he saw Bunty running over to them her face looking troubled. "Bunty?"

"We need to get back to the manor. We have a problem."

"It's ruined," Mrs. Chen said quietly, her head sunken down to her chest, on the verge of tears as she gripped a mug of tea between her shaking hands.

This was the image Cliff, Hans, Bunty, and Gerald—still carrying a large wicker basket filled to the brim with fresh produce and goods from the market—witnessed as they all entered the living room. Sol was in his usual chair, looking unsure of what exactly, if anything, he should be doing, while Kitty sat on the couch beside Mrs. Chen, rubbing her back softly.

"It's going to be fine," Kitty said, turning to glance back at the newly arrived housemates.

Cliff thought she didn't look nearly as confident about that proclamation as she sounded.

"We heard what happened," Hans said.

"Yes, we got your message. How are you, Mrs. Chen?" Bunty asked. "We came home right away."

"It's a bit of a mess," Kitty said.

"I'd hardly call it a mess," Mrs. Chen said. "Disaster perhaps, or travesty." She looked up to Bunty. "You would likely have the right words for all of this."

"Perhaps, but right now, I think it more prudent to figure out a way we can help," Bunty said.

"Help? Not sure how on earth you could help," Mrs. Chen said, in a far more defeatist tone than Cliff had ever heard from the woman.

Whatever is going on has clearly given her a hit.

All Cliff knew was that something was wrong in the garden. Not much had been conveyed via the short phone call Bunty had received from Kitty, informing her that Mrs. Chen had come inside distraught that morning, having done her usual walk through.

It didn't take a detective, Cliff imagined, to come to the conclusion that the torrential downpour from the night before had done some damage to her flower beds. He could hardly imagine just how much damage could have been done to warrant such a reaction from a woman Cliff would best describe as "stoic."

"I'm sure it's not as bad as you imagine," Bunty said, trying her best to remain as optimistic as possible.

"Have a look for yourself," Mrs. Chen said, gesturing toward the door.

Cliff looked at Bunty, then over to Hans and shrugged. Gerald, on the other hand, was no longer standing with them, and at some point after they arrived, must have headed into the kitchen without anyone having any idea that he'd disappeared. The heavy-set man was deceptively light on his feet.

Curious now, Cliff turned and led the way out of the house with Bunty and Hans hot on his tail. Of course, they had all seen the front garden that morning, and once again when they returned, but it was primarily mazed hedgerow with two Japanese maples and fronted with some lavender bushes and some annuals that Mrs. Chen had planted to give it some colour. Upon closer inspection, Cliff did notice that some sections of the front garden appeared to be less protected by the hedges, and some of the annuals had been washed away. Though he would hardly describe the scene as disastrous.

It wasn't until the three turned their attention towards the rear garden that the narrative Mrs. Chen had been building began to take shape. Although there were many sections of the garden that had been protected by the surrounding trees, there were others that looked like someone had tossed buckets of water on them, nearly washing away all the soil and mulch, and taking many of the plants with it.

Some of the more devastated sections gave the impression that something had stomped though like a twisted conga line, buckling the stems of the flowers, so they now drooped to the sides like macabre bows. Washed-out rivers of soil fingered their way through the flower beds like tributaries leading to the base of the flower beds before pooling at the bottom where the ground sloped down. Even the grass hadn't fared well, as their feet squished into the earth as they stepped.

"It doesn't look great," Bunty said unceremoniously, having given it a moment to let the damage sink in.

"Don't let Mrs. Chen hear that," Hans said, shaking his head.

"You think it's salvageable?" Cliff asked, realizing just how much he didn't know about the garden or how long it would take to repair. But based on the work they had done over the last week, and Mrs. Chen's resilience at coming out every morning to tackle tiny sections, Cliff had his doubts. Though he supposed that all depended on when the committee would be coming to judge the garden.

"Yes," Bunty said without hesitation, though her head tilted as she appeared to study the garden a little more intently.

"You do?" Cliff asked.

"Yes. I do. There isn't much a little hard work can't fix," she said with a confidence Cliff had not seen in the woman. She quite literally began rolling up her sleeves. "The hardest part will be convincing Mrs. Chen." She let out a little sigh and turned to head back inside.

Cliff and Hans took a final look at the washed-out garden, and Cliff chose to withhold any doubts he had, most of all because he truly had no idea if Bunty's proclamation was possible. All he knew was that his knees and his back already felt tight at the prospect of what they would need to do to pull it all off.

"We can fix that, Mrs. Chen," Bunty said as she stepped inside the living room. She took the seat beside Mrs. Chen. Kitty was still posted on the other side, her hand rubbing affectionately on her back.

"That's very kind of you, Bunty. But I don't think so," Mrs. Chen said, still reasonably deflated by it all. "I just received word that the judges will be coming this Friday."

"That leaves us six days before they come!" Hans said cheerfully. "Surely that's more than enough time to get the garden in order?"

"Perhaps. If the forecast wasn't calling for rain for the next three days," Mrs. Chen said, shaking her head. "It's a nightmare."

"A nightmare is me having to give a speech in front of the town council in my underwear while Kitty sips tea and stares at me from the side of the stage, shaking her head," Sol said, giving a little shudder.

As everyone in the house turned to look at the usually quiet man, a few smiles appeared, including one on Cliff.

"What we have here is a setback. Best to take those in stride, Mrs. Chen." Sol gave her a firm nod. "You say we have six days to get this garden in order?"

"Three, if you don't count the rain."

"That would require trusting the weatherman, who has one of those rare professions that doesn't require you to be right," Kitty said with a huff.

"True enough, Kitty," Sol said. "But even still, that still gives us three days to plan our attack." Sol didn't skip a beat. "We can either sit around and wait for those days to pass us by, or we can start coming up with a plan to tackle this project."

"We?" Kitty said, her lips curling into a smile as she studied her husband.

"Of course, we! This may be Mrs. Chen's pet project, but the

Limestone Manor is home to all of us, and if Mrs. Chen has put in all of this work to honour our house," Sol said, folding up his paper and setting it on the table, letting out a breath as he squared up his shoulders and held up his chin, "then we all have a duty to help bring her vision to fruition." He finished with a nod.

Cliff could see the pride on Kitty's face as she nodded at her husband. The rest of the room appeared to be equally surprised by Sol's sudden commitment to the garden. In the past, he had tried his best to leave himself parked inside rather than out working in the garden. But whatever the reasons were for the man's turn of heart, it appeared to rally the house, and in particular, Mrs. Chen, who was now propped up, nodding in her seat.

"You're right, Sol. Thank you," Mrs. Chen said, giving the man a nod.

"In the meantime, might I suggest a strategy meeting? I'm thinking The Trillium? Get our minds away from the problem, and look at it from the distance it may very well need?" Sol proposed.

"Excellent idea," Kitty said.

"Perhaps some distance would be nice," Mrs. Chen said softly.

"Perfect. Gerald, we're thinking…" Sol began to shout, but to his surprise, Gerald was already dressed and in the hallway, slipping on his shoes.

"I'll be waiting in the Hearse," Gerald said as he fingered through the small container that held the house's umbrellas until he found his own and pulled it out. With that, he was out the door before anyone had a chance to say anything else.

"There is truly something wrong with that man," Kitty said, shaking her head.

"He's certainly loves a meal." Bunty smiled as the rest of the house began standing up and moving towards the front entrance to get ready to leave.

Cliff, still in his jacket, moved aside to let the others through. Sol approached him from the living room. "Great speech, Sol. Very uplifting."

"Thank you," Sol said, giving Cliff a nod.

"You were hungry, weren't you?" Hans whispered from over Cliff's shoulders, so only the three of them could hear.

"Very much so, yes," Sol said with a weak smile as he shook his head at Hans. "But I meant every word. Mrs. Chen has done nothing but work on that garden for months. If I can help now, I will. And if helping at this moment means having a nice breakfast, then so be it." He sent Hans a wink, and the three of them moved toward the door and began slipping on their shoes and filing out towards the Hearse.

As they stepped out onto the landing, Cliff saw Jan's beaten up old Pontiac turn into the driveway and stop beside the Hearse. Jan hopped out, not caring about the light rain that must have just started up again while Cliff and the others were inside. He walked over to Hans and Cliff.

Hans finished locking up the door and turned, surprised. "Jan?"

"Hi, Opa," Jan said, his voice strained.

"What's wrong?" Hans asked when Jan looked as though he desperately wanted to say something but couldn't find the words. Han's inquiry appeared to lift the floodgates.

"I just found out that the OPP believe they found Pieter VanWinkle's missing will. It was in Mari's apartment. Obviously, she claimed she'd never seen it before, but they don't believe her. Lou said she was trying to get a hold of you, but couldn't, so she sent me the heads-up."

Cliff felt his pockets and realized he didn't have his phone. He must have left it upstairs in his room when he went out that morning. He still wasn't used to having the thing on him all the time.

"That's not ideal," Cliff said.

"Is Mari alright?" Hans asked.

"I haven't seen her. But I imagine she's not doing great, considering she's being accused of killing her father."

"Why would she keep the will? Not just get rid of it or burn it? Anything else?" Cliff asked.

Jan shrugged. "Maybe she wasn't thinking right? Maybe it was an accident?"

"You think she accidently poisoned her father?" Cliff asked, trying not to sound too incredulous.

"I don't know."

"Are you boys coming?" Kitty shouted from the door of the Hearse, as the rain began to get a little heavier.

"Yes. Sorry, Kitty. One minute," Hans called back. He turned to Jan. "We're just on our way to The Trillium. Why don't you come for breakfast, Jan, on me," Hans suggested.

"I probably shouldn't, but…?" Jan paused.

"Just get in the Hearse." Hans chuckled as he began to move towards the house's ride.

"Oh, and there is one other thing. The police also found something at Flynn Stroud's house."

"What?" Cliff asked.

"The company logbooks," Jan said.

"So they each had something from the safe?" Cliff asked, though it was more of a statement for himself than a question. But that didn't stop Jan from answering.

"Yep. And apparently, there's more," Jan said, as the rain intensified.

"Can you just say it, kid? I'm starting to get a little wet out here," Cliff said, pulling his jacket up, as if that would protect him from the rain.

"Right, yeah. Flynn Stroud has been lying about the books," Jan said.

Cliff had already begun piecing together what was coming next before Jan said it out loud.

"So Flynn lied to us, and had the ledgers at his house the entire time!"

21

"Let's not jump to conclusions," Hans said once they had been shown to their table, which consisted of pushing two large tables together to make enough space to accommodate Jan, as well as the rest of them. Apparently, with the rainy morning, it hadn't just been the idea of the residents of the Limestone Manor who thought it would be a good idea to get breakfast. The Trillium was well stocked with a variety of locals, all hoping to get a hot breakfast and possibly a little gossip. Gossip that was sure to spread like wildfire should anyone overhear their table.

"I think it's best if we try to keep our voices down," Bunty said, looking around the diner and likely noticing the same things Cliff had.

"What was that, Bunty?" Kitty asked, her voice cutting through the air despite the chaos of the background noise.

"She said, keep your voice down," Sol said, giving Bunty a nod, partially expecting a "you're welcome," though all Bunty gave him was a shake of the head.

"It's only just…perhaps we should tread lightly, discussing this stuff in the diner. Given the…umm…well…"

"Gossipers?" Mrs. Chen offered.

"Yes. That," Bunty said.

"I'd hardly call it gossip." Kitty, across from Cliff, folded her hands together and placed them on the table over top of her menu, which she, like many people at the table, hadn't looked at, since they already knew what they were going to order.

Unlike Cliff, who, despite ordering the same standard breakfast each time, still found it worth perusing through each time he arrived, on the off chance that something caught his eye.

"Of course, you wouldn't." Sol chuckled, the act receiving a jab to the side from Kitty's pointed elbow, causing him to flinch, though it only served to make him laugh harder.

"Are we not discussing actual things that have happened? How is that considered gossip?" Kitty asked.

"Well, technically, gossip is a casual conversation about people's private lives that are not confirmed as being true," Bunty said.

"But it is true. Jan just confirmed it," Kitty said, gesturing to Jan, who held up his hands in defence, though none came.

"Jan told us his version of what he heard," Hans said.

"You're all so boring. You all discover…what we know…" Kitty said, looking around the diner conspiratorially, "and you want to, what? Ignore it?"

"Not ignore," Bunty said, "But perhaps we can be discreet about it."

"Good luck," Sol said, beginning to read over his menu, though Cliff knew it was more of a distraction than him actually *wanting* to read it. Cliff had discovered that Sol preferred to always appear preoccupied, rather than engage in whatever everyone else was discussing, unless he felt the desire to.

As had been the case for a while now, the housemates had collapsed into their normal formation around the table. It was the same as when they would sit around the dining room table, with the exception of Jan, who was in the extra chair at the end of the table between Hans and Bunty. Kitty and Sol were across from Cliff, which left Mrs. Chen on his right and Gerald, happy on the end, his fingers tapping eagerly on the table while he stared intently at the waitress taking orders nearby.

"If I may, I think what Bunty is trying to say, Kitty," Cliff offered, leaning in towards the table and glancing over at Bunty, pausing to make sure it was alright for him speak for her. Bunty gave him an approving nod. "Is that Jan has given us *a* truth. Items have been found in people's possession. What we don't know is how they got there. Which means we are speculating on speculation. Which can quickly turn into gossip if left unchecked."

"So, what we're doing is not gossiping, it's speculating?" Kitty asked, tilting her head.

Cliff thought about it for a moment.

"And that is not different how?"

"Speculating is to form a theory on a subject, without all the evidence. Gossip is spreading misinformation about peoples' private lives for entertainment," Bunty said.

"You say potato, I say *potato*," Kitty shrugged.

"Well, perhaps it's best if, for today, we all say potato," Hans said, receiving several nods around the table, save for Kitty, who looked marginally unimpressed, and Gerald who still appeared to be ignoring the conversation and focusing on the waitress.

"Jan, perhaps it's best if you tell us again what you know," Cliff said.

"What I know," Jan said, shaking his head, "is that Mari is currently being held for questioning. This version of the will clearly states an equal division of land between Mari and her cousins."

"Why go through the effort of stealing it and not destroying it?" Hans asked, clearly shaken by this information.

"I agree," Bunty said. "It's one of the key items that links her to her father's murder."

"Maybe she didn't have time, or she forgot, or taking it was an afterthought." Cliff shrugged. "The reality is, it was found at her house, and that on its own doesn't look great for her."

"Maybe it was planted," Kitty said. Tapping her fingers against her chin, she added, "That is a thing, isn't it, the real criminal steals something to frame someone else? How do we know she's not being framed. Maybe by one of her cousins?"

"Flynn did have those other documents," Jan said, "and if what Lou told me is true—"

"I didn't know you and Lou we're talking," Kitty said, cutting Jan off and studying the young man, her eyes narrowed.

"We aren't, or we don't. She just had this information and thought I could get it to all of you."

"Why didn't she come herself?" Kitty asked, leaning closer as Jan's face began to flush red.

"I'm...well, you'd have to ask her, wouldn't you?" Jan replied.

"Maybe I will." Kitty leaned back in her chair, her eyes never leaving Jan's, who stammered back to life as he laid out everything he knew about the two incidents.

He started with Mari and the documents, which had stated very clearly that Pieter's wishes for the farm had changed. He had expressed wanting to divide of the farm into three, giving Flynn and Hendrik a share, likely as some recompense for his sister, who was completely cut out of the will by their father. Something, Hans had mentioned, that had always eaten away at Pieter.

He also explained how, according to the documents they found, Flynn had been lying about how much the farms were costing to run and likely pocketing the extra cash. According to Jan, and the information Lou provided, he had been skimming money from the company and looking to use it to purchase another farm nearby, something Cliff couldn't quite wrap his head around.

"So, he has failing farms already, and his response is to purchase another? Why would he do that?"

"Likely depends on the farm he was trying to buy," Hans said. "But there are a few reasons why another farm could help them. More purchasing power, for one. Might have figured it would help reduce the overall cost of goods."

"And if he thought he was going to get a farm from Pieter, perhaps he imagined this was going to be the perfect opportunity to break off on his own?" Bunty suggested.

"But the farms weren't making money," Cliff said, feeling very out of his element here.

"It's normal for farms to carry debt," Hans said, "just as long as you have the assets to prop it up with. If I had to guess, I would say that is where Winkleberry Farm was running into some issues."

Cliff shook his head. "There is just so much I don't understand about farming."

"It's a tricky business if you're not in it. I did it for fifty years, and so much has changed from when I started," Hans said.

"Sorry, it's taken me so long," Zoey, the waitress, said. Zoey was somewhat of a staple here, since it appeared she worked nearly every day. "It's been a busy morning, as you can see."

"We didn't even notice, love," Kitty offered.

"I did," Gerald said, tapping his fingers together, ignoring the glare Kitty provided him with, which Cliff thought was impressive given the woman's intimidating presence.

"Of course you did, hun, and what can I get you?" Zoey said, pulling out her notepad and holding up her pen to stop Gerald before he spoke. "Let me guess, belly buster with white toast and sunny side up eggs, hashbrowns with onions, and a coffee, no water."

Gerald closed and handed her his menu. "Yes. Thank you." He nodded approvingly.

Zoey continued around the table, picking people's brains, knowing what each person wanted without them having to say anything. It was impressive, though not nearly as impressive as her ability to ramble on about the news of the town between orders. It was something Cliff would have had a hard time with in his best years.

"Did you hear about the murder at Winkleberry Farm? I couldn't believe it. I was supposed to take my nephew there this weekend, but given they still haven't caught whoever did it, I can't imagine it's a smart move. French toast, coffee and a water," she wrote down for Kitty, who nodded approvingly. She paused at Cliff briefly before smiling. "Let me guess, you're not sure, but you suppose you'll have the standard breakfast, over easy eggs, sausage, rye toast, and hashbrowns and onions. Am I close?"

"Given the look on his face," Mrs. Chen said, "I'd say you were spot on, my dear." She chuckled, and Cliff remembered that, in spite of everything going on with the VanWinkle family, Mrs. Chen was still trying to sort out what she was going to do about her garden. They'd all agreed to pitch in after a rather rousing speech given by Sol.

"Great, I'll get that in for you all, and hopefully, it will be out as soon."

"Zoey, dear?" Kitty stopped the young woman, much to Gerald's clear disappointment.

"Yes?"

"What else have you heard about the murder?" she asked.

"Not a murder," Cliff said, holding up his finger. Everyone looked at him. "There is speculation, but there is still no proof it was intentional."

"Fair enough," Kitty said with a short nod. "What have you heard about the speculation of murder?"

Cliff still didn't think this was a great way to phrase it, but he supposed, in the end, it didn't matter much. People in town were going to think one way, regardless of what he said here.

"Well, just what everyone else has, I suppose," Zoey replied. "Though I heard a rumour it was someone in his family that poisoned, or is suspected of poisoning, him." She looked to Cliff for some sort of approval he wasn't entirely comfortable giving, so he shrugged, which appeared to appease the young woman. "Poor man," Zoey added. "Oh there was one other thing, but it's all just a rumour, I suppose."

"Mum's the word." Kitty smiled, politely, and Cliff thought that Kitty may have missed her calling as a politician with the way she managed to control the situation.

"Rumour has it they're sitting on some sort of gold mine out there."

"You mean the farm?"

"Yeah. Only I mean a *literal* gold mine. Mr. Roberts said he'd seen some sort of geological survey being done out that way, and the tags on the van said it was gold something or other. He didn't think much of it, but with the murder…who knows, maybe someone wants the gold for themselves." Zoey's eyes flashed around the restaurant. "Sorry, I'd better get this in. Like I said, though, just some rumours, but it certainly makes for a good story." She laughed and ran off, disappearing into the kitchen.

"That can't be real. Gold?" Bunty said, shaking her head.

"A lot of people have killed for gold," Gerald said, a little more vocal now that he was no longer preoccupied with staring down Zoey.

"But could there really be gold there?"

"Canada is well-known for its gold production," Gerald said, shrugging when everyone glanced over at him. "It's an interesting fact."

"He's right. But it's not common in *these* parts," Hans inserted.

"Seems odd though, no?" Cliff turned to look at Hans. "If there were gold on the farm, even a small amount, that Pieter wouldn't have known about it or done anything about it? Isn't it?"

"Maybe he didn't know," Kitty said.

"He had a survey done on the land," Sol pointed out.

"*Someone* had a survey done on the land. You're presuming it was

Pieter, but that may not be the case." Kitty raised her hand as Zoey returned with a round of coffees, water, and a tea for Bunty.

Cliff thought she was suspiciously quiet through all of this, though he thought he could see her mind was like a duck on water, racing under the surface.

"Thank you, Zoey," Cliff said, looking up at the young woman as she placed his coffee down in front of him. "I'm curious, Zoey, what else did you hear about the gold?"

Zoey looked around at the restaurant and, once she was confident she didn't have anywhere to be, she pressed her tray up against her chest and thought for a moment. "Not much, really. Like I said, just some rumours." She shrugged.

"Yeah, but surely there must have been more than just that, no?" Cliff asked.

"Well…" she started hesitantly, then shook her head, thinking better of it. "No, I shouldn't…"

"Just curious, dear," Kitty said, as she mimed zipping her mouth shut.

"You just know how rumours spread in this town."

"True, but eventually, the truth comes out and everyone moves on," Kitty said, trying to reassure the young woman.

Cliff felt bad trying to pressure her into saying what she knew, but whether she understood it or not, she currently had one of the most valuable pieces of information they or anyone else seemed to have on the topic. The fact that she had heard anything about this gold talk was enough. But still, he wasn't in the habit of making anyone do anything they weren't comfortable with.

"It's alright if you don't want to tell us, Zoey, no pressure," he said, hoping he sounded comforting.

"Oh, I *want* to tell you." She laughed awkwardly. "I just…it's just, again, it was Mr. Roberts who was in here yesterday that was telling us about a storm that's come to town. I didn't get it at first, but I began to piece it together. Apparently, Mr. VanWinkle's sister has come back to town and, from what I've heard, she's on some sort of warpath to get the farms handed over to her, since she's technically next in the family, and overturn Pieter's final wishes altogether."

"You mean Cynthia VanWinkle is back in town?" Bunty asked, her eyes nearly bulging out of her head, the entire table turning to look at her unusual reaction.

"Her last name is Stroud now, like the boys," Hans said, looking towards Bunty in surprise.

"I think they called her Cindy, yeah. Do you know her?" Zoey asked curiously, and from the faces of everyone at the table—save for Gerald, who looked as interested as he ever did—they were all wondering the same thing.

"Sort of. Her parents used to drop her off at the library, and all she ever seemed to want to do was terrorize the place. She hated books about as much as she hated this town." Bunty shook her head. "But I haven't seen her since…well, before their father died, at least."

"Same," Hans said. "Though I could hardly blame her for not wanting to come back."

"Why is that?" Kitty asked.

"She was cut out of her father's will. He left everything to Pieter. The oldest son and all that," Hans explained.

"Stupid idea," Kitty scoffed.

"It was a different time," Sol said with a shrug.

"Not that different," Bunty said.

"Since it is still happening," Mrs. Chen agreed.

"Not as much," Sol broke in.

"Not as much isn't *never*," Mrs. Chen pointed out, and her words appeared to have put an end to the conversation regarding the fairness of what happened to Cynthia Stroud.

Cliff understood just how common it was for families to fall apart, especially when it came to matters of money. A problem that persisted no matter where you lived.

"Well anyways, I heard she's back in town and on some sort of mission," Zoey said, glancing around the dining room, her voice dropping conspiratorially. "I even heard a rumour someone spotted her rental car over at the Badger's place just yesterday." Her brows raised in suspicion.

"Interesting," Bunty said slowly.

Cliff had to agree it was rather interesting. Not simply because Pieter hated the Badger, and there was no proof he hadn't been involved with what happened to Pieter. But then again, the other names on the list were her own children and her niece. So, it would be hard to be in town and not see someone under suspicion, he supposed.

"I should get back to my tables. Your food should be ready soon," Zoey said, turning and walking back to the kitchen without another word, leaving a lull in the air.

"Why would Cynthia be going to the Badger's house at all?" Kitty asked.

"I can make a few assumptions." Sol laughed, receiving a whack in the arm from Kitty. "What was that for?" Sol protested.

"You get your mind out of the gutter, Sol Keen."

"It wasn't in the gutter, Kitty," Sol said, sitting up a little straighter in his chair. "I was referring to the fact that she must believe she is in the running for the farms and looking to sell them off to Badger." He turned to look at Kitty. "What were you thinking about, *my love?*" He gave her a mischievous smile.

Even Cliff could see Kitty's cheeks flush red as she shook her head vigorously. "I was thinking the same thing. Obviously," she said hotly.

"Obviously," Sol said with a grin.

This caused a round of laugher at the table, save for Kitty, who was trying to look anything but embarrassed.

Cliff caught a glance of Bunty, who had her hands wrapped around her tea and, although she was laughing with the rest of them, Cliff could tell she was thinking about the information they'd just learned. Cliff knew this because he was doing the same thing.

If Pieter's sister Cindy was, in fact, back in town, and believed she was entitled to the farm along with everyone else, it was likely only going to complicate things. He made a mental note to bring this up with Lou when he spoke with her next. Perhaps she might be able to fill in the blanks where the town's network painted a larger picture.

"As much as I love investing my time into the lives of other people," Mrs. Chen said, tapping the table and leaning in to peer down at everyone, "I hope you've all not forgotten my garden is ruined at the moment, along with my chances of winning this year's garden of the year."

"We haven't forgotten, Mrs. Chen," Hans said.

"What if we can't fix it in time?" Mrs. Chen asked.

"We will," Kitty said with a firm nod, looking happy now that all the attention had moved on from her.

"Of course, we will," Bunty agreed. "All we have to do is assess the damage and take it one step at a time." She clenched her fist and knocked it firmly against the table.

"I appreciate your enthusiasm, but it took me weeks to get it to where it was, and last night nearly ruined all of it."

"It took you weeks of working alone," Hans said. "Now you have the rest of us in your corner, committed to getting it done. Right everyone?"

"Right," they all said, as collective nods came from around the table. Though Cliff thought he spotted Gerald nod rather than actually agree to anything. But, given the determined look on Hans's face, he doubted there was much Gerald could do to get out of helping. And from the resigned look on his face, Gerald knew this as well.

"See, Mrs. Chen, I'm sure everything will work out," Hans said, which appeared to ease the worried expression on Mrs. Chen's face, if only a little.

Cliff wished he shared his friend's optimism, but he'd seen the garden, as well and, given the few days he'd worked on it had nearly destroyed his body, he wondered if the group of them would have it in them to get it fixed up. But he figured this doubt was best kept inside, along with the looming idea that something was seriously wrong.

22

"It's a good idea," Cliff said for the third time that morning as he sat squeezed in between Hans and Bunty in Hans's old pickup truck.

"Are you sure?" Bunty asked. "I just mean with everything going on…" Bunty's voice trailed off. She'd been apprehensive the whole morning, since coming up with the idea of going to visit Hendrik after she'd overheard Hans talking to Mari on the phone.

"Cliff's right," Hans said with a grin, "Hendrik might know something that we don't."

"I suppose. I just feel bad leaving Mrs. Chen," Bunty said.

"Look at it out there," Cliff said, shaking his head, "it's been raining like this for the past day and a half."

"And the radar doesn't look good," Hans said. "I doubt we will see this let up until tomorrow." Hans looked up at the sky. Like all great farmers, Hans was very good at reading the weather radar, since, for most of his life, how and when he worked was dictated by the rain. How on earth someone had the strength to live off the whims of Mother Nature was something Cliff couldn't ever understand. Even now, having to watch Mrs. Chen fret over the state of her garden filled Cliff with anxiety. But doing it repeatedly would have likely driven him mad.

"Poor Mrs. Chen. I mean, all her hard work." Bunty shook her head.

"That is a problem we can solve tomorrow," Cliff said, giving Bunty a gentle pat on the hand. "There is no point in letting another day go by where we don't at least try to figure out what happened to Pieter, right?" He waited for Bunty to give him an affirmative nod. "And honestly, talking to Hendrik is a great idea. I'm just upset I didn't think of it first," Cliff chuckled.

"You did." Bunty smiled, and Cliff looked at her curiously. "You were the one who suggested talking to everyone with keys."

"Did I?" Cliff asked, getting a nod from Bunty. "Right then," Cliff said, although Bunty's admission felt hollow.

Even if he *had* thought of it first, he'd forgotten all about it. Lately, he'd been feeling one step behind, as if he was losing his edge or something. Or perhaps, he was just out of practice. He hoped it was the latter, since he would rather be slower, than losing the one part of himself he'd always been proud of—his mind.

"You're sure he'll be there?"

"As sure as I can be," Hans said as he pulled up to a short, red brick building off James Street.

Cliff had been past it many times, though he'd never paid much attention to the innocuous-looking building.

"Mari said he rents office space here for when he's in town. I guess he has an agreement with the owner." Hans shrugged.

"Well, it's lucky for us he's still in town," Cliff said.

"You don't think he would leave, do you?" Bunty asked. "What with everything going on with his uncle? I mean, isn't he under suspicion, just like everyone else?"

"Yes. Though I don't really know what he has to gain from any of this," Cliff said. "I suspect he's just sticking around as a courtesy to the family."

It wasn't hard to find Hendrik's office once they got inside, since there wasn't much in the building besides a few other small offices, all of which appeared listed on a sign on the way in.

"Hans!" Hendrik said. He shuffled some papers around on his desk and stood to greet the big man. "How are you?" He reached to shake Hans's hand.

"I'm good, son," Hans said, "and I appreciate you taking the time to chat with us."

"I won't lie, I wasn't too surprised to hear from you. I've heard you and your friends here are doing a little side sleuthing into Uncle Pieter's death." He gestured for them all to take a seat, though there were only two chairs.

Cliff opted to stand and look around as Hans and Bunty sat.

"You heard that, did you?" Hans said rather sheepishly.

"You've hardly been subtle." Hendrik laughed. "Mari, Uncle Lucas, Flynn. He was the one who actually called me." Henrik leaned back in his chair and swivelled from side to side, looking relaxed.

"I hope you don't mind—" Hans said, but Hendrik raised a hand to stop him.

"No. Don't apologize for anything. I think we all want to know what happened to Uncle Pieter, though I am a little surprised they think anyone did it at all. I mean, I spoke with the police, and it seems like he just had a horrible accident." Hendrik shook his head.

"You spoke to the police already?" Cliff asked.

"Yeah, a couple days ago. One of the reasons I'm still in town, in case they needed anything more. Though I admit I am eager to get back to the city sooner than later. Anything more than a few days here tends to make me a little stir crazy," Hendrik joked. "I'm sure you understand, Mr. Shaw. I hear you lived in Toronto as well?"

Cliff turned to look at the young man who would certainly be described as handsome, especially with his flashy suit that was quite out of place in a small town like St. Marys. "I was a detective there for fifty years."

"Do you miss it?" Hendrik asked.

Cliff opened his mouth to say the obvious answer that was on his lips. Which was, of course he missed it. The busy streets, people all around, the food. Compared to St. Marys, Toronto was a mecca. It was hard not to miss things about it.

"I don't miss the traffic," Cliff said with a smile. "And the company here is a little better," he admitted, seeing a smile on both Hans's and Bunty's faces.

"Well, I can certainly understand the traffic. It's a nightmare on sixteen lanes," Hendrik chuckled. "Now, what would you like to know?"

Hans looked over at Bunty and back at Cliff, and when Bunty didn't speak but pulled out her notepad, Cliff supposed it was his turn to take the lead.

"Well, I guess you can start by telling us what you remember from the day?" Cliff asked.

"I mean, it was busy. Uncle Pieter was expecting a ton of people, and the place was really starting to fill up. I had decided to take the day off to come help, since I know it was such an important day for the farm."

"I know it meant a lot to your uncle." Hans smiled as the two men shared a moment together.

"What else do you remember?" Cliff asked.

"Not much, I'm afraid. I was just in charge of getting supplies. Yes, I had a key to the shed where my uncle was found, and yes, I was in and out of there for most of the day, and no, I didn't see anything. Sorry, it's just I've already been through this with the police. Besides, I was already in town, unfortunately, when I heard about Uncle Pieter."

"You weren't at the fair?"

"No. I got a call from the office asking me to get some documents signed. I was annoyed, because I was supposed to have the day off, but they pay my bills. Soo..." Hendrik shrugged. "I didn't find out about any of this until Mari called me to tell me what happened."

"That must have been hard," Bunty said.

"It was awful. Honestly, I didn't really understand what was happening, and none of it really felt real until I got to the farm and saw everyone. It's terrible. But for what it's worth, I don't understand how anyone in my family could do this. I said as much to the police."

"You seem pretty sure it was all an accident then?" Cliff asked.

"Well, when the alternative is, you know"—he waved a hand in the air—"yes. I don't want to think about that possibility."

"No one wants to, son," Hans said, shaking his head.

"Yeah." The room fell silent for a second while Hendrik appeared to ponder something, though he managed to shake the thought away. "Look, I don't want to push you out," he said looking at his watch, "but I do actually need to get back to work."

"What do you do again?" Cliff asked.

"I work for Harrison Edwards; it's an investment firm in the city."

"Sounds interesting," Cliff said.

"If you like analyzing company financials, it's the job for you," Hendrik mused.

"I'll leave that to you," Cliff said.

Hans and Bunty stood up from their chairs to leave. Fair enough. Considering Hendrik wasn't even at the fair when Pieter died, it would be very difficult for him to poison him. But perhaps not impossible.

Still, one thing in particular was still weighing on Cliff. "You mentioned a deal to your uncle. What was that about?"

"A deal?" Henrik paused. "Oh, you mean the offer, yeah well, and I suppose it's not much of a secret now, but Flynn had told me about his plans to purchase another farm, and when I asked him how he was going to get the money, he, after some persuasion, told me what he was doing. I told my brother to put the money back and that I would speak to Uncle Pieter about putting some money into the farm for an ownership percentage. I figured I could expand my portfolio. Flynn could have capital to expand the farm and everyone would be happy."

"You were just going to give them money for the farm?"

"I mean, I was going to buy a stake in the farm. It's no secret in my family that I don't really care about farming. But I have the means to help, and honestly, when I heard what that bastard Badger was doing to them, I figured what the hell?" Hendrik shrugged.

"And do you think your uncle was going to do it?" Cliff asked.

"It was a good offer, I think. But I suppose we'll never know."

"Are you still planning on making the offer?" Cliff asked.

"Once all this is sorted out, I don't see why I wouldn't. Hell, it's still the family farm," Hendrik said.

"Thank you for taking the time to talk with us," Cliff said as he stepped out of the office, with Hans and Bunty saying their goodbyes behind him.

"Thank you all for taking an interest in Uncle Pieter's death. I honestly just wish I had more information for you." Hendrik shrugged as he shook Hans's hand.

A few moments later, they were wet from the rain and back sitting in Hans's truck.

"Well, what do you think?" Hans asked, looking over at Cliff and Bunty.

"Besides being obviously from the city," Cliff said, "I don't see how or why he would want Pieter dead."

"Not to mention, he wasn't even there," Bunty said.

"So, a waste of time then?" Hans asked.

"Not quite," Cliff said. "Assuming he was telling the truth, and we have no reason right now to believe he wasn't, then Flynn was planning on putting the money he'd been taking back before Pieter was killed."

"Why does that matter?" Hans asked.

"It means he didn't have a reason for wanting Pieter dead," Bunty said.

"So?" Hans asked, clearly not understanding what the implications of any of this could be.

"So," Bunty said, "it means…" She stopped, and Cliff didn't want her to be the one to have to say it out loud.

"It means, right now, everything points back to Mari."

23

It wasn't until midmorning Tuesday that the rain alleviated enough for them to get out and assess the real damage to Mrs. Chen's garden. Although not an expert, even Cliff instantly realized that the repair work would be extensive, and it didn't take a genius to see that Mrs. Chen felt the same way.

In fact, the only person who appeared mildly optimistic about the entire situation was Hans. Although, in the many years that Cliff had known his old friend, he'd never known him to be very pessimistic about much of anything. It was his best, most annoying quality.

One of the few positives everyone could agree on was that it had at least stopped raining, and the dark clouds were moving swiftly by, breaking up into smaller chunks, allowing ribbons of sunshine to pass through them every now and then. It was actually quite pleasant, Cliff thought, but this wasn't enough to cheer everyone up. Breakfast might have been good for their bellies and for their morning, but seeing the amount of work there was to do, Cliff already felt tired.

Even with all seven members of the house helping, including Gerald, who Cliff perhaps shouldn't have been surprised was quite adept at tending to plants, by the end of that first afternoon, they'd only managed to restore less than a fifth of the damaged garden. Given how much Cliff's body was aching by that afternoon, he couldn't fathom how he was possibly going to last even one more day, let alone three until the judges arrived.

That evening, it was a relatively quiet dinner. It was a nice, hearty minestrone soup Gerald had somehow managed to whip up that afternoon. It was a wonderful contrast to the cold, windy day, and to Cliff, it was just what his body needed. From the looks of everyone else, he believed it was the same for them as well.

"Interesting day," Cliff said, as he placed the last pile of dishes on the kitchen counter. Bunty had already filled the sink up with soap and hot water and was beginning to tackle the small tower of dishes left over from dinner and Gerald's cooking.

"I suppose that's one way of saying it." Bunty gave Cliff a tight smile. "Poor Mrs. Chen." She shook her head, and Cliff suspected her own thoughts were the same as his, that it would be a miracle if they could manage to get the garden done in time. Although no words were said aloud about it, it was just the feeling in the air.

"Yes," Cliff said, passing behind Bunty and grabbing a drying cloth from off the stove handle. "We still have a couple days."

"True," she said, with another thin smile. "I've been thinking." She placed one of the clean plates in the drying rack for Cliff to pick up and begin to wipe down. "Cynthia VanWinkle, or Stroud, I suppose now…" She stopped as if this was a thought on its own. And perhaps it may have been, but not one Cliff was privy to, so after a moment of letting the thought linger, he finally spoke up.

"What about her?"

"Well, it's just interesting, isn't it? That she would come now. After all these years."

"Is it? I mean, from what Hans told me, she didn't leave on great terms. Perhaps she thinks this is her chance to get something."

"You think this is all about money?" Bunty asked.

"It usually is. People do all sorts of strange things when they think they'll get money out of it."

"But her brother just died."

"I think it's more likely Cynthia was told that her sons were going to be left out of the estate, just like she was, and now she's going to take what they deserve," Cliff said with a shrug, ignoring the look of disappointment on Bunty's face.

There was no doubt in Cliff's mind that years of working as a detective had made him more than a little jaded and cynical. And maybe he would be wrong here, but with all the information they had in front of them, he doubted this story would end with a reunited family at the end of it. Especially when it appeared more than likely to be one of them responsible for Pieter's death.

"Anger can cloud our better judgment," Bunty said, as if this clarified the entirety of her thoughts on the matter, and perhaps, in a way, it did.

"Still, I'd love to know more about Cynthia's conversation with the Badger."

"You mean if she did chat with him at all. The gossip around town might be better treated as scripture, best left up for interpretation." Bunty smiled.

"I'm surprised to hear you say that," Cliff mused, knowing this was a woman dedicated to the church and its choir every Sunday.

"It's no history book, and there are far too many 'begats,' and not enough of the women who had to beget them all. A blind spot such as that surely deserves to be open for discussion, no?"

Cliff thought about this for a moment and couldn't argue with her logic. "You may very well be right, but if she did talk to him, I would have enjoyed being a fly on the wall for that. Surely, she must understand how bad it looks to be speaking with him, what with everything going on."

"You don't know Cynthia." Bunty chuckled. "That young woman never did know how to be subtle."

"People change," Cliff said with a shrug.

"Perhaps. But people also have an innate capacity to hold onto grudges for far too long," Bunty said. "No matter what my thoughts were about her as a child, I would never agree with how she was treated by her father. Something like that sits with a person for longer than we would care to admit." Bunty soaked a plate and gave it a scrub with the dishcloth as she shook her head. "Now her sons appear to be treated the same way." She rinsed the plate and handed it over to Cliff. "One could hardly say it's fair."

Cliff took the plate and began rubbing it down. He agreed with Bunty that much of what happened to Cynthia wasn't fair, and he couldn't blame her for being angry.

But what was her plan then?

"I'm confused," Cliff said.

"Not a good sign at our age, Cliff," Bunty joked, giving Cliff an elbow in his side.

"No, not like that," he chuckled. "I mean about this situation."

"Go on."

"Well, hypothetically, if someone deliberately poisoned Pieter, knowing he had a deadly peanut allergy, then who? I know Mari has the most to lose, Flynn was stealing from the farm, Hendrik was proposing to invest the farm. And Lucas and Cynthia both have complicated relationships with Pieter. Then there is Aria, who we saw with Pieter just before he died. And then the Badger, who, despite everything people say about him, doesn't seem like the kind of person who would kill someone over land. Not when he has other means of persuasion."

"So where are you confused?"

"I don't understand why anyone would want him dead."

"You just gave plenty of reasons," Bunty said.

"Did I though? People are upset, and I know you don't want to think it"—Cliff felt guilty even bringing it up, but in his mind, these were the facts—"but only Mari had any real reason to want her father dead. Between the new will, which cuts Mari's share of the farm down, and the prospect of at least some of that remaining share going to Hendrik if Pieter were to sell, it doesn't look all together that good for Mari."

"But the others?" Bunty said, obviously frustrated by this line of thought, but there wasn't much Cliff could do to make her feel better.

"I know, but if Flynn wanted to keep his dealings a secret, surely killing Pieter would have only shone a light on what he was doing. Hendrik would have needed Pieter alive to purchase ownership in the farm, and Cynthia and Lucas are angry, but his farm is only worth a couple of million—if that, after the debts—and they are not in the will anyway. None of which is enough to warrant a death."

"What if it isn't about money?" Bunty asked. "Maybe someone just wanted him dead?"

Cliff took another plate from Bunty and began wiping it down. He didn't say it, but he certainly wasn't convinced this wasn't somehow about more than just Pieter's death. It seemed strange to him that anyone would just want this man dead for no reason. Perhaps there were a few people in his family who may have had enough anger to want to hurt him, or even destroy his business. But to kill someone is entirely different, especially when you realize that, in order for them to do it, they had to plan it out, make sure Pieter was somewhere no one could help him, and give them time to get out of there unseen. That takes planning and thought. No, whoever did this figured they could get away with it, and the payoff would have had to be worth the risk.

"What do you make of this gold idea?" Cliff said, bringing his mind back into the kitchen.

"Seems like a neat story," Bunty said with a shrug.

"What? So no gold then?" Cliff asked.

"A little unlikely that there would be gold on the property that no one has noticed until now."

"But Gerald was right, Canada is known for its gold production."

"Yes. But mostly up north. Down here, it's not really something you see," Bunty said, and Cliff remembered that Bunty was the type of person who picked up on a lot of things. Knowing her husband had been in the industry must have given her a little more insight into this world than Cliff, who had spent most of his life living in the city.

"So, no gold then?" Cliff said unable to hide the disappointment in his voice.

"Unlikely," Bunty said with a shrug as she handed Cliff another plate. "But that doesn't mean there isn't something else there. Assuming the survey was done and isn't just another rumour."

"How could we check that? Can we check that?"

"Umm." Bunty stopped her work to give it some thought. "No," she answered after a minute, before picking up another plate and dunking it into the sink. "Surveys done on private land don't need to be processed through the municipality, unless you want to use them for development of some kind."

"How do you know that?"

"I worked in the clerk's office for a summer before I realized that working for the town was not my calling. And given how difficult it is to get the rules changed, I am suspecting that this also hasn't changed."

"So, hypothetically, if someone had a survey done, it wouldn't need to be recorded anywhere."

"Other than a record with the company who completed the survey, but you couldn't get your hands on those documents unless you owned the land the survey was conducted on."

"So does that mean Pieter would have needed to be the one who requested the survey?" Cliff asked, trying to wrap his head around this idea that could also be a complete waste of time.

He was starting to feel like his brain going around in circles, his body was aching from the work in the yard that afternoon, and all he really wanted to do was go to sleep. But still, there was a minute portion of his brain that he believed was putting the pieces of the puzzle together, even if he didn't quite have the whole picture yet.

"Yes," Bunty said as she dumped a plateful of utensils into the soapy water.

Pausing, he reflected, "Though I guess if you had access to the land, you could get something done. It wouldn't necessarily be by the book, though."

"Great. So anyone could have done it."

"Maybe. If they knew someone who was willing to come in and do it for them," Bunty agreed. "But they would still need to know them, since it is illegal to do it without the landowner's permission."

"But if they thought the landowner knew, then they could get away with it?"

"In theory. I suppose..." Bunty thought for a moment. "Couldn't the police just get a warrant check? We could ask Lou."

"They could. But Lou would have to tell them why, and given our history with Captain Marks, I can't imagine he would be all that keen on ordering a search warrant because we heard a rumour at a diner. Do you?"

"No. But..." Bunty stopped when they heard a knock on the front door. "Who could that be?"

Cliff shrugged as he finished wiping down the last plate and set it on the clean pile. Tossing the towel over his shoulder, he made his way towards the front door.

The first thing he heard was Kitty, sounding annoyed as she stood by the open front door.

"You do realize that it is the evening, do you not?"

"I'm sorry to come so late, Kitty. But it's important."

Cliff immediately recognized that it was Jan, sounding more than a little flustered.

"What is so important, Jan, that it couldn't wait until a decent time of day to come visit?"

"This," Jan said.

Cliff peered around Kitty just in time to see Jan waving a manilla folder in the air.

"Paperwork, Jan. Honestly. At this hour," Kitty scoffed.

"It's not… I mean it is…technically," Jan said, as he tried to navigate his way around Kitty. "It was delivered to the paper, to me."

"Sounds like it should be a *you* problem then." Kitty attempted to close the door, but Jan put a hand out to stop her.

"Please, Kitty, I just need to talk to Cliff for a moment," Jan said.

Cliff sighed as Kitty shot him a look that appeared to imply this was somehow all his fault.

"Just let the boy in, Kitty," Sol shouted from the other room. "This crib game isn't going to finish itself, and I would like to get to win before I go to sleep."

"It's cute that you believe you'll win," Kitty shouted back. "Alright then." She waved her hand for Jan to enter.

"Thank you, Kitty," Jan said, shoving the folder in front of Cliff's face as he entered the house. "You are not going to believe what is in this folder."

"Must be something good to risk Kitty's wrath at this time of night, Jan," Cliff said.

He heard Bunty's light footsteps behind him and, turning, saw her eyes falling curiously on the folder, savouring the moment. Cliff knew that Bunty enjoyed all of this nearly as much as he did. Perhaps even more.

He led her and Jan into the library, where they sat as Jan dramatically tossed the folder on the table.

23

"It was delivered anonymously…to me!" he said, not bothering to hide his excitement. "Can you believe it? Someone delivered me a news scoop."

"What's in it?" Cliff asked.

"I'm not sure. I haven't opened it," Jan said, his enthusiasm not fading.

"You haven't opened it?" Bunty asked.

"No."

"So, how do you know it's important?" Cliff asked.

"Look at it, Cliff. It's a manilla folder. Anonymously dropped off at the paper with my name on it. What else could it be?"

"Literally anything, Jan," Cliff said, shaking his head. "Why didn't you look at it?"

"I was nervous. It's never happened to me before," Jan said.

"I can tell you're excited," Cliff said, placing a hand on Jan's shoulder, "but for all you know, it's someone interested in putting wedding photos into the paper." Cliff watched as the wind got knocked out of Jan's sails.

"Well, perhaps we should open it up and see," Bunty suggested as she picked up the folder and began to open it.

"Wait!" Jan shouted, causing Bunty to flinch.

She stopped and looked up at him.

"Jan!" Kitty shouted from the other room.

"Sorry. It's just, what if there's something dangerous in it?" Jan asked, his head swivelling between Bunty and Cliff as Bunty paused to share a look with Cliff. He could see the concern in her eyes.

"We're in St. Marys, not Chicago in 1926. I'm sure we're fine," Cliff said, but noticed this did little to appease Bunty, who appeared to be re-examining the folder.

Cliff put his hand out, and she reluctantly handed it over to him. Carefully, though he wasn't sure why, since he was confident it would just contain papers, but a small part of him was slightly embarrassed by the fact that he was nervous, he opened the folder. "If this is how I go, please don't tell anyone." He smiled grimly as he peered inside the envelope and pulled out a bundle of papers.

"What is it?" Jan asked, leaning in towards Cliff as he laid the papers out on the table between them.

"Documents?" Bunty asked. She picked one up and began to examine them. "Old documents." She pointed to the now-faint date at the top of the page. "1956."

Jan grabbed another one of the pages and began to read it. "I knew it was something important."

"We don't know what they…" Cliff started, but was cut off by Bunty.

"Cliff." She held out one of the papers she'd been reading.

"What is it?"

"I think Jan might be right. These documents are all for Winkleberry Farm."

24

"How did you get these?" Cliff asked, sifting through the contents of the papers now laid out on the table between them.

"I told you, they showed up on my desk," Jan said, his fingers fanning out like he was performing some sort of magic trick.

Cliff looked up at him and shook his head.

"What? I'm telling you, I don't know who dropped them off."

"You don't have any cameras or anything?" Cliff asked.

"We aren't overly concerned about theft, considering we don't have much in the building of any value."

"So that's a no then?" Cliff took a seat in his chair as he scanned the documents. There must have been a few hundred pages in the folder.

"Some of these go back to the fifties," Bunty said, the excitement in her voice energizing Cliff, who couldn't remember the last time he'd been given anonymous papers. Even he had to admit it was a bit of a rush.

"You haven't looked though any of these, Jan?" Cliff asked.

"Nope, brought it over here, in case there was something I was supposed to do with them." Jan shrugged.

"You should take them to the police," Cliff said, though he didn't sound as convincing as he should have. He was retired, and the local police were in charge of this murder investigation, not him. But when someone drops off mysterious papers, it's hard not to get wrapped up in the intrigue of it all.

"I did." Jan smiled, gesturing to Cliff.

"You know that's not what I mean," Cliff smirked.

"I know, but if I did that, I doubt they would let me go through them, and I have to imagine there was a reason someone decided to drop them off to *me* instead of going to the police. It felt disrespectful to not at least look at them." Jan moved in and picked up a few of the pages and sat down in the chair next to Cliff.

Skittles entered the room and leapt up to sit, inconveniently, on the remaining pages.

Historically, Cliff wasn't a pet person, but he had to admit he rather liked having the little guy wandering around. And the fact that he mostly kept to himself suited Cliff very well.

"Shoo, Skittles," Jan said, waving a hand in Skittles's general direction. The cat simply waved its tail and stared absently back at him. "Cats." His head shook and he rolled his eyes, as if this summed up the entirety of the species.

Cliff continued to review some of the pages in front him, though he was having trouble understanding what most of them were. He could tell they all had something to do with Winkleberry Farm, since it was referenced in many of the pages. But they looked a little like some sort of legal document.

"It's a will," Bunty said finally. "At least, I think it is." She pulled out one of the pages for Cliff to take. Like the others, it was older and some of the writing was missing, but it wasn't all gone.

"Pieter's will?" Cliff asked.

"No. Too old for that. Pieter's father's, perhaps?"

"What about Johan?" Hans asked as he stepped into the library, looking around the room before his eyes settled on Jan. "I'm not sure if I should be jealous you're not here to see me, or just happy to see you, Jan."

"Sorry, Opa, I just got carried away with all of this," he said gesturing to the pile of papers, most of which were being spread out on the table as Skittles rolled over them.

"What are they? Besides something to do with Johan VanWinkle?" Hans asked, walking over, tilting his head to look at the papers.

"We think maybe a will or something. It was left on my desk at the office," Jan said.

"Very cloak and dagger," Hans laughed. "And you think it's a will?"

"Or some other sort of legal document. There are a few legal clauses on that page there." Bunty gestured to the sheet Cliff was now holding, though he hadn't had a chance to look at it himself.

He had faith that Bunty did know what she was referring to, plus Cliff had seen enough evidence on his pages to come to a similar conclusion. Why someone would be dropping off fifty-year-old legal documents to Jan still made little sense to him.

"Umm," Hans said, glancing down at one of the papers on the table, "I think you're right about legal documents." He bent over to pick up a paper he'd spotted using one hand to brace his back as he did.

"You alright, Opa?" Jan asked.

Hans lifted Skittles off the page, barely fazing the old cat. He continued to stare up at them all with what Cliff assessed to be mild annoyance.

"Fine, just a long day in the garden. Mrs. Chen's flowers got hit pretty hard by rain, and we have been trying to salvage them before the judges come this week," Hans said, giving his lower back a light rub as he held up a paper.

"That's terrible. Do you think she'll be able to repair it?" Jan asked.

Cliff, Hans and Bunty all shared a look. None of them seemed to want to say what they were thinking aloud.

"We'll have to see what tomorrow brings, but I'm sure it will all work out," Hans said, giving Jan a thin smile. It didn't really satisfy the young man, but he didn't press the matter further. "This, on the other hand, is something that I can answer," Hans said, a more genuine smile coming to his lips.

"What is that?" Bunty asked.

"Well, I can't speak to the other pages, but this was the header for one of the old surveying companies in the area, MacDunn's. They used to do all the work in this area before they were bought up."

"How do you know it's theirs?" Bunty asked, squinting as the page which, like the others, was very worn out.

"It's faint, but I can see their old insignia on the page, and you can barely make out the name under it, but I'm sure that's who it was."

"What did they do?" Cliff asked.

"Surveyed farmland, created legal documents to protect borders for land ownership, changed land designations. Pretty much everything someone would need to adjust something on their land, these guys did."

"So why would someone give us a bunch of worn-out land documents?" Cliff asked.

"Maybe they want us to find something?" Jan said. Everyone looked at him. "What?"

Cliff didn't have to say it, since he knew Bunty and Hans were all on the same page in the understanding that someone wanted them to find something. But with no leads on what to look for, or the ability to read all of the documents, since some of them were so worn they would have been lucky to get twenty-five percent of it, it would be a challenge.

"Well, I mean, obviously, they want us to find something," Jan restated, as he must have clocked the amused expressions on their faces. "I just mean it must be in here somewhere, right? Even if it all seems a bit...faded?" Jan gestured to a nearly bare sheet of paper.

"Perhaps," Cliff said looking over the pages. "But without any idea what we're looking for this could be…"

"Tedious," Bunty offered.

"Yes," Cliff said, giving her a nod.

"What is tedious?" Kitty asked, as she stepped into the living room with Sol behind her.

"We've got all these pages, and we're not sure what we're looking for," Bunty said.

"That *is* tedious," Kitty said shaking her head. "Why exactly are you reading all of these papers?"

"We're not sure yet, but we think it might have something to do with Pieter's death," Jan said, which received some glares from Hans and Cliff. "What I said is, we *think*…which means we don't know. Which we don't," Jan said, holding his hands up in defence.

Kitty stepped over to the table and picked up one of the sheets and began reading it. "There is nearly nothing in these pages," she said, waving the paper.

"We know," Cliff said, letting out a heavy sigh.

"Well," Kitty said, picking up a couple more pages and handing them over to a very confused-looking Sol before picking up some more.

"What is this?" Sol asked.

"We can hardly let them do it alone. They'll be up all night."

"Kitty, you really don't have to…" Hans started, but Kitty's hand was already shushing him.

Sol looked as though he was about to object, but the look Kitty shot him sent the man back down to the couch instead, where he began reading.

"What's the system here, Bunty? I presume you have one?" Kitty asked.

"System for what?" Mrs. Chen asked. She came in, wrapped up in her house coat and holding a cup of tea in her hands.

"We're trying to find information in these documents," Jan said.

"And no, we don't know what we're looking for exactly."

"Sounds tedious," Mrs. Chen said.

"Very," Kitty agreed.

"Yet here we are all the same," Sol said with a thin smile.

Mrs. Chen approached the table and picked up a small stack of pages.

"Mrs. Chen, you should get some rest. You've had a long day," Hans said, putting a hand up to stop her from taking the pages.

But she pushed it aside. "I have. But I could use the distraction at the moment," she said, giving him a tired smile.

Cliff got the sense that, despite holding it together for most of the day, the reality of the situation with the garden was very upsetting to her. He could hardly blame her, since she'd spent the better part of a year planning it out and it took all of two nights to nearly ruin all of her hard work. He wondered if her body and mind would even let her sleep if she tried.

As it turned out, Bunty did, of course, have a system she believed would be the most effective for the type of search. Since, of course, they didn't know what they were looking for, and they couldn't be sure what was or wasn't useful.

"What we need to do is scan the papers and sort them by relevance. We'll keep it simple. We will have four piles. One for unread pages. One that has been scanned once with no references, one that has been scanned twice with no references, and lastly, a pile for pages that reference the farm or the land or that contain something we think is useful," Bunty said, signalling small sections of the table. "We can narrow down the field of relevance as we go until, hopefully, something makes sense."

"Tedious indeed," Kitty said, but despite her head shaking, she settled into a couch and began reading.

Cliff wondered if the library had ever been so full in its history, with all the available seats being used, along with the window banquettes, and an old-looking chaise longue that Cliff had never really noticed. It was being occupied by Sol, who, on more than one occasion, nodded off with a paper blocking his face. He may have gotten away with the sleeping had it not been for the not-so-light snoring that was often short-lived before Kitty smacked him awake.

Sol wasn't the only one who was tired, and by the time they'd managed to get three-quarters of the papers done, it was nearly eleven at night and well past all of their bedtimes. One of the saving graces was Gerald, who Cliff had assumed had gone off to bed. But he returned with some light snacks and tea for the house. Perhaps even more surprising was that he picked up a stack of papers and began reading.

If Cliff hadn't be so tired, he might have felt something along the lines of pride in his housemates for all coming together at this time. But as it was, with the work in the garden and now this little game of spot-the-inconsistency, he wasn't feeling much of anything. But it was when he began to catch himself reading the same line twice, he knew from experience he was nearly done. At a certain point, he knew they would have to call it off and let everyone get some sleep and revisit it another time.

Looking at the table, he saw the dwindling stack of papers, though they hadn't dwindled enough that they would finish tonight. There might have been only a couple of dozen papers left, but everyone was exhausted. Sol was oblivious, as he'd propped himself up with a free pillow and was blissfully sleeping.

"Perhaps it's best if you all go to bed," Jan said, stifling a yawn.

"What? Now?" Kitty said, gesturing to the pile. "When we're so close?"

"I can finish it up tonight, and we can all go over it in the morning," he said, forcing a smile.

"How will we know if we've found what we're looking for?" Mrs. Chen asked.

"I'm not sure," Jan said. "Cliff?"

"I was kind of hoping it would jump out at us when we found whatever it was."

"You thought maybe we would find some sort of admission of guilt from sixty-year-old documents?" Kitty joked.

"Maybe not admission, but something to point us to why all of this might have happened."

"Like what?"

Cliff put a hand over his mouth to block his yawn as he struggled to speak. His mind was like molasses and each thought came slowly to him. "Who knows, something with the farm, or, I don't know, anything."

"It is a farm, isn't it?" Bunty said almost imperceptibly and mostly to herself, though that didn't prevent everyone from turning to look at her, causing her face to flush red.

"Yes, Bunty, Winkleberry Farm is a farm," Kitty said, causing a deeper shade of red to brush Bunty's cheeks.

"Of course. It's just something I thought I read in one of the pages. I didn't think much of it at the time, but now I can't believe I missed it," she said, rummaging through the pages, until she found the page she was searching for and held it up. "Yes. Here." She pointed to the page.

"What is it?" Cliff asked.

"It's the land designation for the farm," she said as a smile came to her face.

"It's late, Bunty. I believe it would be best to be direct," Kitty said, waving a hand towards the paper. "What is it you're saying?"

"I'm saying that, according to this document, Pieter's father had the land designation changed in the sixties from farmland to EI. I can't believe it slipped my mind, but it seems so obvious now that I'm looking at it."

"Still not obvious to the rest of us," Kitty said.

"It is to me," Hans said, shaking his head.

"Care to fill the rest of us in?" Jan said.

"All farmland in Ontario is either A1 or A2 designation. It basically means it's zoned for agricultural use," Hans said.

Cliff, who knew very little about land designation, was starting to feel his brain tighten up as it tried to understand the significance of it all, which only made him realize just how tired he was.

"So what is EI then?" Cliff asked.

"It means extractive industrial," Bunty said, with an enthusiasm which was utterly unmatched by the rest of the house except for Hans. "Right, well, it's the designation you need to set up a mine."

The pieces suddenly clicked into place in Cliff's mind, and from the sounds made around him, the others seemed to draw the same conclusion.

Gold.

<h1 style="text-align:center">25</h1>

The conversation had diminished at the prospect of gold being found anywhere near St. Marys and, given the late hour and the fact that Sol and Gerald had both fallen asleep, it seemed best that everyone should go and get some rest. Cliff wasn't surprised by the fact that, when he woke the next morning, he entered a very lively household.

Mrs. Chen was already in her gardening boots, with her wicker basket, complete with pruning shears and gloves sitting beside the door, as she finished up her tea on the living room couch. The conversation she'd been sharing with Sol and Kitty was impressively animated for six in the morning.

"They don't call it a gold mine for nothing," Sol said, shaking his head.

"Surely, they wouldn't just allow them to tear up such a beautiful farm," Kitty said.

"Never underestimate what one is willing to do for money," Mrs. Chen said, as she tapped the side of her tea mug and glanced out the window.

Cliff could tell that her mind was split between the present moment and all the work she would need to get to today to have things ready for the judges coming in just two days. Today was going to be a long day for everyone, but with any luck, they would be back in time to assist Mrs. Chen in the garden.

No matter how much my body might protest.

"You're all up early," Cliff said as he passed through the living room heading for the kitchen, where he was happy to find a full pot of coffee. He wasn't questioning their reasons, as he suspected the unusually busy morning was for similar reasons as to why *he* was up and ready to go.

"Who could sleep with all that's going on?" Kitty said, taking a sip of her coffee.

"Me," Sol said, shaking his head. "I could have slept, had it not been for the endless questions."

"Well, pardon me for finding a little intrigue in the situation, Sol," Kitty said, swatting his arm, which he pretended hurt much more than it likely did, playing it up to the others.

"You see what I was dealing with?"

"It certainly is interesting though," Mrs. Chen said, her hands hugging her tea as she shook her head with mild confusion. "I just don't understand what any of this has to do with Pieter's death. I mean, surely this all can't be about land."

"It's about revenge," Kitty said.

"Here we go," Sol chuckled.

"Don't you chuckle at me, Sol Keen."

"What do you mean, Kitty?" Cliff asked, curious to know what prompted Kitty to be so animated at this hour of the morning.

"Thank you, Cliff. At least one person appreciates my input." Kitty's chin shot up as Sol rolled his eyes and waved a hand as if to say *fine get on with it.* "What if it was a setup?" Her voice dropped low and conspiratorial as Cliff took a seat on the couch beside Mrs. Chen.

"A setup for who?"

"Pieter."

"But Pieter died," Cliff said.

"Exactly! And the first obvious culprit is Mari, who appears to have the most to gain from all of this."

"Except she loved her father," Sol objected.

"Exactly!" Kitty said, as if they were all following her mind. "But if you can make it look like she didn't…"

Cliff thought he understood where all of this was going now, but he thought it best to let her finish.

"…then she would take the blame, and the entire farm would go to the next ones in line, Cynthia and Lucas. Both of them were snubbed by their father."

Cliff also knew that Lucas's entire life had been torn up, and there was a chance that Pieter was the one who ruined it. He didn't know much about Cynthia, but from what he'd heard so far, she was good at holding a grudge. Though none of this was built on evidence, it was sounding like plausible story.

"So, what do they do? Devise an elaborate plan to seek their revenge and finally get their hands on what they believe they deserve," Kitty said with a nod of satisfaction.

The room was quiet for a moment. Cliff, who was busy poking holes in this theory in his mind, imagined the others were doing the same. None of them appeared to want to speak up about it first.

"It's an interesting thought, Kitty," Cliff finally said, which earned him a smile, though he knew it would be short-lived. "It's just, there may be a couple of issues with your story."

"Like what?"

"Well, for one, Cynthia lives in Calgary and, from what we know, was there at the time of Pieter's death. Which means she would have had to convince Lucas to kill Pieter, but since the land transfer is to the next eldest, Lucas wouldn't have had anything to gain from helping her. He would have been putting his faith in someone who was willing to kill their brother, taking all the risk, without any guarantee of the reward."

"Perhaps Cynthia is very convincing?" Kitty suggested.

"I'm not sure anyone is that convincing," Sol said.

"Can you get me more coffee, my love?" Kitty asked.

Sol glanced down at his own barely touched coffee. Still, he stood up to grab her a coffee. "Of course."

When Sol left the room, Kitty smiled. "Women can be very convincing." She let out a little laugh as the others joined in.

"I think it is an interesting theory, Kitty. But, unfortunately, we don't know enough to say what happened one way or another."

"It would help if we knew what the police were thinking," Kitty said. "Speaking of, have you heard from Lou at all?"

"Not in a couple of days, and I suspect she's been told to avoid us, or rather, has been avoiding any confrontation with Captain Marks on account of us." Cliff said, though admittedly he'd been wondering the same thing. Since learning that the police presumed Mari was the culprit, Lou had all but disappeared, and he found himself wishing he could have more information. So far, everything they had was circumstantial, and nothing pointed to a clear culprit.

"What is his problem?" Kitty said as Sol dropped off her coffee, his own topped up as well. "Thank you, my love," she said, sending a wink toward Cliff and Mrs. Chen.

"I don't want to know." Sol shook his head.

"You're right." Kitty smiled. "As I was saying, you would think the important thing is to find the person responsible. Surely, if we can assist with that, then it is helpful, no?"

"It's not really police policy to invite civilians into investigations, let alone a possible murder." Cliff shrugged.

"I still can't believe he's gone," Hans said appearing in the doorway by the kitchen as he wiped his hand on a rag. "I was thinking about it this morning, and it still feels…"

Cliff didn't have to look very hard to see the sadness behind the big man's eyes. None of them were strangers to death. It was an inevitability, and with each passing year, more and more names were added to the list of those who passed on. Each of them understood this in the innate way only someone who has lived a long life could. But it was still difficult to watch those who had years left to enjoy go early and in such a horrible manner.

"I'm sorry, Hans. We shouldn't be talking about this. We know Pieter was your friend," Cliff said.

"No. It's okay, really," Hans said, forcing a thin smile. "Don't forget, I'm the one who asked you to investigate it. But I still find it all so strange, like he shouldn't be gone. You know?"

The room nodded in collective agreement as each of them appeared to remember someone they'd lost. Cliff hadn't ever kept too many people close to him to lose. Besides his brother Davy and his parents, Cliff had somehow managed to separate himself from the sadness of losing people. He'd always assumed it was some sort of coping mechanism, something preventing him from getting too close and ever feeling that pain again. After all, the pain never served him very well in the first place. It was just something he carried around with him, like a bag of rocks. Useless and burdening.

He'd told himself it was because of his job, that caring too much about his work would only ever make it difficult to do what needed to be done. But now that he was finished working and no longer had to worry about that, he still found his walls up and as sturdy as ever. He was starting to realize that, maybe, there was more to his safeguards than he understood.

"It's easy to imagine this as some sort of game," Kitty said softly, "but I do recognize we are talking about real lives with real consequences."

"Sometimes it's easier to treat it like a game," Cliff said. "If you think about the truth too much, it hurts."

The room fell silent for a moment, until finally Hans jumped in.

"So, you going to chat with Lou? Find out what's going on?" he asked, which appeared to free up the air in the room.

"I suppose I could try messaging her again, but she's been very distant lately." Cliff shrugged. "It would be nice to know what's happening."

A knock at the door startled all of them and nearly caused Sol to spill his coffee.

"Good lord, it's not even six thirty in the morning," Kitty said. "Who could that possibly be?"

"I'm not sure," Hans said, walking over to the front door and opening it up.

"Jan?" Cliff heard Han's voice from entrance way.

"Coffee first," said a very groggy-sounding Jan as he stumbled into the living room, his eyes drooping as he let out a stifled yawn. "Morning, everyone."

"Jan? Why are you here so early?" Cliff asked. "Any news on the…?"

"No. I'm not here for that. I thought Mrs. Chen could use some help today, so I brought some help."

"Help?" Kitty asked.

"Who?" asked Mrs. Chen.

"Mari?" Hans said.

"Morning." Mari's voice came from the front door, sounding much more awake than Jan. "I hope you don't mind, but I thought Aria and I could help out too."

A moment later, Mari and a very quiet Aria stepped into the living room and gave a wave.

"Jan told me about the trouble you all had with the rain the other night and, given what I'd heard about the work you've done on the garden, Mrs. Chen, I figured the least we could do was to come and help out for the day."

"That's very kind," Mrs. Chen said, "but you girls really don't have to—"

"We insist. Besides, what better way to spend a day off?"

"I can think of plenty of other things I would rather do," Sol said, chuckling.

"Yes, but that's because you're useless." Kitty grinned.

This caused some laughter around the room, though Cliff was more intrigued by the genuine look of surprise on Mrs. Chen's face. Clearly this was not something the older woman was used to, and she tried hard to quelch the tear in her eye. It was the most emotion Cliff had ever witnessed from the woman.

"It is very kind of you all to come and help. I am very grateful," Mrs. Chen said.

Cliff caught her dabbing the corner of her eye before she jumped to her feet.

"I suppose there is no time like the present."

"But I haven't finished my coffee yet?" Sol said. Even so, he was pulled up on his feet by Kitty, and he reluctantly gulped what he could before setting the mug down on the table. "But hey, who needs coffee?"

"I do!" Jan shouted from the other room, which sent a wave of laughter through the living room, until Mrs. Chen stopped.

"Only one problem," she said. "I'm not sure I have enough equipment for all of us."

This time it was Mari who laughed. "Don't you worry about that. I got us covered."

Mari did have it covered, as it happened, having brought the farm with her, so to speak. The back of her truck was complete with spades, gloves, hoes, and everything else Mrs. Chen would have loved to have but didn't.

"Very impressive," Mrs. Chen said as she surveyed the equipment and helped herself to a couple of items with extendible poles. "This will save my back."

"It will do more than save mine," Sol said, picking up a stand-up cultivator.

"Mari, it was very kind of you to bring all this stuff," Hans said, looking at the younger woman with pride and, although Cliff could tell the words were there, he just couldn't seem to find the courage to say out loud that her father would also be proud.

"Well, I couldn't have got it all here without Aria's help," Mari said shifting the conversation away from herself and diverting the attention.

This was the first time that Cliff had seen Aria since the day at the market, and before that, he'd spotted her walking with Pieter the day of the festival. As far as he understood it, Aria, who was born in the Netherlands, was here to work on the farm and gain some experience before eventually going back home. At least that was typically how it worked, according to Hans. Every now and then, they decided to stay and continue to work over here.

Other than that, Cliff knew little about the young woman. She was apparently a hard worker, and she was quiet. Admittedly, he discovered this last part for himself, having seen her speak only the smallest amount of Dutch to Hans before she curled up into herself when Mari tried to show her any sort of attention.

"What is this?" Bunty said, stepping outside in a green and yellow flowered dress and a cotton gardening apron, fit with pockets and gloves, looking every bit the gardener.

"You look prepared," Cliff said, admiring the woman in front of him before catching himself staring and turning away to focus on the gardening tools, hoping that the warmth in his cheeks was only in his mind and not coloured on his face.

If she noticed, Bunty gave him the courtesy of not mentioning anything as she joined him and reached into the box of tools, picking out her own short spade and cultivator, along with a portable bench.

"One must always look prepared," Bunty said with a smile. "It is the first step to being prepared."

"Very sensible way of living," Cliff said.

"I believe so." Bunty turned to look over at Mrs. Chen, who, to Cliff's enjoyment, seemed excited for the first time since the rain had started to fall. "What's the plan, Mrs. Chen?"

"Firstly, I would like to thank you all for being here. I know some of you"—she sent a courtesy nod towards Sol—"would much rather be doing other things."

"He's happy to help," Kitty said.

"Helping can't be worse than the hell Kitty would give me if I didn't." Sol smiled politely.

"As I said, he's happy to help." Kitty smiled thinly.

Cliff heard the front door closing, followed by the sound of shuffling feet on the driveway and was genuinely surprised, and a little taken aback, to see the portly Gerald jogging around the corner in what appeared to be a beige safari outfit and a beekeeper's helmet and veil. The look might have been surprising if he hadn't already been so surprised to see the man outside at all. Gerald and heat were not something Cliff connected very often.

"Gerald?" Mrs. Chen said.

"Let's not make a big deal of this, shall we?" he said. Cliff could already see beads of sweat forming on the man's brow, despite the gentle morning breeze.

"You look...prepared," Mrs. Chen offered.

"Won't you be hot?" Sol asked.

"I should be fine. It's the same outfit I wore when I traversed Egypt," Gerald said, adjusting the face mask. "Save for the mesh net. That was for something else entirely."

"What were you doing in Egypt?" Mari asked.

The question seemed to draw the attention of not just the youngsters, but all the house as well. She wasn't the only one who would love to learn even just a little about the mysterious past of Gerald. The enigmatic housemate appeared to have lived hundreds of lives before arriving in St. Marys, and not one of them was known in any great detail by anyone in the house. Cliff had always assumed he was the only one who didn't know about their housemate, but the longer he lived in the house, the more he realized just how in the dark *everyone* was.

"Working," Gerald said with a shrug.

"On what?" Mari continued.

Cliff wondered if, perhaps, she was about to have more success than the rest of them ever had, but that thought was very short-lived.

"Well, it wasn't this garden," Gerald said, picking up another long gardening rake from the back of the truck. "Now, what's the plan? Because you know what they say..."

"A failure to plan is a plan to fail," Mari and Aria said almost to themselves, the two women sharing a look.

If Cliff had to guess, he would think Aria was a good fifteen or so years younger than Mari, but in that moment, both shared the same youthful exuberance in what was surely a shared memory.

"It was something my father used to say," Mari said.

"It was something your *grandfather* used to say," Hans said, chuckling to himself.

"I like that," Gerald said. "I'm going to use that."

"What were you going to say, Gerald?" Kitty asked.

"No plan is a dumb plan." He shrugged. "But that one was much more elegant."

"Perhaps it's time we stopped talking about the plan and actually made a plan?" Sol suggested, earning a nudge in the side from Kitty, though it did serve the purpose of getting things moving.

Cliff wished he had thought about talking to Mrs. Chen beforehand so that he could have paired up with Mari, since it would have been a great opportunity to learn more about her and, perhaps, gather more information about the family farm. But as it turned out, this was not the case. He was paired instead with Gerald, who looked indifferent to his grouping, along with Aria. Neither of them appeared to enjoy chatting very much. On the upside, Cliff noticed Bunty had been paired with Mari, and he hoped whatever facial expression he'd had on when he shared a look with her, would be taken as a *please get more information* look.

Bunty moved off to work alongside Mari, Mrs. Chen with Sol, while Hans, Jan, and Kitty completed the other group. Each group was given a section of the garden to focus on, prioritizing the areas most affected by the rainfall first and working their way through it.

Cliff, who hadn't spent as much time in the garden, imagined that a group this size, with the addition of some better-functioning youngsters, should have the entire garden finished by early afternoon.

But this was a fallacy short-lived, as they began working through their own section. Even with the three of them tending to the garden, including Aria, who proved to be a well-accomplished gardener in her own right, and Gerald, who was unsurprisingly competent, it was still very slow moving.

"You're very good at this," Cliff said to Aria as he wiped sweat from his brow. The cooler morning air was starting to make way for the more intense morning sun. By midday, Cliff suspected it would be well above twenty degrees Celsius.

"I would hope so," Aria said as she groomed the soil around a particularly washed-out bush root. "I do it for a living," she chuckled. "Would be disappointing if I wasn't."

"I suppose that's true," Cliff acknowledged.

"Were you good at what *you* did?" she said, not looking up from her work.

Despite her thick Dutch accent, he had to admit her English was great. Cliff wondered if she already knew what he'd done and was simply being polite or if she was perhaps genuinely interested. It didn't matter too much either way, he supposed.

"I was objectively good, yes."

"Whose objectives do you use to gauge your work?" she asked.

Cliff paused to give it some thought. *That's a rather interesting question.*

"I'm not sure," he chuckled, still honestly considering the question. "I mean, I solved crimes, and well, I'm not sure, I suppose we all think we could have been better at our jobs, no?"

"If you solved crimes, it's not really all that objective then, is it?" she asked.

"No. Maybe. I'm not sure," Cliff stumbled, not loving talking about himself or his work in such a critical way.

"You're not sure if you were good?" she asked.

"I think I was good at what I did," Cliff said with more conviction than he would have ever given himself credit for.

"Then you were good." Aria shrugged.

Cliff had to admit that her blunt nature was rather refreshing.

"How long have you been working on the farm?" Cliff asked.

Aria thought about it a moment. "This farm for just over a year. But I've worked on farms for most of my life."

"Why?"

"Because I like it." She shrugged. "And I am good at it."

"Two wonderful reasons," Cliff said.

"They've worked for me."

"You don't get tired?" Cliff asked.

"Everyone gets tired." Aria smiled, and Cliff felt a little ridiculous for asking such a simple question. "I just like being *this* kind of tired. Working with my hands, being outside. In the sun." She gestured to the sky. "What more could you want?"

Cliff could think of a bunch of things he might want more than feeling the stiffness in his back from the work they were doing, though he knew there was truth to what she was saying. After all, getting out and working hard was a great way to keep your mind active.

"Was it Pieter who brought you over?" Cliff asked, and he watched as she paused for a moment while the words hit her consciousness. "I'm sorry, I didn't—"

"No. It's fine. I don't think it is bad to talk about him. Remember him in some way," she said as she let out a breath. "Yes, Pieter was… ummm…well, he was a family friend from back home, I guess. He knew my mother. They grew up together. He would visit whenever he came to Holland."

"Is your mother still back in Holland?" Cliff asked, as he dug out a trench around the rim of the garden to help remove some of the pools of water still left over from the storm.

"My mother died last year. Cancer," Aria said, bending over to loosen a patch of soil around a rose bush.

"I'm sorry to hear that," Cliff said, a morsel of guilt settling in the pit of his stomach. Even though he hadn't known, he didn't love the feeling he got of bringing it up with Aria. "What about your…?"

"He's dead as well," she said evenly, as she stood up and brushed herself off at the knees. "It looks like we need more topsoil." She turned and walked back towards the truck.

"You ask too many questions," Gerald said, as he tossed a bunch of plant clippings into a small weed bucket.

"How was I supposed to know?" Cliff asked, feeling a little like he was on the defensive.

"You weren't." Gerald shrugged. "But not everyone wants to share their life story with you."

Cliff got the sense that his housemate wasn't just referring to Aria in this moment.

"I know that," Cliff countered.

"Do you?" Gerald asked, setting the pruning shears he had been holding beside the trim bucket. He headed off towards the house.

"Where are you going?" Cliff asked.

"To prepare lunch," Gerald said. "I'm starving."

"It's not even ten a.m. yet."

"Good food takes time," Gerald said, continuing towards the house, "and you can hardly expect me to cook on an empty stomach, now can you?" he tapped his fingers together eagerly, no doubt his mind was already ruminating on what would likely be his next meal, leaving Cliff standing alone in their allotted patch of garden.

"You really know how to clear a room," a voice said from around a high bush behind Cliff.

He poked his head around to find Jan touching his toes and

stretching his back.

"You heard that?"

"Every awkward second," Jan said with a sad smile.

"I didn't mean…"

"I know you didn't," Jan said, raising a hand and wincing as he did.

"What's wrong with you?" Cliff asked, trying to turn the conversation away from himself and placing it instead on the stretching mass of Jan.

"Mrs. Chen has me moving bags of topsoil around the garden. So far, I've moved twenty bags, and she just insisted I pick up another twenty more. I'm a writer, Cliff, not a body builder." Jan rubbed his biceps. "Have you given any more thought to those papers we found?"

"What papers?" Cliff turned to see Lou walking up the path beside him with Dan close behind.

"What are you doing here?" Jan asked, ignoring the annoyed look on Lou's face.

"Dan and I were getting breakfast at the diner, and Zoey told us about Mrs. Chen's garden. So, I thought we would come see if we could help."

"I think we have all the help we need, thanks," Jan said as he stood, arms crossed against his chest.

"Funny, I didn't realize I…*we* were here to help you with *your* garden?" Lou said, folding her arms across her chest to match Jan.

"Shouldn't you be off policing or something?" Jan said.

"It's my day off. You mind telling me why you're being such an….ass right now?" Lou said.

"I don't know. Maybe it's because you've all but disappeared on us? We've not heard anything from you about Pieter's case in over—"

"I'm a cop, Jan. I'm not here to tell you what's going on in any case, because it's not my job to keep you informed."

"Have you found anything new?" Cliff asked, trying to move this more-than-a-little-awkward discussion away from the pair of them. He might have felt sorry for Dan, but he appeared oblivious to all of it as he just stood in the back, looking around at the garden.

"I can't talk to you about that now," Lou said, her eyes shifting to Dan, who missed it altogether. "I'm just here to help with the garden."

"I think we got that covered," Jan said again.

"Weren't you just saying you could use help moving bags?" Cliff asked. "Dan could probably—"

"No, I'm good," Jan said, raising his hands to Cliff, who was pretty sure he'd also puffed his chest out a little.

"But you just complained about—"

"No…not complaining, just taking a break."

"You need help moving things?" Dan asked. "'Cause I can do that. Can't say I'll be all that helpful with the plants."

"No," Jan said at the same time Cliff said, "Yes."

"Confusing." Dan shrugged.

"Perhaps it's better if we go," Lou said. "I didn't realize you already had people here." Lou's eyes glanced over towards Mari's truck, feeling, perhaps, that Mari might find it strange to find the police, who had been speaking to her earlier about her father's death, here now.

"We have lots of help," Jan said.

Cliff shoved an elbow in the young man's side.

"Ouch."

"The more help the better. There are bags of topsoil that need to be moved around the garden," Cliff said. "And lots of soil that we need to loosen up."

"You just tell me what to carry and where," Dan said, rubbing his hands together.

"I've got that covered, so it's not that big a deal," Jan said, waving a hand in a rather sad attempt to be nonchalant.

"Nonsense, I'm happy to help," Dan said, "It's just…" He looked down at his white t-shirt and jeans. "I'm not really dressed for this," he laughed.

"Such a shame. It was a kind offer though, Dan. But we wouldn't want your shirt to get dirty." Jan shrugged.

Both Cliff and Lou shot him a disapproving glare. But if Dan was insulted, he didn't let it show. He simply smiled and shrugged.

"You're right, Jake. It's just a shirt," he said.

"It's Jan."

"Right, sorry. So, Jan, where we going?" Dan said as he began to lift his shirt off.

"What are you doing?" Jan asked, stopping him.

"I don't want to get it dirty. Like you said," Dan said, pulling his shirt over his head.

"I didn't mean…"

"That's better." Dan folded his shirt over his arm, shirtless in the middle of the garden. "Let's get to work."

27

"Where do you want this?" Dan asked, as he approached Kitty with four bags of topsoil hanging over his shoulders. Even with Gerald off preparing lunch, the extra hands of Lou and Dan were really making a dent in the garden.

The only person happier than Kitty at this moment was Mrs. Chen, who was smiling more than Cliff had ever seen, as she watched her garden slowly returning to its usual high standard. The entire morning felt like a success, save for a minor confrontation between Lou and Mari, who rightfully, wasn't all too thrilled to have one of the officers investigating her working alongside her. Though, with some assistance from Hans, and some assurances that the garden was big enough that they would not have to be around one another, everything moved smoothly.

"Just over there, Dan." Kitty gestured to a small area just beside a hydrangea bush.

"You got it, ma'am," Dan said, casually moving to where'd she'd pointed before swinging the bags down to the ground.

"Please, I have been telling you all morning to just call me Kitty. No need for the formalities," Kitty said, shooing Dan away playfully.

"Sorry, it's just how I was raised, I guess." Dan wiped some sweat from his body, though not nearly as much as Cliff would have had, had he been the one moving sixty pounds of soil around the gardens.

"And weren't you raised right!" Kitty blushed. "We're so lucky to have such a strapping young man here to help us."

"What about these, Kitty?" Jan said, his own body drenched in sweat as he struggled with the two bags over his shoulders.

"Anywhere over there, Jan." Kitty waved indifferently in the direction of Cliff and Lou, and Jan hauled in a deep breath to carry it down the garden.

"You look parched. How about some water or lemonade?" Kitty asked.

"Would love some," Jan sighed as he dropped the bags.

"I was talking to Dan," she said. "You know where the glasses are if you'd like some, Jan." Kitty looped her arm through Dan's and pulled him off towards a small table that had been set up for drinks.

"What am I? Chopped liver?" Jan slumped down to take a seat on the grass beside Cliff.

"You're not new and shiny, son. Don't get too hung up on it," Cliff said, giving him a pat on the back.

"Still, I'm helping too." Jan pouted.

"People don't appreciate the things they expect as much as the things they don't," Cliff shrugged. "I wouldn't think about it too much."

"I just don't see what Lou sees in him."

"You mean besides the fact that he's kind, great with people, saves lives for a living, and is fit as all hell? You're right…I don't know what I see in him either," Lou said, causing Jan to jump up.

Cliff couldn't tell for sure, because of Jan's physical exertion, but he thought perhaps his face turned an even darker shade of red.

"I wasn't… I mean…" Jan stammered.

"Jealousy is not a good look on you, Jan."

"I'm not jealous. I couldn't care less who you're with. I just think… you know…look at him…he's trying too hard," Jan said, his face contorting, as though he'd smelt something terrible.

"Wow," Lou said, shaking her head.

"What?"

"I mean, he's here on our day off, helping, even though he has no reason to, other than to be kind. He got Kitty that calendar because she asked, and he's making your life a hell of a lot easier by carrying all those bags. And you sit there and criticize him, for what? Having a six-pack?"

"I'm not..."

"You're pathetic, Jan," Lou said. She stormed off, walking to meet Kitty and Dan, who were at the table, but not before turning to stick a tongue out in Jan's direction.

"Well, that was childish," Jan said.

"Yes, it was," Mrs. Chen said, startling both Cliff and Jan this time, as she walked up to the bag of topsoil and cut the top open. With a little effort, she tilted the bag off the ground and emptied it in the garden, swatting Jan's hand away when he tried to help.

"Thank you, Mrs. Chen. She was being..."

"I was talking about you," she said, tossing the empty bag of soil on the lawn before reaching for the other one and repeating the process.

"Me!?" Jan said, wiping his face with his shirt in an attempt to remove the sweat, but only managing to smear the dirt instead. "But she's the—"

"You don't need to be old to realize that you're jealous of Dan."

"I'm not jealous of him... I'm... Cliff?" Jan said, looking to Cliff for help.

But Cliff raised his hands, extracting himself from the conversation, happy for once not to be the one dishing out the hard truth.

"Don't hide behind him," Mrs. Chen said, looking back at Cliff. "This one has his own blind spots." She shook her head.

"Hey, I happen to like Dan," Cliff said with a shrug.

"My point exactly," Mrs. Chen said, giving her head a shake.

"How did I get roped into all of this?" Cliff asked.

"You can't just do nothing and expect the results you want." Her eyes drifted from Cliff to Jan, neither of whom appeared to understand the reason for their sudden lashing.

"Are you talking about Lou?" Jan asked. "Because last time I checked, she rejected me and hates me. For good reason," he added when both Cliff and Mrs. Chen appeared to want to point out that Jan had, in fact, asked Lou out on a date, only to use a quote from said date, in a later article, completely breaking her trust. "But I've moved on, and I think it is great that she has too. I just think that the whole 'great body' thing is a little predictable is all. I just imagined her to be into something different."

"Tall and awkward?" Mrs. Chen asked.

"I'm not awkward!" Jan protested.

"Who said I was talking about you?" Mrs. Chen feigned confusion, which only flustered Jan even further.

"I wasn't… I mean…not me…"

"Good. Because I don't think that you and Lou are right for each other," Mrs. Chen said, fully knocking Jan off his heels, as he scrambled to understand what exactly was happening.

All Cliff could do was watch and admire the way Mrs. Chen appeared to control the situation and be thankful that, for the moment, her attention was solely on Jan and not turned back on him. And in order to keep it that way, he was content to remain silent.

"Not right…? Me and Lou?"

"Lou and I," Mrs. Chen corrected.

"Right, but I already know this."

"Do you?" Mrs. Chen asked.

"Yes?" Jan said, though he didn't sound nearly as convincing as Cliff suspected he would have liked.

"Good," Mrs. Chen said, using a long rake to start spreading the topsoil.

"Good," Jan said, trying not to look as confused as he clearly was. "But just out of curiosity, why do you think it's not a good fit?"

"Why what isn't a good fit?" Bunty asked, approaching.

"Nothing," Jan said quickly, but it was in vain.

"Jan and Lou," Mrs. Chen said, not bothering to look up from her work.

"Awww. Right." Bunty shook her head.

"How did this become about me?" Jan asked.

"It's always about someone," Mrs. Chen said, shrugging. "Today it is about you."

"You really are a confusing woman, you know that?" Jan said, as he picked up another bag of soil and opened it up.

"Thank you." Mrs. Chen smiled. "Just over there." She gestured to a small patch of garden a few feet away from where she'd poured the last one. "How are we doing in your section, Bunty?"

"Nearly finished, I think." She smiled, though her eyes shifted to Cliff and her smile faded.

"We might actually get this finished in time," Mrs. Chen said, her smile beaming.

"I think so!" Bunty said cheerfully. "Do you mind if I steal Cliff for a moment?"

Mrs. Chen waved a hand as she moved the soil around a small patch of black-eyed Susans.

"Do you need me too?" Jan asked, slight desperation in his voice.

"You stay," Mrs. Chen said. "Tell me what you know about the other gardens."

"I don't know anything about the other gardens." Jan shrugged.

"Aren't you writing a piece on the home garden competition?"

"No, I don't think so," Jan said.

"You mean, not yet." Mrs. Chen smiled. "You can start with the winning garden. Mine."

Cliff didn't hear how the rest of this played out, as he and Bunty moved off towards the swing, where she took a seat and signaled for him to do the same across from him. They began to rock back and forth.

"As much as I appreciate the rest, what's going on?" Cliff asked, watching as Bunty wrung her fingers together.

"I'm not sure," she said. "It might be nothing, but it might be something."

"Sounds interesting."

"It is. Maybe. I'm not sure."

Not for the first time today, Cliff found himself utterly confused by the situation he was in and wondered why on earth it was so hard for people to just say what they wanted to say.

"Bunty. Are you okay?"

"Yes. It's just something that Aria told me. Have you spoken with her?"

"Briefly," Cliff said, recalling that his interaction might not have gone as well as he'd hoped. "Just about how she is from Holland and how she came to work here."

"How her family is gone?" Bunty asked.

"Yes, I knew that," Cliff said, wondering where this was heading.

"There was just something about the way she was talking about Pieter to me that got me thinking..."

Bunty appeared to be actively avoiding the section of the conversation she really wanted to get to. This did little to help Cliff understand what the point of all of this was. He'd also talked to Aria that morning and, though it might not have gone the most amicable way, he had just chalked up her desire to not want to discuss Pieter to it being a sore subject for everyone at the moment.

"Bunty, where are you going with this?" Cliff asked, confused as to why she would feel the need to pull him aside just to tell him what he already knew. Aria, like everyone else on the farm, was upset that Pieter had been killed.

"It's just, I remember seeing them at the festival, you remember?" she asked.

Cliff only vaguely remembered seeing Aria with Pieter during his little confrontation with the Badger on the day of the festival.

"She was with him when—"

"When the Badger was trying to get him to sell the farm," Cliff agreed absently. As much as his knees were enjoying the respite from the work in the garden, he was starting to feel a little guilty—and perhaps a little tired now that he was sitting down. He began to wonder if a nap would be in his future, which in turn, caused him to stifle a yawn as the cool summer air brushed by him.

"Yes. What else do you remember?" Bunty asked.

"I'm not sure?" Cliff tried to think about it, but couldn't get further than wondering where all of this was heading.

"Think," Bunty insisted.

"Ummm…I don't know. Pieter and the Badger were yelling at each other, and then Aria pulled Pieter away when it looked to be getting heated." Cliff closed his eyes and tried to visualize what he could about the interaction, while simultaneously attempting to understand why on earth any of this mattered to Bunty.

"Yes."

"Bunty, I'm tired. Can you please just tell me what you're thinking?" Cliff's shoulders slumping in defeat, while his brain tried to compute what was happening. When she didn't say anything, Cliff forced himself to think harder. "I don't know, she grabbed him and pulled him away."

"She didn't just grab him. She grabbed his hand."

"Wait, you saw them arguing too?" Cliff asked wondering how this was the first he'd heard of it.

"Yes, it happened just beside the tent I was buying my yarn from. Not one of those things you can just pretend not to see, you know?" Bunty shook her head.

"I still don't understand why any of this matters," Cliff said. "She wanted to pull him away."

"I agree, but if you saw two people fighting and wanted to pull one away, you would go for the shoulder or the upper arm, something to control their movement. Aria went for his hand. Which is much more intimate than just the arm."

"Is it?" Cliff asked.

"The hand is one of the most intimate parts of the body. Think about any time you have ever reached for someone? Did you grab their hand? Wrist? Arm? Really think about it," Bunty said.

Cliff obliged, though he had to admit that, between the shade and the cool breeze, most of what his mind was thinking about was going for a nice long nap. Still, he tried to think about all the times he'd ever had to step in to defuse a situation. Having been a policeman and detective for the better part of fifty years in Toronto, that was more than a few times.

"I suppose I wouldn't usually grab someone's hand."

"Why?" Bunty asked.

"I don't know, I just wouldn't."

"Because it is an intimate act. It isn't something someone does naturally, not unless you have a bond with that person. It is truly one of the most non-sexual, intimate acts humans share."

Cliff was still more than a little confused about why any of this should matter or what it might have to do with Pieter's death. Or that's what he *assumed* they were talking about.

"You think this has something to do with Pieter's death?" Cliff asked.

"I'm not sure. But I think it's important."

"What? Like you think that Aria and Pieter shared…an intimate bond?" Cliff asked, his brows lifting with the very awkward insinuation rolling around in his mind.

"Yes," Bunty said, but when she caught Cliff's expression, she retracted. "I mean, no. Not that."

"Then what is it you're trying to say, Bunty?"

"Aria told me her father died recently," Bunty said, giving Cliff a slow, pointed nod.

"Yes, she told me." Cliff pinched the bridge of his nose as he started to become annoyed by this back and forth. Normally Bunty was so good at simply explaining what she meant, and he couldn't understand why suddenly it was so difficult for her to get to the point.

Cliff only vaguely remembered seeing Aria and Pieter together, though Bunty had already proven to him that her ability for recalling information was far superior to his own. But he still couldn't understand why any of this was important, or why it would matter if Aria took Pieter by the hand or why it was important that her father had died recently.

Cliff sprang up. His eyes met Bunty's as the implications Bunty was presenting began to settle in.

"You think Pieter…?" Cliff asked.

Bunty put a finger to her lips.

"You don't think anyone knows?" he whispered.

Bunty shook her head.

"Do you think she…?"

"I don't know." Bunty shrugged. "I'm not even sure if any of it is true," she admitted, "but if it is, then you would have to admit it's a little strange that no one is talking about it. No?"

"Assuming anyone actually knows? Sure, yeah, it would be," Cliff said as he began to think about what this all meant. "You don't think—" Cliff's thought was dismissed by the sounds of shouting coming from the front of the house.

"What are you doing here?" cried a voice Cliff thought maybe he recognized, but he couldn't quite figure out who it was.

"What's going on?" Bunty asked, standing up abruptly, causing the swing to smack Cliff in the back of the legs, knocking him off balance, and causing him to nearly collide into Bunty.

"I'm not sure." He stood up on his toes, like the additional height would somehow allow him to see more of what was happening. It did not. There was a hedgerow blocking his view.

"I have every right to be here," shouted another voice, and this time Cliff *knew* it was Lou speaking.

What in the world is happening?

Cliff and Bunty shared a quick look before they both walked down the garden. All thoughts of Aria and Pieter went out the window as they tried to root out the source of whatever was troubling the house.

Cliff caught sight of the house's newest visitor. Flynn had one finger pointed right at Lou, but his attention shifted to Mari, who was standing, arms folded, glaring at him.

"What are you doing with her? You realize she is one of the ones who thinks you killed Uncle Pieter, right? Or did you forget that?"

"I don't think anything. I'm doing my job," Lou said, shaking her head.

"What are you doing here, Flynn?" Mari asked.

"What are *you* doing here? Both of you?" he said, this time gesturing towards Aria, who was trying her best to stay quiet and out of the way.

"I'm here as a favour to Hans. Not that it's any of your business," Mari said.

"You know these people are investigating Uncle Pieter's death, don't you?" Flynn said, looking around at the group. "Yeah, don't think I don't know what you're all up to."

"We just want to know what happened to Pieter," Hans said.

"Has anyone stopped to think that maybe it was an accident? That maybe he grabbed the wrong drink? Uncle Pieter was old…"

"Old enough to forget he was allergic to peanuts?" Mari asked. "You think my dad, the man who ran our farms, was so forgetful that he just forgot what drink was his and then managed to lose his EpiPen?"

"I don't know. Maybe?" Flynn said. "It's better than thinking someone did it, isn't it?"

"Not if some actually *did* it!" Mari shouted.

"Look, I didn't come here to argue with you." Flynn shook his head.

"Then why did you come?"

"I need to speak to you," he said, looking around at the small group that had gathered before adding, "privately."

"Why?"

"Because I do."

"What does it matter, Flynn? Whatever you tell us is going to come out anyways, or did you forget that this one is a cop?" she said, hooking a thumb in Lou's direction, which clearly made Lou even more uncomfortable than she already was.

"Look, I'm just here to help out my friends, not—" Lou started.

"But it's true, isn't it? Whatever he says is going to come out, or they will think we're hiding something."

"This doesn't have anything to do with Uncle Pieter's death," Flynn insisted.

"Everything has to do with it until we find out what the hell happened to him. Don't you understand that? Just like I know how you've been stealing from the farm," Mari said, causing Flynn to take a step back.

"I'm not stealing…I'm…"

"Just taking money from the farm."

"I was trying to buy more land."

"More land is what got us into this issue in the first place. The farm was fine where it was, but no, you had to convince my dad to buy all that land that we couldn't afford, sinking our farm into it all. And for what?"

"Mari, this really isn't the place," Flynn said.

"Look, Flynn!" Mari said, taking a step towards him slowly. "I am tired, sad, and very angry, and the last thing I want to do is deal with any of this. I want to grieve my father's death, but every day is like a sick reminder that he is gone, and I don't know why. So please stop all of this and tell me why you're here."

"Fine," Flynn said, his hands flaying out. "Fine. It's my mom."

Cliff watched as Flynn looked deflated, and all the frustration he'd been carrying around with him melted away. What was left was a very sad and weak-looking young man. But no one, especially not Mari, was prepared for what he had to say next.

"She's sold the farm to the Badger."

28

"What do you mean?" Mari asked, her head shaking as her brain attempted to catch up with the reality of the situation.

A reality Cliff himself was having trouble understanding. He wasn't a lawyer, by any means, but surely, Cynthia Stroud couldn't simply sell a farm that wasn't hers. And from the looks around him, he wasn't the only one having this thought.

"Mom just called to tell me that she's had a meeting with the Badger to sell him the farms," Flynn said.

"But she can't. She doesn't even own them," Mari said dismissively.

"Not yet, apparently. But she could if your dad's will can't be sorted out. Then, all of the land will be split between her and Lucas, who she's already convinced to sell," Flynn said, shaking his head.

"I don't understand," Hans said. "Mari is the only child. Shouldn't everything go to her?"

Cliff and Bunty shared a look with one another. Mari was, in fact, the only *known* child of Pieter. But if their suspicions were correct, then things might get a little more complicated. He couldn't keep from glancing over at Aria, who seemed to have disappeared into the background. If she was a half sibling to Mari, she didn't appear to be the kind of person who wanted everyone to know about it. *But why?*

"Not if Mari is under suspicion of killing her father," Lou said.

"And who the hell thinks that's true?" Flynn said bitterly, causing

265

Lou to step back, her arms going out reflexively to ease her position.

"Look, it's not me who believes it. We just have to go off of the evidence," Lou said.

"Right. The evidence that shows either Mari or me, or one of our other family members, killed Uncle Pieter because we wanted his land? Is that what you mean?"

"Yes," Lou said. "You may not like it, but it does appear that someone killed your uncle, and it's our job to figure out who it was and why. Don't blame me because you might have something to hide."

Flynn took an aggressive step towards her, but both Jan and Dan stepped between them. This successfully stopped Flynn's movement, but also angered Lou enough to push both men aside and take her own step towards Flynn.

"Believe it or not, we're trying to help you. Just because you don't like it, doesn't mean it's not going to happen. You claim to care about the farm, and yet here you are about to lose it, and I might be one of the few people who could actually help you save it. If you'd let me."

Flynn looked as though he wanted to say something, but stopped himself, which was probably for the best. Considering Lou was still a police officer and he was still a viable suspect in Pieter's death.

"Lunch is ready," Gerald said, stepping out of the front door, looking surprised when the agitated party all turned to face him. "Did I miss something?" he asked with a little shrug.

"Flynn," Hans said, taking a step towards the young man, who pulled away. "Look, why don't you stay for lunch. We can talk about this and maybe figure out what's really going on."

"Why on earth would I ever stay for lunch?" Flynn asked.

"Because Gerald is one of the best chefs that I know, and I feel as though now might be a good time to clear the air about all of this business," Hans suggested.

"All of this business is about trying to figure out who killed my father, Hans," Mari said, sounding frustrated.

"I know that, Mari."

"Do you? Because you said that you could help me find out what happened to Dad, and so far, all anyone thinks is that Flynn or I did it. At this point, it doesn't even look like any of it matters, since, even if we do find out who did this, Winkleberry Farm is finished. I mean what's the point of any of this if it means the farm is gone?"

"The farm's not finished," Flynn said.

"Flynn. Thanks to you, we're broke. Dad's gone and your mom's already got plans to sell it," Mari said, shaking her head. "From what I can tell, it's hopeless."

"Nothing is hopeless, young lady," Mrs. Chen said gesturing around her. "Yesterday, I thought this garden, which I have been working on for over a year, was destroyed after a single night of rain. But with all your help, look at what we have accomplished."

"With all due respect, Mrs. Chen, I don't see how these two things are comparable."

"Hopelessness is a state we put ourselves in when we don't see a way out on our own. But you're not alone. Neither was I. We are all here to help you…if you want it," Mrs. Chen said with a smile.

"I'm sorry. But I just don't see a way out of all of this," Mari said as she started to walk away.

Flynn reached out to stop her but dropped his hand. "Mari's right, this is hopeless. And it's all my fault. If I hadn't tried to borrow from the farm, or—"

"Flynn, son," Hans said, "whoever killed Pieter is responsible for all this. You made a mistake—"

"A big one," Flynn interjected, "and now…" He shook his head, pausing when his phone began to ring. He looked around at everyone before saying, "I should take this." Flynn answered and walked away, his voice carrying back to the group. "Hey. Ya, I know. I don't want mum to sell it either, but you know what she's like. Yeah, she's mad. I don't know. Yeah, I'm heading to the farm now." His conversation faded off as everyone watched him and Mari leave.

"I should probably go too," Aria said, as she tucked her hair behind her ears and smiled awkwardly at everyone.

"Please, stay for lunch," Bunty said.

"Which is getting cold, by the way," Gerald said.

"Shush, Gerald!" Kitty shouted.

Gerald gave a shrug and went back inside, mumbling to himself, no doubt heading inside to prepare his own lunch, since he showed no interest in the situation at hand.

"I wouldn't have a ride back to the…"

"Jan will drive you," Kitty said with a smile.

"I will?" Jan looked confused, but the look Kitty gave him appeared to set the record straight for him. "I mean, I will. Absolutely."

"See, it's settled. All your hard work deserves a meal," Kitty said. "And Gerald, despite his horrific manners, does make a great meal."

"She's not wrong." Hans smiled.

"I suppose I am a little hungry." Aria returned his smile.

"Great, it's settled," Kitty said.

"Where are you two going?" Mrs. Chen asked, as Lou and Dan began to slip away.

Dan quietly gestured towards his shirt, which was folded on a table outside.

"I think we've caused enough drama for one day," Lou said, glancing over at Aria.

"Nonsense. We need to celebrate this triumph," Mrs. Chen said. "You're staying, and that's final."

"I am pretty hungry," Dan said, rubbing his stomach—or six-pack rather—causing Jan to let out an audible sigh, which was not missed by Lou, who shot him an annoyed look. Dan, on the other hand, appeared oblivious to it all.

"Come on, let's eat," Cliff said. He started ushering everyone inside, feeling his own tummy rumbling.

He turned to spot Bunty standing quietly behind him. "You coming, Bunty?"

She looked deep in thought but snapped out of it when Cliff reached out and touched her arm.

"What? Yes, sorry, I'm coming. I just had a thought."

"What kind of thought?"

"Not sure yet. But once I know for sure, you will be the first to know," she said with a grin.

"Is it about the case?"

"Not sure yet. I'm just going to make a call," she said.

"You want me to wait for you?"

"No. I'll just be a minute." She reached out and placed a hand on his forearm. Her touch felt warm on his skin, even with the midday sun beating down on him. "I promise I'll tell you what I find." She gave him a wink as she nudged him away.

Cliff didn't know exactly what was going on, and he wasn't really used to the people around him having ideas before him. He did have to admit that Bunty had a particular knack for linking things together. She had suggested it was due to the long list of books she had read over the years, but Cliff didn't think it was only that. Bunty was observant and paid very close attention to detail. Something Cliff had always prided himself on in the past. *So, what exactly did I miss?*

He knew this would distract him for the rest of the day, or at least until Bunty decided to share her thoughts with him.

By the time lunch ended, Cliff was very full and dreaming of his bed and a nap. He was no closer to figuring out what Bunty had been thinking about. Having returned inside she was, unfortunately, seated a few spots away from him, though he occasionally caught glimpses of her examining Aria from the corner of her eye.

He suspected that, whatever it was that had clicked in her brain, had something to do with that young woman, and yet, for the life of him, he couldn't figure out what it was. Even worse was the rigid onset of an aching pain that was spreading throughout his body from the work they had put in the garden. Glancing at the exhausted expressions on the faces around the table, he wasn't the only one who was feeling the work. The only two people who appeared to be unscathed from the morning work were Aria, no doubt because this was hardly work for her at all, given what she did on the farm every day, and Mrs. Chen, who beamed with joy every time she glanced out the window.

Cliff was thrilled to see her so happy after everything that had happen over the last few days. It was nice that they were all able to help at least one person get what they wanted. Cliff wished he could say the same for Pieter and his family, but the more they uncovered about his death, the further away they were from solving who actually did it.

He also wished he could have a moment alone with Lou to ask her some extra questions about what the police were making of all of this, but since she'd arrived, her time had been occupied by others, and it didn't feel entirely right to pull her aside for a private conversation while Aria was there.

Cliff wasn't sure how much he enjoyed doing the whole detective thing working from the outside. At least, before, he was entitled to a certain amount of information to do his job. But here, in this small town, where he was no longer a police officer and knew almost no one, all he really had to go on was what he could gather on his own or from the people in his house. It didn't seem to be a lot. Even Bunty was having better luck then he was. At least she had some understanding of the farming world. If Cliff was being honest with himself, he was beginning to feel a little like a fish out of water. A very tired fish out of the water at that.

"I would just like to say," Mrs. Chen said, pushing herself up from her chair and looking over at everyone around the table, "I wish everyone could have stayed for lunch, but for those of you who did, I would like to thank you all from the bottom of my heart for what you did for me today." Her normally unflappable exterior cracked slightly from the emotion she was feeling. "To have the chance to present our garden this year…well, it's everything."

Cliff could see her hand gripping the back of her chair, and he couldn't tell if it was the exhaustion or if her emotions were getting the better of her. He supposed it was likely a little of both. After all, at this point in their lives, nothing was guaranteed, and to lose the opportunity to present her garden this year would have been a terrible blow. It was something Cliff and their fellow housemates understood all too well. To them, there wasn't much more she needed to say.

"To tomorrow," Hans said, raising his glass of water.

"To tomorrow," the room echoed.

After some deliberation, Hans finally convinced Aria to let Jan give her a ride back to the farm, while Cliff decided that it was time for a much-needed nap. Though when he finally made it up to his room and climbed into bed, his brain wasn't listening to his body. He tossed and turned for the better part of a half hour before finally giving up and heading back downstairs.

The house was very quiet. He hadn't been the only one who had snuck off for a rest. Given the amount of work they had all done in the garden, it wasn't a surprise. He was, however, surprised to find Bunty sitting in the library with Jan, looking through the files that Jan had brought over.

"What are you two doing?" Cliff asked, stifling a yawn as he leaned against the doorframe to the library. Skittles hopped off the windowsill and wrapped himself around Cliff's legs.

"Jan was helping me find something," Bunty said.

"What?" Cliff asked.

"A clue. I think," Bunty said with a sheepish smile.

"What is it?" Cliff asked. "Maybe I can help."

"I'm not sure. What if it's a waste of time?" Bunty said.

"What if it isn't?" Cliff proposed.

Bunty began to ponder. "Fair enough. But we'll know more once I hear back from my friend."

"You two are being very secretive right now." Cliff chuckled to himself.

"Not fun being on the outside, is it?" Jan said with a grin.

"No, it isn't," Cliff admitted.

Being on the outside was not a place he'd been in some time, not since he was a young detective, and in his later years, he simply tended to work alone, where he was never on the outside, because he had no one to share it with. He understood that wasn't really what Jan and Bunty were talking about.

Cliff could appreciate wanting to have a firm grasp on an idea before sharing it, and, as Cliff was becoming painfully aware, his relationships around town—or rather, lack of them—hardly put him in the best position to get answers. In Bunty's shoes, he'd have gone to Jan, too, as his job at the paper gave him access to more information. But he had to admit, it stung a little to be left out.

"I just don't want to waste your time if it ends up being nothing," Bunty said, pushing her falling glasses up on her nose, while she gave Cliff a thin smile.

"I can understand that," Cliff said, "but I'm here and I can't sleep. I've been thinking about what you said."

"But I didn't say anything." Bunty's head tilted curiously.

"I know, but sometimes the mystery is in what we don't say." Cliff stepped over Skittles as he took a seat in one of the high-back chairs and picked up a loose paper that had been resting on the table. "You clearly spotted something important. But for the life of me, I can't figure out what it was."

The paper he was looking at was some sort of old order form for the farm, showing feed for the cattle. Cliff picked up another from the same side of the table, which looked similar, and guessed this was the less interesting side of the table.

"I'm assuming you're not just looking at old order forms," Cliff said, setting the sheets back on the table.

"No," Bunty said. "I'm trying to find a form I saw last night. I didn't think it was anything at the time, but if my suspicions are right, it might be confirming my thought about Aria," Bunty said.

Cliff glanced over at Jan.

"Bunty told me." Jan shrugged. "Though I'm not sure why all the secrecy around it."

"Pieter has a secret daughter in Holland that the family doesn't know about and then she comes to work on the farm and then he ends up dead?" Cliff said, his brows raised.

"Well, when you frame it like that…" Jan said. "But Aria was with us all morning. She hardly seems like the type of person who would murder someone. Besides, if no one knows about her relationship to Pieter, then what does she have to gain from all of this? I mean, I could understand if she was telling everyone to try and get her hands on the farms, but she isn't doing any of that."

"Good point," Cliff said.

"I don't think Aria killed Pieter," Bunty said, still flipping through pages. "But if we can prove that she is, in fact, Pieter's daughter, then at the very least between her and Mari, it will slow down whatever plans Cindy Stroud has for selling the farms. She can't sell what isn't hers."

"Because the farm would go to Pieter's kids first," Jan said with a smile., "Smart."

"Got it!" Bunty said, waving a sheet of paper around in her hand.

"So what is it?" Cliff asked, reaching for the paper.

Bunty handed it over. "Work permits for Aria, signed by Pieter," she said. "I didn't think of it at the time, which was silly of me because it seems so obvious now, but in the file, it lists Aria as family. But look there." She gestured halfway down the form, and Cliff spotted it clearly.

"What is it?" Jan leaned over to peer over the paper, though, to him, the entire thing was upside down and probably completely useless.

"Pieter has Aria listed as 'daughter' on relations."

"Come on!" Jan said, clapping his hands. "Wait? So does this mean Aria being Pieter's daughter isn't a secret?"

"Not necessarily," Bunty said. "I don't see why anyone other than him would see these documents."

"Well, it doesn't matter, does it?" Jan said. "We show them this document, and boom, another hurdle for Cindy to jump and we have a little more time to figure out who did it." Jan dusted his hands together, as though this were the simplest thing in the world.

"Maybe," Cliff said thoughtfully.

"Come on. It's a good plan," Jan said.

"It is. I don't disagree with you."

"But?" Bunty and Jan said with a sigh, and had it not been so important, Cliff might have even found this amusing.

"But what if there's a reason Aria isn't telling anyone about being Pieter's daughter? This could create a problem for her. We may think that she's not capable of killing, but take it from a former detective, the police certainly will put her at the top of the list, especially if they think she was trying to hide this information from them," Cliff said.

Bunty took the sheet from Cliff's hands and read it over thoughtfully. "I hadn't thought about that," she said softly. "So, what do we do?"

"I'm not sure."

"Well, it's obvious, isn't it?" Jan shrugged his shoulders.

Cliff and Bunty shared a look. If it was obvious, only Jan saw it.

"I mean, we just need to figure out who did it. That way, Aria can keep her secret and share it when she feels ready."

"Isn't that what we've been trying to do?" Bunty asked.

"Yes, but we just need to be more proactive about it," Jan said.

"What do you suggest?" Cliff asked.

"Well, it wouldn't hurt to go back to the scene of the crime. Maybe we missed something?"

"That might not be a bad idea," Cliff said.

"I doubt that they are going to just let us walk through a crime scene, though," Bunty said.

"It's unlikely Captain Marks is going to let us do much of anything over there." Cliff chuckled to himself, knowing the chief of the local OPP was not a huge fan of him or his friends.

"So...what?" Jan asked.

Cliff smiled. "We don't ask Captain Marks."

...

"Absolutely not," Lou said, loud enough that Cliff guessed both Jan and Bunty heard it, despite the phone not being on the speaker.

"All we want to do is have a look around, Lou," Cliff said, like he wasn't casually asking her to break all the rules.

"No," Lou said dismissively. "You, of all people, should know I can't do that."

"I know it's a big ask, but..."

"A big ask? Cliff, you want me to take you to an active crime scene."

"I know. But I wouldn't be asking if it wasn't important."

"Important? You're a private citizen, retired. As in not working anymore. Why do you need to go?" Lou asked.

"I promised Hans I would look into it. As a favour," Cliff said.

"Well, you shouldn't have been promising Hans to do anything illegal."

"I would hardly call it illegal," Cliff said, though even he couldn't argue that it wasn't exactly "by the book" either.

Still, he'd made a promise to a friend, and if he was being honest with himself, he was becoming a little annoyed by the fact that he seemed to be getting nowhere with who had done it. Despite all of the evidence pointing this murder at the family, he didn't feel like any of them had it in them to kill Pieter. Not least of all because he wasn't sure why the farm was worth killing for. And if he wasn't killed for the farm, then why was he killed?

"Semantics, Cliff, you know that." Lou sighed. "I'll be crucified if I get caught."

Cliff took a positive from her contemplation of the idea, which was all he needed.

"What if we made a trade?" Cliff said.

This caused both Jan and Bunty to perk up a little in front of him.

"What kind of trade?" Lou asked. The bait was set, and he'd got his nibble; it was time to reel her in.

"Documents. About the farm."

"What? No!" Jan said, but Bunty silenced him with a calming hand on his and a finger pressed to her lips.

"You're with Jan, aren't you?" Lou sighed heavily. "Who else? Bunty? The rest of the house?"

"It doesn't matter," Cliff said.

"What documents do you have? And if they are important to this case, why have you not already handed them over to the police?"

"They we're given to Jan, and he has every right to hold on to them to protect his source."

"But I don't…" Jan started, but Cliff shot him a look and he stopped.

"I should have known Jan had something to do with this."

"We have files from the farm. We're pretty sure they're Pieter's," Cliff said.

"Who would send you Pieter's files? And why?"

"We can't tell you that," Cliff said, which wasn't really a lie, considering neither he nor anyone else knew who had dropped the files off to Jan.

"What's in the documents?"

"Land deeds, personal documents, farm history. There is a lot to go through, and we hardly have the resources to do it and make sense of it." Another white lie, since they had managed to skim through many of the files and find some interesting information. But there was still no way of knowing what any of this had to do with the murders.

"I'm not sure," Lou said, but her tone suggested she was at least entertaining the idea, so Cliff continued to push.

"Come on, it's a simple trade. You show us around, we don't touch anything, and you get to bring a whole set of new documents to Captain Marks. It's a good deal, Lou," Cliff said.

He waited patiently on the phone, knowing that, if there was any chance of this working, he would know in the next few moments. Mercifully, Lou broke the silence first.

"Fine. Come to the farm tomorrow morning at eight a.m.. Bring the files."

Cliff signalled Jan and Bunty with a thumbs up, each one looking mildly triumphant and a little nervous.

"Cliff. Please don't make me regret this," Lou said.

"You won't," Cliff said. "I promise."

The phone fell silent and Cliff hung up, letting out a breath he hadn't realized he'd been holding in.

"Tomorrow morning at eight a.m.," Cliff said with a grin.

"But we have to give them the files!" Jan said. "If we do that, then…"

"Then they could learn about Aria," Bunty finished for him when he didn't.

"I know," Cliff said. It had been on his mind, but he couldn't see another way.

"Couldn't we just keep this document?" Jan asked. "Give them everything else?"

"No," Cliff said firmly. "If we keep information now, it will only hurt all of us and Aria. The best thing we can do for Aria is discover who did this before the police uncover this information." Cliff knew that what he was saying was only meant to placate the other two in the room, who appeared to feel quite certain that Aria couldn't have done it. But Cliff knew that, when it came to situations like these, there was no telling what people were capable of, and this included Aria.

In Cliff's experience, poisoning someone took some thought, effort and premeditation. It wasn't a crime of passion, or some spur-of-the-moment crime. It required hate and strength. And though these were not words Cliff would have used to describe Aria, it hardly meant she was innocent. She may not be trying to get the farms, but that didn't mean she wasn't angry enough to want Pieter dead. After all, he was hiding her, for some reason, in plain sight. Who knows what that does to a person? And given the right push, it could be more than enough cause to want someone dead.

This was the realization Cliff had gathered from this situation, and there was no doubt in his mind that the OPP would as well. Which meant, if she was innocent, they would only have a limited amount of time to figure who was guilty before Aria was taken in for questioning. Then there was no telling what would happen to her. Maybe they would send her back to Holland, or worse, prison.

"If we do this, we have to give them everything. If Aria didn't do it…"

"She didn't," Bunty said confidently, and Cliff knew she had an idea of who did, but she still hadn't shared it with him, which he did not like.

"Right. Are you going to tell us who *did*?" Cliff asked, annoyed by his petulant tone.

"Not yet. But I promise I will soon." Bunty smiled softly.

He knew the last part was for him, but it still didn't help how he felt about it now.

"Okay. But then it's up to us to prove it, before they realize what's in those documents," Cliff said.

"We will. I know it," Bunty said optimistically.

Jan smiled. "Of course we will."

"Yeah, of course we will," Cliff said, unsure if he shared their confidence.

30

Cliff grimaced as he attempted to miss yet another pothole on the gravel road heading towards Winkleberry Farm. He glanced sheepishly at Bunty to his right and tried his best to ignore the tight grip she'd been keeping on the door.

"Not used to gravel roads, are we?" Bunty said through a bout of nervous laughter.

"It's been a while," Cliff acknowledged, shaking his head.

He didn't want to admit it, but since he'd moved to town, he'd not had much opportunity to sit behind the wheel of a vehicle. Although technically the driving duties for the Hearse were supposed to be divvied between all the residents, it was an unspoken agreement that Hans would be the one who drove them everywhere, since he had the most practice in large vehicles and still had his eyesight.

Thankfully, Cliff wasn't driving the Hearse. Instead, Hans had lent him his truck to take out to the farm, which was by no means a small car, but it was certainly more manageable than the Hearse. Though the way Cliff was driving, he wondered if that might not be entirely true.

"What do you think we're going to find out there?" Bunty asked.

"Hopefully, something that gives us some indication as to who is to blame for Pieter's death." Cliff shrugged. "But if you would be willing to share with me your insights into who you think is behind it, then maybe…"

"Maybe you'll be persuaded to link them to whatever we find?" Bunty offered with a smile. "I think it is best to see if you're able to come to the same conclusions I did on your own. Seems like the smarter approach."

Cliff couldn't fault her logic. It was true that the human brain was likely to fill in patterns that might not be there, just to help fit the narrative it already believed. But it didn't mean that he wasn't annoyed by it. He was also annoyed that she had shared her insights with Jan, but only on the condition that he not share them with Cliff. This only added to his frustration.

"Can you at least give me a clue?" Cliff begged.

"I already told you all of the information I used to come to my conclusion," Bunty said, chuckling. "You really don't like this, do you?"

"No. I do not," Cliff agreed. "Cause the thing is, I went over everything I thought I knew about the case last night…twice." He held up two fingers, further showing his point, but regretted having to remove his hand from the steering wheel and quickly returned it. "Nothing new came to mind. I mean, we have the kids, and Mari's potential fate with the farm, Flynn stealing files to hide his theft—"

"Which he agreed to put back," Bunty said, as if this absolved him of the act.

"But only after he was caught." Cliff shook his head. "He *stole* evidence."

"He took files from his own safe," Bunty corrected.

"You know what I mean."

"I do, but it is fun to see you get so flustered," she mused.

"You are cruel," Cliff joked.

"Oh stop," Bunty said, giving Cliff a playful smack on the arm, which he hammed up slightly for effect. "Go on. What else do you know?"

"Well, we know Hendrik knew about Flynn stealing money and offered to bail out the farms for part ownership, in order to save his brother the humiliation of having to tell Pieter what he was doing. And there is their mother, Cynthia, who apparently wants to sell all the farms to the Badger, and the Badger has a history of pressuring small farms to sell to him by driving up prices of goods or just buying up all the stock they need to run. It's ruthless, but not necessarily illegal."

This received a scoff from Bunty. "Well, it should be."

"Agreed, but that might not be our fight," Cliff said.

"Fair. What else do you know?"

"You're enjoying this, aren't you?" Cliff said.

"Immensely," Bunty replied, as Cliff swerved to avoid another pothole.

"Right, well…there is Aria, who is the secret daughter of Pieter, who no one knows about, or at least we suspect that's true. His brother, Lucas, who allegedly covered up for an accident Pieter may have caused when they were younger, which may have been the reason Lucas wasn't left any of the farm when his father died. Maybe he held a grudge?"

"Perhaps. But you would think, over the years, he would have had plenty of ways to kill his brother and make it look like an accident on a farm—falling equipment, barn fire, equipment malfunction—so why now and why poison?" Bunty said, counting the ways on her finger like she was listing books she'd once read. And perhaps in some ways she was. But that didn't prevent her face from blushing bright red the moment Cliff glanced over at her.

"Remind me not to get on your bad side," Cliff joked, receiving another smack across the arm.

"You know what I mean. Poisoning his drink? Seems off," Bunty said.

"Perhaps you're right. Well, there is always the possibility it was an accident, and *no one* did it, and this was all just a tragic misunderstanding and we're doing this for nothing," Cliff said, wondering if he was starting to lose his edge or if that was beginning to look like the most reasonable cause.

He'd seen people kill for a lot of reasons, but he'd always thought he could tell the types of people who were willing to kill. From what he could tell of the family, although mildly dysfunctional—and certainly hiding things—none of them seemed a plausible killer.

According to Hans, and what they found in those files, the farm might have been worth a couple million at most, split between so many people it hardly felt worth it to kill for. He'd seen people kill for *tens* of million in the past, but a few hundred thousand hardly seemed worth the risk of going to jail.

Unless there was something more to this gold theory. But all they had was a fifty-year-old document with zoning changes and a story from a diner waitress, and for all any of them knew, the van people saw was for a plumber not a surveyor.

"You really believe that?" Bunty asked.

"I'm not sure what to believe anymore. I used to think I was good at all of this." Cliff laughed coldly. "But I don't understand any of this."

"You're only saying that because you think I know something you don't," Bunty said, and Cliff was sure she was trying to be sincere about it, but he had to admit it did bother him.

"Well, you do," Cliff said.

"No, I'm just thinking about things differently. Or perhaps you missed it."

"But it's my job not to miss things," Cliff insisted.

"No, it *was* your job. Now your job is to be retired and relax and perhaps, on occasion, when the opportunity arises, help people in need."

"But I hardly see how we're helping."

"And perhaps you won't until we help them." Bunty shrugged. "Besides, if I'm correct, then I have all the confidence in the world you'll come to the same conclusion as me. Or you won't, and that will be less desirable."

Cliff chuckled to himself as he rounded the laneway that took them down to Winkleberry Farm. It was a shame not to see many cars in the parking lot, not that he'd been expecting lines of vehicles, but from what he'd heard about the farm in the past, he expected a couple more. Instead, there was one truck and two police cars.

...

"You brought a friend," Cliff said to Lou as he cautiously stepped out of Hans's truck. Although it wasn't one of those new massive trucks, he still had to take his time getting out.

"I'm sorry, Cliff," Lou said, her face looking flushed as she clenched her hands beside her boss and Cliff's number one fan, Captain Marks.

"Did you think I wouldn't find out what you were planning, Mr. Shaw?" Captain Marks said, shaking his head. "How about we skip the part where I remind you that you are no longer a police detective and you just go ahead and give us whatever documents you have." He gave Cliff a pitying look.

"I would," Cliff said as he shut the door and approached the large man, "but I don't have them." Cliff shrugged.

"Then *you* have them?" he said, turning his attention to Bunty, who appeared to have no issues getting out of the truck, though it did require some finessing, considering her smaller body and the larger step. Cliff wished Jan had been kind enough to lend them *his* car, but after Jan's obvious disappointment about not coming with them, Cliff didn't have the heart to ask him for his car as well.

Bunty smiled. "I don't have them either."

"Well, truthfully, I don't care who has them, as long as it's me who has them next," announced Captain Marks, his patience clearly running thin. It was a terrible habit the man possessed.

"And you will," Cliff said, "just as soon as you hold up your end of the bargain." Cliff smiled.

Captain Marks snapped the false façade he'd been playing at and dove straight into anger. "This isn't a game. I could have you arrested for withholding information from the police. Now, please stop messing around and give me the files."

"No," Cliff said firmly.

"Cliff, please," Lou said. "I know you want to help, but this isn't the way to do it."

"It's the *only* way to do it. We have something you need, and you have something we need. It's a fair trade. You both know it and, as for the legality of the trade, I think you and I both know Jan, who is a member of the free press, is under no direct obligation to share his information with you unless you have a court order. Which could take some time. And we have an opportunity to avoid all of that if you just show us around." Cliff nodded in the direction of the storage room where Pieter's body was found.

"Give us the documents!" Captain Marks shouted.

"I will," Cliff said. "After you show us around."

"For Chr—" Captain Marks stopped himself and turned away, face pink. He placed his hands on his waist, gripping his belt so hard Cliff thought he might bruise his own palms. "Did you know about this, Polaski?"

"I had no idea, sir. They told me they were bringing the files," Lou said, her face sheepish as Captain Marks examined her closely. "I swear it, sir."

"Argh. Fine. Ten minutes. Then you're out of here," he said through gritted teeth.

"Ten is all we need." Cliff grinned, which only annoyed the captain even further.

"Take them in. I need a minute," he stormed off, heading towards his car, mumbling under his breath and shaking his hands violently.

"You sure you don't—" Lou began, but he turned and looked at her.

"I'm sure. Ten minutes, Officer Polaski. That's it," he shouted as he opened the door to his car and slammed it shut behind him.

"Yes, sir," she said, turning to walk towards the storage room, waving for Cliff and Bunty to follow.

"That went well," Bunty whispered to Cliff.

"First hurdle down," Cliff whispered back.

They moved to catch up with Lou, who was walking silently towards the shed. Her hands were clutching her vest tightly. It was early in the morning, so it was still cool, but Cliff guessed Lou shouldn't have been sweating in her gear until at least midafternoon. Which meant the sweat he spotted on her brow was because of them.

"Don't be nervous, Lou," Cliff said.

"I'm no—" She stopped herself. "I'm sorry," she whispered softly, looking back, as if she wanted to say more, but Cliff already guessed where this was heading and eased her down.

"You're fine. I figured this would happen. It would be too risky not to tell your boss. That's why we left Jan with the folder in town," Cliff said. "The last thing we wanted was for you to get in any trouble for helping us. And now you won't."

"You mean you knew I would tell him?" Lou sounded annoyed.

"It was the right thing to do," Bunty said. "And we figured you would do the right thing."

"But if we'd told you, then it wouldn't appear genuine to the captain when he asked," Cliff said.

"And what if I didn't tell him?" Lou asked.

"But you did," Cliff said.

"So you're not mad that I...that I betrayed you?"

"On the contrary, Miss Polaski," Bunty said, grabbing onto Lou's arm for support. "You played your part perfectly. Not to mention, I believe Cliff enjoys angering our dear friend Captain Marks."

"I wouldn't go so far as to say 'enjoy it,'" Cliff chuckled. "But I have to admit he's a simple man to agitate."

"Well, you certainly have more nerve than I do, messing with him like this," Lou said.

"Everyone needs a hobby." Cliff shrugged.

Lou had to stifle a laugh as she glanced back at Captain Marks, who was sitting in his seat, eyes closed, and appeared to be breathing heavily. His hands didn't get the message, as they were wrapped tightly around the steering wheel.

"Well, be careful, or you may give him a heart attack," Lou said.

"He'll be fine." Bunty smiled and waved a hand passively. "Right now, we need to figure out what happened here."

"What exactly are you looking for?" Lou asked. "'Cause we've been over this place more times than I can count and, honestly, there's not much." She shook her head.

"We'll know it when we see it," Cliff said. "For now, I just want to know what you've found."

"Well, prepare to be amazed," Lou said

From her tone, Cliff wasn't very optimistic.

31

Cliff's instincts had been right, and from what he could tell, there hadn't been many changes to what had been found when he'd last walked through the space, save for the yellow and black caution tape surrounding everything, and tiny, numbered, yellow A-frame stands, showing where various clues had been found.

But it was obvious from the sporadic nature of the signs that they didn't have much idea what was important and what wasn't. At first glance, Cliff counted ten of these stands, and he wagered that number would double as he progressed further in.

"Very thorough," Cliff said, catching a shake of Lou's head from the corner of his eye.

"Seems random to me," Bunty said. Despite being the only one not accustomed to seeing crime scenes, she still found an issue with the scene.

"Why do you say that?" Cliff said, raising a hand to prevent Lou from saying anything. Cliff was curious what someone, particularly Bunty, had to say.

"Well, I don't know," she said, wandering around, careful not to touch anything. "It just seems a little…discombobulated. Like they weren't entirely sure what was relevant and what wasn't." She peered around, pushing her glasses up from her nose to glance down at some sort of smear on the floor.

"Why do you think it appears random?" Cliff asked as he took a stroll around, trying to clock the various tags in the room. He was up to sixteen now.

Lou, having likely walked the scene more than a few times, stood near the doorway with her arms folded against her chest, listening. Cliff could tell from the way her mouth kept opening and shutting that she was trying hard not to interject.

"It's just, well, the body was found here," she said, gesturing to a chalk outline of the body. "He was clearly trying to get here." She pointed to an evidence marker on the ground.

"Why do you say that?" Cliff asked. Bunty hadn't ever been in this room before, and therefore, wouldn't have known about the EpiPen that had been on the ground, now labeled with a number "1" marker.

"His body's positioning on the ground, and this is the first evidence tag. Most people don't crawl towards danger. So, whatever was here, he must have assumed could help him," Bunty said.

Cliff chuckled. "Not bad."

"It was his EpiPen," Lou said from the door.

"Right. Because of the peanuts," Bunty said, more to herself than anyone else. "So, I would assume this was his drink." Bunty gestured to an area labeled "2" with a crusty, dried patch of milkshake on the ground.

"Correct," Lou said. "You're not bad at this, Bunty."

"I enjoy puzzles." Bunty grinned as if that somehow qualified her to be good at spotting details in crime scenes. "Then you have the safe." She gestured to the back wall. "But after that, the numbers begin to scatter, marking random scuff marks, items along the floor. Nothing really points to a singular location. It just seems, to steal from the English, higgledy-piggledy."

"What's that mean?" Lou asked.

"Disorderly or confusing," Bunty stated.

"In other words, like you're unsure what you're looking for, and therefore, you look at everything." Cliff glanced at Lou, who confirmed the notion with a thoughtful tilt of her head.

"In our defence, multiple people have access to this room. We don't know what it was like before the incident and, for whatever reason, there are no cameras here." Lou shook her head.

"It's a farm in the middle of the country," Bunty said. "More people are after the expensive farm equipment than a potential few thousand in a safe."

"Still, you would think, if you had a safe with money in it, you would want to have it watched, no?" Lou said incredulously.

"Not if the camera equipment would be worth more than what you're trying to protect." Cliff shrugged, understanding that, sometimes, the most logical isn't necessarily the most cost-effective.

"Would have made this all a lot easier though." Lou sighed.

"Not necessarily," Cliff said, taking a lap around the room and having a look at all the marks left over by the police. Even he had to admit that it seemed difficult to associate what may or may not be a part of the crime scene. When you didn't know what exactly you were looking for, everything appeared to be helpful, even if it wasn't. He didn't envy the team responsible for having to tag everything, that's for sure. "If you think whoever did this had access to this room, there is no reason why they also wouldn't have had access to the camera footage, which means they would have likely deleted that as well."

"Oh well, then in that case..." Lou said shaking her head.

"Sorry, old habit."

"Well, any of those old habits giving you any insight into who did this?" Lou asked.

"Not yet," Cliff chuckled.

The room felt smaller than he remembered, but then again, it was just a few of them inside, now it contained the remnants of the police who'd worked to document the scene. But still, there were things he remembered, and lots of things he'd clearly missed as well.

It was a large, rectangular room, with shelving units on either side and boxes piled up near the door. The area where Pieter had collapsed was closer to the door than Cliff remembered.

"He looked as though he was crawling somewhere." Bunty said.

"Towards his EpiPen." Lou gestured to a yellow number 1 on the ground. "We think he realized what was happening, but he must have dropped it and it rolled over here."

"So, whoever did it must have watched him try and grab it," Cliff said.

"Or they left him in here." Lou suggested.

"And risk him living to tell everyone what happen? No, more likely they stayed."

"And did nothing to help," Bunty added, her voice bitter.

"Murderers don't usually try to help their victims," Lou pointed out.

"No. They don't," Cliff said absently, his mind looking over the area from a different perspective.

"What?" Lou asked. She must have noticed the shift in Cliff, because she took a step in, clearly thinking that, whatever Cliff was pondering was of importance.

He didn't know if it was though. Right now, it was just an idea.

"Well, we are all under the impression that Pieter was killed deliberately," Cliff said.

"Because someone poisoned his drink."

"What if they didn't? What if that was just an accident?"

"What? So no one killed him?" Lou said shaking her head.

"Perhaps no one *saved* him," Bunty said, her eyes following Cliff's. "How does his EpiPen end up on the floor behind these boxes?"

"Exactly," Cliff said.

"It's more like someone *tossed* it over here," Bunty said.

"We checked the EpiPen for prints," Lou said. "Only had Pieter's prints."

"Maybe they kicked it," Bunty said.

"So, what? Someone was in here talking to him and watched him die?" Lou asked.

"A crime of opportunity," Bunty said.

Cliff nodded. "What else did you find in the room?" Cliff asked Lou. "Anything else out of the ordinary?"

"Nothing, just your usual things, some footprints, some clothing fibers on some shelves, but nothing obvious." Lou shrugged.

"Solve the case yet, old man?" Captain Marks came in, appearing to have calmed himself from the frustration of not getting the files he wanted.

"I'm not a wizard, Captain Marks," Cliff said shaking his head. "I only see what you see."

"Cliff suspects whoever did this might not have done it on purpose," Lou said, and from the look she gave Cliff, he imagined she thought this was helpful. But knowing what he did about Captain Marks, this certainly wasn't the case.

"Oh good. So, we have a reluctant killer on our hands." Sarcasm practically rolled off his lips. "Any other insights? Accomplices maybe? One to poison and one to watch?"

"I understand you're frustrated, but it's no reason to take it out on us." Bunty berated the younger man as if he'd been a child in her library. But they weren't in her library and Captain Marks wasn't a child.

"My frustration is that you've been withholding evidence on a case, because you think whatever this"—he waved a hand in their general direction—"game it is you're playing, is more important than actual police work. So, forgive me for not indulging you all in this little fantasy. Now, you've had your look around. You've come up with your little conclusions. Can we please move on and get those documents so the *real* police can do their jobs?" His voice had an edge to it that made Cliff realize now was not the time to test this man.

So instead, Cliff pulled out his phone and messaged Jan.

"The files are being dropped off now," Cliff said.

"Good. Thank you. Now get the hell out of my crime scene." Captain Marks pointed towards the door.

Cliff shared a look with Bunty and headed toward the door, but was surprised when Bunty turned to look at Captain Marks.

"There is a rumour around town that some sort of survey company was seen up on the farm. Something Gold," she said, tilting her head. "I just thought you might be interested to know."

Cliff hadn't been sure what Bunty was going to say, but it certainly hadn't been that.

From the mildly amused look on Captain Marks's face, it wasn't what he was expecting either.

"Thank you for letting us know about the rumours amongst the villagers," he said with clear mockery.

"We're a town. Not a village," Bunty said. "And you, sir, are an idiot," she added before walking out the door, not bothering to wait for a response.

Captain Marks looked as though his head was going to burst from anger, but somehow, he managed to contain himself and simply let them walk away. It helped when his phone went off, and from the sound of the conversation, it appeared, as instructed, that Jan had dropped off the files.

Bunty was a few paces ahead of Cliff, and it took some extra-long strides to catch up to his friend as she strode forward with determined focus.

"That man is…well…" Bunty looked flustered as she tried to find the word to use to describe Captain Marks.

Cliff had a few words *he* would have chosen, but he doubted very much that they would have suited Bunty. His assumptions were correct as she seemed to find the word she was searching for.

"Imbecilic. That's what he is." She shook her head.

"He is. Though in fairness, I can't imagine he's all too happy to have us running around his crime scene." Cliff shrugged.

"You saw it in there. It looked like they were grasping at straws. Old shoe prints, stains on the floor, clothing fibers…it's a farm, and a storage unit of course…"

"Clothing fibers?" Cliff asked curiously.

"Yeah, that was the clothing fiber Lou mentioned. Likely torn off on one of the shelves," Bunty said passively.

"Cliff! Bunty!" Lou shouted, striding up to meet them. They hadn't quite made it to their truck. "I'm sorry about him. He's…a little stressed."

"You don't have to make excuses for him, dear." Bunty smiled thinly. "He's an adult, who should be able to manage his feelings by now. No need to be rude just because he can't figure out what's going on."

"You may be right, but I'm sorry all the same."

"Well thank you, Lou," Bunty said.

Cliff's mind was still swirling around that fabric. *Was it on the shelf?*

"Lou, you mentioned fabric? What kind of fabric?" Cliff asked.

Lou thought about it for a minute before shaking her head. "Not much really. Just some shirt caught on one of the shelves. It's"—she opened up a notebook and read through it—"100 percent cotton, white and blue—at least that was the sample—but that's it. Hard to get much out of it without the rest of the shirt," Lou said.

Cliff nodded politely.

"Why, do you know something I don't?"

"A cotton shirt is a nice material. Very breathable," Bunty suggested, glancing over at Cliff. "But most people know that, I assume."

"Why do I feel like you're not telling me everything?" Lou asked, her eyes narrowing as they shifted between Bunty and Cliff.

"I think it's best to assume I'm never telling you everything, my dear," Bunty said, her voice cool and casual.

Lou shook her head. "Did I mention, I don't think I like this." Lou pointed a finger between Cliff and Bunty.

"What's that?" Cliff asked.

"You two…it's annoying," Lou chuckled.

Cliff shrugged. "If it makes you feel any better, she's not telling me either."

"It doesn't," Lou said.

"The mind can be very suggestive," Bunty said. "Plant an idea too early and it will be all you see. That's not helpful."

Cliff couldn't agree more. It was always better to have as many minds as possible trying to solve the problem on their own, rather than many minds stuck on the same path. Too many times, Cliff had been in situations where obvious things got overlooked because of group biases and blind spots. Keeping as many avenues open as possible only served to better lead to the right conclusion. Cliff had his theories, as did Bunty and the police. Everyone running down different paths and getting to the same finish line could only better serve the justice Pieter deserved.

"I agree," Cliff said, giving Bunty a nod. "If we know anything for certain, Lou, you will be the first to know, I promise. But until then, it's best if we don't sway your judgement. You have all the information we have now, and hopefully, we can figure out who is responsible for Pieter's death." He gave Lou a pat on the arm.

"You're right about that," Lou said, looking over her shoulder nervously, but Captain Marks must have still been on the phone inside the storage room. "There is something you may want to see."

"What's that?" Cliff asked.

Lou pulled out her phone and started to scroll down until she found what she was looking for. She handed it over to Cliff. Bunty pressed up beside him as they both struggled to read the tiny document.

"Whatever happened to good old-fashioned paper?" Bunty asked, shaking her head.

"The scans make it easier to share. But that's beside the point. When we retrieved the files from Flynn Stroud, this was one of the documents inside. We didn't think much of it, because we knew that Flynn was having issues with the farm. It made sense to be having a land survey done if they were thinking they might need to sell the land to pay off debts or borrow more money against it. At least that's what our analyst said."

"Before you realized he hadn't spent the money yet. He was just trying to get enough to buy more land," Cliff said.

"Which doesn't make it right. But yes, we know that now."

"Still, your reasoning makes sense," Bunty suggested. "If Pieter knew what Flynn was doing, then he might have thought selling it was the only way to fix their problem. But that would depend on how deep of a hole Flynn had them in."

"It was deep," Lou said, shaking her head. "Flynn's agreed to put the money back, but the farm is still in trouble."

"Not if the Badger buys it," Cliff said.

"You mean all that stuff Flynn was talking about at your house is true?" Lou asked.

"Apparently so," Bunty said.

"Well, that would be a bad idea," Lou said.

"How's that?" Cliff asked.

"Check out the fourth document. I assumed it was just another survey, but take a look at the company," Lou said.

Cliff scrolled down the phone, finding it difficult to navigate as the screen kept starting and stopping, then flipping through many pages.

He used his phone the absolute minimum and trying to flick through documents was not something he did. He could call, text, and get on the internet, and even then, he found it difficult at times.

But finally, with a little help from Bunty, who had surprisingly nimble fingers, they landed on the page Lou mentioned. It looked to be another survey of the farm, only this one was done by a different company. One called Gold Standards Inc.

"You said someone in town saw a van, Gold-something, right? Maybe this was it," Lou said. "Only this one isn't for land boundaries."

"It's the mining perspective," Bunty said, sending Cliff a sideways glance.

"You know something about this, don't you," Lou asked. "What?"

"We know what you know, Lou," Cliff said as he read through the document. He landed on something he thought was interesting, but before he could react to it, Lou pulled her phone back.

"Tell me," Lou said.

"You're a smart woman, Lou," Cliff said. "Trust your instincts."

"It would just be helpful if you could give these instincts a little push," Lou grumbled.

"Go through the files, Lou. See what you find," Cliff said.

"We should get going," Bunty said, pulling on Cliff's arm.

Lou looked as though she was going to pull him back but refrained.

"You two are the worst," Lou said as Bunty and Cliff walked to Hans's truck.

Neither of them said anything until they were both seated in the truck. Cliff's mind was racing with the information on the document he'd just read over. It had taken every ounce of willpower not to react in any way, but he should have known that Bunty would see right through it.

"You saw it, didn't you?" Bunty said, not bothering to look over at Cliff.

"I did."

"So, you…?" Bunty started.

"I think so," Cliff said, his mind flipping through the possibilities to try and understand if what he was thinking could be the truth. But even in his mind, all roads led to the same conclusion. The same one he imagined Bunty had arrived at days earlier. All he needed to do was prove it. "But how did you…?"

"I paid attention to the right things." Bunty shrugged, causing Cliff to chuckle.

He still had no idea what Bunty could be referring to, but knew instinctively that they'd arrived at the same conclusion.

"I think we know who killed Pieter VanWinkle," Cliff said. "All we need to do is prove it."

32

"You have to trick them."

It was Gerald who finally said it aloud, though it was clear from the affirmative nods around the dinner table that the rest of the house agreed. Even Cliff, who was hoping for something a little more concrete, was beginning to think that, if there was any chance of catching Pieter's killer, then they were going to have to be creative about it.

After returning from the farm, Cliff and Bunty had confirmed that each of their suspicions were the same. But there were still a few major problems. The first being that, just because they agreed on who'd done it and why, it wasn't obvious "how." This would mean the best chance they had at catching them was to force a confession. Obviously easier said than done.

"How do you suppose we do that, Gerald?" Kitty asked.

"I never said I knew how to do it. I simply said it was the best way to do it. Given the information, or lack of information, it makes the most sense," Gerald said, scooping out some mashed potatoes to have with his plate of braised short ribs that he'd managed to "whip up" that afternoon.

Cliff, after having a bite of his own, had decided it was one of the best things he'd ever eaten and, for the life of him, he couldn't understand why Gerald wasn't working in a high-end restaurant rather than a communal home with a bunch of old people.

"Gerald, you've outdone yourself tonight," Sol said, shaking his head as he cut off a piece of beef and ate it.

"Just the one serving for you tonight. Doctor told you to lay off the red meat," Kitty said.

"The doctor never had this dinner." Sol smiled. "It might be worth the reduced time."

"Don't you dare. We still haven't won our bridge league. That would be embarrassing," Kitty said.

"Food is life, Kitty." Gerald smiled as he worked his way through a second portion, nodding for her to eat.

Kitty reluctantly took a bite as the group watched. Her shoulders slumped low as she chewed and let out a heavy sigh. "My lord, Gerald, you are an odd man, but you are a gifted chef."

"I think that's the nicest thing you've ever said to me," Gerald chuckled.

"Don't get used to it," Kitty mumbled between bites.

"I think we can all agree that Gerald is a great chef," Hans said, "but I would very much like to get back to the matter of Pieter's death. Not least of all wondering just how correct you are on all of this? I mean, we're playing with people's lives here."

Cliff understood that Hans was not a big fan of the situation, since it meant a member of Pieter's family had killed him. And assuming Cliff and Bunty were correct, that Hans knew them well.

"I know this is difficult, Hans." Bunty placed a hand on top of his. "But we've told you what we know, and I think that it's important that, if we move forward, it's with the understanding that this might not be the outcome you were looking for."

"Truth be told, I didn't know what the outcome would be. I just thought I wanted to know, regardless."

"Ignorance is bliss," Cliff said softly.

"True enough." Hans shook his head.

"We still don't know if you're right about all of this," Sol offered. "Perhaps there's another option we don't know about. One that isn't so bad."

"Sol's right," Kitty said. "This could all be a terrible accident."

"You're right," Cliff said. "I would hardly say we're working with all the information. We could just let the police do their job and see what they find?"

"So what? All your work was done for nothing?" Kitty asked.

"I would hardly say nothing," Bunty said. "We could tell Lou what we discovered and allow them to decide if it all lines up."

It was one thing to try and help a friend. It was another thing entirely to use that information to accuse someone of murder. Cliff had been a detective for most of his life, and he had seen people do terrible things for all kinds of reasons. But he never had much of a personal connection with any of the suspects. Now, faced with having to accuse someone so close to one of his oldest and dearest friends…it was slightly more difficult.

"I agree. We're not the police. We may not have all the information. Perhaps they have an alibi, or someone saw them elsewhere. I would hardly say it was possible for us to do all our due diligence, because we don't have access to everything the police do," Cliff said, trying to make the case that it wouldn't be hard for them to walk away. If that was the decision they made.

"So, you just let the cards fall where they may?" Kitty asked. "Seems a bit anti-climactic, no?"

"Well, we would tell Lou. Right, Cliff?" Bunty asked.

"Of course," Cliff said, feeling the shift in the room and, though selfishly he would have liked to figure this one out, he understood the reluctance behind it. Everything was more complicated when it got personal. "Assuming that's what Hans wants?"

"Hans?" Bunty asked.

All heads turned to look at the big man, who clearly did not like all the attention.

"Well, I asked you to do this," Hans said softly.

"And we were happy to help." Bunty patted his hand.

Hans looked as though he was thinking over his response as Gerald leaned over to grab a slice of bread.

"For heaven's sake, Gerald!" Kitty shook her head.

"What? It didn't feel like the right time to ask for help." He shrugged, running the bread through the juices from the beef on his plate.

This caused Hans to chuckle, then Sol, and soon the laughter rippled around the table before finally ending, as all good bouts of laughter do, with a collective sigh.

"There is a third option," Mrs. Chen offered. Everyone turned to face her. "Tomorrow, the judges come to look at the garden, which, thanks to all of you, is ready to be presented. We could let this new information sink in and decide tomorrow how we want to proceed."

Bunty smiled. "A very sensible solution, Mrs. Chen."

"Perhaps that would be for the best. Give us a chance to think everything over," Hans said, though it was clear he still had his hesitations, or perhaps he just felt guilty at having Cliff and the others investigate, to only have them stop now.

"We will respect whatever decision you make, Hans." Cliff gave his friend a firm nod, hoping it conveyed the honesty behind his words.

"I, for one, will be quite happy once this judging is complete," Sol said, giving his shoulders a rub. "Any more work out there, and you all may have to start digging a hole," he chuckled.

"Big enough for two," Cliff said, giving his knee a rub, though it was his entire body that ached.

"Have you not been doing your stretches?" Bunty asked. "I'll never understand why you boys would rather live in pain than take ten minutes to stretch." Bunty shook her head.

Sol shrugged. "We've got better thing to do."

"Like what? You're retired. All you do is sit around and play cards," Kitty said.

"Exactly." Sol grinned and took a bite of beef, as once again laughter filled the room.

When it finally settled, the conversation shifted away from Pieter's death and focused on the garden and the various plans for the weekend. Not that the weekend plans differed so much from the weekday plans in the house.

It amazed Cliff how easy it was to get swept up in all the conversation spinning around in his mind, although they were never far from Pieter's death. He watched as Bunty fell back into her quiet, reserved self, which he was beginning to understand was less her being shy, and more her being very observant. If working on this mystery had taught him anything, it was that Bunty rarely missed much.

...

"Good morning, Cliff. Beautiful day out there," Mrs. Chen said, as she came into the living room, her cane in one hand and a tea in the other. She was dressed in a nice sundress and must have been up for a while, as Cliff noticed she'd already prepared her gardening basket and placed it by the front door.

"Good morning, Mrs. Chen. It would appear the day has been kind to you," Cliff said, admiring the morning sun coming through the window. "What time are you expecting the judges?"

"Ten a.m. Or there abouts," she said.

"Nervous?" Cliff asked.

"Not in the least. Hardly feels worth it. I believe I've exhausted my emotional expenditure for the week." She chuckled. "Whatever happens today, I will be proud."

"What a wonderful attitude to have," Bunty said as she entered the living room and took a seat on one of the chairs across from him.

Cliff knew they'd decided to wait till the judging was over to decide what to do, but still he wanted to find a moment to speak with Bunty just the two of them. He'd been thinking about it all night and was wondering if the best thing for them to do was talk to Lou and tell her everything. Then, with any luck, the police would sort it out. But he didn't think it was fair to do that without talking to her first. Since she had been so critical in finding everything. In fact, she'd done most of the work.

"I have a feeling today is going to be a good day," Kitty said. She sipped her coffee and looked around, waiting for nods of approval from her housemates.

Cliff was all too happy to provide one also.

It wasn't till after breakfast of eggs, toast, and bacon by Gerald, that Cliff finally found a moment alone with Bunty. She was in her chair knitting, with Skittles the cat curled up on her lap.

He'd hardly had a chance to sit down, before, without skipping a stitch, Bunty said, "I think it's best if we give what we have to Lou." She paused momentarily to glance up to read Cliff's expression, which he wagered was something between confusion and relief.

"I was thinking the same thing. I just know how much work you—"

"*We* put in." Bunty smiled. "And I think that's why it would be good to tell Lou. I would hate to be wrong and, like you said, we may not have all the information."

"Do you think we should tell Hans?"

"Bunty already has," Hans said as he rounded the corner. "We spoke this morning in the shop about it. I agree. These are people's lives and, honestly, it was unfair of me to ask you both to do any of this."

"Hans, you know I…*we* are happy to help," Cliff said, sending a sideways glance towards Bunty, who nodded her agreement. "Truth be told, I was enjoying it." Cliff sighed and leaned back in his chair. "It's been nice to have something to focus on. Don't get me wrong, I've enjoyed living here, but I'm starting to realize that I don't have anything to do. You have your knitting"—Cliff gestured to Bunty—"you have your woodworking, Mrs. Chen her garden, Gerald his cooking, Sol and Kitty have cards."

"Don't forget endless debating," Bunty mused.

"That too," Cliff laughed. "I just feel like I'm not really doing this whole retiring thing very well. All I have ever had is my work. I'm not sure what I'm supposed to do here."

Cliff was surprised when Hans started to laugh. Cliff wasn't sure if it was at him or the situation, but it didn't stop him from feeling a little embarrassed.

"Cliff, you've been here a couple months. You can hardly expect yourself to just slow down and fit right in. You need to give it time. Being retired isn't easy. You think I just walked off the farm and into the woodshop?"

"Yes, actually," Cliff said, feeling a little ridiculous now.

"I didn't. I tried working on the farm part-time for nearly three years, slowly becoming increasingly more useless. After that sidestep, I found myself with eighteen-hour days and nothing to do. I tried everything—reading, writing, gardening, and yeah, eventually, woodworking. All I'm saying is, you've never been retired. Why would you think you would be good at it right away? Give yourself a break, try some things. Maybe remember what it's like to be bad at something," Hans said, giving Cliff a pat on the shoulder.

"I used to think I was a good detective, but it would appear Bunty has surpassed me in that regard."

"Oh hush, you," Bunty said, playfully slapping his arm. "I had some advantage on you. Besides, I would never have known where to start.

Although I must admit, I understand why you enjoyed your job. Save for the people dying part, of course."

"Do you think they will catch Pieter's killer?" Hans asked.

"I do," Cliff said, giving his friend a firm nod. "And if it turns out our assumptions are right, we will be right here to support you, my friend."

"I appreciate that."

Death had a funny way of lingering over people, once the shock of it all wore off. There came a time when all anyone really needed was closure. From Cliff's experience, he knew his friend was not finished grieving, he'd simply put it on pause—as he was sure the rest of the family had—until they knew what had happened. Then the reality of it all would sink in, that Pieter was no longer with them.

He hoped, for all of their sakes, that they would get closure soon and, more than anything, that they were wrong about everything.

33

"Welcome," Mrs. Chen said as three judges stood at the front gate of the Limestone Manor.

The wrought iron fence was the final barrier between them and the front garden. Cliff and the rest of the household stood behind the judges, along with Jan, Mari, Aria, Lou, and Dan, who all came to offer their support to Mrs. Chen, although she'd said she couldn't, for the life of her, understand why anyone would want to turn up to watch her show off a garden.

Cliff couldn't be sure, but he got the impression that at least two of the judges—a tall, slender woman with glasses, wearing a floral sundress, and a stylish man in a powder-blue linen suit, pink paisley flowered shirt, and thin black glasses—looked excited by the prospect of looking through the garden. They were anxious to get around the house to the main attraction. The third, a shorter, serious woman, who also wore a flowery dress with a matching sun hat, stood at the front of the party and gave little of her personal emotions away. If Cliff had to guess, she was the one Mrs. Chen would have to impress the most.

"Wonderful hedge work," Cliff heard the man say, which received a nod from the taller woman and a subtle tilt of the head from the shorter one, which Cliff hoped was a positive first step.

"If you wouldn't mind following me, I can show you to the rear garden," Mrs. Chen said, opening the front gate and directing everyone in.

The small party moved one at a time through the small gate and hedgeway, slower than Cliff ever would have, but he supposed he'd never had to judge a garden before. It amused Cliff to realize that, in all the time he'd had spent living at the house, this was the first time he'd ever used, or seen anyone enter, the front garden via the gate. He wouldn't have been sure it worked, had Hans not greased the hinges prior to everyone's arrival.

"This is all kind of exciting," Bunty whispered to him as they strolled down the pathway.

"A tour of our own house," Gerald muttered to himself.

"You know, Gerald," Kitty said, tapping the man on the shoulder. He turned to face her suspiciously. "Perhaps it would be a better use of your time if you were to prepare sandwiches and lemonade for everyone for after the tour."

"Interesting thought," Gerald said tapping his chin. "It would be a proper way to end a garden tour, and I am feeling rather peckish myself. But I wouldn't want to take away from Mrs. Chen's day," he said, pondering the idea.

"Nonsense," Kitty said. "I'm sure she would love it."

"Well, Kitty, if you think it would help, then who am I to stand in the way?" Gerald said.

As they reached the pathway to the rear garden, he ducked out to move around the group, heading wordlessly into the house. If Mrs. Chen noticed, it didn't appear to trouble her.

"What a great idea, Kitty!" Bunty said.

"It was either that or listen to him mutter on about the heat all morning," Kitty chuckled.

"Kitty!" Bunty admonished the other woman.

"Oh shush, you know he's happier in there anyways."

"Thank you all for coming today. I feel confident enough in saying that, due to the rainfall this past week, it would be very unlikely the garden you are going to see today would be worth visiting, were it not for the help of my housemates and the others who gave up their time this week to help me. Thank you," Mrs. Chen said, her smile beaming as she looked out over the small gathering in front of her.

Bunty began to clap, and, so she wasn't alone, Cliff joined in. Soon enough, there was a light smattering of clapping, save for the judges, who looked more confused than anything.

"Without further ado, I would like to present the back—"

Mrs. Chen was cut off by a large pickup truck pulling into the driveway, followed by two police cars, which stopped along the road, and finally, a jacked-up black Ram truck that parked in front of the Anglican Church.

A moment later, the small gathering had nearly doubled, as Captain Marks, along with two other police officers—one of whom Cliff recognized as Officer Prescott, the officer who had watched over him when he'd been arrested—joined them, along with Lucas VanWinkle, the Badger, Flynn, Hendrik, and a woman Cliff assumed to be Cynthia Stroud. All of them approached, looking very concerned.

"I'm sorry, but what is all of this about?" asked the short, serious-looking judge. "I'd hardly say theatrics are going to help your garden."

"I truly have no idea what this is about," Mrs. Chen said, looking at the rest of the housemates, all of whom turned to look at Lou, who looked equally as bewildered as the rest of them.

"Mari VanWinkle?" Captain Marks shouted over the murmuring crowd.

Mari raised her hand and took a tentative step forward. "Right here. But what's—"

She didn't get a chance to finish, as Captain Marks gestured towards her. Officer Prescott and the unknown officer walked up behind her and began handcuffing her.

"Mari VanWinkle, we are arresting you for the murder of Pieter VanWinkle. Anything you say can and will…"

"What?" was the collective murmur of the crowd, as Mari, clearly unsure what to do, let the officers place the cuffs around her wrist.

"What do you think you're doing?" Bunty demanded, stepping out from the crowd and approaching Captain Marks.

"My job, ma'am," he said coldly. "Now, if you would please excuse me—"

"But Mari didn't do it!" Bunty shouted.

"On the contrary. She did," Captain Marks said.

"But why would I kill my own father?" Mari said, appearing to find her voice again.

"All of this will be explained down at the station," Captain Marks said.

"I would like you to explain it now," Bunty said, stepping between Mari and the police.

"Mr. Shaw, would you please explain to your friend here that I am not under any obligation to explain myself to her," Captain Marks said. "But I am well within my right to arrest her for obstruction, should she desire that instead." He smiled coldly.

"I don't think that is necessary, Captain," Lou said, stepping forward and putting an arm around Bunty's shoulder.

"Officer Polaski. I should have guessed you'd be here."

"I'm here to support my friend, Mrs. Chen. And you are currently ruining the presentation of her garden," Lou said, with more gusto than Cliff would have ever had when talking to a superior.

"Oh, don't mind us," the man said calmly.

"Yes, this is rather exciting," said the tall woman. "Not that your garden wouldn't be, Mrs. Chen. It's just been a dull morning since the rain did so much damage to—"

"We are not supposed to discuss other gardens, Nancy!" snapped the shorter woman.

"Right. Sorry, Vera."

"And Kevin, wipe that smile off your face. It's not a parade. A woman is being arrested, for Christ's sakes." She swatted at the man, whose face immediately took on an embarrassed expression.

"She is *not* being arrested," Bunty said firmly.

"Yes. She *is*," Captain Marks retorted, while the two had a good stare down.

"Perhaps you could explain to us why she's being arrested?" Cliff said.

Captain Marks's ire turned on him. "As I said—"

"I know what you said, and you are correct. But I think you're making a mistake here."

"Do you now?" Captain Marks mused "Oh, I'm sorry, but is that what you think? You think you and your friends are the only ones capable of solving a crime in this town?"

"Of course not. I'm just curious why you think it was Mari. Because I think you're wrong."

"Arrest them *all*!" Captain Marks shouted, which caused more than a few confused looks, primarily from the two officers, who began counting the number of people, which obviously meant more handcuffs than they'd brought with them.

"Maybe we should all take a moment to breathe," Cliff said, looking towards Captain Marks, whose face was bright red now.

"Fine! Mari VanWinkle killed her father in order to keep the farms for herself. She was the only one not accounted for at the time of the incident. She had the keys to the building and was supposedly in her office, but no one saw her there. She was well aware of her father's allergies and was the first to find the body, giving her ample time to get rid of any evidence before we got there. She was aware her father was planning on selling the farm to her cousin Hendrik and, if he did that, she would be left with nothing. Since this is exactly what happened to her aunt, she was desperate not to have a similar fate. Oh, and we have it from numerous sources she'd been arguing with her father about the plans to develop the farm. She had the opportunity, the motive, and means."

"But I didn't do it!" she shouted, her hands behind her back.

"That's what everyone says," Captain Marks pointed out.

"You said everyone else was accounted for?" Cliff asked.

"Yes." Captain Marks rolled his eyes but continued. "Lucas VanWinkle was working on a tractor in the field; a number of families saw him there. Aria was helping out in the flower centre, and Flynn and Hendrik Stroud were having a meeting in the barns."

"Wait? Sorry. Say that again?" Cliff said.

"No. This isn't a Q&A, Mr. Shaw."

"It's just, you said Flynn and Hendrik were together?"

"Yes."

"But Hendrik told us he was on his way into town when Pieter's body was found," Bunty said. "How could he be with Flynn then?"

Cliff and the rest of the people in the crowd, at least the ones who knew who he was, turned to looked at Hendrik. Cliff's mind was racing now to connect all the pieces.

"Yes. I was with Flynn before, and then I left to go to town. Like I said," Hendrik said, his voice even.

"But then Flynn wouldn't have an alibi at the time of the murder," Bunty said.

"I was with Hendrik. He literally just said that."

"Did anyone else see them in the barn?" Bunty asked.

"What exactly is going on here?" Cynthia Stroud asked as she took a step forward. "Because if I'm reading this correctly, you're implying that it was my son who killed Pieter, which is ridiculous. Why would he?"

"Mrs. Stroud, may I ask why you are here with the Badg...Mr. Wilderman?" Cliff asked.

"Not that it's any of your business, but we were discussing the possible sale of the farm.

"But *you* don't own the farm," Cliff stated.

"Maybe not yet. But I'll be damned if I'm not going to get what's rightfully mine this time around. I've been booted out once already. I'm not about to let that happen again."

"But the farm would go to Pieter's kids before it would go to you."

"Not if Mari killed him, which is looking more and more likely, despite the fact that you, whoever you are, keep pointing your finger wrongfully in my son's direction," Cynthia said.

"His name is Detective Clifford Shaw," Bunty said, stepping up beside Cliff.

"Retired," Cliff added.

"Well, if it isn't the librarian. I see you haven't changed much," Cynthia said. "Still butting your nose into other people's business."

"Encouraging kids to stand up to a bully is hardly nosy, young lady," Bunty said, receiving a scoff from Cynthia.

"I'm not sure what's happening right now," Captain Marks said, shaking his head, "but does any of this have a point, or can I go?"

"The point is..." Bunty said, turning to look at Aria, who appeared to be curling up into herself.

Cliff knew this wasn't the time to be dragging this young woman out in front of everyone. She had her reasons for keeping her relationship with Pieter a secret, and who were they to decide when she told them?

Bunty must have noticed as much, as she stammered over herself "The point is... Cliff?"

"The point is, you claim that Mari is the only one with motive. But that isn't true," Cliff said.

"The point, please, Mr. Shaw."

"Winkleberry Farm was in trouble, because Flynn Stroud was stealing money to double down and buy more land in a last-ditch effort to grow their operations in order to compete with Mr. Wilderman."

"I admitted to all of this," Flynn said. "Hendrik offered to invest capital into the farm in exchange for ownership. I was going to put the money back."

"But Hendrik was never going to do that, was he?" Cliff asked. "Because Hendrik wasn't just buying a *part* of the farm. He wanted the *entire* family farm."

"It was a good deal. He'd let Mari run the farm, and I'd have enough capital to expand. Everyone wins."

"Not everyone. Not Mari, since she would end up with nothing."

"I'm not sure how any of this is helping Ms. VanWinkle's case, Mr. Shaw," Captain Marks said. "And my patience is wearing thin."

"You see, this is why this case baffled me. Why would anyone want someone dead over a couple of farms worth a million or two at best? I mean, sure, that's a good chunk of change, but only if you knew without a doubt it would be yours. Seems hardly enough to ruin your life over. It just never made any sense to me."

"Just like this isn't making any sense to the rest of us?" Captain Marks sighed.

"Mrs. Stroud, in your agreement with Mr. Wilderman, did you offer to sell him all the farms?" Cliff asked.

Cynthia looked annoyed and she rolled her eyes. "No. I'd *planned* on selling them all. But when Hendrik explained his proposal, how he thought the farms should stay in the family, I agreed."

"What?" the Badger said, clearly confused at this news.

"Sorry, Badge, but it's family."

"To hell with you all," the Badger said, storming off towards his truck, muttering about a *waste of time* and *stupid family* before climbing in his truck and driving off.

"Baby," Cynthia said with a grin.

"Why, Hendrik?" Cliff asked, everyone looking at him. "Why would you want the family farm?"

"I'm sentimental."

"But you hate farming. You were chomping at the bit to get back to the city."

"It's our legacy," Hendrik said.

"So, it has nothing to do with the fact that Winkleberry Farm is sitting on a gold mine?"

"What?" There was a collective gasp from everyone not living at the Limestone Manor.

"Cliff, there isn't any gold on Winkleberry Farm," Mari said.

"No, there isn't," Cliff admitted, "but there is a fairly high-density limestone deposit on it, isn't there, Lucas?"

All heads turned to look at Lucas, who looked more annoyed at being talked to than anything else.

"At least, I presume you're the one who delivered all those family documents to Jan at the paper?"

"Uncle Lucas?" Mari asked.

"Sure. Yes. I dropped off the papers. And yes, I knew there was something. I didn't know what. Just that Dad had the farm zoned for mining back in the day, but Pieter convinced him not to do it, said he wanted to run the farm, not sell it off. But he never changed its status either, and so when I saw the surveyor in there, I figured maybe he'd changed his mind. Only he told me he didn't hire a surveyor."

"Because he didn't. Flynn Stroud did," Cliff said.

"No, I didn't!" Flynn protested.

"Lou, any chance you have those documents on your phone? The ones you showed us?"

"Sure," Lou said, stepping forward. "But what was the…?"

"Gold Standard," Bunty said.

"I don't see what any of this has to do with Uncle Pieter's death," Hendrik shouted.

"You don't?" Cliff asked.

"Got it," Lou said, handing the phone over to Captain Marks, who reluctantly read it.

"So, Flynn Stroud had a survey of his own land done." Captain Marks shrugged. "Why does that matter?"

"But I didn't," Flynn protested.

"No, you didn't." Cliff agreed, "Your brother Hendrik did and forged your signature to make it look like you did after discovering the farm was zoned for mining. Something he knows a little more about, since his firm handles small capitalization mining companies."

"That's not a secret," Hendrik scoffed.

"But then you'd know better than anyone here that the family farm isn't just worth a million dollars."

"How much is it worth?" Flynn asked.

Cliff caught him glancing towards Hendrik, who was glaring at Cliff.

"I'm not a geologist, but given the density of the deposit, and your unique proximity to a cement plant," Bunty guessed, "low side ten million."

"You son of a..." Flynn hurled himself at Hendrik, gripping his suit jacket as he threw him to the ground. "I trusted you! You bastard."

Everyone around them spread out as Captain Marks and Lou jumped in to separate the two men.

"You used me!" Flynn was shouting now.

"Shut up, Flynn!"

"You made me watch him die! You told me we were in it together." Flynn was caught somewhere between rage and tears now.

"I said shut up, Flynn!" Hendrik shouted.

"We did it!"

"Flynn, no!"

"It wasn't on purpose. We'd brought the smoothie and maybe we mixed them up or something, but we just wanted to talk about options. We approached him about our plan and he refused. He said he would never sell the farm. I just thought it was because he was stubborn. I'm not sure. All I know is, we were shouting. But he was fine, and then the arguing sorta stopped, and Uncle Pieter started coughing. His face started to go red and puff up, and he just collapsed on the ground."

Flynn was rambling now that the faucet had been turned on and was flowing openly. Cliff was confident, given the furious look on Hendrik's face, that, if he wasn't being restrained, he would be ready to attack his brother.

"It took me a minute to realize what was happening, and then he dropped his EpiPen. I saw it roll on the ground. But he"—he pointed at Hendrik—"started to tell me how maybe it was for the best, that we could leave and no one would need to know that I was stealing, and we could work it all out with Mari. He said I would go to jail if we saved him, since he knew I was stealing, that all we needed to do was *nothing*, and all our troubles would go away. I panicked. I watched Hendrik kick Uncle Pieter's EpiPen away, and I just stood there watching as he crawled to get to it. Then Hendrik picked up his drink and told me to get rid of the files from the safe. We just assumed people would think it was an accident or something. But then things started to get carried away, and you were all looking at Mari, and we just..." Flynn was shaking now. "Hendrik said it was all going to be fine, that no one would be blamed, and just to stick to our story. So, I did. I swear I didn't want this to happen, Mari! I swear, I just... I didn't know what to do and I panicked. I'm sorry, I'm so sorry!" He was in tears now, curled up on the ground.

The crowd around them was in stunned silence and, for a long moment, no one could speak.

Finally, it was Captain Marks who took charge. "Release her," he said, gesturing to Mari, whose face was ashen white. "And cuff both these men. Flynn Stroud, Hendrik Stroud, we are arresting you for suspicion of manslaughter. Anything you say…"

His voice trailed off as Cliff turned to look over at Bunty. Her face was difficult to read, and no doubt, her mind was trying to understand what had just happened. Cliff's own brain was struggling to catch up with the whirlwind of emotions.

"That was…intense," Nancy, the tall judge, said, shaking her head.

"I think I need to sit down," Mari said. She reached out and gripped Hans's forearms. She stumbled a little and looked up at Hans. "I think I'm going to…"

Mari collapsed into Hans's arms before she could finish.

Luckily, Hans caught her. Dan, who was certainly no stranger to shock and stress, swooped in and scooped her up in his arms and, with some direction from Hans and the other housemates, carried her inside.

34

"I still don't really understand," Mari said. She was propped up on a pillow on the couch as Bunty arrived with a cold glass of water. The living room was far busier than a typical sunny Friday morning.

They should have all been outside exploring the garden, not holed up in the living room of the house, attempting to understand why and how a good man had to die.

Or so Cliff thought, being one of the many distraught and confused faces surrounding Mari on the couch.

"What's there to not understand?" Gerald asked. Although he'd been inside cutting the crust from his prepared sandwiches, in true English high tea fashion, he'd had a fairly good rundown of events as everyone poured into the house. "After Hendrik attempted to manipulate your father and his own brother into selling him the one true thing of value in your family, Flynn simply admitted to everything," Gerald said bluntly. "Pretty ruthless endeavour, I have to admit."

"I think she is more in shock about *why* any of this happened, Gerald, not how," Kitty said, helping herself to a sandwich and napkin from the plate now being passed around.

"Fair enough. Though I imagine it had something to do with the ten-plus million he would have got from the land." Gerald tilted his head curiously when Kitty shot him a disapproving look.

"For heaven's sake…"

"No, he's right," Mari said shaking her head.

Gerald turned, giving Kitty a snarky smile of his own before placing the sandwiches on the centre table and helping himself, placing two of them on a napkin and slipping away to tuck himself into the nearest empty corner.

"I just can't understand how on earth he could have done it. After everything my father did for him."

Cliff supposed she was referring to Flynn, who had been working on the farm since he was a teenager.

"Money has a sad way of getting in the way of families," Lucas said from his own corner of the living room, where he'd cozied up with a beer.

Cynthia Stroud had disappeared after Flynn and Hendrik had been hauled down to the police station. Cliff supposed she'd left to follow them. From everything Cliff had witnessed, Cynthia wasn't the kindest person in the world, but he still couldn't help but feel a little sorry for the woman.

"You said Dad knew about the limestone?" Mari asked.

"Not exactly," Lucas said. "All we ever knew was that it had been zoned for mining, but we agreed that wasn't what we wanted. We just wanted to keep the family farm going. Though I'll admit that kind of money is very tempting." He chuckled to himself.

"It's not nothing," Hans said.

"Ten million." Mari whistled.

"On the low side," Cliff said. "That's right, right Bunty?"

"Well, take my knowledge with a grain of salt, but a high-density limestone quarry with a short haul to a functioning cement plant?" Bunty thought for a minute. "It's been a few years for me, but yes, at *least*."

"That's a lot of strawberries," Lucas chuckled.

"Uncle Lucas, why didn't you say anything?" Mari asked.

"I promised your dad I wouldn't. He wanted to be the one to explain it to you, so that when the time came for you to take over the farm, you could make your own decision," Lucas told her. "But then…he never got the chance. And I honestly didn't know what to do."

"But why would you agree to letting Aunt Cynthia sell to the Badger?"

"That was *never* going to happen," Lucas said.

"How could you be sure? Up till a few moments ago, I was the primary suspect. After that, the farm would have gone to you and Aunt Cynthia. Right?"

"Not quite." Lucas sent a glance towards Cliff, Bunty, and Hans.

"What do you mean?" Mari asked, glancing around at each of them. "What are you not telling me?"

"Land transfers are clear. Immediate family, then closest relative," Bunty said.

"I know that. But it's just…" Mari's brow creased as she wiggled uncomfortably in her seat. "Earlier you said kids. When you were talking to Captain Marks. But Pieter didn't have *kids*. He only had me." Mari's head swivelled in confusion, unsure of who she should be speaking to now.

"The documents Lucas sent over to us had all kinds of farm information in them. Zoning designations, deed transfers, as well as personal files from your father," Cliff said, feeling as though he had some sort of obligation to take the lead on this, since, after all, he had the most experience breaking difficult information to people.

From the looks on the faces around him, including Aria's, who was silent in the corner, someone needed to tell Mari the truth.

"There were a few other documents in there. One of which was—"

"Wait," Aria blurted out. She'd been tucked in beside Lucas, silently watching since they'd all come inside. Now she stepped cautiously forward, approaching the table that separated her from Mari on the couch, with a fearful yet determined look set into her face.

It was a look Cliff knew well and couldn't have been more relieved to see on anyone else in that moment.

"This isn't how I…*we* wanted to tell you. But we were planning on it, I swear."

"Tell me what, Aria?" Mari asked, as she scooted herself to the front of the sofa with a look of uncertainty as she stared up at Aria.

"Umm, well, it's just…you've been so great to me since I came over here. And I didn't want to ruin that. But we'd been talking about telling you for a while, and I was starting to get excited." The words ran out of her mouth like a waterfall, as if she feared, if she stopped now, it would never come out. "But then Pieter died, and I got scared that people would think I did it, or worse, *you* would think I did it."

"Why would I think you would do anything to my dad, Aria?" Mari said, though Cliff thought, for a brief moment, that a small look of understanding crossed Mari's face.

"Because he was…ummm…" Aria looked around the room, clearly uncomfortable with this kind of attention.

Cliff felt bad that this information had to come out with so many people around.

"He was *our* dad." Aria stood, staring at Mari along with everyone else, waiting to catch her reaction.

Mari's face was unreadable as she slowly got to her feet and walked around the small table separating them. She stood in front of the young woman, just starring at her, and Cliff had no idea what she was going to do. Finally, she pulled Aria into her arms and wrapped her up tightly in a hug. The action appeared to take Aria by surprise, but eventually, she embraced her sister. The pair rocked silently in front of a silenced crowd, before Mari pulled away and grasped Aria's shoulders. Both women were in tears now.

"I have a little sister," she said softly.

"I don't want your farm," Aria blurted out, as if this was the big question everyone needed the answer to. "It's never been what I wanted. I swear."

"I believe you," Mari said, chuckling to herself. "You've been with us for a year." She shook her head. "How could I not know?"

"I wanted you to get to know me first. Without, you know… everything else," Aria said. "I just thought maybe you might hate me. Or Pie… Dad." Aria said the familiar term like a sigh of relief.

Cliff wondered just how long she'd wanted to say that but never could.

"I mean, I wouldn't mind some explanation, but maybe another time? I've had enough surprises for one day." Mari laughed, wiping a tear from her eye.

"Agreed," Aria said, using the sleeve of her shirt to clear her own eyes.

"I suppose I owe you all a thank you. For everything you've done," Mari said, turning to look at the room. "Without you, I'm not sure what would have happened. So, thank you." Mari looked thoughtfully around before landing on Hans. "And you…" She moved over to sit beside the big man on the couch, dragging Aria to sit beside her, as if she was unwilling to let her sister go. "I truly can't thank you enough."

"I hardly did anything." Hans smiled, looking up at Cliff and Bunty behind him.

"We know that isn't true," Mari said, giving him a kiss on the cheek before turning to look at Cliff and Bunty. "And if it wasn't for you two…"

"It was a group effort," Cliff said, feeling uneasy about taking any of the credit.

"We were all happy to help," Bunty added.

"I have one question that's been bothering me," Gerald said, an empty plate in his hand as he stepped forward to grab another sandwich.

"And I know this isn't any of my business, but I am very curious about it."

"What is that?" Mari asked.

"Well, it's you, Lucas." Gerald looked towards Lucas, whose eyes were red, as if he was struggling to contain his emotions. Cliff supposed he wasn't the sort of man who loved to get emotional, and certainly not around people.

"What's that?" he said evenly.

"Well, you seemed to know about Aria, and the zoning, and presumably a little about the value of the land. And clearly you wanted to help, or else you would have never sent Jan those documents. Yet you remained silent and never made an effort to gain anything from the chaos of it all."

"Is there a question in there?" Lucas asked head tilted in confusion.

"Yes. Why would you do that?" Gerald asked. "It doesn't make any sense. This entire case was about greed, and you had the most to lose and potentially the most to gain. All you would have needed to do was nothing, and you could have been a very wealthy man."

Everyone turned to stare at a very uncomfortable Lucas.

He picked away at the label of his beer. "I don't care about money. I just wanted to work hard, farm, and hoped one day that I'd be worthy of forgiveness. And I made a promise to Pieter that I wouldn't get involved."

"You kept a promise to your dead brother, even when you were suspected of his murder?" Gerald asked.

Cliff agreed it was rather confusing.

"A promise is a promise," Lucas said quietly. "I may have bent the rules a little giving the information to Jan, but I kept my promise, I didn't get involved."

"But—" Cliff couldn't help himself from asking, but he was cut short.

"But why help at all?" Lucas shook his head. "You asked me about the accident, when my friend was killed. You heard the rumour that it was Pieter who was driving the truck. That isn't true. I *was* driving the truck. I killed him and injured the others. And I live with that regret every day of my life. At the time, though, Pieter wanted to say it was him, to protect me. It was no secret I was a bit of a screwup. Everyone knew it. Even our father. But Pieter always believed in me, and didn't want people to judge me for my worst actions. I knew I couldn't let him throw his life away because of me. He was always there for me; he was my big brother. He looked after me, no matter what. I just wanted to be there for him the same way he was for me. You know?" Lucas stared down, tapping the side of his bottle absently. "I was supposed to be there for him. He wasn't just my brother; Pieter was my best friend. I would have done anything to protect him, but I failed him. I failed to protect him when he needed it most. All I had left was a promise I made to him."

The pain and suffering behind his eyes as he fought back his emotions tore into Cliff as he watched the young man within struggling with the man he was now.

"I should have done better."

Mari got up and ran over to give him a hug. Lucas, despite his imposing size, crumbled like a small boy, slowly sinking into his niece's embrace.

"I'm sorry, Mari," he said softly. "I'm so sorry."

"You're a good man, Uncle Lucas. Dad would be proud," Mari said, and it was as if a small piece of Lucas's burden was lifted, although Cliff doubted the man would ever allow himself to be entirely free of his past.

"I do hate to be the one to ruin all of this," said a voice from behind Cliff.

He, along with everyone else, turned to see the three judges in the living room doorway, two of them with tears in their eyes, while the third, Vera, examined her watch.

"We are on a rather tight schedule today," she said. "Perhaps it would be better to reschedule for another time…"

"Absolutely not!" Mari said, wiping away her eyes. "Mrs. Chen, I will not let us be another reason that you're unable to show off your beautiful garden." She clapped her hands. "I think what we all need right now is some fresh air and beautiful flowers." She walked over to offer a hand to Aria, who took it gladly, pulling herself up to her feet.

"Are you sure, because it really looks like there is a lot going on here, and time is—"

"Nonsense. You heard the young woman. You're going to love it," Mrs. Chen said, gesturing to the door with her cane. "If you would all be so kind as to follow me, I believe you will particularly like the flower combinations in the east garden." Mrs. Chen strode out of the house with purposeful determination.

"*Allons-y!*" Bunty shouted as the small mass of people trudged out the front door.

The sunshine hit Cliff's face as he stepped out, breathing in the fresh air, and he wasn't sure if it was the sunshine or the aroma of the flowers, but for the first time in a while, Cliff felt as though things were beginning to look up.

35

"Well, that was an interesting week, to say the least," Bunty said from her chair in the library, where she sat knitting with a hot cup of tea beside her.

Cliff sat beside her with his coffee, staring up at the bookshelf, the morning paper in his lap. For the first time, he didn't have to share the paper with Sol and Kitty, as Jan had taken the liberty of delivering plenty of copies to the house that morning.

"I'm not sure I like our home depicted like this," Kitty shouted from the living room. "Who agreed to this photo in the first place?"

"I don't think it's about us, my love," Cliff heard Sol say.

The pair broke off into a lively debate about who should be entitled to approved an image in the paper.

"'Mysterious Murder Solved by the Limestone Manor.' Not entirely true, but it is certainly a catchy title," Cliff chuckled as he read the headline.

"I'm sure Captain Marks is thrilled," Bunty agreed with a laugh.

"The important thing is we all got to the bottom of it," Cliff said.

Bunty rolled her eyes at Cliff. "I'm sure that's the only thing he cares about."

"Personally, I'm a big fan of page seven," Cliff said, opening the paper. "'The Limestone Manor Takes First Place in Perth County Home Garden Competition.'" He turned the paper to show Bunty the photo of Mrs. Chen standing in front of her garden, holding the large blue ribbon awarded to first place. Cliff and everyone else believed that it should have just been her in the photo, but Mrs. Chen was insistent that everyone in the house, along with Mari, Aria, Lucas, Lou, Dan, and Jan, be in the picture as well. It was clear she wasn't going to take no for an answer.

"Mrs. Chen has already started planning for next year." Bunty shook her head. "I swear that woman will never slow down."

"And who knows what she can accomplish with her new budget." Cliff chuckled, knowing that, along with the blue ribbon, first place also came with a $1500 gift card to Hennigan's Garden Centre.

"It's not about the money," Mrs. Chen said, as she came out of the kitchen, her wicker basket in one arm and her cane in the other. "I mean, it will certainly help," she mused.

"You can't possibly be going to work on the garden today, are you?" Cliff asked incredulously.

"Nonsense. It is time to enjoy the spoils of victory," she said with a grin. "I think we all deserve a break." She smiled as she walked to the door and opened it. "A week should suffice." She nodded before walking outside and closing the door behind her.

"She was joking, wasn't she?" Sol said from the other room.

"Hard to tell with her," Kitty said.

"She was," Cliff called back before turning to look at Bunty. "Wasn't she?"

Bunty just shrugged and gave Cliff a playful smile.

"Sweet Jesus." Cliff shook his head.

"Mr. Shaw!"

"I said he was sweet." Cliff raised his hands defensively in the air, as Bunty shook her head at him.

"You know I've been thinking a lot about what you said," Cliff said.

Bunty turned to look up at him, momentarily pausing her knitting project. "And what exactly did I say?" Bunty picked up where she left off as if there had been no interruption at all.

"About me getting a hobby," Cliff said.

"Is that what I told you?"

"Isn't it?"

"I suppose it couldn't hurt," Bunty said.

Cliff was officially confused, since he was confident that it was Bunty who told him he should find something to pass the time. Find a hobby.

"If you think it's a good idea to have a hobby, then who am I to stand in your way?"

"Didn't you…? Isn't that…?" Cliff shook his head.

"Confusion isn't always great at our age," Bunty smiled.

"I'm not. I just mean I think it would be good for me to have something to do. Something to distract my mind from not working."

"I'd love that for you, Cliff. Excellent idea."

"I know what you're trying to do here, Bunty, and it won't work," Cliff insisted.

"And what exactly am I trying to do?" Bunty asked, laying her knitting down on her lap to look over at Cliff.

"You're trying to make me think it's my idea to find something to do, not yours."

"Is that what I'm doing?" Bunty asked, her face void of any expression.

Cliff was beginning to question if he knew what was happening.

"If you think having a hobby will help you in your retirement, then I think that's a great idea."

"It's not like I haven't been trying."

"And you've succeeded at finding the things you *don't* want to do," Bunty said. "You, of all people, should know, Cliff, little steps lead to big outcomes."

"Why me of…?" Cliff began to laugh, which seemed to cause Bunty more than a little concern.

"Are you okay?"

"Yeah, it's just…well, I'm trying to figure out why women in my life keep telling me this," Cliff mused.

"You have other women in your life, Mr. Shaw?" Bunty asked, her brows lifting playfully.

"Not like that. No. It's just…it's a long story." Cliff couldn't figure out a good way of explaining how a psychic, who was right about so many things in his life, including a murder, might have helped Cliff take his first steps towards understanding what was important to his life, or *who* was important, for that matter.

"Well, if you ever want to share it, you know where to find me," Bunty said.

"That I do," Cliff leaned back in his chair, glancing over at Bunty, watching as she tied off the end of her row before starting a new one.

"I did have one question for you," Cliff asked.

"Just the one?"

"For now. What if I was thinking of taking up knitting?" Cliff asked.

"Then I would suggest you keep thinking." Bunty smiled. "Who knows, maybe another mystery will pop up and offer you a fresh distraction."

"I think it's best if I leave the mysteries to the police from now on," Cliff said. "As you said, I'm retired now, Bunty."

"That's right. You're retired," Bunty said, looking over at him with a grin. "But you're not dead."

The End

Acknowledgments

There are many people I would like to take a quick moment to thank for helping to pull this book together. As always none of this would be worth doing if it wasn't for everyone who has taken time from their lives to give this book a read. There are millions of books in the world and the fact that you chose this one means the world to me.

I was so excited to get the opportunity to follow up this series with a second book and I know this is in large part due to you the reader and the countless people from the Town of St. Marys who showed up to support this Author at the launch of the Limestone Manor. I am truly grateful that so many people have supported this series and enjoyed it over the past couple of years. But it all started with the wonderful and generous support of Betty's Bookshelf in St. Marys. If you ever find yourself strolling through the streets of St. Marys, please pop into Bettys! It is a wonderful store run by some incredible people, Jan and Wren, I appreciate all that you have done for me.

I would also like to take this opportunity to thank my family and friends for all of their support during writing this book. Particularly I would like to thank my Dad for his tireless support, and his trust that I am actually spending my time writing. Also, my incredible partner Hilary who always takes the time to read and proof notes and to provide me feedback on every book I write. I feel eternally grateful to have her in my life to encourage me and to tell me when I am wrong. Lastly, I would like to send my deepest thank you to my mum, Jessie, who has, and continues to be the first person to edit and read everything I write. To have someone in my life who is so generous with their time and willing to support me and the journey I am on is incredible. I feel so grateful for all of the people who I get to surround myself with and love. Thank you all. GJJSHLRDTLAHBKA LLNGKGRHTHDPGRJHKC

As for my creative team, I would like to thank my editors, Keenan and Shannon. Both of them spent a lot of time going through and fixing up the story, further editing it and cleaning it up in order to share it with you the reader. Honestly, if you could see the progression from the first to final version of these stories, your mind would likely blow. It goes through so many variations and drafts, each one making it the best story it can be. Thanks to you all for your hard work on this story.

Thank you to Colleen, my incredible cover artist. This is their second book in the series, and I hope there will be many more to come. When I first reach out, I just like to give them a few things I think would help describe the story I am trying to tell. After that I let their imagination lead them and I am always so thrilled by the outcome. Thank you for your contribution to this project. We will do it again soon!

The final piece of the puzzle would be the beautiful and wonderful town of St. Marys, ON. Although all of my stories are fiction and none of the people are real, nor are they in anyway linked to anyone real in town, I have used some wonderful points of reference. The Limestone Manor is a beautiful home nestled near the churches which I have always admired, the Town Hall- which is actual limestone, and the beautiful riverside walk where Cliff and Lou seem to have all of their clandestine meetings are just a few. In fact, most of the stories I think of come as I walk around the town and try to just get inspired by how beautiful it all is. And although, this book took us a little out of the town, I do promise we will return soon. In the meantime, I hope one day you get the chance to visit, meet the people, and see for yourself. It really is one of the most charming towns I know. So, thank you for all of your inspiration. And to all the farmers who read this book, I apologize if I messed anything up. I tried my best to be as accurate as possible but if I missed anything glaring, please don't hesitate to send me an email. Jonny@jonnyonthepage.com.

I'm not always the best at finding the words to express myself, stories are much easier to come by in my experiences. The expectations seem less daunting. But all of these people, and places, I have mentioned including all of you reading this now mean so much to me since none of what I do here on my computer or in my imagination, while walking my dog around the Grand Trunk Trail in St. Marys, would mean anything if I couldn't share it. So, thank you for reading.

Until next time,

Jonny Thompson

About the Author

Jonny Thompson is an award-winning writer living in Ponamogoa titjg/Dartmouth, NS with his partner Hilary and their dog Henry. Jonny was born in England and grew up in the traditional lands of the Anishinabewaki and Attiwonderonk nations now St. Marys, Ontario.

Jonny attended Dalhousie University, where he received a BA in Theatre. He's worked professionally in stage and film for over thirteen years, including five extremely exciting years travelling the world as a puppeteer.

Jonny's debut novel *Ash and Sun* was released in October 2022. His novels Atlantis and the Limestone Manor were released in 2023, while Firefly: Book two of the Ash and Sun trilogy was release in 2024. He has written various novels, novellas and short stories which can be found on his website.

He is continuously working through new projects and looks forward to sharing them with you soon. Thank you for reading!

You can connect with me on:

🌐 https://www.jonnyonthepage.com

f https://www.facebook.com/Jonnyonthepage

🔗 https://www.instagram.com/jonnythompson.author

Also by Jonny Thompson

Ash and Sun

After a 200-day suspension, all Senior Agent Adam Jennings wanted was a win on his return to the Global Investigation Bureau (GIB). But when a simple warehouse fire begins to look more like a homicide investigation, he is forced to watch as the entire case begins to unravel, slowly revealing the dark underbelly of a world that should not exist.

Firefly: Book 2 of the Ash and Sun Trilogy

Senior Agent Adam Jennings is ready to leave the past behind and move on. But when his partner Ali is kidnapped, Jens' hand is forced as lives suddenly hang in the balance. Unwelcomed truths are revealed, leaving Jens isolated, no longer knowing who he can trust or what he should believe.

THE LIMESTONE MANOR

When retired police detective Clifford Shaw hesitantly steps off the train in his former hometown of St. Marys, Ontario, the last thing he expects to greet him is a murder. The only thing worse than being inadvertently roped into the investigation is the surprise he receives when the too-good-to-be-true room rental from his lifelong friend Hans has one massive catch. It's in a shared house with six other retirees. Already hesitant about returning to the town he swore he never would, Cliff has one week to figure out if he wants to refuse the room or give his old town one last chance. All this while he helps unravel a mystery to save 'The Town Worth Living In'.

Atlantis

In a high-stakes race against time, Master Sailor Clive Davis has only twenty-eight days to locate a world-altering weapon hidden in the technologically advanced city of Atlantis. Disguised as a deep-sea welder, he delves into the mysterious depths, determined to thwart billionaire Grace Alice's sinister plan. As Clive unravels the city's secrets, he grapples with his purpose and must race against the clock to separate truth from fiction. Time is ticking, secrets are unravelling, and Clive is our last hope. Will he save the world, or will Atlantis be its undoing?